"...easily one of the most intriguing books I've read all year..."

Writerlea Book Reviews

"*Empire's Daughter* is a story that enriches the imagination. A compelling tale of survival and strength in unity."

Avril Borthiry, author of *Triskelion*

Empire's Hostage

"A bold vision of historical fantasy written beautifully from start to finish; *Empire's Hostage* takes us on an epic journey that is at once intriguing, convincing, and deeply affecting."

Jonathan Ballagh, author of *The Quantum Door*

"A fantastic sequel."

Cover to Cover Book Review

"*Empire's Hostage* is as immersive as Marian L Thorpe's first book *Empire's Daughter*. Filled with beautiful imagery and well-developed, realistic characters, *Empire's Hostage* surpassed my expectations."

D.M. Wiltshire, author of the *Prophecy Six* series

Other Books by Marian L Thorpe

Empire's Daughter: Book I of the Empire's Legacy Series

Visit my website

marianlthorpe.com

find me on Facebook

https://www.facebook.com/marianthorpe/

tweet me

@marianlthorpe

Marian L Thorpe lives in a small city in Canada

with her husband and two cats.

When not writing or editing,

Marian can be found either birding,

an avocation that has taken her to seven continents,

or taking courses on the landscape archaeology of Britain.

EMPIRE'S
HOSTAGE

BOOK II

OF THE

EMPIRE'S LEGACY SERIES

For Chiava, with my vegans,

Marian L Thorpe

[signature]

Arboretum Press

for

Drs. Tomer Feigenberg, John Radwan, and Sarah Rauth,

&

the entire team of surgery, nursing, and radiology staff

at the Carlo Fidani Cancer Centre,

without whose expertise

I would not have been alive to write this book.

'Thank you' seems completely inadequate.

Acknowledgments

Thanks are due to many people: to those who wanted Lena's story to keep going, and kept asking for this book; to my beta-readers Katie Thorpe, Liis Scanlon and fellow author D.M. Wiltshire, for their insightful comments and suggestions; to the Minett family of Guelph, owners of The Bookshelf Café, who provide local writers with quiet writing space on Monday mornings, where most of this book was written; to other 'Writing Room' writers for support and long discussions over lunch; to the Friends of Vocamus Press Sunday afternoons and even longer discussions, and to my cover artist, A.J. O'Brien, for understanding and translating my vision.

For the Battle of the Tabha, thanks go to historian Jeffrey Duff for graciously allowing me to adapt his description of the Battle of Stamford Bridge: (http://medieval.stormthecastle.com/the-bad-fall-of-1066-part-3-the-battle-of-stamford-bridge.htm); battles are not my strong point, and his article was clear and descriptive.

And, as always, my deepest thanks to my husband Brian Rennie, who saw nothing odd about a March trip to Hadrian's Wall so that I could understand what it felt like in the cold and wet.

The sea-eagle is for you.

†††††

Cover Design by Anthony O'Brien

Cover Image: Taiga/Shutterstock
Used under License

Map by Marian L Thorpe

The Characters of *Empire's Hostage*

Characters whose role is important in the story are in **bold**.
Characters mentioned by name but not a direct part of the story are in plain type.

Character	*Pronunciation*	*Allegiance*	*Role*
Birel	**Bih-*rell***	**The Empire**	**Casyn's soldier-servant**
Callan	**Kah-lan**	**The Empire**	**Emperor**
Caro	**Kah-ro**	**The Empire**	**cook**
Casse	Kahss-uh	The Empire	Hunt-leader at Tirvan
Casyn	**Kah-sin**	**The Empire**	**General, advisor & brother to the Emperor**
Colm	Koh-lm	The Empire	Advisor and brother to the Emperor, castrate, deceased
Cormaic	Kor-myak	The Empire	Officer overseeing the prison at Land's End fort
Darel	**Dah-rell**	**The Empire**	**cadet**
Daria	*Dah*-ria	The Empire	Woman of Karst
Dern	Dehrn	The Empire	Captain of *Skua*
Dessa	Deh-ssa	The Empire	Boatbuilder at Tirvan
Dian	Dee-yahn	The Empire	Guardswoman
Elga	El-gah	The Empire	Fisherwoman at Berge
Finn	Finn	The Empire	Soldier
Galen	**Gay-len**	**The Empire**	**Soldier, Lena's father**
Garth	Gah-rth	The Empire	Lena's cousin and past lover, Maya's brother
Gwen	**Gwen**	**The Empire**	**Lena's mother, midwife and healer to Tirvan**

CHARACTER	PRONUNCIATION	ALLEGIANCE	ROLE
Halle	**Hall-uh**	**The Empire**	**Guardswoman**
Ianthe	Yan-thay	The Empire	Tice's sister
Kira	Kee-ra	The Empire	Lena's sister
Kyreth	**Ky — reth**	**The Empire**	**Marta's apprentice**
Lara	Lah-ra	The Empire	Siane's daughter
Lena	**Lee-na**	**The Empire**	**Guardswoman**
Marta	Mahr-ta	The Empire	Midwife and healer to Berge
Maya	My-ah	The Empire	Lena's partner at Tirvan
Pel	Pel	The Empire	Tali's youngest son
Rikter	Rick-ter	The Empire	cadet
Risa	**Ree-sa**	**The Empire**	**Shepherd at Berge**
Siane	Shah-nah	The Empire	Dessa's partner, deceased
Tali	Tah-lee	The Empire	Lena's aunt, mother to Maya and Garth
Tice	Tice (rhymes with dice)	The Empire	Potter at Tirvan, deceased
Turlo	**Tur-low**	**The Empire**	**General, advisor to the Emperor**
Valle	Vahl -uh	The Empire	Garth's son with Tice
Ardan	**Ahr - dahn**	**Linrathe**	***Canri'ad* (lieutenant) to Donnalch**
Bartol	**Bar - toll**	**Linrathe**	***Eirën* (farmer) of Bartolstorp, Gregor's father**
Cillian	**Kill-yan**	**Linrathe**	***Dalta* (student)**
Dagney	**Dag-nee**	**Linrathe**	**Teacher**
Donnalch	**Dunn-*alch***	**Linrathe**	***Teannasach* (leader)**

CHARACTER	PRONUNCIATION	ALLEGIANCE	ROLE
Gregor	Greg-orr	Linrathe	Soldier, Lena's guard
Huld	Huhld	Linrathe	Toli's daughter
Isa	Eye-sa	Linrathe	Cook at the Ti'ach
Jordis	Yor-dish	Linrathe	*Dalta* (student)
Kebhan	Kev-*ann*	Linrathe	Lorcann's son
Lorcann	Lor-*kann*	Linrathe	Donnalch's brother
Miach	Mee-yach	Linrathe	Soldier
Niav	Neeve	Linrathe	*Dalta* (student)
Perras	Perr- *as*	Linrathe	*Comiádh* (professor) of the *Ti'ach* (college)
Piet	Pete	Linrathe	Fisherman
Ruar	Roar	Linrathe	Donnalch's son
Sorley	*Sore*-ley	Linrathe	*Dalta* (student)
Toli	Toe-lee	Linrathe	Bartol's son, Gregor's brother
Torunn	Toh-*runn*	Linrathe	Bartol's wife, Konë (headwoman) of Bartolstorp
Åsmund	Ess-mund	Marai	Fritjof's brother
Fritjof	*Freet*-yoff	Marai	*Härskaran* (king)
Herlief	Herr - *leaf*	Marai	*Härskaran* (king)(deceased)
Leik	Lake	Marai	Fritjof and Rothny's son
Niáll	Nee-*yall*	Marai	Soldier
Rothny	Roth-nee	Marai	*Fräskaren* (queen)

Vocabulary

The language of Linrathe and Varsland is based on a mix of p-Celtic and q-Celtic languages, with some Scandinavian influence. The language of the Marai is based on Scandinavian languages. Pronunciation does not necessarily follow the conventions of any of these languages.

WORD	PRONUNCIATION	MEANING
Abhaínne	Av-*anne*	river
Af	Av	with
Ag	Ag	with
Allech'i	A-leck-*hee*	please
An	An	the
Arnek	Ar-neck	arnica
Athir	*Att*-hurr	father
Basi	Ba-*shee*	pass
Be'atha	Bay-*att*-a	food
Bluth	Blutt	blood
Cailzie	Kall-*yah*	capercaillie
Canri'ad	Kan-ree-*ath*	lieutenant
Colúir	Col-*oo*-urr	pigeon
Comiádh	Ko-mi-*ath*	professor
Dalta(i)	Dal-ta(tay)	student(s)
Danta	Dan-tha	saga
Deir'anai	Day-*urr*-an-i	(we will speak) later
Din	Deen	your
Dhuarach	Thurr-a-*rahsh*	dull, dulled
Dhur	Thurr	dark
Eirën	Aye-er-un	farmer (male)
En	An	an
Flodden	Vlod-*den*	river
Fo	Vo	from
Föla	Vo-lah	blood

WORD	PRONUNCIATION	MEANING
Forla	Vor-*lah*	sorry
Fräskaren	Vre-skar-*an*	queen (literally, female ruler)
Fuádain	Vwa-*dai*-een	falcon
Fuisce	Vwi-*schah*	whiskey
Geälis	Gi-*ah*-lish	shining
Gistel	Gee-*stel*	hostage
Glaéder	Glee-there	welcome (literally, you gladden)
Halla	Hahllah	hall
Handa	Hantha	direction, position
Harr	Harr	headman
Härskaran	Herr-skar-*an*	king (literally, male ruler)
Ja	Yah	yes
Konë	Koon-eh	headwoman
Ladhar	Lath-*ar*	lute
Leannan	Lee-annan	dearest
Lissande	Lish-*and*-eh	shining
Liun	Linn	heather
Lys	Lish	light
Marái'sta	Mar-uh-*ee*-stah	of the Marai (referring to language)
Marren	Mah-*ren*	south
Mathúyr	Mat-oo-*urr*	musician
Mattai	*Math*-ay	dull, dulled
Meas	May-as	thank you
Mer heithra	Mer hett-ra	I am honored, you honor me
Merliún	Mer-lee-*oon*	merlin
Min	Min	mine
Mot'ulva	Mooth-ul-*fa*	arnica

Word	*Pronunciation*	*Meaning*
na	Na	of, named for,
na	Nah	no
Scáeli	*Schaa*-lee	bard
Snámh'a	*Shnav*-ahh	dipper (a type of wren)
Sostrae	Shost-ree	sisters
Takkë	Tack-uh	thank you
Tar'an	Tahr-*ann*	bread
Te	Tay	to
Teannasach	Tee-*na*-shah	chieftan
Ti'ach(a)	Tee-ash(a)	college(s)
Tien	Tinn	a
Torp	Torp	hamlet, farmstead
Torpari	Tor-*par*-ee	farmworkers, peasants
Tuki	Too-kee	prop (for a falcon)
Vaëre	*Fah*-ur-ay	please
Vann	Fahn	water
Yn	Un	and

THE WORLD OF EMPIRE'S HOSTAGE

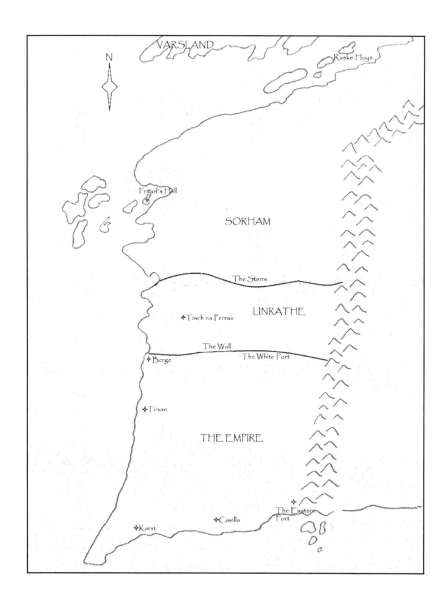

The swallows gather, summer passes,
The grapes hang dark and sweet;
Heavy are the vines,
Heavy is my heart,
Endless is the road beneath my feet.

The sun is setting, the moon is rising,
The night is long and sweet;
I am gone at dawn.
I am gone at day,
Endless is the road beneath my feet.

The cold is deeper, the winters longer,
Summer is short but sweet;
I will remember,
I'll not forget you,
Endless is the road beneath my feet.

-Tice's song

Chapter One

THE RAIN SLASHED DOWN UNCEASINGLY, half ice, stinging exposed skin and making it nearly impossible to see anything in the grey light. When the sun, hidden now behind the thick layer of clouds, set—*not long now*, I estimated—the stones of the Wall and the native rock would lose what warmth they held, and begin to ice over. Night watch would be treacherous, tonight. I counted it a small blessing that my watch had begun after the midday meal.

I wiped a gloved hand over my eyes yet again and scanned north and eastward, not focusing on anything, but looking for motion, or for something that didn't belong, as Turlo had taught me; something that moved against the wind, or a shadow that hadn't been there yesterday. I listened, too, to the sounds beyond the noises of the fort and the babble of the stream behind me: the hoarse cry of a raven, the soft chatter of sparrows settling into their roost. No alarm calls. I walked the few steps across the watchtower to begin my scan again, to the northwest.

Footsteps sounded on the wooden stairs. I did not turn. Only when my relief stood beside me, looking out, could I look away.

"I think the minging gods have forgotten it's the first day of spring," Halle said. "Anything I should know?"

"There's a raven in the usual tree," I answered, still looking outward, "but it's just making conversational croaks occasionally. I saw a fox about an hour ago, when I could still see, and its mind was on finding mice in the rocks. No owls today, but maybe they're not hunting in this rain. There could be forty northmen out there, and as long as they moved with the wind and stayed low, I wouldn't know. But I don't think so. I'm guessing there is one, or maybe two, watching us, no more."

"Wrapped up in their cloaks, under some rocks or furze," Halle said. "I'd rather be here."

"So would they," I reminded her.

She laughed, but without mirth. "Go and get warm," she said. "The hunting party brought back a deer, so there's venison stew to be had." I glanced over at her. Her eyes were on the land beyond the Wall, watching.

"Good luck." I took the stairs down from the watchtower as quickly as I felt safe; the movement warmed me, slightly. At the bottom, I stepped over the gutter, running with rainwater, and onto the cobbled walkway that ran along the inner side of the Wall. The Wall itself broke the wind, and the rain fell with less force. Still, I pulled the hood of my cloak over my head as I walked to the camp.

All the discipline of the Empire could not build a finished fort in a time of war, and while the tents and a few stone and timber huts stood in orderly rows, most of the roads and pathways between were earthen—or mud, right now. Since the skirmishes had died down, some weeks earlier, work had begun on paving the main thoroughfares through the camp. A narrow, cobbled track ran from the Wall to the centre of the encampment, just wide enough for two people to pass. I noticed it extended a few feet further into the camp than it had when I had left for watch duty. I stepped off its comparatively clean cobbles onto the slick surface of the hard-packed earthen path. It had been built to drain, and two ditches ran on either side of it, but I could feel mud sticking to my boots.

At the kitchen tent, I scraped the mud off my boots on the iron blade mounted outside, and shook the worst of the rain off my cloak. Ducking inside, I met a blast of welcome heat. I stripped off my gloves and cloak, and the thick tunic I wore beneath the cloak, piling them on a bench. A gust of cold air told me someone else had come in. I turned to see Darel already loosening the clasps of his cloak. He'd been on watch duty at the tower east of the camp.

"Quiet?" I asked. He nodded, concentrating on pulling his tunic over his head.

"Very." His red hair, streaked with rain, stood up in clumps. He sniffed the air. "I hear rumours of venison stew," he said. Caro, on servery duty, spoke up.

"More like thick soup," she said, "but, yes, it's venison. With some root vegetables and barley in with it. Sit down, and I'll bring it over."

We did as directed, and soon enough two bowls of food stood in front of us, with a loaf of dark, hard bread. Darel cut the loaf in half with his belt knife, passing one piece to me. I ripped off a chunk, and dipped it in the soup, eating hungrily.

Caro brought over two mugs of thin beer, and for a space of some minutes we did nothing but eat. Others had come in as we ate, and the smell of damp wool began to overpower the scent of venison stew in the tent. No-one said much; another day of rain and cold and mud dampened spirits as much as it did hide and stone. *I'm sick of rain,* I thought, listening to its ceaseless drum on the tent. *If the sun would come out, I'd feel better.*

Caro put more fuel in the brazier and then slipped onto the bench beside me. We had ridden north together, from Casilla, half a year earlier, when Dian had come south to requisition food and horses and other supplies for the army. I hadn't really known her. She had worked at one of the small food stalls near Casilla's harbours, and sometimes on my way to or from my work on the boats I had bought something from her.

"How's the soup?" she asked.

"Fine," I said. It was; thick enough to be satisfying, and reasonably spiced.

"It was only a yearling," she said. "Not enough meat to go around, really, so we had to make soup."

Food, I knew, was becoming a problem. At the end of the winter, with almost all the army ranged along the length of the Wall, game within a day or two's hunting was scarce. Sending men—or more likely women—south to the villages for provisions meant fewer of us to defend the Wall if another raid occurred. The truce, called ten days ago, could end at any moment; the Emperor and his advisors spent their days at the White Fort, east of our camp, negotiating with the leaders of the northmen. Fifteen months of war: eight to drive the invaders back beyond the wall; another seven, now, keeping them there, until the ravages of winter, little food, and the deaths of so many, on both sides, had led to the request, and agreement, to parley.

"Who brought it in?" I asked idly.

"Dian," Caro replied. "They got two, both yearlings, but one went to the White Fort. Have you had enough to eat?"

I shrugged. "Enough," I said. Food was for energy, nothing more, and what I'd eaten would suffice. "Is there any tea?" Darel looked up.

"I could eat more," he said, "if there is any?" Darel was so young, and growing, and thin as a starveling cat. All the cadets looked the same.

"There's a bit," Caro said judiciously. "Give me your bowl, and I'll bring it back, and your tea, Lena." She slid off the bench to return to the servery. Darel stretched. "Dice?" he suggested. "After we're done eating?"

I shook my head. "Not tonight," I said. "My tunic needs repairing. One of the shoulder seams is splitting." Caro came back, and Darel fell on his bowl as if he hadn't eaten the first helping. I curved my hands around the mug of tea. It smelled of fruit: rosehip, I thought.

I sat, sipping the tea. It warmed me, as much as anything did, these days. Darel finished his soup, wiping every trace of liquid from the bowl with the last piece of bread, and pushed his bench back. He took his beer and joined a pair of cadets at another table, pulling out his dice. They would sit here, playing, all the rest of the evening, if Caro let them. The servery tent was warmer than the barracks, and there was always the chance of some scraps of food.

I finished the tea, idly watching the dice game. "Minging dice," one of the cadets growled.

"Language!" Caro warned. She allowed no obscenities in the kitchen tent: another slip and she'd make the cadets leave, and they knew it. I'd got used to the casual swearing among the troops; 'minging', a lewd term for urination, was one of the most frequently heard. I even said it myself, now. I stood to take the mug back to Caro, along with Darel's forgotten bowl. Suddenly, the clatter of hooves on the cobbles rang out in the night. "Who?" Caro breathed. The cadets dropped the dice, standing. The tent flap parted, and Turlo—General Turlo, now, and advisor to the Emperor—strode in. Darel straightened even more: the presence of his father always made him conscious of his decorum.

Turlo blinked briefly in the light of the tent. "General?" Caro said. "Would you like food, or drink?"

He smiled at her. "We ate well enough at the Fort," he said, "but thank you. No, I came in search of two soldiers, and I've found them. Guard Lena, Cadet Darel, please go to your barracks, pack your possessions and come back here as quickly as you can. You two—he nodded to the other dice players—go to the horse lines, please, and bring back two mounts. And then retire to your barracks," he added. "Go!" he said, not unkindly; the cadets scurried to do his bidding.

Darel had not moved, but looked over at me. "General?" I said. "What is happening?"

"I will tell you," he said, "when you return with your packs. Bring anything you cannot live without, and your warmest clothes and boots, if you are not already wearing them. Quickly, mind!" It was mildly said, but still an order. I glanced at Darel; he had already turned to put on his outdoor clothes.

We dressed hurriedly and went out into the night. The cadet barracks lay in the opposite direction to mine—the Guards being the women who had come to support the army of the Empire—but Darel hesitated. "Lena," he whispered, "what do you think is going on?"

"No idea," I said. "But we have orders to follow, and very little time to do it in. Be quick, Darel!"

I half-ran to the Guards' barracks, trying not to slip on the slick path. I was in luck; the three women I shared my room with were somewhere else. Halle, at least, was on duty; I wasn't sure about the other two. No questions to slow me down. I pulled my pack from under my cot, looking inside: spare underclothes and socks, another pair of breeches and a shirt lay folded. The pack doubled as storage in this small space. I picked up my indoor slippers, putting them in the pack. From the small wooden chest beside the cot I took a few other things: my comb, my sewing kit, the soft absorbent cloths I used every month during my bleeding, the small supply of anash from which I brewed a tea to lessen the cramps that came with the bleeding, my pen and ink. Then I picked up the last two items that lay inside: two books. One was the history of the Empire, given to me by Colm, the Emperor's advisor and castrate twin; one was my own journal. I stuffed them down inside the pack, buckling it closed.

Outside the servery tent two horses—my Clio, I noticed, was not one of them—stood saddled and bridled beside Turlo's horse. Inside the General sat alone, a mug of beer on the table. Caro had gone. Turlo looked up at me without smiling, nodding for me to sit. Darel came in a minute or two later.

"Now," Turlo said, "I will be brief. The talks have been fruitful: there is a truce that both the Emperor and the Northmen's leader, Donnalch, can agree to. *Teannasach* of the North, he styles himself; so be it. I remember when he was a stripling leading raiding parties for sheep, but no doubt he remembers when I was a stripling too, scouting up their glens. If you do this long enough, old adversaries are almost friends." He grinned. Nothing, ever, seemed to keep Turlo's spirits down. "But the treaty, my lad, and lassie," he added, "requires hostages. Donnalch's son, and another, to us, and two children of our leaders, to them."

Darel found his voice first. "We are to be hostages? Sir?" he remembered to add.

"But I am not a child of our leaders," I protested, not understanding.

"Aye," Turlo said. I wasn't sure which one of us he answered. He looked at Darel. "You are my son," he said, "and therefore must stand as hostage. And you, Lena," he said, switching his gaze to me, "Casyn asked for you to stand as his surrogate daughter. His own daughters are in Han, with their own children, and the Emperor has fathered no sons, or daughters, for that matter, in all his years."

Casyn had asked for me. The words echoed in my head. I had met my own father only once; he served at one of the easternmost postings on the Wall. In the almost two years I had known and worked with and served the General Casyn, I had come to regard him, and to love him, I had acknowledged, as I might have my own father, had I known him. I had had no conception that he might have thought of me in a similar light. Something pushed through the dullness of my spirit. *This time,* I thought, *you will not fail him. This time, you will go.*

"What does it mean, to be a hostage?" I asked. I saw something flicker in Turlo's eyes. He grinned again.

"Exchanging the children of high rank as hostages is an old and honoured tradition," he answered, "although not one we have

8

respected, in some generations, and in truth needed to be reminded of. We'll treat Donnalch's son, and the other boy they are sending—his brother's son—with every courtesy. They will lodge in the White Fort for now, and then be sent south to the Eastern Fort when the weather improves, to learn with our senior cadets. Darel, you will basically live the life that Donnalch's son would have, whatever the education, in arms and tactics and books, they deem appropriate. That is the gist of it: we exchange our heirs, in surety for each side's good behaviour. You will not be mistreated, but, understand, neither will you be truly free. "

"And me?" I asked. "I cannot see the northerners teaching me arms. And I am not a child."

"You are right, of course," he said, his voice graver. "I must be honest and say I do not really know. We have not concerned ourselves, over the years, in gathering much intelligence on how the women of the north folk live their lives, except to know they live with their men, and perhaps divide the responsibilities of daily life much as we did here once in the Empire, before Partition. But," he said, his voice brightening, "you will bring us back much valuable information, as a result."

"Am I to spy, then?" I tried to keep the exasperation out of my voice.

"Of course," he said simply. "Both of you. Do you not think that the northern boys will be doing the same?"

I realized the truth of what he said. "Why must we go so quickly?"

"I will tell you as we ride," he said, standing as he spoke. "Mount up, now."

Once we had ridden past the tents of the camp Turlo spoke again, his voice raised slightly against the wind and rain. "You asked about the need for haste," he said. "Donnalch would brook no delay. The exchange had to be done tonight, before he would sign the papers of truce. Callan had little choice but to agree, since Donnalch's son and nephew were already at their camp, close to the Fort on the northern side."

"I wonder," I said thoughtfully, "how long those two boys have known they would be part of the truce?"

"And what their instructions have been?" Turlo said. "As always, you are quick, Lena. If Colm had been here," he said, a trace of grief in his voice, "he would have seen the probability that an exchange of hostages would be part of any agreement, I believe, and we could have prepared the two of you too. But we did not see it, until earlier today, and there was no way to let you know."

"Is the truce fair?" Darel asked.

"It is," Turlo answered. "I cannot tell you much tonight; the proclamation will be tomorrow at mid-day, at the White Fort. You'll be there, front and centre, by the bye, as proof to all the good will between our two sides, so hold your heads up and be proud ambassadors for the Empire, when all the eyes are on you."

"I hope they let us have baths, then," I said.

Turlo laughed. "No doubt they will."

We rode through the gates of the White Fort, stopping outside a large stone building. Soldiers—cadets, really—stepped forward to take our horses. We dismounted, shouldering our packs. The horses were led away. I glanced at Darel: he looked as nervous as I felt.

"General," I said. "How long are we to be hostages?"

He looked from me to his son. "Half a year," he replied. *That long?* I thought. But Turlo still spoke. "Half a year, from now till harvest, to give the northerners a chance to plant and harvest: food runs short on both sides of the Wall. Time for us to hold Festival, and let the villages know our needs for food and supplies. And in that time Callan and Donnalch—and advisors on both sides—will hammer out the terms of a final peace, or not."

"But this is an order, and my duty," Darel said, his voice steady. "I understand, General."

"Good lad," he said. "And you, Guardswoman?"

A mix of emotions roiled through me: a thread of pride, fear, reluctance. When I had ridden north to the Wall the previous autumn, I had sworn fealty and service to Callan, the Emperor, for the duration of the conflict with the northmen. He had not released me from this, and therefore I too had an order and a duty to follow. I had thought I might die as a Guard, so why was I of two minds about this? *But when was the last time you really wanted to do anything?*

"General," I said, "will it be known, that I shall be a hostage to the northmen?"

Turlo's eyes softened. "You are thinking of your mother, and your sister?"

I nodded. "Yes," I said.

He understood. "My belief is you will be allowed letters," he said, "at least to your family and other women. I will find a way to send word, to Tirvan. Will my word suffice?"

"Of course," I said, grateful for his comprehension and compassion.

"Is there anything else?" I hesitated. "Tell me," he insisted.

"Well, if I could, if it's allowed—could I have my mare? Clio?" At least she would be something familiar. My stomach roiled. *Why had Casyn asked this of me?*

He laughed. "Is that all? Of course you can; you'll need a horse, no doubt. I'll have someone bring her over in the morning, and her tack. Darel, is there a particular horse you would like?"

Darel grinned, his teeth bright in the moonlight. I saw the resemblance to Turlo in that grin. "I rather like the skewbald with the white eye," he said, "but so does Rikter. Still, I don't suppose he'll have much chance of revenge, if I'm away with the northmen."

Turlo reached out to cuff his son lightly on the shoulder. If he had heard the fear behind the bravado, he didn't acknowledge it. "Good man," he said. "The skewbald it will be. Now, they are waiting for us, and we can delay no longer." He pulled open the great wooden door, beckoning us inside.

We walked into a hall. Torches in black iron sconces gusted high in the rush of air from the open door, and then subsided to flickers against the grey stone. Turlo led the way to another pair of doors, his boots loud to my ears on the stone flagged floor. Apprehension knotted my stomach. He knocked, but, not awaiting an answer, pulled the doors open and strode inside.

I stopped, Darel beside me, just inside the door. Like the hall, stone blocks formed the walls, but the ceiling curved above us, twice the height of the hall, huge beams supporting it. Fireplaces burned at both ends of the room, and torches, this time in gleaming bronze sconces, lined the walls. *But the floor!* It was flagged, around the periphery, but otherwise an intricate picture, in tiny fragments of stone and ceramic and glass, made up the rest of the surface. The colours gleamed in the firelight. Faces and sea creatures and designs—and under my booted feet I could feel warmth. Into my dazzled mind the words carved on the stone gates of Casilla came unbidden: *'Casil e imitaran ne'*. 'There is only one Casilla' was the common understanding of the words, which were in no language of the Empire, but a very old woman I had met in the marketplace had told me a different translation: 'Casil this is not'. I had puzzled over those words, but something about this room resonated with them. It did not look as if it belonged to the Empire I knew, but to something older, perhaps greater.

I forced myself to look up at the men seated at a long table. I saw the familiar face of Casyn, and beside him his brother, the Emperor Callan. Beyond Casyn, the empty chair that should have been Colm's: it was Turlo's, now. On the other side of Callan sat a man, tall but slight, with greying dark hair and no beard, dressed in a woven, woollen tunic and breeches, a cloak, also of wool, over one shoulder. The cloak was pinned to his shoulder with an intricate, enamelled pin, and around his neck he wore a twisted gold ring. Like the floor, the brooch and the gold of the torc glittered in the firelight. Two more men sat beside him, one clearly a close relation; the other, younger and blond-haired, and stockier. And beside them, two young men, bracketing, I thought, Darel in age. My heart beat hard against my chest. I willed my breathing to slow.

Callan stood. "Thank you for your speed, General," he said. "Guardswoman Lena, Cadet Darel, of the third, welcome to the Council of the White Fort, where after long days we have agreed to a truce between the Empire and the Northmen. Has the General Turlo explained your roles?"

Callan had named me, the elder, first. "He has, Emperor," I replied, hoping my voice was steady. He nodded.

"Yes, Emperor," Darel answered. He had served at the Emperor's winter camp, in the time before the invasion, and was less in awe of his Emperor as a result than some of his fellow cadets might have been.

Darel shared many traits with his father, I was beginning to realize, and Turlo rarely stood on ceremony.

The slight man spoke, his voice surprisingly musical, and conversational. "This is your son, Turlo, then? Not that I need to ask: I can see it in his face. Who is his mother?"

"Arey, her name is, from Berge," Turlo replied. "And before you ask, Donnalch, her hair is brown and Berge's records say her forbears, for as many generations as they have records, are from south of the Wall." Donnalch grinned.

"Aye, but who would tell of a child got by a northman who had slipped over the Wall?" he said. Then his voice became serious. "And the woman, Casyn? You ask for her to stand surrogate for your own daughters?" My breath caught in my throat. I swallowed.

"I do," Casyn said, in his grave voice. "If Lena will have it so. My daughters are both mothers, with small children; even so one might have agreed, but they are several days' ride away, in Han village. And had I the right I would be proud to name Lena my daughter." He smiled at me, with those words.

"Hmm," Donnalch mused. "Lena," he said, in his lilting voice, "You are from Tirvan, am I right?" 'Teeerrvaan', he pronounced it, not our shorter, flatter 'Turvan'. I nodded. "How old are you?"

I cleared my throat. "Nineteen," I replied. I could not remember the title Turlo had mentioned. "Sir," I added, in case he thought me lacking in courtesy.

"And you have skill with weapons, I am told," he said.

"Some," I said. *Hold your head up*, Turlo had said. "I have learned the sword, and the use of a secca, in these past two years. The hunting bow I learned as a girl. I am reckoned a good shot with a deer bow," I added.

He studied me for some time, without speaking. I kept my eyes on him.

"But I cannot put you with the boys," he said, half to himself. He paused. "Will you read? And write?"

"Of course I can," I said, too startled to be more polite.

"No, lassie, that's not what I asked," he said, spreading his hands. "I asked if you will. Do you like to do such, I should perhaps have said."

13

"Yes," I said slowly, with a quick glance at Casyn. "I have learned to like both; I have been reading the stories of our Empire, and I keep a journal, a private record of the happenings of my life."

"Then," he said, with a quick confirming look to his advisors, "I know what to do with you. You were a bit of a puzzle, lassie, but now I have it: I will send you to a *Ti'ach*; a house of learning, as we do with one of our own sons or daughters who are drawn to the written word. Will that suit you?"

He was asking me about where I would like to go? I glanced again at Casyn, and this time saw him make the briefest of nods. "Yes, sir," I said. "It would suit me." *Would it? What had I just agreed to*?

"My title is *Teannasach*," he said easily. "But 'sir' will do fine, until your tongue is more comfortable with our language. Now, these two youngsters"—he indicated the two boys—"are my son, Ruar, and his cousin Kebhan. They go as hostage to your Empire, to be cadets. You two come as hostage to the North, to Linrathe. We of the North hold to more of the old ways, and not all the agreement between us can be of the Empire's shaping. So, this exchange of hostages is a symbol, but it is also a surety, for us both, that the agreement we have made here will hold from planting to harvest. If it does not, then the lives of our heirs—of Kebhan and Ruar, or of Darel and Lena—may be forfeit. Is this understood?"

I swallowed. I looked at Darel; he had paled, but his face was resolute. Then I glanced over at the two northern boys. They looked solemn, but not shocked. *They had known in advance*, I thought. "Yes, sir," I answered.

"It is growing late, *Teannasach*, and there is much to do if our truce is to be announced tomorrow." The Emperor spoke; his voice sounded weary, but not strained. I regarded him: even in the forgiving light of the torches, he looked tired. His face held more lines, and his hair more grey, than when I had first met him over a year earlier. Time had brought betrayal and loss, and the relentless battle to push the northmen back and reclaim the Wall for the Empire. But he had done it, against enormous odds.

"Aye," Donnalch agreed. "Shall we have a few minutes with our children, to say our farewells, and then we can commit this agreement to paper, and sign our names to give us a season of peace?" He pushed back his chair to stand. Immediately his two companions and the boys followed suit. "We will leave this room to you, Emperor," he said. "As it's your fort," he added. I watched the five of them leave the room by a door in the far wall. It closed with a click of its latch.

"Darel, Lena," Casyn said. "Please, come, and sit. Leave your packs." We did as we were told, taking the chairs just vacated by the northmen. My legs felt suddenly weak. Casyn poured two glasses of wine, passing them to us. "There is food, if you would like," he said. I shook my head, as did Darel, which surprised me. *He must be as nervous as I am.* Casyn poured more wine, for himself and Turlo and the Emperor. He glanced at Callan, who nodded.

"You will be wondering why we agreed to this, and with such haste," he said. "We have been talking, now, for nearly twenty days. At first, we were trying to create the terms for a lasting peace, but there is too much we do not agree on. What we could agree on was the need for a hiatus, for the reasons stated, so we began talking about the terms for a temporary truce. We had reached an agreement late this afternoon, and then Donnalch made the demand for hostages."

"I could not let the truce fail on such a request," the Emperor said. "The *Teannasach*, I think, needed to put his mark on this agreement, and as he proposed his own son and his brother's son as their hostages, saying that his people would see this as binding, in their tradition, I believe he offers this in good faith."

I had a dozen questions, but none could be asked, here and now. I wished I had some time with Casyn, alone; I needed advice. I gathered my thoughts.

"May I ask a question, sir?" I said.

"Of course," Callan said.

"What am I—we—to pay attention to, wherever we are sent?"

"Ah," Callan said. "I could answer that better for Darel than for you, Lena. For you, Cadet," he said, turning to Darel, "there are two things: the state of their supplies, whether it is food or weapons or men, and, perhaps more importantly, what the men are saying. They will forget, eventually, to hold their tongues in front of you, and the boys your age will repeat what they hear from their fathers and uncles. Commit it to memory: do not write it down in plain words, at your life's peril. Now, go with the General Turlo—your father," he amended, in a rare acknowledgement of the relationship, "who will tell you what you can write, if you are allowed letters."

Turlo beckoned Darel over to a corner of the room. The Emperor turned his eyes to me. I had seen those eyes gentle in compassion, pierced with anguish, cold in anger and judgment. Now I just saw fatigue, and perhaps a mastered regret.

"Donnalch said he would send you to a house of learning," he said. "What we know of these is limited. There is no code to brief you on, no knowledge to pass on, or even much advice I can give you. Listen to what is said, about Donnalch's leadership, about the war, about what they wish to change. Exchange views on Partition, on your life as a woman of the Empire, our histories. Colm would have known more," he added, "and I believe he would have envied you this opportunity."

"I will do my best, sir, to remember that." I felt the prick of tears behind my eyes. Colm, who had just begun to show me complexity of our own history, and the cost and consequences of our choices. *I could not fail him, either.*

The Emperor regarded me in silence for some moments. I waited. "Listen to your instincts, Guardswoman," he said finally. "You will do well, I believe."

"Yes, sir." I hoped he was right. I heard footsteps crossing the room: Turlo and Darel. They joined us. The two men stepped aside to confer in hushed voices. I looked at Darel. He tried a grin.

"Another adventure," he said, in a passable imitation of his father.

Fatigue and apprehension began to dull my mind again. The northmen joined us, and after some further conversation among the leaders, Birel—Casyn's soldier-servant—led us through a warren of dark lanes to our beds for the night. Darel's bed was in a shared room, but I had a small, dark chamber to myself. The room felt clammy, but when I pulled back the blankets to climb into the narrow cot, I realized someone—likely Birel—had put a heated stone wrapped in cloth in the bed.

I pulled the blankets over my shoulders and wrapped my feet around the stone, then doused the single candle standing on the small table beside the cot. The mattress below me rustled, a thin pallet of straw on a rope web, suspended from a wooden frame. If I were lucky there would be no vermin sharing the straw. *Where would I sleep tomorrow night?* I shivered, more with anxiety than cold, burrowing deeper into the blankets. I would not think about tomorrow. Instead, I began to count in my mind all the beds I had slept in, this past year, since I left the one I had shared with Maya, and then Garth, in Tirvan.

The first had been the bed at Keavy's inn, a day's ride from Tirvan, with Garth beside me in the night. Then more inns, and camps, for several weeks, and then? The shared room at the Four-Ways Inn, I remembered, and then the bed with old Ione at Karst. My camp bed at the Emperor's Winter Camp. Back to the Four-Ways Inn, riding as Emperor's Messenger now, a brief sleep in Freya's own bed. Then Karst again, and then Casilla: one night in a hostel near the gates, and then months in the Street of Weavers, sharing a house with Tevra and Ianthe, and Garth's son Valle, and Maya, after she joined us. The memories of these rooms and houses and beds blurred and shifted. Sleep claimed me.

I awoke to a knock on the door. The room held no light, and I had no sense of the time. "Yes?" I called.

"Time to get ready, Guardswoman," I heard Birel say. "I've brought wash water. Shall I leave it outside the door?"

"Wait," I said, pushing back the blankets to sit up. I fumbled on the table, and by feel lit the candle. Then I walked the three paces to the door, opening it. I stood aside, holding the candle high, to allow Birel to bring in the water.

He had also brought soap and a towel. "I'll return shortly," he said, "to guide you back to the great hall."

This part of the White Fort had only communal latrines for the men, and so I used the chamberpot before washing. I combed water through my hair and dressed in my clean clothes. Then I repacked my pack, and waited for Birel.

He returned promptly. I shouldered my pack, following him through the damp morning. Around one corner he stopped to knock on another

17

door. Darel opened it, and stepped out. He too had dressed in clean clothes, and smoothed down his red hair.

"Good morning," I greeted him. "Sleep well?"

"Of course," he said. He had learned the soldier's knack of sleeping anywhere and anytime, whether in a shared barracks or curled up under the Wall during a brief halt. "And you?" he asked.

"Yes, fine." I had slept, solidly, fatigue trumping apprehension, and my sleep had been dreamless, as far as I remembered.

We followed Birel to the great hall. This morning the light came from the high windows, and the floor, while still magnificent, did not shimmer and glitter; the images lay still. *Sleeping*, I thought, and then dismissed the fancy. The men of the Empire and the North sat at the long table, but the focus at this moment was breakfast, not diplomacy.

Turlo greeted us by name. "Come and sit," he said, "and eat. There's fresh bread, and some dried fruit. Eggs and cold venison, too. " Places were found for us, and food brought, and I made as good a breakfast as I had had for some months. Birel, unasked, brought me tea, smelling of mint.

I saw Birel take Casyn's plate and pour something steaming into his cup. Turlo nibbled dried fruit. The Emperor's place had been cleared; he studied papers before him, a pen in his hand. At the other end of the table the servers repeated the work, clearing plates, pouring drinks. The Emperor looked up.

"Now," he said, "we had better talk of today." I saw, from the corner of my eye, Birel gesture to the servers. They left the room, Birel alone staying, standing against the wall.

"Keep eating," Callan said, as Darel moved to push aside his plate, "but listen." The Emperor looked down the table at the northmen; they stopped their conversation to focus on Callan. Donnalch rose.

"I'll sit with you," he said easily, and walked along the table. Casyn, with a glance at his brother, shifted over. Birel brought another chair, and Donnalch took the place beside the Emperor. The gesture, with all its implications, made me uncomfortable. I could not think of this man as the Emperor's equal.

"We are lucky with the day," Donnalch remarked, as he sat. "The sun is shining, and by all the signs there will be no rain before the afternoon. It's best if we can do this outdoors, where as many men can see and hear as possible."

Callan acknowledged this statement with a nod of his head. "If we speak from the watchtower west of this fort," he said, "the land is nearly flat for a good space on both sides. Will that serve, do you think, *Teannasach*?"

"Aye," Donnalch said. "Your messengers are ready to ride?"

"They are," Callan said. "And yours?"

"Mine also," Donnalch agreed. "The copies of the treaty are ready too, the ones entrusted to my scribes, and yours also, I believe?"

"Done," Callan said, "and the exchange has been made: the copies are here." He indicated the papers in front of him. "I have read and signed them; there are no errors of copying that affect the meaning of the truce; your scribes are to be commended." He spoke quietly and politely, but I thought his voice lacked spirit. He did not quite sound defeated; resigned might be a better word. I wondered what the treaty said.

"And yours," Donnalch said. "I read through the copies from your scribes earlier, and wrote my name on them all; I wake early. So now, Emperor," he challenged, "how will we determine the speaking order? Who has precedence?" He smiled as he said this, but something in his face told me this was a serious question. Donnalch's men, I noticed, had become very still.

"*Teannasach*," Callan said calmly, "as you yourself said last night, it is my fort. And my wall, and my watchtower. Your incursions into the Empire were repelled, and you and your men retreated to your historic lands. I think our positions are clear, and therefore the precedence. Would you not agree?" He kept his eyes on Donnalch as he spoke. The hall was very quiet. I had the sense that this conversation had happened before

Donnalch held Callan's eyes for several heartbeats. Then he inclined his head, a half-smile on his lips. "As you say," he said, his voice courteous. "I will give precedence to the long years of history, and the remnants of the greater Empire that this room reminds us of." I frowned. *What did he mean?* I glanced at Casyn. He looked grim. I repeated Donnalch's words in my mind, and heard this time the subtleties: precedence not to the Emperor, or even to his superior military position, but to history. I watched the men, holding my breath, feeling the precarious balance in the room.

Callan stood, his hand lightly resting on his sword, his eyes still on Donnalch. I heard chairs scrape as around both men their supporters stood too. Belatedly I realized I too had better stand, although I had only my secca on my waist. I could hear Darel's breathing beside me, not quite even, and the thumping of my heart. Very slowly, Donnalch came to his feet.

"The remnants of a greater Empire we may be," Callan said, "and myself a pale echo of those Emperors who came before, but the soldiers of the Empire do not forget. If it is that history you would acknowledge, then will you face east with me, and bow to that memory, and to what may still lie beyond the mountains and the seas?"

"I will," Donnalch said, "and my men with me. We do not forget either." The men moved out to the centre of the hall, facing the windows where the morning light was brightest. Callan and Donnalch stood beside each other, their swords in front of them. I followed Darel to stand behind the men. I had absolutely no idea of what they spoke, or what this meant.

Callan's voice rang out. "To the Empire unconquered," he proclaimed, bowing deeply. I followed suit, a memory surfacing of Colm's burial: Callan and the soldiers facing east and bowing. *What did they bow to? What greater Empire? Where?*

The brief ceremony seemed to be over, but the men remained standing. Donnalch turned to Callan. "Perhaps, Emperor," he said, "we should make this acknowledgement again, when we announce our truce. It would help, I think, to remind both sides that we come from a common history, although we have taken different paths. Perhaps, one day, we can find a road that we can all walk on, without enmity, and the truce we sign today may be the first step on that road." He spoke simply, with no trace of the challenge or posturing I had heard earlier.

Callan nodded. "Perhaps."

A line from Colm's history of the Empire came back to me: 'When there had been silence from the east for many years...'. I had thought, when I read it, that it had referred to a previous threat that had gone quiet, and had not asked Colm about it, although I had meant to. I wracked my brain. *What did I know about the east?* The mountains, the Durrains, which formed the eastern boundary of the Empire, and were said to be uncrossable. The Eastern Fort, where I had never been. Something more: *the eastern fever.* I heard the words in my mother's voice, but I couldn't place the context; something, perhaps, overheard as she instructed Kira. And what had the Emperor just said? *What still may remain beyond the mountains and the seas? What was he talking about?* I shook my head in frustration.

The movement caught Turlo's eye. He turned to look at me, frowning slightly. I coloured: did he think I disagreed with Callan, or Donnalch? I made a small gesture of placation; he nodded slightly, returning his attention to the leaders. Callan and Donnalch still faced each other, silent. Finally, Donnalch inclined his head slightly, a faint smile crossing his lips, and turned again to sit.

The men spoke quietly now, looking at papers. I watched for some minutes, but when I saw Kebhan and Ruar begin whispering to each other, I turned to Darel.

"Darel," I murmured, "this bowing to the east, what's it all about?"

"Don't you know?" he whispered back, surprise evident even in the hushed tone.

"No," I said. "Would I be asking, if I did?"

He remained quiet for a moment. "I suppose," he whispered finally, "it doesn't matter, to the women's villages. I can't tell you everything here, so this must do for now: once, many hundreds of years ago, maybe longer, we were part of a larger Empire, whose Supreme Emperor ruled from a city far to the east. What happened to that city, and those Emperors, we do not know. But what we know, the men, I mean, of command and strategy, and of fighting, we learned from them, and Callan and our Emperors before him take their titles in subservience to the Eastern Emperor, whether he lives or not, and remembers us if he does live."

I stared at him. "But what happened?"

He shrugged. "I told you, we don't know. Just that all messages, emissaries, trade, they all stopped. A very long time ago. We learn

21

about it as cadets, and then we forget about it again, except in ceremonies, and at burials."

"But why does Donnalch know about it, and honour the memory? The north is not part of the Empire."

Darel shook his head. "I don't know. Maybe they have learned it from us in the long years there have been soldiers on the Wall?"

"Maybe," I murmured. My mind went back to a conversation I had had with Colm, months before. We had spoken of the building of the Wall, and how the northern armies had included men who had chosen to move north, rather than live under the rules of Partition. *Perhaps*, I thought, *they brought the knowledge of the Eastern Empire, and the traditions around it, with them, and they have been maintained there to this day, as they have been here.*

And what did it matter? This Eastern Empire had been gone for centuries. Rituals called upon many things: some invoked gods I did not believe in, and a long-disappeared Empire wasn't that different. I would take the knowledge north with me: perhaps it would help in finding common ground with those who would be charged with my keeping. It might be useful to know this, in a house of learning. I felt glad, suddenly, that I was not the village girl I had been before the day, nearly two years ago, when Casyn had ridden into Tirvan. I had known nothing then of our history, beyond a few bare facts, and nothing at all of the world beyond the borders of Tirvan. Since then I had learned to defend the Empire, ridden its length, lived in Casilla, served the Emperor. *I had learned lessons of the heart, too,* I thought, *about love and loyalty, duty and obligation, and how difficult it was to separate them.* I would take all that north, and learn what I could, for my Emperor, and for myself.

Chapter Two

A WEAK SUN BRIGHTENED THE DAY, but gave little warmth. The stones of the road and the Wall gleamed damply, drying in the stiff northwest breeze. I rode beside Darel in the middle of the entourage. His attention was mostly given to controlling the wall-eyed skewbald that had waited for him, tacked and restless, when we left the White Fort. I had been glad to see my Clio, although I needed both my voice and hands to keep her calm.

Darel's horse shied, skittering sideways over the flagstones. Clio danced away from the larger horse. I heard Darel swear, hands and heels efficiently bringing the skewbald back into line. I felt the northerners' eyes on us; they sat their rougher hill ponies easily, and would know that our mounts' skittishness came in part from our own apprehension. Although, I noted, Kebhan and Ruar's ponies trotted calmly.

Ahead of us the commanders and their advisors had noticed nothing. As we approached the watchtower where the proclamation of truce would be made, the crowd of soldiers deepened. We slowed to a walk, and then pulled up. Dismounting, I handed Clio's reins to Birel, who had appeared beside me; he took the skewbald from Darel as well, motioning us forward.

I followed Darel to the base of the watchtower, and up the wooden steps. I could hear more footsteps behind us, echoing on the thick planks. As I turned the corner onto the top of the tower, the cold wind snatched at me, carrying the scents of smoke and pitch: the beacon-fires had been lit, to call the people in. My eyes watered. I looked northward. A horde of men and some women stood on the moorland below the tower, looking up. Southward, an equal number watched, although almost all were men.

Watchtowers held, usually, one to three men: eight of us crowded the space. The Emperor, and beside him Casyn; Donnalch and his brother—whose name, I realized, I did not know—and the four of us who stood as hostage. From the end of the platform I saw a red head on the top of the Wall below: Turlo, with more men beside him. I guessed the Wall ramparts on both sides of the tower supported men, watching, guarding. The crowds on both sides shifted; voices rose and fell.

Casyn had told us, before we left the White Fort, what we were to do: step forward when our names were announced. Beyond that, nothing. Given the wind and the crowds, all proclamations were to be made twice, once facing north, once south, repeated by both the Emperor and Donnalch.

From the wall rampart below us came the wild moan of the elbow pipe, a sound that belonged to these windswept moors and valleys. The crowds on both sides of the wall gradually fell silent, except for the shifting of bodies. Together, Callan and Donnalch stepped forward, to the north, first. My gut tightened. I looked at the backs of the two men, Callan a head taller than Donnalch, and heavier. Neither man wore armour. Callan's grey cloak, trimmed with white fur, hung to his knees; around his neck was the silver pendant denoting his rank. Donnalch's robe encompassed the greys and fawns and purples of the moor, as effective a camouflage as the feathers of a grouse hen. The gold torc caught the light. His dark hair lifted in the breeze.

"People of the north," he said, his voice pitched to carry. He followed it by something in a language I did not know, the words sliding together, sounding somehow as wild and sorrowful as the pipes. "People of the north," he said again. "I stand here today—no, we stand here today, to announce a truce, between myself and Callan, the Emperor of the lands south of the Wall, and between our peoples. Listen now, as together we tell you, in our common language, of the terms of this truce." He turned slightly to face Callan. "Emperor," he said, gesturing.

"My thanks, *Teannasach*," Callan said. "These, then are the terms. For six months, we will lay down our arms; your people will return to your villages and your fields, to your byres and pastures, and mine will do the same, before starvation finds us on both sides of the Wall. I give my word here, and the *Teannasach* will give his, that no raid nor battle will be undertaken by either side during this time of truce, nor any action that leads to the death by violence of a man or woman of our opposing side." He stepped back slightly. The mass of people remained, for the most part, quiet. *Waiting*, I thought, *to hear more.* Donnalch raised his voice again.

"In those six months, I and Lorcann, and the Emperor Callan and his brother the General Casyn, will meet, and talk, with the intent and the hope to find a way to a permanent peace between us; a peace, mind you, not a treaty that makes one side a vassal state to the other. Only if we are equals, in the tradition of the fallen Empire of the East that both our lands revere, can there be true peace. In surety of this truce, and our hopes for a lasting peace, I send my son Ruar, and my nephew Kebhan, to live with the cadets of the Southern Empire." At a nod from the man I now knew was Lorcann, the two boys stepped forward. Now the crowd did react: no-one shouted, or cried out, but a slow murmuring began. Donnalch raised an arm, and slowly, it subsided. The boys stepped back beside Darel and me.

Callan spoke again. "I have no children," he said, calmly, "to my sorrow. The Empire sends Darel, son to the General Turlo, and Lena, who stands as surrogate daughter to the General Casyn, to live and work and learn with you, and as hostages to the Empire's intentions. Here they are." I took a deep breath, and with a brief glance at Darel, stepped to the edge of the watchtower. Hundreds of eyes looked up at us.

"Thank you," I heard Casyn murmur, and we stepped back. I let my breath out. Donnalch spoke again.

"Look," he said, holding up a rolled paper, "here is the truce. Watch, now, as the Emperor and I sign it in your sight." He unrolled the paper, spreading it on the rampart of the watchtower. The wind caught at it. Casyn and Lorcann held in down, and first Donnalch and then Callan signed the document. *It would have to be signed twice*, I thought, *for both sides to see.* The paper was rolled again, and held up in Donnalch's hand.

"This truce begins now," he cried, "and the penalty for any man or woman who breaks it is death: not only yours, mind, for you may be willing to make that choice, but remember that you could be choosing death for my son and nephew too, and that is not your choice to make. As your *Teannasach*, chosen by you to be your leader, I command you: uphold this truce, and leave here today with nothing more in your hearts and minds than your families and the sowing of your crops. We have made history here today, with you as witness; remember that and rejoice." He said something else, in the same tongue, with its undercurrent of music and mourning, and handed the scroll to Callan.

We all turned, then, to face the soldiers and guards of the Empire. Callan and Donnalch repeated the same words, Callan announcing the truce, and then Donnalch giving the terms. Only in the minor changes needed for the speaking order and the audience did the speech differ from what had been said to the northerners.

"I send Darel, son to General Turlo, and Lena of Tirvan, who stands as surrogate daughter to my brother the General Casyn, to live and work in the north, as hostages to the Empire's intentions," I heard Callan say. Again, I took a deep breath, and stepped forward. The eyes before had been those of strangers, assessing, curious. Now the eyes of those I served with, my companions and friends, looked up. *This was harder*, I thought. I saw Halle in the crowd, met her eyes. She smiled, gave a quick nod. I swallowed. I did not look for anyone else.

I heard Casyn's quiet cue to step back. The same formal signing of the document occurred, with Lorcann and Casyn holding the paper against the wind. Callan said the final words, reminding our people that my life, and Darel's, were forfeit to truce-breaking. I heard the words, but I could not make them real. I wondered where Callan and Donnalch would meet; here, on the Wall, I supposed. *Who would guard the Wall now? Soldiers from both sides, surely?*

A clatter of boots roused me. The Emperor and the *Teannasach* descended the steps from the watchtower, followed by their supporters. Darel stepped forward just at the same moment as one of the northern boys—Kebhan, I thought. They both stopped.

"It is your Wall," Kebhan said softly, and with a slight bow. "You go ahead."

Darel hesitated. He looked at the steps, and then back at Kebhan. "The way is wide enough for us both," he said. "Shall we walk together?"

Kebhan smiled slightly. "A diplomatic solution," he replied. He wore woollen clothes like his father's, woven in shades to blend with the moorland, and deerskin boots, and this close to him I could see

Donnalch in the shape of his chin and his eyes. He turned to his cousin. "You will walk with the lady Lena, Ruar," he said.

"I am not called lady, Kebhan," I said, "nor are other women you might meet in the service of the Emperor."

He glanced at Ruar. "That is good to know," he said. "How should I address you, then?"

"By my rank, which is Guard," I said, "or just by my name. You may also meet women who serve the Empire's army but are not part of it. Such a woman you would call by her role: Cook, or Smith, if you did not know her name."

"I see," he said in his soft voice. "In our lands, La...Lena, a woman of rank, and you must have such, if you stand as surrogate to the General Casyn's daughters, is addressed as my lady, or Lady. You should expect this."

I frowned. "Rank in the Empire does not come from our fathers," I said, "so if I had any rank, it would be from my mother, who is a council leader in our village. But we do not use such terms: rank and titles belong to the Empire's armies, not the women's villages."

"We both have much to learn," Kebhan said. "We must all try not to take offense at usages and customs not our own." I frowned again: *was he chastising me?* But he turned away. "Come, Darel; Cadet Darel, yes?" he said. "We should follow our *Teannasach* and your Emperor down these steps. Are you ready?"

Darel grinned. "Ready, Cadet Kebhan." They descended shoulder to shoulder, heads high. I looked down at Ruar. *Eleven, maybe twelve,* I thought. In the Empire, he would be choosing his path to service, whether on the boats, or as a cavalry cadet, or training to be a medic, just as I at twelve had chosen my apprenticeship. I wondered what the customs were, in the north.

"Come, then, Guard Lena," Ruar said. *A quick learner.*

"Cadet," I replied, and we turned and walked together down the stairs.

††††

Clouds scudded across the hills. We rode with the east wind in our faces, the thin spring sunlight holding little warmth. The track we followed was muddy; we kept the horses to a walk, and even so could not avoid being splattered.

Near mid-morning our leader, Ardan, held up a hand to stop. Turning in his saddle, he called to me. "Lena, ride up beside me." I did as he asked. We had stopped at the crest of what had felt like a gentle rise, but below us lay a long, deep valley, and in that valley stood a complex of buildings, built of grey stone. An L-shaped hall made one side of the complex, standing three storeys high and roofed in lichened, mossy slate; from each of its wings ran lower structures, and two or three free-standing smaller buildings surrounded the central courtyard. Trees sheltered it, and the rocky valley side. It looked, to my eyes, very old.

"The *Ti'ach*," Ardan said, gesturing. "Also called *Ti'ach na Perras*, for Perras, who heads this house, and to distinguish it from the others. Here you will live, for the duration of the agreement, and be treated as any other woman who had come here to learn."

Looking down, I swallowed my apprehension, studying the buildings to make sense of what I saw. Smoke rose from several chimneys. Someone came out of one of the smaller buildings, a basket in her arms, and began to peg out washing on a line. Others worked in what I thought was probably a garden plot, preparing the ground. It looked peaceful, nestled in its valley, undisturbed.

We rode down a switch-back path and over a stone bridge. The stream below ran rapidly, in full spring spate. In the paved courtyard, we dismounted. I held Clio's reins, looking around me. On seeing us riding down the path, the woman hanging washing had left her basket to go into the large house, calling something as she went, so by the time we reached the courtyard several people had emerged from inside. I saw two young women—one no more than a girl—and a man a few years their senior, flanking a grey-haired man leaning on a stick, and an upright older woman beside him.

It was the older woman who spoke. "Ardan," she said. "Welcome back. We were not expecting you. Are the talks completed then? Is there peace?"

"My lady," Ardan said. "There is a truce: six months to replenish our food supplies, on both sides of the Wall. Our *Teannasach* and the southern Emperor have proclaimed it, and during this truce, they will negotiate a longer peace, it is hoped. For surety, hostages have been exchanged. One has been sent here. I bring her to you: this woman, Lena, who stands hostage for the General Casyn."

As Ardan spoke I stepped forward, Clio obediently following. In the silence, I could hear her mouthing her bit. The older woman smiled.

"Welcome to *Ti'ach na Perras*, Lena," she said. "I am Dagney, and this," she gestured to the man beside her, "is Perras, *Comiádh* to this house. Ardan, will someone take Lena's horse, please?" I felt Clio's reins taken from my hand, heard her turn away. "Come," Dagney said, beckoning. She and Perras turned to walk back into the house. One of the younger women waited. "Come," she repeated. "I am Jordis. Are you tired, from your ride?"

I bristled at the implication of weakness. "No, my lady," I answered. "I am used to riding; I am a Guard in the Emperor's troops, and have ridden the length of the Empire twice. A few hours in the saddle is nothing."

"Oh, dear," she said, flushing. "I have offended you. But, a Guard? I did not know women served in the troops. Please forgive me...will you tell me more?" I realized she was flustered, and younger than I had thought. I stopped bristling.

"It is I who should apologize," I said. "You only asked what anyone would of a traveller. I am happy to tell you more, but," I looked over at the doorway, "should we not go inside, as the Lady Dagney indicated?"

"Oh. Yes," she said. I followed her up the shallow steps into the house. The door opened into a wide hall, lit only by small windows. The air smelled of stone and a smoke that was not woodsmoke, but something sharper. As my eyes adjusted I could see a long table and chairs standing on the flagged floor. At one end of the room a huge fireplace dominated; cabinets lined the opposite wall. Perras and Dagney, and the other man and girl waited, standing, at the table. The room was cold.

"Jordis," Dagney said gently. "Please go and fetch tea. Lena, will you sit?" Chairs were drawn. I took the one that Dagney indicated, draping my cloak over the back. Everyone sat, the young man last, after helping Dagney with her chair.

"Let me introduce you," Dagney said. "This is Niav," she indicated the girl, "and," nodding to the man, "this is Sorley. They are students here, as, I assume, you are to be?"

"I suppose I am," I said, "my lady. Your *Teannasach*," I stumbled a bit over the unfamiliar title, "said I should come here." I tried to remember his words. "He said he would send me here, because I like to read, and write, and this is where sons and daughters of your land come, if that is what they are drawn to."

"The *Teannasach* was a student here himself," Dagney said, "for a while. He still visits, when he can. Now, Lena, tell us a bit about yourself. Where are you from?"

"Tirvan," I said. "It's a fishing village, on the coast, south of Berge and Delle." I saw Perras nod. "I had a boat there, with my partner. We were separated, in the preparations for the invasion by Leste, and later I went south, to find her, and for other reasons. The search took me to our Emperor's winter camp, and I was there when..." I hesitated. *What did I say to these people? It had been their men we had fought against.*

"When the *Teannasach* took his men through the Wall," Perras said, his voice precise and measured.

"Yes," I agreed. "When that news reached us." I warmed to Perras, coming subtly to my aid as he had.

"And you came north, to the fighting?" Dagney asked. "I also did not realize women fought at the Wall."

I shook my head. "Not at once. I was given a task to do, to ride to the southern villages, to ask for women to ride north. I came north, to the Wall, later." *That would do,* I thought. *They did not need to know all my history.*

"The General Casyn is your father?" Perras asked. "You are hostage in his name, did I hear?"

"I am," I said, "but he is not my father." I saw Jordis return, carrying a laden tray. "He asked me to stand instead of his daughters, who are mothers with small children, and some distance from the Wall. It was Casyn who trained us, at Tirvan, and we rode south together, for part of the way. Now he is—" I stopped. "Was, I suppose," I amended, "my commanding officer."

Perras nodded. Jordis put the tray on the table and for a minute or two the distribution of tea and small oatcakes, spread with a soft, pungent cheese, occupied us. I sipped the smoky, unsweetened tea.

"What languages do you speak?" the young man—Sorley, I thought—asked.

"Only that of the Empire," I said. He raised an eyebrow, but said nothing.

"What books have you read?" Jordis asked.

"Schoolbooks," I shrugged. "My mother has books of healing—she's a midwife—but I haven't read those. There were not many books in Tirvan, except those, and some on husbandry."

"But why, then, were you sent here?" Sorley asked. "Forgive me if I sound rude, but you have less learning than one of our children in their tenth year."

I put my cup down and took a breath. "I came late to an interest in books," I said, trying to remain calm. "In the weeks I spent at our Emperor's winter camp, I was given a history of our Empire by the Emperor's brother and advisor, Colm. Reading that, I began to want to know more. So, I may know very little, but I am eager to learn."

"Colm's history?" Perras said, his voice a shade less measured. "You have read Colm's history?"

"I have," I said, "and discussed it with him, just a little."

Perras shook his head. "He and I exchanged a few letters. His loss was more than unfortunate," he said. "What do you remember? Could you write it down?"

"I could," I said. "But I have a copy, if you would like to read it."

Perras put his cup down. No-one spoke.

"You have a copy of Colm's history?" Perras said. I could hear the disbelief.

"Yes. Colm gave it to me to read, and after he was killed, the General Casyn told me to keep it. He said the Advisor had meant for me to have it. It's in my saddlebag."

"I would be..." Perras hesitated. "most grateful if you would let me read it. Would you consider allowing it to be copied?"

What would Colm think? I wondered. *He and this man had corresponded.* "Yes," I said, "I would, as long as it is done here. And I can keep an eye on it," I added.

"I will do the copying myself," Perras said. "As I read it; it will help me in considering and remembering what is written, and allow me to annotate as I go. Is that acceptable, Lena?"

"Of course."

"Would you like more to eat or drink?" Dagney asked. "If not, then I will have Jordis show you to your sleeping chamber, and you may wash and change after your ride. And then," she smiled, "perhaps you could bring the book down to Perras. He will be in his workroom, waiting as patiently as he can." I heard the gentle teasing, and the affection behind it. I glanced at Perras. He acknowledged me—or Dagney's comments?—with a nod. I smiled.

"I will be as quick as I can," I said, standing to turn to Jordis.

"This way," she said, pointing. I picked up my cloak, following her out of the room and up a flight of wooden stairs. The sound of my riding boots echoed against the stone walls; Jordis, I saw, was wearing deerskin slippers. We reached a landing. At the third door, she stopped.

I stepped through the door. My saddlebags sat on a low chest against one stone wall. A narrow bed, covered by a woven woollen blanket, faced a small fireplace, with a sheepskin on the flagged floor. A table and chair filled the space under the one window, and a wardrobe and washstand lined the other wall. Simple, but more than adequate, and much better than my shared quarters at the Wall.

"I am next door," Jordis said. "Is there anything you need, Lena?"

I shook my head. "Just a few minutes to change, and perhaps to wash my face and hands. Is there water in the jug?" I stepped over to the washstand. The jug was full, and a towel hung on the bar. "I see there is. Then, no," I said, and then realized there was. "Wait," I said. "Yes, there is. Jordis, I assume there are no servants here? We empty our own slops, and the chamberpot?"

"Yes, of course," she said. "Except for the *Comiádh*, because of his infirmity. I will wait for you in my room. When you are ready, knock on my door, and I will show you the back stairs, and the well and laundry." She hesitated. "Are you used to servants, Lena?"

"No!" I said. "I am far more used to doing for myself, and happy to do so, once I know the house. But should I not take the book to Perras first? And is that what I call him?" There was a familiarity to this, learning the protocols and ways of a new place. I had grown used to it, over the past year.

"*Comiádh* is better," Jordis answered, "at least at first. The older students, those who have been here for some time, often call the *Comiádh* by his name, but I am not comfortable yet doing so. I think I am waiting for him to invite me to." She coloured a little.

"Com-i-ath," I tried. "Is that right?"

"Almost," Jordis said. "The emphasis is on the last part, though— Com-i-ATH. Do you hear the difference?"

"*Comiádh*," I stressed the last syllable of the title.

"Good," she said. "And yes, take him the book first. We can do the other later. Should I wait for you, or can you find your way back?"

"If you don't mind waiting," I said, "while I think I can find my way back to the hall, I do not know where the *Comiádh* will be. Will you show me? I'll be quick in changing; soldiers learn to be."

"I'll wait. I'm that side," she indicated with a movement of her head. She closed the door quietly behind her.

I took a deep breath, valuing the brief solitude. I walked to the window. It had a view over the yard. The wind had picked up a bit, and the laundry billowed in the weak sunshine. I looked out, beyond the valley, to the hills where the play of cloud and sun dappled the grey-green of their slopes. A lone bird—a buzzard, I thought—rode the air.

I stepped away from the window to pull off my riding clothes. Quickly washing in the cold water, I dressed again in my clean tunic and trousers. Hair freshly combed, I pulled my indoor slippers onto my feet, and picked up Colm's history.

Jordis had left her door open. I knocked lightly; she turned from where she sat at her table. I saw she had been reading. "That *was* quick," she said. She looked down at what I held. "Is that the history?"

I held it out to her. "Do you want to see it?"

Her eyes widened. "Not before the *Comiádh*," she said, with a quick shake of her head. She stood. "Come."

I followed her down the stairs and through the hall. She led me to a door I hadn't seen, obscured between the cabinets by shadow, and knocked lightly.

"Come," I heard Perras say. Jordis opened the door, ushering me in before her.

Perras sat in an armchair beside a fireplace, where a fire glowed, warming the room and giving off a rich, unfamiliar smell, not unpleasant. On both sides of the fireplace, shelves held many books, and some objects. Writing tools and paper, and an open book lay on a large table.

"Lena," Perras said. He stood carefully, steadying himself with the arms of the chair. "You were very quick."

I held out Colm's history. "I thought it important to you." *And I have been trained to not keep those who outrank me waiting,* I thought, but did not say. Perras took the book from me. He turned slightly to the firelight, and opened it. I knew by heart the words that began the first page: 'In the third year of the reign of the Emperor Lucian...'.

We stood in silence as Perras read, turning pages carefully. After a few minutes, he sighed, closing the book. "I must not be greedy," he said, "but I have waited a long time to read this work."

"You never met Colm?" I asked.

"No," Perras answered. "We exchanged a few letters, as I think I said, a few years ago, about what our records and our memories say about the building of the Wall, but we never met. I had hoped we would. We would have had much to discuss." He glanced down again at the book in his hands. "So much," he echoed. Then he raised his head to smile at me. "Please sit; it is easier for me." he said, his voice firmer. He nodded toward a second chair, facing his, on the opposite side of the fireplace.

I did as I was bid. Perras settled himself back into his armchair, looking up at Jordis. "You may go," he said gently. "My thanks for bringing Lena to me."

"My pleasure, *Comiádh*," she answered, and slipped from the room, pulling the door firmly closed.

I waited for Perras to speak. The warmth and flicker of the fire threatened to make me sleepy. I suppressed a yawn. The *Comiádh* appeared deep in thought.

"I think," he said, "that I would like you to sit with me each day, for a few hours, as I copy this history. That way I can ask questions of you, and discuss what you remember, as I read it." He smiled. "And you can keep an eye on your book, as you requested. Does that seem reasonable, Lena? I can see the book is precious to you."

"Yes...mostly because Colm gave it to me, and because both the book and he taught me things I had never known about our history." I stopped. Perras regarded me intently. I felt a need to explain. "In our village school, we learned just the simple facts: that the Partition Assembly was held, and some of the reasons why, and why we now live the way we do. That was all I wanted to know, at ten or twelve. But now..." I stopped.

"But now the facts are not so simple, and you are questioning whether they are facts at all." Perras finished for me.

"Yes," I said. "*Comiádh*, as we go through this book together, would you tell me what you know, from beyond the northern Wall? I would like to hear your side, too."

I saw a flicker of surprise in his eyes. "It will not make things simpler," he warned. Then he smiled again. "Beyond the northern Wall," he repeated. "Perhaps that is the first thing we must question." I frowned, puzzled. "Turn around, Lena," he said, "and look at the map."

I turned my head. On the wall behind me hung a large map. I looked at it, not recognizing anything. I stood to examine it more closely. A blue expanse to the right of the map was water, I realized, and there was blue, as well, at the top edge and at the bottom. I saw the pointed symbols for mountains running down the centre of the map, veering left. Islands of brown dotted the blue near the bottom of the map. I frowned.

"Where is this?" I asked. Perras stood, slowly, making his way over to stand beside me. He laid one hand on my shoulder, pointing with his cane.

"Here," he said, "is what you call the northern Wall. And here we are," he pointed to a spot below the line he had called the Wall, "and here is your home village, Tirvan." He indicated a place on the right-hand side, where the land met the sea.

"But," I started to say, and then I saw. "It's upside down," I said, in wonder.

"From what you are used to, yes." Perras agreed.

He had taken his hand from my shoulder, and so I took a step forward. I scanned the map. I found the roads I had ridden, and Karst, and followed the road with my eyes back to the Wall. Then I let my eyes travel down toward the bottom of the map. I could not read the names, but I could see the line of another wall, and named villages, and then a gap of ocean where the islands lay, and then just the edge of another land.

"There is another Wall!" I said. "And what lands are these, here?" I pointed to the bottom of the map.

"The land to the far north, at the bottom, is Varsland, and the islands belong to it." Perras said. "The other Wall—it is not a stone wall, or not mostly, but an earthern dyke for the greatest part—is The Sterre. The land below it is called Sorham—the South Home of the men of Varsland, for to those people it is south; and between The Sterre and the Southern Wall is this land, Linrathe."

I stared, trying to take it all in. Questions swirled in my mind. I didn't know what to ask first. My eyes returned to Tirvan, trying to fix a point in this new image of my world. I heard Perras make his slow way back to his chair and settle himself. I traced again the road to Karst, and found Casilla, and let my eyes come back to the Wall. I followed the Durrains from the sea to where they bent eastward, and studied the islands and the northern lands, then brought my eyes up again to where The Sterre was marked, dividing the land from the Lantanan Sea on the west to the mountains.

"Does the map show the same distances everywhere?" I asked without turning. "Would it take as long to ride from The Sterre to the northern sea as it does to ride from the Wall to Casilla?" The distances looked the same to me, on the map.

"Were there roads of equal quality, and the land equally flat or hilly," Perras said, "then, yes. The map is accurate, or as accurate as our mathematics allows it to be."

"Then," I said, "Sorham is as big as The Empire, and this land—Linrathe?—only half the size of either. Am I right?"

"You are," he answered. "Come and sit down, Lena, and tell me what you are thinking. Turn your chair, if you like, so you can see the map."

I did as he asked; I was being rude, standing with my back to him. I moved the chair so I could see the map with a turn of my head.

"What are you thinking?" Perras repeated.

"Too many things," I said. "That the world is not what I thought I knew; and how can I not have been taught this, at home or by Colm? That your land is walled between two larger lands, so why then do you raid south and not north? Who are the Varslanders, and why have they not sailed south to the Empire?" I shook my head, like a horse trying to dislodge an irritating fly. "Too many things,"

"Good," Perras said gently. I looked up. "Now I know what we should teach you in your time here. You will find more questions, as we work together, but we have a starting place. But that is enough, for today. Can you find your way back to your room?"

I wanted to object, but I knew Perras was right; I had learned more than enough for today. "I can," I said. I stood up. "Thank you, *Comiádh*." I hoped I had got the pronunciation right.

"Thank you, Lena," he said. I crossed the room, pulling open the door. I glanced back before I closed it; Perras had Colm's history open on his lap, his face rapt.

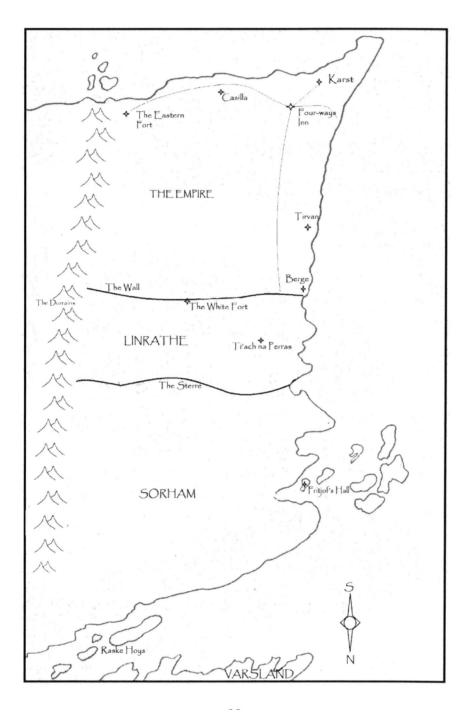

CHAPTER THREE

THE HALL WAS EMPTY. I walked across to the outside door to pull it open. The sun had begun to wester, but I estimated several hours of daylight remained. I wanted to check on Clio.

Outside the clouds were still moving quickly across the sky. It had rained briefly at some point; damp patches showed on the flagstones. I looked around, wondering where the stables were.

I had better find someone to ask, I thought, setting out for the nearest range of outbuildings. I poked my head into an open door: the laundry. No-one was here, but I could hear voices close by. I walked along to the next door, and opened it. As my eyes adjusted to the dim interior light, I realized I had found the bath-house.

Ardan lay in a large metal tub, his legs hanging over the end. Gregor, another of our party, occupied the tub beside him. A jug of something—I guessed beer—sat on a table between them, and two large mugs. I averted my eyes. "My apologies," I said. "I was looking for someone to tell me where the stables are."

"Walk down to the end of these buildings, and you'll see a path that goes off to the north," Ardan said. "Follow it, and you'll find the stables. But your mare is in the field behind the stables; I gave her a rub-down, and an hour or so in the stall, and then turned her out." He sounded unperturbed by my presence.

"Thank you," I said. "I like to see her, in a new place."

"Aye, you're well trained," he said. "Close the door as you go, to keep the warm in, if you would." I recognized the dismissal, and did as he asked.

The path took me to the stables, as Ardan had said it would. Just below the crest of slight rise. Clio stood among a group of horses, one hip cocked, resting. When I called her, she ambled over to the fence and blew happily as I scratched her poll and withers. Tatters of hair hung from her heavy winter coat. After a few minutes, I gave her a gentle slap and she wandered away from the fence, back toward the other horses. I went in search of her tack.

I found it hanging in a space that doubled as tack and feed-room, neatly stowed, and cleaned, albeit the quick cleaning of a working day. I wondered if Ardan or Gregor had cleaned it. I needed to thank them. I would give the tack a thorough cleaning—and Clio a thorough grooming—as soon as I could.

I heard a sound from the end of the stables, the familiar scrape of pitchfork on stone. I walked down the range; at the end stall, I found Sorley clearing out soiled bedding.

"Hello," I said. "Sorley, isn't it?" He looked up, straightened.

"Lena," he said. "Can I help you?"

I shook my head. "I came to see my horse," I said. "Although, would you know where Jordis is? She was going to show me around."

He glanced up at the sun. "She'll be with the Lady Dagney, in lessons," he answered, "for another hour, I would think."

"Oh," I said. "What should I do, then? Do I have time to curry Clio?"

"You should," he said. "Did you see the tack room?" I nodded. "You'll find what you need there, but why don't you bring her down this end—you can tether her there," he said, pointing to a ring in the wall between two stalls, "and talk to me at the same time. If you would like," he added.

"All right." I went to fetch Clio and the currycomb. By the time I brought her back, Sorley had finished cleaning the stall, and was propping a barrow up against the end of the stable.

He looked at Clio. "She's a nice little mare."

"She is," I agreed. "Her name is Clio, and she was bred at Han, in the north of my country." I began the task of easing out the undercoat. As I worked, sparrows flew out from under the eaves of the stable and began to pick up bits of hair for nest-building. After a few minutes, I glanced at Sorley. He sat on an upended bucket, watching.

"Tell me how things work here. What are the days like, and who decides what we do?" I thought he might give me a more balanced view than Jordis; he was older, exuding calm and competency.

"The *Comiádh* and the Lady Dagney decide what we do, if you mean with whom we study. What we study depends on our own interests, for a large part, although there are some common subjects, such as how to write well, and how to take care of books and scrolls. Did the *Comiádh* say who your tutor would be?"

"I am to work with him." I said.

He looked mildly surprised. "Then it is history, and politics, that interest you?"

I considered. "I suppose. History, anyway. What does the Lady Dagney teach, then?"

"Languages, and music, and the *danta*."

"What are *danta*?"

"Long poems set to music," he explained, "that tell stories about past kings, or battles, or other things; our history, in a way, but with a lot of other things—magic, and giants, and winged horses—mixed in. Sometimes they are fairly horrible, like the song about Ingjol, who killed his enemies by burning down the hall they slept in, and sometimes they are more like stories for children."

I moved to Clio's other flank. "And are there other teachers?"

I saw the negative movement of his head. "No. Although sometimes a student who has been here for some years, like me, will work with newcomers, if we are asked."

"I see," I said. "How long have you been here, Sorley?"

"Five years. It will be time for me to leave, soon."

"To do what?" I wondered if my question was an intrusion.

"I will go back home," he said. "Help my father, instruct my brothers and in the school a bit, learn be the *harr*...I do not know how to say that, in your language. Leader? Of the family, and the village?"

"I don't know, either," I said. "In our village, we had headwomen, but they were elected by the council, and the title was council leader. But I think I understand."

Clio flinched as I tugged on a mat of hair, and I realized I had not been paying attention to the task. I soothed her with voice and hands, giving my attention to detangling the knot.

"How do you learn, then? You do not have places like the *Ti'acha*?"

"No," I said. "In my village, in Tirvan, girls go to school from the time we are seven, until we are twelve. We learn to read and write, and do sums, and some history. We learn the rules that were set down at Partition, both for the Empire's men and women, and for the villages.

In our last year, we choose an apprenticeship, and after that we learn as we work, practical skills."

"And if a girl truly wanted to learn more, from books, I mean? Is it against the rules?"

"I don't know," I said slowly. "It has never happened, as far as I know. Although my mother—she is the midwife and healer, as I said—sometimes said she wished she knew more, or had more books." *Would she have gone beyond the village to learn, if the chance had been there?*

"If we can find peace, beyond this truce, I mean," Sorley said, "then she could go to the *Ti'ach na Iorlath*, where healing is taught, for a season, if she would be allowed to."

"But she is more than twice my age," I said.

He shrugged. "Age does not matter," he said. "The *Teannasach* himself comes here when he can, to discuss and debate matters with Perras, and the Lady Dagney, and to read more books, which leads to more discussion and debate." I heard the bucket scrape as he stood. "The lesson will be nearly done. Do you want to turn your mare loose again, or stable her?"

"Turn her loose. She has spent too long picketed, or in stalls." I untied the lead rein to walk Clio back down the stable block to the paddock, stopping briefly at the tack room to put away the currycomb. She looked a lot better, I thought, as I watched her trot away across the field. I turned to Sorley.

"She will need shoeing before too long. Who does that, here?"

"There's a smithy a few miles north of here," he answered. "But will she need shoes? You won't be going anywhere; couldn't you just take her shoes off for now?"

Anger spurted through me. *Who was Sorley, to tell me what I could or couldn't do?* I bit back a sharp retort. *He was right, of course. Although...*

"Do you not ride to hunt? I am skilled, both with the hunting bow and with a knife. I would like to help with that, if I could."

He looked down at me, raising one eyebrow lazily. "Women don't hunt here," he said, "except for hawking. Can you fly a kestrel, or a sparrowhawk?"

"No," I said coldly. "But I can take down a deer with one arrow, and I have killed both game and men with my knife." I looked up at him. "Your women may not hunt, Sorley, but I am from the Empire, and the Empire's women hunt."

He flicked his eyes away from mine. "The decision will be Perras's," he said. "My understanding of a hostage is that you live by our rules, while you are with us. But I may be wrong."

Casyn had told me much the same. "You are probably right," I admitted. "I am not accustomed, yet, to this role of hostage."

"Nor do we really know how to treat you." We walked a few steps back toward the house in silence. "Have you really killed a man?" he asked, suddenly.

"Yes," I said. "Two, actually. But I would rather that was not common knowledge. I don't like talking about it." I no longer had nightmares, but the memories were not good ones.

We rounded the corner of the outbuildings that held the bathhouse and laundry, and there was Jordis. "Lena! I was looking for you."

"I was at the stable, seeing to my horse."

"I can show you around now," she continued. "Sorley, the Lady Dagney is waiting for you."

"Then I better go. I will see you later, Lena." He walked off in the direction of the hall.

"Where do we start?" I asked.

I spent the best part of an hour with Jordis, first touring the rest of the outbuildings—fuel-store, toolshed, cidery—there was an orchard somewhere—and the chicken coop, where the hens that provided eggs for the *Ti'ach* were housed at night, against weasels and foxes. Then we went inside, and I was shown the kitchen, and the stillroom, and Lady Dagney's teaching rooms and the adjoining music room, where Niav was practicing a stringed instrument. We did not go to the third floor—the male pupil's rooms, Jordis explained, and off-limits to the girls and women of the *Ti'ach*. That part, at least, reminded me of the inns of the Empire, where men's rooms were also separate, and often—as here—with a separate staircase for access.

Finally, the tour was done. We had returned to the kitchen; at about this hour every day the household gathered for tea, Jordis explained.

Two trays were waiting in the kitchen: one with a large pot of tea and mugs, one with a plate of buttered bread and another of oatcakes. We each took a tray, carrying them through to the hall. Jordis went back to the kitchen to return with a third tray, this one with small plates. She distributed them around the table: I counted nine.

"Nine?" I said to Jordis. "I haven't met everyone, then?"

"Oh," she said. "It's only Cillian, from the *Ti'ach*. He is a pupil of the *Comiádh*, like you, but he is older. I don't know who the other two plates are for—perhaps some of your escort?"

My question was answered as the household began to gather. Ardan and Gregor came in from outside; Sorley, Niav and Lady Dagney from her rooms. At a look from Dagney, Sorley walked over to Perras's door, knocking before opening it. "Tea, *Comiádh*," I heard him say.

We took our seats. Dagney looked around. "Where is Cillian?" she asked.

"He rode over to the smithy," Sorley said, "several hours ago."

"We won't wait," Dagney decided. She poured mugs of tea and we passed them around the table, followed by the plates of bread and oatcakes. Following the lead of others, I took one piece of each. My stomach had been rumbling for a little while. I wondered if I had missed lunch, or if mid-morning and mid-afternoon tea replaced that meal here.

"What have you done this afternoon, Lena?" Dagney asked me. I gathered my thoughts.

"After I met with the *Comiádh*, my lady," I answered, "I went to see my horse; I like to do so in a new place. She needed grooming, so I did that, and talked with Sorley, who was also at the stables. And then Jordis found me, and showed me around, until just a few minutes ago."

"And what do you think of our *Ti'ach*?" she asked. I wondered what the question really meant. I doubted she wanted a polite, meaningless answer.

"It seems very peaceful," I said, "and organized so that there is time for both learning and work in and out of the house. The way the building is designed reminds me of some of the inns which I have stayed in, on the road, except for the stables being more distant than would be usual. Beyond that," I shrugged slightly, "it is only my first afternoon, but those are my first impressions."

"I am glad you find it peaceful," Dagney said, smiling. "We do strive for that. It will be a change for you, will it not?"

"It will, my lady."

"Lena is to study with me," Perras said to the room. He looked around. "But it appears you all knew that—except, perhaps, you, Niav?" She nodded. "It will be good for me to have a second pupil, and one who brings a different knowledge than most. But, Lena, you should also spend a few hours a week with the Lady Dagney—I am thinking of languages—you speak only one, and it would be useful if you had at least a basic understanding of our language, and that of Varsland."

"If you wish." A thought struck me. "Am I making you all speak my tongue, because I do not understand yours?"

Dagney smiled. "Not entirely. When a student leaves here, it is our hope that he or she will be comfortable in speaking three languages: our own; that of the Marai, the people of Varsland, and yours. So, in conversation at mealtimes, and in lessons, we may speak any of the three. We will speak your language for a week or two, both for your benefit, and for Niav's, as she has had no chance to converse with a native speaker." I glanced at Niav, who coloured slightly.

"Also," Perras added, "many of our books are written in your language, or a version of it, so it is important that students learn to read it, as well."

I wondered how many of our soldiers could speak or read these other two languages, or at least the language of Linrathe. *Turlo, perhaps, and borders scouts, and those with long service on the Wall?* It could not be wise to deal with an enemy who could communicate in your language, without learning theirs, too.

"I will be off in the morning, with your leave," Ardan suddenly announced. I looked his way, but he was addressing Perras. "Gregor will stay, as the *Teannasach* directed. I see no reason to leave two men."

"Nor do I," answered Perras. I frowned. *Why was Gregor staying?* But then I realized: he was my guard, to ensure I did not leave. I opened my mouth to protest, and then closed it. *As the* Teannasach *directed,*

Ardan had said. Ardan could not change the order, even if he had wanted to. Darel would be guarded too, and, I reflected, so would Kebhan and Ruar, on our side of the Wall.

The room was darkening, and I heard rain against the window. Niav brought candles from the sideboard and lit them. I glanced toward the window. "*Comiádh*, sir?" I said. "May I go to stable my horse? I would prefer her not to be out all night in the rain, as there is a stable for her."

"We'll go," Ardan said, before Perras could answer me. "No point in us all getting wet."

"Thank you, Ardan, Gregor," Perras said, but even as the men stood the hall door opened. A tall man stepped in, his dark hair dripping rain onto a heavy sheepskin jacket.

"Cillian," Dagney said. "You are late. Is all well?"

"Yes, my lady," Cillian replied, his voice soft. He walked into the low candlelight, and for a moment I thought he was someone I had seen before—*but where?* "Just that the rain has come from the north, and so I rode back from the smithy at a walk as the path was slippy, and then I took the time to stable the horses in the paddock, and ensure they had a bite of hay. But a hot mug of tea would be welcome."

Niav had gone to the kitchen at Dagney's words. Ardan and Gregor hesitated, and then sat again. "That was kind of you," Perras said. "You have saved these two soldiers a wet trip." The two men murmured words of thanks, but Cillian shrugged them off. "No matter," he said, shedding his wet coat and hanging it on the back of an empty chair. *No, I decided, I did not know him.*

Niav returned with hot water to fill the teapot. She brought Cillian a mug, and the last of the bread and oatcakes. He smiled at her, and ate hungrily. The room was silent.

After a mouthful of tea, he looked up. "I am being rude," he said. "We have visitors."

"Ardan and Gregor you will remember," Perras said, "as soldiers of the *Teannasach's* guard." Cillian nodded. "And this is Lena, Guardswoman of the Empire, one of the two hostages exchanged in surety for the truce. The *Teannasach* has sent her here, and she will be studying with me, so you have interests in common."

I saw the flash of surprise in his eyes, followed by a cold, evaluative look. "Another student of history, and a woman of the Southern Empire at that," he said. "You will be busy, *Comiádh*." He spoke no word to me.

"Now, Lena," Dagney said. "The hours between our afternoon tea together and supper are not scheduled; this is time for all of us to use as we please: in study or practice, conversation, or solitude. There is a rota for the duties of the house each day, but you will not start on those until tomorrow. You are not bound to the house; you may, in this time, exercise your horse or see to her other needs, if you wish, but the *Teannasach* has asked Gregor to accompany you if you ride out by yourself or with others of the *Ti'ach*. We are glad you are with us, but scholars and teachers of the *Ti'ach* cannot be responsible for your safety; that is Gregor's job. I hope this will not distress you?"

"No, my lady," I answered, glad I had realized Gregor's role earlier. I might have been less calm, otherwise. I had had little to do with Gregor on the ride here, but he had always been polite. I judged him to be about thirty, a lean man of middling height with a relaxed air to him. I wondered how he would find life at the *Ti'ach*, guarding one woman in a school. *Ardan—or the* Teannasach—*must have had reasons to choose him,* I thought.

Niav and Jordis rose to gather the plates and mugs. Sorley stretched, speaking to Dagney. "My lady, will I disturb you if I practice the *ladhar* for an hour? I can take the instrument to my room, if it will."

"It will not," she said. "And the practice room will be warmer."

I stood too, uncertain of how to take my leave. "Thank you," I said finally, "my lady, *Comiádh*, for such a welcome to the *Ti'ach na Perras*. I am looking forward to my time here."

Dagney looked surprised. "Your presence here graces us," she said. "We will learn together, for you have things to teach us, too."

"I am eager to start tomorrow," Perras said.

I smiled. "Thank you," I said again. I smiled, too, at Cillian, making the overture.

Then I walked up the stairs to my room, pulled off my boots, and collapsed on the bed.

I drifted into a light, dreamless sleep for a while, but the room was cool and I had not pulled the blanket over me. I woke to cold hands and feet. No fire had been laid in the hearth. I remembered Dagney's words to Sorley about the practice room being warmer, and guessed that fires in our rooms were reserved for the coldest months alone. Fires had been a luxury in the barracks, too. I was used to the cold. I lit the candle on the table.

I pulled my journal out of my pack; pen and ink stood in a stand on the table, beside the candle. But I was not ready yet to write down my feelings and impressions. I turned my pack out onto the bed, putting my few possessions away in the wardrobe and chest. Then I sat at the table, opening my journal.

But still I did not write. I stared out into the darkening world, past the candle's reflection, letting the thoughts and impressions of the last week swirl through my mind. Casyn's request that I stand as hostage in his daughter's stead; the room at the White Fort, with its floor of pictures; the rituals that invoked an Eastern Empire; the map on Perras's wall. A world turned upside down.

CHAPTER FOUR

IN THE END, I WROTE ONLY A FACTUAL ACCOUNT of the past few days. I could not marshal my thoughts to do more. I had not had a chance to write since Turlo had come to the servery looking for Darel and me, and so even the facts took a long time. My hand ached as I reached the end.

I glanced over what I had written, and picked up the pen again. *Why have I never heard of the Varslanders, when they are closer than Leste?* I wrote. *Why do they not trade with us? What peace treaty exists between them and the Northmen—the people of Linrathe?* All questions I could ask Perras.

There was one more thing. *Ask Perras about the Eastern Empire.* Not yet: for some reason, I felt it was not something I could broach with him, until I knew him better. But the ritual at the White Fort haunted and frustrated me. I felt like a child again, kept from grown-up mysteries.

From downstairs, a deep ringing 'boom' sounded. I guessed it was the signal for supper. I lifted the candlestick and in its flickering light made my way down to the hall.

Supper was mutton stew and barley bread, and more oatcakes served with cooked apples. A thin beer accompanied the food. Perras and Dagney led the conversation, directing questions at the other students about recent lessons, and what conclusions they had drawn from what they had learned. I guessed this was the usual pattern at the evening meal.

But at the end, as we were finishing the oatcakes and apples, Perras cleared his throat. "Tonight, we will not have our usual entertainments after supper, for there is something you all should hear: the words of the treaty our *Teannasach* and the Southern Emperor have signed. So, let us have the table cleared, and, I think, wine poured for everyone, and then I will read the treaty to you."

"Do we ask the kitchen-folk to join us?" Jordis asked, already gathering plates.

Perras shook his head. "No. I will gather the cottagers tomorrow, and they will hear it then."

Cillian went to one of the cupboards and brought back goblets that caught the firelight, making several trips with the fragile objects. As he placed them on the table, I realized they were glass, something I had never seen except for some tiny, square, medicine bottles my mother had. From the same cupboard, he brought a flagon made of glazed pottery, and poured a small amount of dark wine into each glass. He did not distribute them.

Ardan moved a candle from the centre of the table closer to Perras, and handed him a tied scroll. The older man loosened the ties, and unrolled it, reading the words to himself. I saw him nod, slightly, and then he looked at me.

"Lena," he said, "you among us, save for Ardan and Gregor, will have heard these words before. When I have read them, I would appreciate it if you would tell us how they were received, by the gathered soldiers of the Empire. I will ask Ardan to do the same, for our men."

"I will do my best," I murmured, glad of the forewarning.

"'Herein are the terms of the truce between Linrathe and the Southern Empire, agreed this first day of spring at the White Fort, between Donnalch, *Teannasach* of Linrathe, and Callan, Emperor of the South,'" Perras read. I listened, hearing the words again, letting them wash over me as I watched the faces around the table: Dagney intent, focused; Sorley frowning occasionally; Jordis nodding. Only Cillian showed no reaction, his face set, although a muscle jumped in his jaw at the mention of the Eastern Empire.

"'The penalty for the breaking of this truce by any man or woman, from Linrathe or the Southern Empire, is death for the transgressors, who also risk the lives of the hostage of their land. Remember this, and maintain the peace.'" Perras paused. "It is signed by both the *Teannasach* and the Emperor," he finished. No one spoke.

"The wine, now, I think," Perras said. Cillian and Sorley rose and distributed the glasses, Cillian serving the end of the table away from me. I watched how Perras cradled his, cupping the bowl in his hand gently. I copied him, the glass feeling cool and smooth against my hand. I held it lightly, afraid of its fragility.

"To a temporary peace," Perras said, "and may a lasting one arise."

"To peace," Dagney said, and took a sip of her wine. The rest of us followed her lead. The wine, rich and smooth, warmed my throat. I put the glass down carefully.

"Now, Lena," Perras said, his voice conversational. "What can you tell us of the reaction, from the Empire's men? And women," he amended.

"I had only a few minutes to see," I said slowly, "and you must remember that soldiers are trained not to show reaction to orders, and the truce, read out by our Emperor, is an order. So, I may be guessing here, a bit, but what I think I saw was relief. We have been at war for over a year; many have died, and food is scarce. I think nearly everyone wanted and welcomed a truce."

"And did you?" Perras asked.

"Yes," I said. "For the same reasons." *And because I had begun to think the war unwinnable.* I did not say that aloud. I suspected many on the Wall felt the same.

"Ardan?" Perras said. "What did you see and hear?"

"Much the same," he answered. "I also saw pride, when the *Teannasach* spoke of a treaty of equals. They—we—have great faith in him, and look to this as a beginning of change for Linrathe, in our dealings with both the Southern Empire and with Varsland."

"Lena," Perras asked, "what will happen now, for your soldiers? Where will they go? The treaty speaks of returning to fields and villages, but that is not your way, is it?"

I shook my head. "No," I said, "not for the men."

Niav leaned forward. "Is it true," she asked, her voice hushed, "that women do not live with men in your land, by law? And that they do all the work of men?"

"It is," I answered. I saw her eyes widen in the firelight.

"But why?' she asked.

I glanced at Perras. "Go ahead," he said. "The others know what our history teaches; it will be instructive for us all to hear what you were taught about Partition."

"I would have told a different story, not too long ago," I said. "But briefly, then: many long years ago, men and women of our Empire did live together, much as I imagine your people do here. But military service was mandatory, and the Emperor of the time, Lucian, wished to expand his Empire, except that he needed the approval of the people to do this: those were the laws, at the time. Village councils were in the hands of women, as so many men were away so much of the year, and those councils overall did not want the Empire to be expanded at the cost of more lives. So, the Emperor called for an assembly, and, after long discussion and debate, a proposal was made that divided the laws that govern men and women: women would live in the villages, farm and fish and provide food, much as they already did, and be governed by their councils. Men would fight: the army would govern them. It is called the Partition Assembly, as it divided not just our laws, but our lives."

I glanced at Niav, watching me, wide-eyed. I took a breath. "What I did not know, until this past year, is how many objected. For many people of the Empire, men and women, Partition was not the answer. But by our laws, those people either had to submit to this new decree of the Empire, or choose exile. Many chose exile, and most, I believe, crossed into these lands. Some of us in this room may share common ancestors; your *Teannasach* and our Emperor may be distant cousins, for all I know. But to live separate lives has been our lot for twenty generations or more, and it seems normal to us now." *Or it had, until the invasion from Leste.* "Does that answer you question?" I asked Niav.

"Yes," she said. "So, you can do everything? Build a wall? Shoe a horse?"

I laughed. "Well, not me personally. But in my village, in Tirvan, there were women who did those things, and who built boats and houses, and ploughed and harvested the fields. I fished, with my partner, from our boat."

"And you can fight," Sorley said. "After all, you are a soldier now."

"Yes," I answered. "I can fight, and I have. I can handle a sword, and a bow, but my specialized training is with the secca, the knife, in close combat."

"Sorley," Perras said quietly, "we are diverging from our purpose here tonight, with these questions. You will recall I asked Lena what would happen now, for the soldiers of the Southern Empire."

"My intent was to remind us that there are now women among the Empire's soldiers," Sorley said, "and that perhaps what happens for male and female soldiers might be different."

"As it will be," I agreed, not waiting for Perras to speak. "Women will return to their home villages, to the work they left. The men will return to their duties, whether that is teaching cadets, or patrolling the Wall or the Durrains, or building roads, training horses, or making swords, I suppose."

"But they will continue to be soldiers, training and planning, for the next six months, while our men will not, for the most part," Cillian said. "Which could be giving the Empire an advantage."

"Do not underestimate the *Teannasach*," Ardan said sharply. "Do you think he would not have thought of that?"

"The Southern Empire has had professional soldiers for many generations," Perras pointed out. "And yet we have fought to an impasse. Will one summer change that?"

"Is not the point," Jordis said, "that there should be no more fighting? The *Teannasach* and the Southern Emperor will spend this summer talking, looking for a permanent peace. And another winter war? Remember what Halmar wrote:

war in winter sends sorrow soaring;
hunger hurts, cold kills:
ravens rejoice, wolves wait;
men moan, women wail:
death in darkness, glory gone...

"And if the intent is to find peace, then perhaps the *Teannasach* did not see harm in the soldiers of the Southern Empire returning to their usual duties?" she finished. Her insight surprised me—*unfairly so*, I admitted to myself, as I barely knew her.

"Do you think the *Teannasach* can negotiate a permanent peace, under the conditions he has laid down? An agreement of equals?" Perras asked. It was Sorley who answered.

"If he does," he said, "then surely it would challenge the terms of our peace with Varsland, with the Marai?" he said. No-one responded.

"Forgive me," I said, "but I do not understand. What are the terms of the peace with Varsland?"

Dagney answered. "Linrathe pays tribute, or tax, if you like, to Varsland," she said. "In return, the Marai—the ship-warriors of Varsland—do not raid into Sorham, and leave landholders such as Sorley's father, and my brothers, in peace. It was not always so."

"Is that why there is another Wall? The Sterre?" I asked, remembering the map.

"It is not why it was built," Dagney answered, "but now, yes, it defines the border between Sorham and Linrathe. The Marai do not cross it, although they may enter Sorham for peaceful purposes, seeking trade or marriage. People of Sorham travel north, too, to Varsland or the islands, for the same reasons. My own mother was born on Naermest, one of the islands of Raske, or the Raske Hoys, as they are named there. Many—if not most—of the folk of Sorham carry the blood of the Marai."

"So," I said slowly, working through it, "Linrathe has a peace treaty with Varsland, but by the terms of this treaty Linrathe is," I hesitated, looking for the right word, "subservient to Varsland. The Marai are paid to leave Sorham in peace. But is it Linrathe, or Sorham, who pays the tribute? Who does Sorham belong to, if not itself?"

"Long years ago," Perras said, "Sorham was conquered by Varsland, if conquered is the right word. The Marai moved south from Varsland, settling on some unclaimed lands, raiding into claimed lands, taking wives and fathering children. But folk also moved north from Linrathe, especially when our numbers swelled at the time of Partition in the Southern Empire. Conflict ensued, and after some years the current agreement was reached: the Marai withdrew with the promise of peace, leaving Sorham to Linrathe, for a price."

"I believe our *Teannasach* thinks," Cillian interrupted, "that if he can negotiate a treaty of equals with the Southern Emperor, then it will be time to challenge the terms of our treaty with the Marai. Their king is old; there will be a new one soon, so what better time?"

"Aye," Ardan spoke softly. "That is how I see it, too."

"If our two countries find peace," Cillian said, "then is not the very reason for the Southern Empire's army gone? What happens to an army when there is no enemy to fight?"

No-one replied. I took another mouthful of wine. Candles and shadows flickered in a small movement of air, from beneath the door or a loose window. *Cillian was wrong*, I thought. *Enemies could still arise, as Leste had.*

Perras broke the silence. "I think that is enough discussion for this evening," he said. "Perhaps one song, before we retire? Lena, is there a song of the Empire you could sing for us?"

I had not expected this. "I have not much of a voice," I said, stalling.

"No matter," Dagney said. "Sorley, would you fetch a *ladhar*? Sorley will follow you on the instrument," she explained, as he went toward the practice room, "or accompany you, if the tune is one we know."

"I hope you can recognize it, if it is," I said. I wondered what to sing, reviewing in my mind the songs sung at Tirvan. Only one stood out.

Sorley returned, and moved a chair back from the table. He ran his fingers over the strings of the *ladhar*, and adjusted one tuning peg. Then he nodded. I stood.

"This is not a song of my village," I said. "I learned it from our potter, Tice, who was from Karst, at the southernmost reaches of the Empire." I took a breath, and began.

The swallows gather, summer passes,
The grapes hang dark and sweet;
Heavy are the vines,
Heavy is my heart,
Endless is the road beneath my feet.

I heard the notes of the *ladhar*, as mournful as the song. I glanced at Sorley; he nodded. I continued, the instrument now in time with my voice.

The sun is setting, the moon is rising,
The night is long and sweet;
I am gone at dawn.

I am gone at day,
Endless is the road beneath my feet.

The cold is deeper, the winters longer,
Summer is short but sweet;
I will remember,
I'll not forget you,
Endless is the road beneath my feet.

Sorley plucked a few more notes from the *ladhar*, letting them fade away into the night. Silence held, for a minute.

"Thank you," Dagney said. "The tune is known to us, but not those words. Would you write them down for us, Lena? And anything you know about the song?"

"Of course," I said. "Tice said she had learned it from a retired general of the Empire. And I heard it sung at the Emperor's winter camp, but that is all I know. I think it is a southern song, though, because of the line about the grapes."

"You may be right," Dagney said. "You will find paper and ink, and a pen, in the box on the table in your room. If you should run short, just ask for more. And now, I think, it is time for us to retire. Lena, you will hear the breakfast bell in the morning; before that, your time is your own, as is the time now until you choose to sleep." She stood, as did Perras. "Good night to you all," she said.

"Good night," Perras echoed. "Don't stay up too late, children." I saw a quick flicker of a smile on Cillian's face as he stood to fetch Perras a candle, a smile that brought again the feeling that I knew him from somewhere. He saw me looking at him, and the smile vanished. Perras, organizing himself with candle and stick, looked from Cillian to me. "Cillian," he murmured. "Would you light me to my room? I find myself unsteady tonight." He handed the candle back to the younger man, and together they walked slowly to Perras's study door.

Ardan had also risen. "Bed for me too," he announced, "I've an early start. Sleep well, all." Gregor, with a nod to us, accompanied his commanding officer.

No-one spoke for a moment, until Sorley broke the silence. "Cillian holds a grudge against the Empire," he said quietly. "It's not personal, Lena."

"I'm glad to know I wasn't imagining it," I said tartly. "Am I allowed to know what that grudge is?"

The students looked at each other. "I suppose so," Sorley answered. "We all know. His mother—she was very young—died after giving birth to him. His father was a soldier of the Empire, but whoever he was, he never returned to see how his lover had fared. Cillian has not forgiven him, and, by extension, the Empire."

"I see," I said.

"Perhaps," Jordis said, "if he had known you were coming, he might have had time to prepare himself."

"I think the *Comiádh* is speaking to him now, about this," Sorley said quietly. He stretched. "I am going to practice the *ladhar*," he said. "Niav, do you want to join me?"

The younger girl shook her head. "I would rather talk to Lena," she replied, and then shot a doubtful look my way. "If that is all right?"

Did I want to talk? Inwardly I sighed. But I had had my time alone, and my journal, and I did not think I had anything more to write tonight. "Of course."

Sorley grinned. "Niav loves stories," he said. "She'll turn them into songs, though, Lena; be warned." He left us, raising a hand in farewell as he did.

"What would you like to know?" I said to the two young women sitting with me.

"Everything," Niav burst out. "What your village is like, and how you learned to fight, and about your travels. And how it feels, to be told you must live in these villages, and not marry."

"That is too much for one night," I said slowly. *Is that how she sees us?*

"Tell us about your travels," Jordis suggested. "Tell us about Casilla—you have been there?"

"How do you know about Casilla?" The question surprised me, but I welcomed the change of topic.

"It's on the map," Niav said, as if it were obvious. "We learn the geography of your country too, as well as ours, and Varsland." She sounded put out, as if I had under-estimated her. *Then again,* I thought, *I had.*

Casilla, I thought. *How to begin?*

"When the wall was breached..." I stopped. "When it was opened to your soldiers," I amended, "I was at the Emperor's winter camp, for the Midwinter celebrations and proclamations. As the army prepared to ride north, I was asked to ride as messenger, to the southern villages, to ask women who were willing to ride north too. That task took me some time, and when I was done I stayed for a while at Karst, the grape-growing village of the south."

"Why did you not ride north?" Niav demanded.

"Hush, Niav," Jordis said. "Lena will tell us what she wishes. Do not pry."

"It's all right," I said. "I did not know, yet, if I wanted to fight again. Defending my village was one thing; it was personal, and those threatened were my family and my friends. I was not yet sure I could raise weapons in a larger cause."

I remembered my conversations—arguments, really—with Halle, who had seen no choice but to ride north. Nor had she wanted one: she wished to be a soldier, and could not understand my reluctance. I had not liked her then, and could not tell her how my actions as a cohort-leader, which had led to the death of my friend and cohort-second Tice, had made me doubt myself. I did not want to tell this to Niav and Jordis, tonight.

"So," I said, resuming my tale, "I stayed in Karst for some weeks. My cousin Garth had a son there, and I stayed with the woman raising him—his aunt—and another friend. The child's grandmother, however, made life difficult for the child and his aunt, and when she decided to go to Casilla, I chose to go with her." I paused.

"Casilla is walled," I continued, "with enormous gates to let in the trader's carts. The gates and the watchtowers are of stone, and they gleam white in the sunshine, and the flag of the Empire flies at each tower, snapping in the wind from the sea. Inside the gates there is a wide road, running down to the harbours: it divides the city in two, into the women's section, and the men's. At one point, there is a wide square where the market is held." I stopped, unsure if I was being clear, trying to marshal my thoughts.

"Harbours?" Jordis said. "More than one?"

"Yes. The fishing harbour, on the women's side, and the quays and anchorage for the ships of the Empire, on the men's side, and between them the traders' quays." Saying this, I remembered the scream of gulls, and the shouts of men and women working on and around the boats, and the salt, pungent smell of the sea and of fish.

"This divided life." Jordis said, "It's hard to imagine. Everything must be duplicated, then? Cookhouses and bakeries, shops and inns?"

I nodded. "Yes. There are two cities, really, and the separation is maintained, except at the market, and during Festival. I had wondered, too, how it might work, but the rules of Partition are held."

"How strange," Jordis murmured. Niav said nothing, but instead sang a stanza, softly:

O we forbid ye, maidens all,
with flowers in your hair,
To go or come by Kertonhall,
for young Fintaill is there.

The tune was haunting. "That's lovely," I said. "Is that from a *danta*?"

"Yes," Niav answered. "It's from a long song, that tells how a maiden won her true love back from the fair folk, angering their queen in doing so. The Lady Dagney says it is very old, and that we share the story with the Marai. I will learn it in their language, soon. But how did you know about the *danta*? "

"Sorley told me," I explained.

"Tell us more about Casilla," Jordis said, a shade impatiently, I thought.

"On the main gates," I said, "there is an inscription, in no language I know. It says *'Casil e imitaran ne'.*"

"'Casil this is not'," said a voice behind us. We all turned to see Cillian standing there. He repeated the words I had spoken, but his inflections made them sound very different. "Or," he continued, "'Casil is not equalled here', if you prefer a more elegant translation."

"So, the old woman was right," I said, half under my breath.

"What old woman?" Niav demanded.

"In Casilla," I said slowly, "those words are generally taken to mean 'There is only one Casilla', but an old woman I met there told me they meant exactly what Cillian just said: 'Casil this is not'."

"And they do," Cillian said. He pulled out a chair and sat. "Do you not learn Casilan?" he asked.

"No," Jordis said sharply. "There were no languages taught in Lena's village. We talked about that over tea, before you arrived."

"And it would seem that is true throughout the country, if the inhabitants of Casilla believe the gate inscription to mean 'There is only one Casilla'," Cillian commented. "Casilla, Lena, is a diminutive, meaning 'Little Casil'. Perhaps once it was meant to rival Casil, but the gate inscription indicates that someone realized it did not."

"And where is Casil?" I asked. But as I spoke I realized the answer. "In the Eastern Empire?"

Cillian raised an eyebrow.

"So, you have learned some things," he said. He was, I thought, striving to be polite. I wondered what Perras had said to him. I shook my head.

"Not really," I admitted. "I heard of it only in the last weeks; it was something Donnalch—your *Teannasach*," I added, stumbling again over the unfamiliar word, "and our Emperor spoke of at the White Fort. They gave an oath to 'the Empire Unconquered'. Darel—the other hostage, a cadet—told me it meant the Eastern Empire."

"Is that all he told you?"

"Cillian, is this not what the *Comiádh* will instruct Lena in?" Jordis said quietly.

He looked at her. A small muscle in his jaw twitched. He nodded.

"Jordis is right," he said. "You should discuss this with Perras, not with me."

"No!" I said, too forcefully. "Please, can't we talk about it now? It has been puzzling me."

Cillian sighed. "Tell us what you know, then."

I thought back to what Darel had said. "There was an Empire in the East," I began slowly, "and a Supreme Emperor, to whom the Emperor here owed allegiance. He—the Supreme Emperor—ruled from a city in the East—that would be Casil?" Cillian nodded. "And then one day all trade and communication—all contact—stopped. But the Emperor and the troops still pay homage to the memory." I shook my head. "That's all I remember."

"It's a fair summary," Cillian said. "But Perras will tell you more, and be glad of your interest." He stretched, and ran a hand through his hair.

"Was Linrathe part of that Empire?" I asked, remembering what had puzzled me at the time.

Cillian shook his head. "Not that I was taught," he said. "Ask Perras, Lena; he has the stories. I am no lover of Empires, lost or current." The chill had returned to his voice. He stood. The chair scraped on the flagged floor. "Sleep well, *daltai*. I will see you at breakfast." He stalked away, not to the stairs, but to the door. A breeze, a taste of night air, and he was gone.

CHAPTER FIVE

I SLEPT WELL. I HAD GONE TO BED shortly after Cillian left, pleading fatigue, and had fallen asleep almost immediately. I woke to the chatter of sparrows outside my window, and faint sounds from the house.

Downstairs, I helped Jordis and Sorley bring food from the kitchen to the hall: bowls of thick oat porridge, jugs of milk, dried fruit. Niav took a tray to Perras's rooms, Dagney explaining quietly to me that he was stiff and sore in the mornings, and preferred to eat alone. There was little conversation over the meal, at least until the food was finished and most of us were drinking a second cup of tea.

"Now, *daltai*," Dagney said, using the same plural of 'student' that Cillian had the night before, "most of you know your duties or lessons for the morning. Lena, Perras wishes you to go to him, but he will not be ready for you for another hour, and unlike the others you do not have work to be getting on with. So, Sorley, will you take Niav for her lesson in the first hour, and then I can work with Lena?"

"Of course, my lady." The others excused themselves, heading off to work, practice, or lessons. Cillian had said nothing during the meal, and did not look my way as he left. I waited for Dagney to speak.

"Shall we go to my rooms?" she asked, rising. I followed her from the hall and through the music practice room, into the teaching room. Like Perras's room, this appeared to be her study as well as her teaching space. Many bookcases stood against the walls, but here the shelves held instruments as well as books. Larger instruments hung from pegs. She gestured me to a chair facing her desk.

"We had spoken of you learning at least the basics of our language, and perhaps that of Varsland. Does this seem sensible to you, Lena?

"It does," I agreed, "at least, it does for your language. I am not sure about Varsland's, not at the same time, unless they are very similar?"

"They share some words," she said, smiling, "but, I see your point. You have not learned another language, even a few words, at all?"

I thought back to the weeks guarding the Lestian captives. Had I picked up any words? *Not really*, I admitted to myself.

"No, my lady." I explained about the Lestians. "I don't think I even thought to try to learn their words. I just let their captain translate."

"So," she said, "it is unlikely you have a predisposition to learning languages. But no matter; it will be more work for you, but far from impossible. You are older than most who learn another language, and that will slow you down. You are in for a challenge." She smiled. "Let us begin, then. We will start, as you did so long ago, with the letters and the alphabet—we do not use different letters than you do, do not worry—but we do pronounce them differently, and use them in different combinations and with different accents, and those are the first things you should learn." From a drawer of her desk she brought out a written sheet and handed it to me.

For perhaps forty-five minutes I learned the alphabet again. I expected to just say the sounds, but Dagney had me think about how my mouth's muscles and my tongue worked to make the sounds, and what happened when I used them differently. "Good," she said finally. "You can practice with Niav: she can correct your pronunciation, and you hers in your language. But there are three words I would like you to learn before we end. Can you guess what they are?"

I thought about what I would want to be able to say. *Food? Water?* But I could point to those, or make signs.

"Please and thank you?" I hazarded.

"Very good!" Dagney said. "Yes, those two, and one more—'sorry'. Those three allow you to be polite, and good manners smooth many an awkward discourse."

"They do, my lady," I answered, thinking of Casyn, always thoughtful, always polite.

"So," she directed, "repeat these after me, and then try to use them as often as is reasonable. 'Please' is '*allech'i*'."

"*Allech'i,*" I repeated.

"Further back in your throat," Dagney prompted. I tried again, generating a more liquid sound and a nod from Dagney.

'Thank you'—*meas*, and 'sorry'—*forla*—took up another quarter of an hour. Finally, Dagney sat back.

"Enough for today. You have been a good student. Go to the kitchen now, and ask for tea with honey; your throat needs it. Perras will be expecting you, but have your tea, and do whatever else you need to, before going to him."

"Thank you, my lady," I said. She smiled in response, but I could see her mind was already elsewhere, her eyes slipping down to a musical score on her desk. I closed the door quietly behind me and went, as directed, to the kitchen. It was empty but for one woman, who sat at the long table peeling root vegetables.

"Hello," I said. I didn't remember seeing her earlier. "I'm Lena. The Lady Dagney sent me here for tea with honey, for my throat."

"Yes, my lady," she replied, her accent thick. She stood and went to the stove, moving a kettle forward and opening the door to give the coals inside a poke. She reached for a mug, and from a canister added something dried. The kettle sang; she poured hot water into the mug, and a spoonful of honey, before handing it to me.

"*Meas*," I hoped my accent was passable. She smiled. "*Allech'i*, may I know your name?" I added.

"Isa," she answered. "I am Isa, my lady."

"*Meas*, Isa," I said. "But in my land, I am not addressed as 'my lady'. Just by my name, Lena."

"But you are in our land now, my lady, and I must. It is the custom."

I nodded. "Yes, of course. *Forla*. I should have realized." *I should have, too,* I thought, hoping I hadn't embarrassed Isa. But when I glanced at her; she had returned to scraping parsnips, unbothered. I took a tentative sip of the tea; rosehip, the traditional winter tea for colds and sore throats. The heat and sweetness felt good on my slightly scratchy throat. I stood awkwardly, not knowing if I should stay or go. Isa looked up.

"Sit, if you would like, my lady," she said. I pulled out a chair and sat, cradling the mug. Isa smiled at me. "Are you here to learn music, like my niece?"

"Your niece?" I asked, puzzled.

"Niav," she answered. "She is my sister's youngest. She came for a visit last year, and the Lady Dagney heard her telling stories and singing to my little ones, and offered her a place here at the *Ti'ach*. We were all pleased, but I lost my helper with the babies." She laughed.

"But there are always girls for that! So, are you here to learn the songs and stories?"

"No," I said. "I will learn history while I am here, with the *Comiádh*. But he and the Lady Dagney thought I should learn your language as well, so I will be working with her as well." I took another swallow of the tea, thinking back to what Kebhan had said when he too had called me 'lady'—'a woman of rank.' Did being a pupil at a *Ti'ach*, a *dalta*, confer rank? Or was it my status as hostage, guarded by a man of the *Teannasach's* troops? I thought of asking Isa, but somehow it did not seem appropriate.

"Like Cillian, then," Isa said. I noted the lack of any honorific.

"A better balance," I said lightly. "Two students for the *Comiádh*, three for Lady Dagney." A thought struck me. "Are there usually so few students, Isa?"

"Nae," she answered, shaking her head. "There should be half-a-dozen more, but the war took them; the boys away to fight, were they old enough, or to home to do the work of those who went. The girls also went for home, to be another pair of hands on the farms, or in the workshops. So, we are not what we should be, here at *Ti'ach na Perras*," she finished, her voice sorrowful. "Only the lady Jordis, and Niav and Cillian, and the lord Sorley—and I hear he is soon for home too, and now you, my lady."

Well, I thought, *I had my answers, to both questions.* I finished my tea and put the mug on the table. "*Meas*, Isa," I said. "I should go to the *Comiádh* now; he is expecting me."

"*Allech'i*, wait a moment, my lady." She got up. "I will make tea for you to take to him. Would you like a bitty more, as well?"

I declined, and in a minute or two left the kitchen carrying a steaming mug for Perras. I knocked at his door.

"Come," he called. I opened the door and went in.

"I have brought you tea, *Comiádh*," I said.

"Ah, Lena, welcome," he said, from his seat at the table. "And thank you for bringing my tea. You have had some?" I nodded, and he took the mug from me and placed it on the desk before him. A banked fire warmed and scented the room.

"I have been transcribing the history," he told me. "Now you are here, I suggest we do this: I will read to you what I have transcribed, and you will follow along in the history, and tell me if I have made an error. And please, ask questions as we go. Do you think we can do that?" He handed me the volume of Colm's history, gesturing to another chair at the table.

"Of course, *Comiádh*," I answered. I sat across from him, and opened the book. He took a long swallow of his tea, and straightened the papers on the table.

"To begin," he said, and began to read.

"'In the third year of the reign of the Emperor Lucian, when there had been silence from the East for many years, consideration was given to the expansion of the Empire's lands, as the villages and towns grew crowded. The Emperor's eyes turned to the northern lands, bleak and mountainous as they were, and he offered free land there to any man who would join him in the conquest.'"

Perras read the words, but it was Colm's voice I heard. Tears pricked my eyes. I did not need to check the text in front of me; I knew these opening words off by heart. I realized Perras was waiting.

I nodded. "That is correct," I said.

"Any questions?" he asked. I shook my head.

"Not now." I wanted to ask about the East, but it seemed too soon.

Perras nodded and continued to read. This time I did drop my eyes to the book I held.

"'Many joined Lucian, for the offer of land was tempting. But they did not find the conquest of the northern lands easy, for the inhabitants knew well the hills and valleys, forests and caves, and used them to their advantage to repel Lucian's army.'"

"Go on," I said. Perras cleared his throat. His voice, I thought, was strong for a man of his age.

"'After several years of skirmishes and small battles, a spring came that was cold and wet throughout the land, and crops and cattle suffered.'"

"Stop." He looked up. "The text says, 'both cold and wet,' I explained, and you read 'cold and wet'." He nodded.

"Thank you." He made the correction before continuing to read.

"'But there were many men to feed in the troops, and Lucian, his thoughts fixed on the northern lands, decreed a higher tax of food from the villages and farms. The headwomen of the villages said 'No' to this tax, almost as one voice, arguing thus: You have taken our strongest men; the rain and cold are unceasing; how are we to feed you? They demanded an Assembly, and the Emperor, bound by the laws of the Empire, had to grant it.'"

"Now I do have a question."

"Yes?" he encouraged.

"What Colm wrote here, that the tax of food from the villages came before the Partition vote—this isn't what I learned, at Tirvan. There, I learned that the army fed itself for some years, before taxing the villages."

"You did not ask Colm about this?" Perras asked.

"No," I answered. "We talked of other things that day. I had meant to," I finished.

"Someone wrote once that those are the saddest words that can be said," Perras said gently. "I too had meant to talk more to Colm." He sighed. "We must shoulder that regret, and go on. I think the answer to your question may be two-fold, Lena. Firstly, in your village—was this history written?"

"No," I said, "not that I know of. It was told to us; we learned all our history that way."

"Tales spoken, even when those who tell them believe them to be true, can often stray from what actually happened. But they often retain much of the truth, and it is possible that there were two sets of taxes; the one before Partition vote, and one, later, that increased the tithe even further, and that over the years the two have become confused, conflated into one event. We may never know," he finished. I could hear what I thought was a trace of frustration in his voice.

"Is there nothing in your books that speaks of this?" I asked.

"No," he said. "Those who wrote our histories were not terribly interested in what was happening in the southern Empire. Although the Partition vote and its results—the laws dividing your lives into women's villages and compulsory army life for boys and men—did warrant mention. It was rather drastic," he added.

"I suppose. It was just normal, for us, until these past two years."

"But it was not normal, at the beginning," he reminded me. "Shall we go on?"

"'For ten days and nights women and men met and debated.'," he read. "'The men supported the Emperor in his quest for more lands, arguing it was needed. The women argued there was land enough; careful husbandry would make it sufficient. Finally, Lucian suggested a parting of the ways: men would fight; women would fish and farm. A vote was taken and by a small margin passed.'"

"Not quite six in ten," I said. Perras looked up, his eyebrows questioning. "That is what the Emperor told me," I explained.

"How did he know this?"

I thought back, to that first meeting, and the unexpected turn the conversation had taken. "He said Colm had found the records. In a storeroom, somewhere."

Perras leaned back in his chair. "I think," he said, "I will include that, as a footnote. I did not know how close the vote was, and it is worth recording." He wrote for a minute.

Should I tell him, I wondered, *that Callan had planned a new Assembly, to consider and vote again on the Partition agreement?* Nevin or Blaine would have sent word of this north, had they both not died that Midwinter's Day, executed as traitors. *And there was my answer. I was not a traitor; I could say nothing.* I regretted even making the comment about the vote. But the Emperor had told me to exchange views on Partition and our histories—did that mean I should talk about it? *No,* I told myself firmly. *It's not our history; it's our future. And he told me to trust my instinct, and my instinct tells me to say nothing.*

Perras finished his writing and looked up again. I hoped my confusion did not show in my face; to hide it, I glanced down at the book in my hands. "This next paragraph," I said, forestalling any comment from Perras, "I have always wondered about what it says." This was not strictly true: it had been Niav's comment last night, about marriage, that had caused me to wonder.

"Let us check my transcription," he said, "and then please ask what you wish; if I can answer your questions, I will."

"'But the decree from the Emperor after the Partition vote was not to the liking of many men and women, not even some men senior in the army and long trusted by Lucian, even though that disagreement meant their death by the laws of the Empire'," he read. "'All men would serve in the Emperor's armies, whether they wished to or not; all women would fish and farm, or run the inns and workshops. Marriages were ended and families sundered. Twice a year only, war allowing, could the men visit their homes. Many fled the lands governed by Lucian, going east over the Durrains, or taking boats south; some even fled north, to the wild lands and people there.'"

"It is correct?" he asked. I nodded. "And what did you want to ask?"

"Several things," I said, prevaricating. Suddenly I did not feel I could ask what I had originally wished to, about marriage; not yet. "The people who fled east," I said instead, "across the Durrains. Where would they have gone? What lies beyond the mountains?" I turned, to look at the map that hung on the wall behind me. It showed the Durrains, but the land beyond them was blank.

"Ah," Perras said. "It is not on that map, Lena. But if you go to that third shelf," he pointed at the bookshelf to the right of the fireplace, "and get down the blue box, I will show you." I stood to do his bidding. I pulled the blue box from the shelf and placed it on the table. The *Comiádh* opened it, taking out a rolled paper, tied with faded ribbon. He loosened the bow and spread the paper—the map—out, weighing the edges with the box on one side and his inkwell on the other.

"Come and stand beside me," he said. I did as he asked, peering down at the map. It was old; the paper browned and spotted, the colours faded.

"Here are the Durrains," Perras said, indicating a line of marks on the map. It was oriented in the way I was used to, the mountains running down the map to the sea at the bottom. But to their right, where the map Casyn had drawn for me long months before had ended, more land was shown; land and rivers and towns, occupying most of the sheet. In large letters, extending over most of the lower portion of the map, was the word 'cadenti'.

"What does that mean?" I asked, pointing at the word.

"Conquered," Perras said.

"Conquered?" I said. "By whom? When? What language is that?"

"By the Eastern Empire," he said, "half a thousand years ago, at least. And the language is Casilan, the language of the East, the archaic version of your tongue, to answer your questions in order."

I stared at the map. "I did not realize. I thought we were part of that Empire, yes, but conquered by them? Who were they?"

"The Casilani ruled much of the known world," Perras said. "They were, from all we know, a people of order, literate and learned, who sought to expand beyond their borders, perhaps at first to feed their growing population. From this city, here," he pointed to the far-right edge of the map, where 'Casil' was inscribed in faded gold lettering, "they marched and sailed armies east, and conquered almost all the lands you see here. They brought learning and order with them. They established subordinate Emperors in their colonies—your Emperor Callan is heir to that position—to oversee the army and the food shipments and the taxes. And then, quite suddenly, they disappeared."

This was much as Darel, and then Cillian, had told me. I looked at the map again, noticing this time that the lands to the north of where the Durrains bent eastward were shaded in grey, not the faded green of most of the map. I moved my eyes to the left, where the land I recognized as my own lay: it too was shaded green, but to its north, the map again was grey.

I pointed to that grey. "Is this Linrathe?"

"What is Linrathe now, yes," Perras answered.

"Does the grey mean it was not conquered?"

"It does," he said.

"Why not?" I demanded. "How did these lands hold out, if my own did not?"

"For much the same reasons, I believe, that your Emperor Lucian's armies could not: 'they did not find the conquest of the northern lands easy, for the inhabitants knew the hills and valleys, forests and caves well, and used them to their advantage'. It is a wild land, Lena, and very difficult, and more so as you go north. But they did try; the Sterre, the other wall you noticed yesterday on the wall map: they built it, but could not hold it for more than a dozen years, if that. Their armies retreated south, and left these lands in peace, more or less."

70

As Lucian had, and now as Callan needed to. Was it just the land that made Linrathe so unconquerable?

"At the White Fort," I said slowly, "the morning of the proclamation of truce—I was there. The Emperor, Callan, and the *Teannasach* debated who should speak first, at the proclamation. Callan claimed precedence, and Donnalch granted it, but I didn't understand his reasons." I struggled to remember. "He said that we came from a common history, and that he and his men did not forget the greater Empire either. What did he mean, if Linrathe was not conquered?"

"Sit, Lena," Perras said, "and I will attempt to explain." I did as he asked. When I was seated, he went on.

"Linrathe—or what would become Linrathe—was not conquered, no," the *Comiádh* answered. "But in the dozen years the Empire of the East's armies occupied this land, the leaders here saw much to admire in the Empire's ways, although they had no wish to be ruled by Casil. They sought—both during and after the occupation, for the Eastern Empire continued its presence in your lands for another two hundred years—to learn from the East, from their writings, from observation and likely from the interchange of ideas, and adopted what seemed good and appropriate for our people. These schools, for example, are part of that tradition. So, yes, the *Teannasach* spoke truly, when he spoke of a common history, although we have moved on from that common history in very different ways."

"I see," I said slowly, my thoughts whirling. My confusion must have shown on my face, for Perras put down his pen.

"I think," Perras said, "that is enough for today. You have much to think about, and the mind does not learn if it is force-fed. There is still over an hour until the mid-day meal. It is your time, of course, but perhaps you might go riding? I used to ride after lessons, especially difficult ones. It helps settle one's thoughts."

My mind cleared at the thought of riding, of action and movement. Clio would be sufficiently rested. I stood.

"*Meas, Comiádh,*" I said. "It is a good idea."

"*Meas*, Lena, for helping me with the transcription," he replied. "Come to see me at the same time tomorrow, and we will continue."

I closed the door quietly behind me. The hall was empty. Upstairs, I changed into my outdoor clothes and boots. From my bedroom window, the sky gleamed grey; *not threatening rain*, I thought, *just a grey day.*

After a quick visit to the latrine I began to walk toward the stables and paddock. A moment later, I heard footsteps behind me, and turned to see Gregor following me. *Of course,* I thought. *I won't be alone; he has to go with me.*

"The *Comiádh* told me to go for a ride," I said, "as a break from my lessons. Since you must come with me, do you know this area well enough to lead me somewhere to gallop? I am in the mood for a run."

"I can do that, my lady," he answered. I didn't bother to correct him. We walked in silence to the stables. The horses grazed in the paddock, but as always Clio came to me when I called her. I scratched her head, wishing I'd brought her a piece of bread, and led her out of the field and to the tack room.

Gregor followed with his solid bay, and tacked the gelding up with the economical, practiced moves of a cavalry soldier. He mounted, not waiting, I was glad to see, to offer me a leg up. I swung onto Clio's back and followed Gregor away from the stable.

The path ran down along the edge of the stream, its surface pocked by the hooves of sheep. The stream itself gurgled and splashed along a bed of dark rock, running fast with the early spring rains and the melting snows of winter. A small brown bird with a brilliant white throat hunted in the moving water, walking into the stream and diving below the surface.

"What bird is that?" I called to Gregor. He reined up and looked where I was pointing.

"A *snámh'a*," he said. "I don't know its name in your language." He shrugged. "It swims? That's what its name means."

"Swimmer?" I hazarded. "Swimming bird?"

He nodded. "Something like that."

"*Meas*, Gregor," I said, and was rewarded by a moment of surprise on his face. Mentally I chastised myself for forgetting to use 'please' before my question. *Next time,* I told myself.

Ahead I could see a stone bridge spanning the stream; beyond it, the track led into a wide valley, with the stream at its right edge. We clopped over the bridge; at its far side, Gregor glanced back at me. "We can gallop here," he said. "Do you want to set the pace?"

"No," I said after a moment's consideration. "You know the land better. We'll follow." He nodded, and urged his bay into trot, and then quickly into a gallop. Clio tossed her head, and galloped after them.

When was the last time I had galloped for pure pleasure? Somewhere in the grasslands, riding south with Garth, I thought. It felt like a lifetime ago. I leaned a bit further forward, and gave myself up to the sensation of speed and power.

It took us about ten minutes to reach the far end of the valley, and sweat lathered along both horses' reins when we pulled up. The valley had narrowed toward the end, the land rising more steeply on the left side. Gregor pointed up the hill. "If we go up there," he suggested, "there's a good long view. It might interest you."

"Let's," I said, and Gregor turned his horse's head to the hill. We followed a track that zigzagged back and forth across the slope to reach the top, an easy climb. The hilltop was flat. Sheep grazed, scattered across the plateau, and a strong wind blew from the west.

I gazed northward. I could see a line of hills a long distance away; snow lay on their peaks; the highest were shrouded in cloud. I thought I saw a glint of water before them. Gregor spoke.

"I was born in those hills. That's home, or was. My da has sheep, like most there, and my ma and the women weave the wool."

"Some women in my village were weavers, too," I said. "They made blankets, and sails, and material for clothes. Is that what the women in your family made?"

"Not sails," he said. "But the other, yes."

"Do you miss them?" I asked impulsively. He did not answer immediately. "*Forla*, Gregor," I said. "I should not have presumed to ask that."

"It's fine, my lady," he said, and the tone of his voice told me he was not just being polite. "I was just collecting my thoughts. Do I miss them? Yes, I suppose I do; although there is no real place there for me. My brother helps my da with the sheep, and there is not a living there for all of us. So, a soldier I became, when the *Teannasach* asked for men."

I looked up at him, sitting easily on his horse beside me. He was looking north, the wind blowing strands of his dark hair across his face. *Why was he a soldier, and not Cillian?* They were the same age, more or less. 'I am no lover of Empires,' Cillian had said. Surely someone who felt like that would have joined a fight against the Empire? *But was that what the invasion was about?* I realized I didn't know. I had never questioned, never asked.

"*Allech'i*, Gregor," I said. "What does the *Teannasach* want with the Empire's lands? Why did he breach the Wall?"

He looked down at me. "Don't you know?" he said, the surprise evident in his voice.

"No," I said, "I don't. I thought it was to support a faction of our soldiers who wanted to overthrow the Emperor, but it can't just be that. There must be something more for the *Teannasach*, and your people. Is it for land?"

"No," he replied. "Not for land, or for any prizes. We invaded to give you back what your Emperors have taken from you. You live in tyranny, my lady, whether you realize it or not: men and women are meant to live together, to marry and raise families, to work together. And you cannot. There are many here in Linrathe whose ancestors, mine included, escaped your lands to freedom here, and for many generations they have been asking our leaders to free the southern lands. This *Teannasach* has listened, and acted. So, it is all for you, my lady Lena, and not for us at all."

CHAPTER SIX

I STARED UP AT GREGOR, SPEECHLESS. *All for us? But why did they think we wanted this?* I thought of Nevin and Blaine: *was this what they had wanted? Was this why Nevin's son had opened the gates to Linrathe's soldiers? Did the Emperor know? How could he not, after all the long talks with Donnalch?* Too many questions. I had wanted to gallop, to clear my head, but now it pounded with confusion and doubts.

Gregor had turned his horse around, facing back the way we came, to scan the horizon, his soldier's training making these actions automatic. I opened my mouth to ask to return to the *Ti'ach*, to talk to Perras, or Dagney. I had just started to speak when he held up a hand to stop me.

"Look," he said, pointing south. "Horses and riders, moving fast." I looked outward, to where he pointed; two horses on the hilltop above the *Ti'ach*. "That's the *Teannasach*: I recognize his horse. And Ardan with him, I've no doubt. We must go back, my lady; I might be needed."

The horses picked their way back down the hill. As soon as we reached level ground, the walk became a gallop, back across the valley and over the bridge, slowing only as we reached the narrow, muddy, uneven path beside the stream. At the stable, we both had our horses unsaddled and turned out in minutes. The day was cool and we had walked the last distance, so they would come to no harm. I strode with Gregor up the path to the house; we reached the courtyard just as Donnalch and Ardan clattered in.

Gregor said something I did not understand, although I thought I caught the word '*Teannasach*'. The two men dismounted; Gregor took the reins of Donnalch's horse, and again said something, this time to Ardan, who laughed.

"No hurry at all, except that we were hungry," he answered, glancing at me, "and wanted to get here in time for the noon meal. If there is one. Have you eaten today since breakfast, Lena?"

"No," I said. "And there is a noon meal planned."

"Good," Donnalch said, "for a piece of bread at dawn has not much staying power." He grinned, turning toward the hall door. As he reached the first step, the door opened. For a moment, against the dark of the room behind, I could not see who stood there.

"Welcome, *Teannasach, Canri'ad,*" Cillian said. "Food is nearly ready, please come in." *A very formal greeting,* I thought. I glanced back at Gregor, wondering if I should help with the horses. He shook his head and began to lead the two horses away. I followed Donnalch and Ardan into the hall.

As when I had arrived—only two days before, I realized—everyone came out to greet the guests. Donnalch had a word for everyone, even Niav, who blushed and giggled when he spoke to her. Dagney sent her out to the kitchen, and I went with her.

"Two more mouths," Isa said from the stove. "Well, there's plenty bread. Niav, cut a bitty more, will you not?" Niav did as she was asked, slicing a loaf with practiced skill. She piled it into a wooden bowl.

"What can I do?" I asked.

"Take the bread out to the hall," Niav answered. "One bowl at each end of the table."

Out in the hall the elders and Donnalch had gathered at one end of the room. Neither Ardan nor Cillian were to be seen. I placed the bread as Niav had directed. Jordis and Sorley were setting the table, bringing spoons and mats from the sideboard where the glass drinking vessels were kept.

We moved back and forth from the kitchen, bringing a round of cheese and bowls of soup. My stomach rumbled. Jordis went to stand beside Dagney. "My lady?" I heard her say. "The food is ready."

She nodded, and spoke quietly to Perras and Donnalch. They broke off talking to come to the table, Donnalch pulling out Perras's chair and making him comfortable before seating himself beside Perras. He looked around. "Where is Ardan?"

"I sent him and Cillian for ale," Perras said. "I thought you would like a draught. Ah, here they are," he added, as the outside door opened. But it was Gregor who entered.

"Did you see your *Canri'ad*, and Cillian?" Perras asked.

76

"No, *Comiádh*, I did not," Gregor answered, coming further into the room. "Shall I go to look for them?"

"No, sit," Donnalch said. "Ardan had something to say to Cillian; they will come when ready."

"Then let us begin," Dagney said. "Cold soup is not to anyone's liking. Sorley, will you take those two bowls back to Isa, and ask her to keep them warm on the stove?"

The soup, creamy on my tongue, tasted of the parsnips Isa had been peeling earlier, and of a pungent spice I could not name. As I ate, I watched the people around the table, curious as to how they treated their leader. Donnalch, I saw, ate with hunger, seemed happy with the simple food, and spoke to everyone in the same open, unassuming manner. Niav, who appeared awestruck at sitting at a table with her *Teannasach*, watched him closely, and without being asked, slipped into the kitchen at one point to return with more bread. As she put it on the table beside Donnalch, the outside door opened again. I looked up. Ardan and Cillian came in, carrying two earthenware jugs. Cillian looked pale, I thought, and distracted.

"There you are," Perras said. "Mugs are on the sideboard; who would like ale, in honour of the *Teannasach*'s visit?"

Mugs and ale were distributed, but I took only a small amount. The soup for the two men was brought from the kitchen, and we continued eating. I tried the ale. It tasted much like any other ale, I thought; I preferred wine, but had learned to drink what was offered in the last two years. I glanced over at Cillian. He seemed to be eating little, but had drained his ale and was pouring more.

"*Teannasach*, forgive me if I overstep..." Perras began.

"You cannot," Donnalch said. "But I can guess what you want to ask: why am I here, and not negotiating with the Southern Emperor, am I right?"

"You are." Perras nodded, a slight smile on his lips.

"It came to my mind that I needed to visit the *Ti'acha,* and the *torps,* to see what our people thought of the truce, and to hear what they wanted from a permanent peace, if we can reach that goal. Callan of the South accepted this; in truth, I believe he wanted much the same, time to consult his advisors and the villages. So here I am. Shall we go hawking this afternoon?"

"Do you not want to discuss the treaty?"

"I would like to speak with you, Perras, but I am also ready for some fun. We can talk in the dark of evening, and into the night."

Perras raised an eyebrow. "As you wish, *Teannasach*," he said. "The fawkner has kept the birds ready; your falcon was flown last a few days ago, I believe. Will you take the young people, if they wish?"

"Oh, yes, please," Niav breathed. Donnalch laughed. I wondered if she wanted just to be near him, and if he knew that.

"How could I say no?" he teased. "Yes, of course. Who would like to go?"

"I will," Sorley said. He, I thought, was at ease with the *Teannasach*, but I supposed he had met and spoken with him before. Cillian shook his head, but said nothing. *A direct question from the* Teannasach, *and he doesn't bother to speak?* But Donnalch showed no sign of offense.

"And you, Lena?" he asked. I hesitated. I really wanted to stay, to ask Perras about what Gregor had said. I was troubled, too, by what the *Teannasach* had said about Callan: time to consult his advisors and the villages. *Would he announce a new assembly, like he had planned...and I not there to be part of it? But I cannot refuse Donnalch,* I thought; *I am not Cillian, long part of the* Ti'ach *and known to the* Teannasach.

"Yes," I said. "If I may. But I don't know anything about hawking."

"You don't need to. Just come and watch."

We all went, except Cillian, who had remained silent and withdrawn throughout the meal. Ardan and Gregor accompanied us—Ardan to guard the *Teannasach*, and Gregor to guard me, I thought—and the fawkner, a sturdy, sandy-haired man in his forties called Tómas. I followed the others to a long, low building on the west side of the courtyard; Jordis had pointed it out to me yesterday, calling it the mews. Where the hawks are kept, she'd said.

Ardan led Donnalch's horse out, and Sorley followed with his own and a sturdy pony, saddled but also laden with saddlebags and rope. He handed the pony's reins to Gregor. The *Teannasach* and Sorley mounted, then swung their right legs up over the pommels of their saddles, to allow Tómas to fix a wooden support—a straight piece of wood crowned with in a curved piece set at right angles to the base—to the saddle on the right side. I frowned. *What was that for?* I watched Donnalch gather his reins in his left and, and lay his right arm in the curve of the wood. Tómas came out from the mews with a falcon, hooded, and with leather straps dangling from its legs, handing it up to ride on the *Teannasach's* gloved fist. It moved from Tómas's wrist to Donnalch's easily, sitting calmly and quietly.

"Even the weight of a falcon can prove tiring, over an afternoon, with the arm always held up," Gregor said in my ear. "The *tuki* takes the strain and gives the bird a smoother ride. A calm bird will hunt better."

I glanced over at him and smiled my thanks. I didn't know if I should speak; he had not whispered, but his voice had been pitched low. "What are the leather straps?" I murmured.

"They're called jesses," he replied, keeping his voice quiet, but not whispering. "They stop the bird from flying from the hand until its handler wants to release it."

Sorley's bird—smaller, I noted, than Donnalch's, although I thought it the same kind—was handed up. He spoke to it soothingly. It had not, I noticed, transferred quite as well as Donnalch's, shifting its weight back and forth on Sorley's wrist. Sorley stroked its back with one finger, and the bird settled.

"We will wait for you by the stream," the *Teannasach* said. Tómas emerged from the mews with a third, much smaller bird, and swung up into the saddle of the pony. He had no *tuki*, but moved the bird to ride on the saddle's pommel in front of him. They rode off at a walk.

Gregor motioned us forward, and we walked down the path to the stables to saddle our mounts. I wondered how Clio would react to the falcons. *Are the Han horses trained to falconry?* I wondered. *Do officers of the Empire fly hawks?*

As if he had heard my thoughts, Gregor came over to me as I tacked up Clio. "Has she experience of falcons?" he asked.

"I don't know," I admitted.

"Then stay at the back, away from the *Teannasach* and the Lord Sorley," he said. "A frightened horse could scare the birds, and we don't want to lose one." It made sense. I nodded my agreement, and swung up into the saddle.

We rode down the track Gregor and I had followed earlier in the day, and across the same field. Where the land rose, Donnalch turned his horse up the hill, and again we climbed to the flat, windy plateau from where we had seen the *Teannasach*'s arrival this morning. There we halted. I guided Clio away from Donnalch and Sorley, to the back of the group, and caught Gregor's eye. He rode over to me.

"Should I dismount, and hold her?" I asked him in a whisper.

He considered. "Not a bad idea," he said. He glanced over at Donnalch, who was conferring with Tómas and Sorley. "Do it," he said.

I swung down from the saddle to stand at Clio's head, stroking her neck. She blew at me, then dropped her head to nose at the thin grass. I held her reins, watching the men.

Donnalch removed the hood from his falcon and raised his arm. The bird launched itself in one powerful push and flew, not high but directly away from us, across the ground. Clio raised her head and sidestepped, rolling her eye slightly. Automatically I calmed her, my eyes never leaving the falcon. The initial rapid wingbeats gave way to a flat-winged soar, the leather jesses trailing. Suddenly the bird twisted and flew upward, rapidly gaining height, and then folded its wings and arrowed down. I held my breath. *Surely it would crash into the ground?* At the last moment, I saw its wings and legs extend. Fur exploded into the air.

"A hare," Donnalch said. Tómas nodded, and went to the bird. I saw him offer it a piece of meat, then slip a hood back over its head. He raised it to his arm, picked up the hare with the other hand, and returned to the group, handing the bird back to Donnalch.

Gregor too had dismounted and now led his horse over to me. "A good start," he said.

"I thought it would hit the ground. It came down so fast," I answered. Niav and Jordis were talking in normal voices to Donnalch and Sorley, so I didn't bother to whisper.

"You've not seen a *fuádain* hunt before?"

"No," I said. "There are seabirds that dive like that, straight down, but they are going into water. Does it ever miss and crash?"

"She," he said. "That's a female bird; you can tell by its size and colouring. The smaller falcon the Lord Sorley flies is the tercel, the male. And yes, they do miss sometimes, especially when they're learning to hunt. Sometimes one is badly injured and dies. But not often."

Sorley unhooded his bird and I watched again as it flew, rose, dived, taking another hare. Clio did not react this time to the flying bird. A weak sun had broken through the clouds, and the wind had lessened. The *fuádain* took two more hares.

"Shall we move?" Donnalch asked. "I've a mind to try for *cailzie*, and for that we need to be closer to the forest. The cock birds will be thinking of the hens, now, and perhaps out from the trees."

"Aye," Tómas answered. "And perhaps the lassies can fly the *merliún* there, for *colúir*."

I remounted, and we rode east toward a band of dark forest. The land rose as we approached, and at one end of the trees a scarp of clay and rock rose like a wall. Crumbled soil and boulders lay at its foot. I could hear the coo of pigeons from the trees.

We stopped some distance from the trees. Donnalch unhooded his bird and it flew, quartering the ground between the forest and us. The pigeons fell silent. The bird circled, went higher, and then plunged at something I could not see against the dark of the trees.

I lost it for a moment, and then she flew up again, close to the evergreens. A pigeon broke from the shelter of the branches and the falcon was on it, pursuing it towards the wall of rock and clay. She rose, stooped, and falcon and pigeon together hit the side of the escarpment, tumbling down to a tiny ledge.

I heard Donnalch swear quietly. Tómas walked rapidly towards the scarp, swinging something that looked like feathers, wings, fastened to the end of a leather strap. He whistled at the falcon, swinging the lure. She looked up; clearly unhurt, she had begun to pluck the pigeon. Tómas whistled again and held up his arm. She rose on her legs and raised her wings, pushed off—and spun helplessly, twisting on a snagged jess.

Donnalch swore louder. Tómas dropped the lure and ran to the base of the scarp, looking up. "Caught on a root," he said. "Up to the top, and lower me down on the rope."

"That scarp's not safe," Donnalch said. "And the rains will have made it softer."

"Aye," Tómas said. "But you and the other men, and the horses if need be, can take my weight. You nae wish to lose the bird, *Teannasach?*"

"I'm thinking we'd have to be well back from the edge," Donnalch replied. "Do we have enough rope?"

The falcon gave a wild flutter, trying to free herself. Niav and Jordis turned away from the sight of the struggling bird. As the men debated I studied the scarp, my eyes searching the surface. "There's another way," I said. Donnalch turned to me.

"What do you mean, lassie?" he asked.

"I can climb up to her," I said. I pointed. "There's enough of a slope, and hand and foot holds, to reach where she is." Donnalch studied the cliff face.

"Aye," he said after a minute. "I see what you mean. But, Lena, it's a soft clay, and the face will crumble if it's climbed. Better to see if we have enough rope, and send back for more if it's needed. Tómas has rescued birds from worse places than this, over the years."

A shower of clay and pebbles fell. The falcon battered the cliff face with her wings. Tómas made a worried sound.

"She's not hanging calm," he said. "She's bound to break a leg, if she keeps that up." At his words, the falcon beat her wings again, and this time a feather fell with the clay. Donnalch frowned.

"You said you could climb up to her?" he demanded.

"Yes," I answered. "I am trained, and experienced, in rock climbing. There are cliffs at Tirvan, and we had to climb them, in the dark, when Leste invaded."

"If we rope you, can you climb down?" I heard Tómas make a sound of protest. "Lena is lighter than you by a third, at least," Donnalch said. "With the cliff so soft, it will be safer. If you are certain, Lena?"

"I am," I said, "except that I have never handled a hawk."

"Sorley, give me your bird," Donnalch ordered. Sorley passed his hooded tercel over. Tómas, who had gone to his pony, dug in the saddlebags to hand up a pair of heavy leather gloves. "Put those on," Donnalch said. I complied.

"You'll need to hood her," he explained. He slid the leather hood off Sorley's bird and then back on. "Like this. Get your arm where her feet can grasp it; she'll hold on, and right herself as soon as she can. Then hood her. She's upset, so she'll likely go for your hands, or try to, so keep the gloves on. She'll go quiet once the hood is on, and we can pull you up."

He had me unhood and hood Sorley's bird several times. I was clumsy, and tentative, but after a few tries he deemed it good enough. He looked up at the cliff face, where his falcon was still fighting her jesses. I realized the men had already ridden to the top of the cliff, and the girls had withdrawn to somewhere I could not see. Perhaps they had ridden back for more rope, just in case.

I wondered, as I rode to the top of the cliff, if I truly could do this, and why I had offered. The rocks of Tirvan's waterfall had been stabilized and ropes added in the weeks before the Lestian invasion, in preparation for climbing; as well, I had climbed it so many times I knew each rock and crevice. This crumbling cliff face was something very different, and so was the situation. I had climbed the waterfall to defend my village. I was risking my life here for a bird. *Maybe there won't be enough rope,* I thought.

But there was enough rope, Donnalch judged, to lower me. Tómas tied the rope around my waist and shoulders, knotting it in front. Then he knotted the other end around his waist. "You're sure?" he said, quietly, so only I could hear. I nodded. I knew my actions were foolhardy. I knew I was trying to prove something to these men. He held my eyes for a long moment. I wondered if he could see my doubts. Then he too nodded. I walked to the cliff, turned my back to the drop, and when I felt the rope tighten, stepped off.

The rope taut under my hands, I scrabbled for footing on the cliff-face. The unstable clay shifted and crumbled. I had no grip. I pushed off, swung. Pebbles and clods of earth dropped from above, where the rope bit into the cliff edge. I looked up, and then down at the struggling bird, and swallowed my terror. "There's no footing at all," I called. "You'll have to take all my weight."

Foot by foot the men lowered me. More soil and rock fell from above. I swung, pushed, dropped slowly. The bird grew closer.

Suddenly a large chunk of soil fell, barely missing me and trailed by a shower of pebbles. I heard someone shout from above. "Hold on, Lena," Donnalch called. "We need to get something under this rope." I hung, waiting. Looking down, I could see the small ledge and the broken root that the falcon hung from. She had gone quiet. I spoke to her, soothing noises, hoping she was not injured.

"Lena!" Donnalch called.

"Yes?" I shouted. The bird fluttered.

"We must pull you up a bit; we're putting a saddle under the rope, to stop it cutting the cliff edge. If you can brace yourself at all, when we tell you, it will help."

"I'll try," I called. The rope tightened even more, and I was pulled up. I tried to keep my feet against the cliff-face.

"Now!" Donnalch called. I braced my feet against the wall, seeing a large rock protruding at eye height. I leaned in and grabbed for it, catching it under my gloved fingers. It didn't move. I hung on, waiting, breathing hard.

"Good!" Donnalch called. "Down again now." I let go of the rock, and let myself be lowered. No more soil fell from above me. I slid down the cliff face, and my foot found the ledge.

"Stop!" I shouted. I manoeuvred over and got both feet on the ledge. It held. Slowly, slowly, I moved to turn my body on the ledge, shifting my feet and my weight in tiny movements. When I stood with back and hands flat against the cliff, I called up. "Give me just a little slack."

The rope loosened. I slid down to a crouch, my hand reaching out to the root. I extended one leg, and then the other, until I sat on the ledge. I pushed the dead pigeon off the edge to give myself more space. The falcon dangled beside my right leg. Murmuring to her, I grasped the root with my left hand, leaning until her talons could reach my leather-clad right arm.

She grasped my arm immediately, the strength of her claws and feet evident through the leather. She scrabbled around, righting herself on my arm. I straightened as much as I could. The men had the rope just slightly slack. I needed now to let go of the root, and hood the falcon.

I leaned as far back as possible and took my hand off the root, reaching slowly for the hood in my shirt pocket. I couldn't straighten entirely; the jesses were not long enough to allow it. I found the hood, turned it in my fingers, brought my hand to the falcon's head, watching her cold yellow-ringed eyes. She moved on my arm. I held my breath.

But she did not flinch from me. I slipped the hood over her head. She stopped moving. I held my arm up and leaned forward again, finding my balance, my left hand exploring the leather jesses tangled on the root. A slit in the leather had snagged on a small, upright rootlet. I slid the jess up and over.

I sat on the ledge, breathing heavily, thinking. I could not stand again from this position; the men would have to pull me up from where I was. I would need to get my left hand behind me, to avoid scraping against the cliff face, and then turn in the air. *Or should I? What would be safer for the falcon?*

"Is she free?" Tómas voice, from below me. I looked down. He stood at the base of the cliff. He must have run down once I was on the ledge, I thought.

"Yes," I called. The falcon did not move.

"Unhood her," he called. "I'll whistle her down to me."

It would be better to be pulled up the cliff-face without the bird, I realized. I reached over and plucked the hood from the falcon's head. She looked around, her curved and pointed beak too close to my face for my liking.

A sharp, cutting whistle came from below. The *fuádain* swivelled her head, and at a repeated whistle raised herself to launch into the air, gliding down to where Tómas stood, swinging the lure. I watched as she dropped gracefully onto his out-stretched arm.

I took a breath. Sounds from above told me the *Teannasach* and the others had seen the falcon return to Tómas. A pebble fell; I looked up. A face looked down. Sorley. *He must be stretched out on the cliff-top,* I thought.

"Magnificent, Lena!" he called. "Are you ready to be raised up?"

"Yes," I answered. "I can't stand, though; you'll have to pull me from here."

His face withdrew. In a moment, I felt the rope tauten, and I grasped the knot with one hand. I extended my other arm and, once I felt my body leave the ledge, pushed off from the cliff, trying to position myself so I could use my legs to keep from scraping along the scarp. I swung, turning from side to side for a minute, but being pulled upward at the same time. The weight of my body took me hard into the cliff-face. I cried out in surprise and pain as my extended wrist took the brunt of the impact. The upward motion stopped. "Are you all right?" Donnalch called.

I tried to flex my wrist. Sharp pain ran up my arm. "I've hurt my arm," I called. "I hit the cliff-face too hard. Let me see if I can get my feet against the wall, before you pull again."

I swung my body, cursing myself. Whatever I had set out to prove, I was now injured. *Nothing but a fragile woman.* Cradling my throbbing arm to my body, I manoeuvred around until my feet were firmly against the face of the cliff. "Now," I shouted.

Slowly but steadily they pulled me up. My feet slipped twice, jarring my arm and bringing tears to my eyes, and more pebbles and soil from above. But then I was at the cliff-edge. Hands reached down for me, held me under my armpits, dragged me over the edge. My wrist throbbed. I lay on the grass, panting, tears streaming down my face, too drained to worry about looking weak.

"Come, Lena," Donnalch said gently. "We need to get away from the edge." He extended a hand down, and I let him help me to my knees, and then my feet. The other men stood some distance off. I walked beside him, the rope dragging, to where they stood, brushing away the tears with my gloved right hand. The women, I saw now, sat on their horses in a little group behind the men.

Sorley stepped forward to undo the knots of the rope harness, freeing me. I winced as he pulled the loop down over my left arm. Pain radiated up from the wrist to the shoulder. Donnalch saw my grimace. He took my left arm in his hands and pulled off the heavy glove. Then he probed. I bit my lip.

"Turn it," he ordered. I moved the wrist, gasping involuntarily. He felt along the bones.

"Not broken," he said, "but a bad sprain. It will need rest and binding. Bravely done, Lena. *Meas*, for rescuing my falcon, although those words are inadequate."

"Aye," Gregor said. "I doubt any of our girls could have done what you did today."

Something broke in me. "And you think we need freeing?" I cried. "That we live in tyranny, and have no choices about how we live our lives?" I felt the tears on my cheeks, and heard the rage in my voice, but fear and pain and anger overwhelmed reason. "I can climb a cliff and rescue your falcon; I can advise Emperors and speak in council meetings; I can sail a boat and kill men with a knife. Your women can do none of these. And you think the women of the Empire need freeing because we cannot marry? How dare you, *Teannasach*, Donnalch of the North? How dare you presume to know what we want?"

Chapter Seven

I CHOKED BACK A SOB, WILLING MYSELF not to break down completely. I stared at Donnalch. He regarded me thoughtfully. Then he turned to look at the rest of the men. I saw Gregor flush.

"*Forla, Teannasach,*" I heard.

"*Deir'anaí,*" Donnalch answered, his voice firm. Gregor nodded. Donnalch turned back to me. I wiped my face with the back of my hand, and swallowed.

"Well, *Teannasach*?" I said.

"Did you speak to the Emperor Callan in this way?" he asked, his voice amused. I blinked in surprise.

"Yes," I replied. I almost smiled. "Once," I amended. "Only once, in anger, *Teannasach.*"

"And what did he say?"

"He said, 'Those who advise emperors should be able to challenge them as well.'," I answered. I had my anger under control now, although I could feel the aftermath of emotion in the slight trembling of my body. I hoped it was not visible to Donnalch.

"Aye," he said thoughtfully. "That sounds like Callan. Well, lassie, I did not think of you advising me—although I am no Emperor—but perhaps I should have. Now, Ardan, give Lena a sip or two of the *fuisce* you carry, and then we had best go back; Lena needs tea and honey, and the falcon needs her mews."

Ardan appeared beside me with a leather flask. I took a sip of the spirits; smoky and rich on my tongue, the *fuisce* warmed me at once. After a second sip, I felt stronger, the trembling subsiding. I handed the flask back to Ardan. Gregor led Clio forward, and I mounted, holding my left forearm against my body. It was awkward.

"Gregor," I said quietly as I put my foot in the stirrup. "Are you in trouble now, because you told me why Linrathe was invading?"

"Aye," he replied. "And I should be."

I grasped the pommel of the saddle with my right hand, and hauled myself up, half prone across the saddle. Clio moved slightly, flicking her ears. Gregor soothed her.

"What will happen?"

He made a small movement of his head. "Whatever the *Teannasach* decides."

I swung my leg over and sat up in the saddle. My wrist throbbed. I looked down at him. "*Forla*," I said quietly. "I truly did not mean for this to happen."

We rode back to the hall at a walk, Gregor staying close beside me. Donnalch spoke quietly to Ardan, and the others rode in silence. By the time we reached the courtyard I was trembling again.

Donnalch swung off his horse and bounded up the steps, shouting orders. Gregor helped me dismount. "Go in," he said. "I'll see to your horse."

Dagney came out from the hall. "Lena," she ordered, "go straight to the *Comiádh*'s chambers; they are the warmest in the house. Isa will bring tea, and I have liniments for your wrist. *Allech'i*, Jordis, go with her."

Perras' door stood ajar. The fire blazed in the hearth, and I sank into the chair offered me. Jordis found a blanket to tuck around my legs. The tea arrived, Isa clucking her concern. I took the cup gratefully. I sipped. Hot and sweet, with just a thread of a bitter aftertaste: Isa—or someone—had added willow-bark for the pain. My mother would have done the same. I held the cup, drinking the tea slowly.

Dagney arrived with a basket, and sat in front of me. I held out my arm, and gently she pushed back my sleeve and touched my wrist. I winced, shook my head at her murmured apology. "It is a sprain, as the *Teannasach* thought," she said. She dug in the basket, bringing out a pot of liniment. She spread it over the wrist, rubbing it in with circular motions. It smelled astringent. "Heather and witch-hazel," she explained, "and an herb called *mot'ulva*, that we get from the Marai. It will help." Then she bound the wrist tightly with a linen bandage, and finally fashioned a sling for my arm from more linen. "You'll need to keep it bound and in the sling for a week," she announced. "We will salve it three times a day."

She poured me another cup of tea. "What were you thinking, Lena?" she asked gently as she passed me the tea.

"That the falcon needed rescuing, and I was the best person to do so," I said bluntly. As much as I liked Dagney, or thought I did, I was in no mood for lectures on what was right—or wrong—for me to do. Dagney must have heard as much in my voice, for she gave me an assessing look, saying nothing for a moment.

"It was brave," she said, after a pause. "I am sorry for your injury, though."

I shrugged. "I've had as bad, or worse, from fishing, over the years." I was being rude, as truculent as a child. "Thank you, my lady, for your ministrations," I said, trying to make my voice less brusque. "*Meas*," I added, remembering. "My mother would be interested in this salve; the herb you mentioned—*mot'ulva?*—is not one we know, as far as I can remember, or at least, not by that name."

"It is also called *arnek*," Dagney said, "but the herb grows only in the northlands and the highlands, so perhaps she would not have access to it. I can send some home with you, when it is time for you to go. But I did not know you were interested in herbs and healing, Lena."

"I'm not, not really, but I have helped my mother in the herb harvest and still-room as a little girl, and some of it I remember."

"A bit of healing lore is always useful," she said. She stood, gathering linen and scissors back into her basket. The pot of salve she left on the table. "*Allech'i*, Jordis, will you dress Lena's arm again this evening, and three times tomorrow?" she asked. "You saw what I did? Then I will look at it again, in two days."

"Yes, my lady," Jordis said. "I can do that."

A knock at the door, and then it opened a crack. "Can I come in?" Donnalch's voice.

"Yes, *Teannasach*," Dagney answered. "We are done; Lena is resting."

He came into the room, bringing the scent of the outdoors with him. "The *fuádain* does well enough," he said. "A few days of rest, and she will be fine, although right now she favours the leg she hung from. Tomas will tend to her. As the Lady Dagney has done for you, Lena, I see. You also are well enough?"

"*Meas, Teannasach,* I am," I replied. "As you said, it is a sprain and I will heal much as your falcon will."

"Salve and willow-bark, and binding and rest is what Lena needs," Dagney said. I though I heard a warning in her voice. Donnalch was looking at me, though, and I shook my head slightly. A smile twitched at the edge of his mouth.

"I'm thinking she's a bit tougher than you give her credit for," he said. "I'll not be long, Lady, but I want a few minutes with our hostage." Gently said, but it was the *Teannasach* that spoke, reminding both Dagney and myself of my status.

"As you will," Dagney said formally. "Come, Jordis."

"Warm in here," Donnalch pulled his outer tunic off. As he spoke, I realized I too was hot, and pushed the blanket away from my legs, letting it drop to the ground.

"I would offer you tea," I said, "but it has willow-bark in it, and there is not a second mug."

"No matter." He sat in the other chair.

"I am glad the falcon is not seriously hurt," I said. "Does she have a name?"

"Grasi, I call her."

"And it is fine for Grasi to hunt, and kill, even though she is female?"

"It is her nature; she was born to hunt and kill," he said evenly. "But she was also born to mate, and raise her chicks with her tercel. As she will, in another season. I would not deny her that right; it would be cruelty, to go against her nature so completely."

"And if her tercel is gone, will she raise those chicks alone?"

"Aye, of course," he said. "Although only because she must. And almost certainly less successfully."

"Because they are solitary birds," I said, "and no other female will help her raise that brood. But think of foxes, *Teannasach*, where the young from a previous year help feed the new litter, so even if the dog fox is gone the young are raised successfully. What is the nature of one animal is not that of another. And we are neither falcons nor foxes, bound to the roles nature gives us, but thinking, reasoning humans. Why should we not choose how we live?"

Donnalch shook his head. "I see I did right in sending you here," he said. "You argue as if you had been taught by Perras for many years. Where did you learn this, Lena?"

"From the women of Tirvan. Do you think we do not argue, in council and out of it?" *And from Casyn and Colm,* I thought, but I was not about to admit that, not at this moment. "And you are changing the subject, *Teannasach,*" I added.

"Aye, I am," he said easily. "Because you are hurt and tired, whether you choose to admit to such or not. I am truly interested in your thoughts, but I would like them to be considered and calm, and I doubt you can stay so, right now." I started to protest, but he stopped me with a raised hand. "I have two things to say, or, more exactly, one to say and one to ask. Will you listen?"

"Of course, *Teannasach,*" I replied, remembering my place here.

"Sometimes," he began, "a leader must find ways of making a task understandable to minds less versed in history, and what Gregor told you was how I explained my incursion against your Empire to the shepherds and fishermen of Linrathe. Gregor told you there are those amongst them who have been agitating for such a sortie for generations?"

"He did," I confirmed. "Is it not true, then?"

"Not entirely," Donnalch said. "But it brought men to the cause, and bound them to me as a leader who listened to their dreams. I channelled that desire to support my own plans."

"Which were what?" I asked, bluntly.

"Ah, lassie, I'm not about to tell you that, not now." He smiled. "Would you expect me to? I'm only telling you this much so that you don't kill yourself in my care, trying to prove the women of the Empire are a match for our men," he went on. "It was a brave thing you did today, and it will have done the girls here—and the men, too—no harm to have seen you do it. But now, my question. Could you ride, do you think, in two days? Or even one? Long days in the saddle, I mean, not a ride for pleasure or exercise. Answer honestly, please, Lena."

I flexed the wrist again. It hurt, but not as much as it had before it had been salved and bound. "Yes," I said, "if the riding is not at speed, I could manage it, I think." I wanted to ask why, but did not.

Donnalch pushed his dark hair off his forehead with one hand, his manner suddenly more serious. "I would like to talk more with you, but I am constrained by time: I have given myself a bare fortnight to make this journey. But I want to hear your thoughts before that, and so I can see no choice than to have you accompany me, and we can talk on the road." He stood. "I'll find the Lady Dagney, and make the arrangements. We'll be a small party, and all men, unless you want another woman along?"

I shook my head. I was used to travelling with men, alone, and had no concerns about their conduct towards me. On the ride, north from the Wall to the *Ti'ach na Perras*, the men had treated me with respect. "If someone can bind my arm for me, for a few days," I said, "and see to my pony's tack." Donnalch had not, I noticed, asked me if I wanted to go. *I was his hostage,* I thought, *so I suppose he doesn't need to.* I was his to command. *Did I want to go?* I wasn't sure.

"Gregor can do that," he answered. "Rest, now, Lena. We will leave the morning after next."

†††††

Dagney spoke forcefully: either another woman went, or I did not. "It is not your honour I am concerned about, Lena," she explained. "Many who learn of your presence will already have their own thoughts about that, unfortunately," she added, with a small grimace, "but the *Teannasach* cannot be seen to ride alone with a woman." She paused. "I will come," she said. "It has been some years since I went north." She smiled at my expression.

"Don't look so shocked, Lena," she said. "I am capable of the ride, and I will be regarded as a chaperone without peer."

I felt myself blush. "My pardon, Lady," I said. "I wasn't thinking you were too old; I just didn't realize you would leave the *Ti'ach*."

"But how else would I find my *danta*?" she asked. "The songs are not written down, or not all the versions of them, anyhow. Almost each village or *torp* has a slightly different version, of the words, or tune, or both. I visit, and talk, and sing with the people, and write down what I hear. I have recently turned my thoughts to a set of ballads about two sisters, and so I will do my research while we travel. Two pots on one fire."

Privately I wondered what Donnalch would think of this: would it distract from his own purpose? I said nothing, though; it was not my decision. We sat in Dagney's teaching rooms after another lesson in language. I had added a few words—predictably food—*be'atha*, and water—*vann*—and learned to ask for both. My arm ached. I had slept poorly, not finding a comfortable position, and the lesson had gone slowly.

Dagney had gone herself to the kitchen to ask for tea, and Isa had brought it through some minutes before. I held my mug in my good hand and sipped.

"Should I go to the *Comiádh* now?" I asked.

"Soon," she said. "Let us talk a bit, first, about what it is you will say to Donnalch, as we ride north."

"How can I decide that, until I know what he asks me?"

"You know it will be about how women of the Empire live, about your right—or lack of it—to marry, to raise children with their father present, to be part of a family."

"Or," I argued, "about the constraints put on the women of Linrathe, to marry, to have and raise children only with a man, and to believe that is the only family."

"Well," Dagney replied, her face impassive, "even your villages haven't found a way for a woman to have a child without a man, have they?"

I stared at her for a moment, and then began helplessly to laugh. Somehow, I put my tea down without spilling it, wiping the tears of laughter from my eyes. Dagney laughed with me. It took us both a minute to gain control. But even as I laughed, a thought had come to me.

"Tell me," I said when I could speak again. "Is it shameful, here, for a woman to bear a child when she has no man to claim the child? To be the father?"

"It is," she answered, sober again now. "There is shame both in bearing a child without an acknowledged father at all, and in bearing a child to a man outside of a formal partnership, even if he acknowledges the child as his."

"And are these formal partnerships—marriages—permanent?"

"Not always," she said slowly. "A marriage can be dissolved, if both man and woman agree. It is rare, though."

I gathered my thoughts. "So perhaps we are not so different. Our children also need to be conceived in a partnership; children born outside of an acknowledged partnership are shameful for us too. The difference is the length of our partnerships with men; they may last only the week of Festival, or, as in my aunt's case, for many years, until her man—Mar—died. Even though they only saw each other twice a year, they were partnered only with each other. And the men, or their designates, are responsible for their sons, by law."

Dagney considered. "It is an argument," she said finally. "But it does not get to the heart of the question: you have no choice in this. You cannot live with your man, even if you wanted to."

"And can you choose to live without a man?" I said. "Are there not restrictions on our choices on both sides?"

"We can choose to live without a man," Dagney said. "I am proof of that. What we cannot choose to do, honourably, is to have a child in that situation."

"And that is why Cillian is so angry," I said, remembering what Sorley had told me.

"It is," Dagney agreed. "And speaking of Cillian, Lena, I think you should know: he will be accompanying us. The plan was made before the *Teannasach* chose to include you as well."

"That will be awkward. He doesn't like me."

"It's not personal, Lena."

I nodded. "That's what Sorley told me, too. I'm sorry for Cillian. I have some experience of what it means for a child to be unacknowledged in our lands; it is not easy. I expect it is not here, either."

"It isn't," Dagney agreed. "Many come—or are sent—to the *Ti'acha,* because it is thought, rightly, that here we care about scholarship, and not lineage. What should matter now in our country is where Cillian trained; he has even now the right to call himself Cillian na Perras, telling all that he is a scholar, trained in this house."

"Should matter?"

Dagney sighed. "Cillian himself makes it difficult. He will not let his anger go, and accept his life as a scholar. He has a very good mind. Perras tells me he is highly skilled in analysing strategy, and the tactics of battles and their outcomes over time, which is why, I expect, the *Teannasach* has commanded him to ride with him as he visits the villages. But he has been disagreeable ever since Ardan told him he was to go. He dislikes acknowledging any authority, seeing himself as separate, somehow, from our laws and our life, an observer and commentator, and a cynical one at that." She shook her head, frustrated. "I am not expressing myself very well." she said. "I have known him over thirty years, almost since he was born, and I love him, but I worry for him. He is not happy."

There was nothing I could say to that. Dagney also said nothing for a minute, her eyes unfocused, thinking. Then she smiled, brisk and contained again. "Go to Perras now," she said, "if you are finished your tea. Leave the mug there; Isa will come for it, soon."

I rose, a bit awkwardly, my balance uncertain with my arm slung against my body. "Thank you, Lady."

I left the warmth of her teaching rooms and crossed the colder hall out to the even colder latrines, fumbling there with my clothes, one-handedly. Then I reversed my steps back into the hall to knock at Perras's door. "Come," he called, and I opened the door to step inside. The room was warmer than Dagney's had been. Perras sat close to the fire, transcribing Colm's book.

"Lena," he greeted me, putting his pen down. "I understand you are to ride north with the *Teannasach*."

"I am. He has requested it, and I can't say no." I hesitated. "I would rather stay here," I said, wondering if I was being imprudent, "to learn from you. There is so much I wanted to ask."

"And I was looking forward to our talks, too. But what the *Teannasach* wants he will have, and so it must be. You will not be gone that long. This is only an interruption in our learning." He glanced down at the page in front of him. "But I must ask this, Lena: will you leave me Colm's history, while you are gone?"

96

I took a deep breath. I had been expecting this question. "I cannot," I said softly. "I am truly sorry, *Comiádh*, but I cannot. He trusted me with it, and it is all I have of him."

He smiled, sadly, I thought. "I thought that would be your answer. In anticipation, I have been transcribing as much as I could, last night and this morning. At least I have now had a chance to read it. You leave the morning after next?"

"Yes."

"Then I think I can get it done, with Cillian's help in the transcription when my hand grows tired. But it will not leave us time to talk, which I regret."

I bowed my head. "As do I, *Comiádh*."

"But it is only for a short while," he answered, "and the Lady Dagney knows our history well. As do Cillian and the *Teannasach*. You will have time to talk, on the ride."

"I suppose so," I said. Privately I wondered if either man would entertain my questions: Donnalch had his own reasons for taking me along, and I thought Cillian would avoid me as best he could. I doubted my questions about the history of the northlands and the Eastern Empire would be a priority for either man. *But Dagney would indulge me*, I thought.

"My hand needs a rest from writing," Perras said, "so we may talk, for a little while, now. I will leave my questions until you return. So, this is your chance, Lena: what can I tell you, that you would like to know?"

Of all my questions, there was one that puzzled me the most. "What happened to the Eastern Empire?" I asked. "I know all communication stopped, but why? Do you know? How could they just disappear?"

"Ah," Perras said. "The answer to that—or more accurately the answer to why you do not know—lies in fear and superstition. The actual answer is quite simple, but it is hidden, because to speak of it might bring it back."

I looked at him, not comprehending.

"Disease, Lena," he said. "The Eastern Empire fell because of disease."

"Disease?" I repeated. And again, I heard my mother's voice: '...*the Eastern Fever...*'. "The Eastern Fever?" I asked. "It killed them? All of them?"

"How do you know that name?" Perras asked sharply.

"My mother," I answered, confused by his tone. "She is a healer. I heard her talk of it once."

"Openly?" he probed, his tone less severe.

I struggled to remember. "She was talking about anash." The memory played at the edges of my mind...*the council meeting, when we had debated the use of the contraceptive tea for young girls, against rape by the Lestians should our defenses fail.* "Yes, openly," I said. "In meeting. She was giving her opinion about anash's safety for young girls, and she said it had been used against the Eastern Fever, and therefore was likely safe."

"That was all?" Perras queried. "And did anyone ask about the Eastern Fever?"

"No-one," I answered. "It wasn't part of the discussion, and nobody seemed interested."

"Is that all you know?"

"Yes," I said. "It didn't seem to matter. If I thought about it at all, I suppose I thought it was an ague, or a summer fever, that's all."

"I wonder," Perras said thoughtfully. "Have the women's villages forgotten, both the fever and the prohibition against speaking its name? So, you do not know what else your mother might know of it?"

I shook my head. "No."

"How I would like to talk to her, or another healer," he murmured. He sighed. "Dagney will tell you the rest, child, as you ride. I will speak to her. I had best return to the copying, if I am to get it done."

CHAPTER EIGHT

FOG OBSCURED THE WORLD, A FINE ICY FOG that spangled our cloaks with tiny droplets and hid the land on either side of the track. We rode at a walk, letting our horses pick their footing, following Gregor. His horse, he had said, knew this track, and he trusted it to find a safe path.

Occasionally a shaft of sunlight cut through the mist, illuminating moorland or mountainside for a moment, showing us a terrain of grey rock, silver-green heath, pewter water. Except for the quiet clop of hooves and the occasional jangle of a bit, silence reigned. Not even a curlew's mournful cry broke the stillness. I sat Clio passively, my gloved hand holding the reins loose and low on her neck, as I had for the past two hours, being carried.

Ahead of us, Gregor called a halt, his voice muffled by the fog. "Ride up," I heard Donnalch say. He had been riding behind Gregor, followed by Cillian. Behind Cillian was Dagney, and then me, and behind us, taking the tail position, Ardan. "There's space here for us all." I gathered my reins to heel Clio forward, edging in among the other gathered horses and riders. We stood on a platform of rock, bare but for the orange and green of lichens, pocked with depressions and fissures. Beyond and below us ran a wide stream, rushing downhill.

Clio shook herself, a shiver running through her skin from head to tail. "This is the Tabha," Gregor said. "It's too fast and too wide to cross here, so we're going to follow the track downhill awhile, until we can ford it safely."

"But a mouthful of food and drink first," the *Teannasach* said. "Dismount, to rest your horse a minute, and warm you." We did as we were told, my movements awkward due to my injured arm. Clio stood stolidly, used to this now. I took a package of food from my saddlebag, my one hand stiff and clumsy on the leather straps, and unhooked the water skin. I wedged the package of bread and cheese into my sling, and, carrying the water skin in my good hand, found my way over to Dagney. I carried the food for us both, her saddlebags taken up with her *ladhar* and writing tools.

She was checking the wrappings on her instrument, ensuring the oiled cloth beneath its woollen bag was keeping it dry. Apparently satisfied, she turned to me, reaching for the food. "You are not in too much pain?" she asked quietly, unwrapping the package. I shook my head, scattering water droplets from my hood.

"Just a dull ache," I said truthfully. She held food out to me. I put the water skin on the ground and took the bread, layered with a piece of cheese. I took a bite. The bread was dry and stale, but the cheese, earthy and pungent, made from sheep's milk, compensated.

"This damp does it no good," she said, the concern in her voice reminding me of my mother. The memory pained. I pushed it away. Dagney glanced around. "I wish you had seen this in sunlight," she said, as she chewed. "The Tabha tumbles down off Beinn Seánfhear, sparkling and splashing over the rocks, and when the *liun*—the heather—is in flower, in the late summer, it is glorious. Even now, in sunshine, it has a bleak beauty."

"Is there a song about it?" I asked, swallowing the last bite of food. I reached for the water skin to wash it down.

"Yes," she answered, "it is mentioned in several, but there is one specifically about the battle fought here, long ago, and the river's role in ending it."

"Tell me," I said impulsively. The lack of opportunity to talk frustrated me: when the track wasn't too narrow to ride together, the wind or rain had made conversation impossible. Last night I had been too exhausted to talk, falling asleep as soon as I had swallowed some food and Dagney had seen to my arm.

"Not now," Dagney answered. "But once we ford, the land is drier, and if we can ride side by side I will tell you then, or sing it, if I can. A story always lifts hearts, even if my *ladhar* is too damp to play."

"Always?" I heard Donnalch's voice ask. "Even when the chorus speaks of '*an abhaínne geälis dhuarcha ag fóla*'?"

"Yes," Dagney answered evenly. "For the Marai sing the same line: '*Tien lissande flodden, mattai af bluth*'. Both sides found the cost here too high, as you well know, *Teannasach*, and so we have peace. Is that not enough to lift our hearts?"

"Is it?" he said. "I wonder." He raised his voice. "Time to ride. Mount up!"

"What does the chorus mean?" I asked Dagney as we mounted. She hesitated.

"'A shining river dulled by blood'," she replied, and then she was behind me on the path. Inwardly I shivered at the description. *Peace bought with blood...* I leaned back in the saddle to balance my weight as Clio began to descend the narrow path.

The fog began to lift as we came down from the heights. As the visibility improved, I saw that the Tabha flowed rapidly across its rocky bed, swollen still with the meltwaters off the high peaks. I wondered how we were to cross it. But when the land flattened, so did the river, widening into a slower and shallower channel. Waterfowl took to wing as we approached, calling, circling back to land in the river behind us. The faint jingle of a bell drifted across the moorland; somewhere, a flock of sheep grazed. Gregor called a halt: we had reached the ford.

Shallower the river might be, but I judged it still over Clio's knees, and perhaps deeper in the middle. My little mare was obedient, and plucky, but she did not like water and I had only one hand and arm with which to control her. "Gregor," I called.

He turned in his saddle. "Lena?"

"Clio will need to be led over," I said. "She is not good with deep water."

"Will she carry you, or should you come up behind one of us?" A reasonable question. I considered. I wasn't sure what Clio would do, but neither could I see how I could mount up behind another rider with my injured arm. "She'll carry me," I said finally, hoping it were true.

Gregor turned his horse to ride up to me. Dismounting, he took a rope from his pack and looped it through the bit rings on Clio's bridle, knotting it with deft moves. "She knows my horse best," he said, although nobody had spoken. Then he swung himself back up into the saddle, signalling to his bay to move forward, down the shallow bank and into the water.

Clio snorted as the water lapped at her hooves, but she moved forward obediently. Gregor kept his gelding to a slow walk, letting it pick its own route across the stony bottom of the ford. The water reached higher on Clio's legs. She faltered, swinging her head against the tautening lead rope. I urged her forward with my feet, encouraging and, I hoped, calming her with my voice at the same time. Another step forward, and another. I could feel water, cold against my boots. Clio flattened her ears. I brought my hand down to the pommel of my saddle.

My mare stopped, water lapping at her belly, her muscles tensed. Gregor felt the lead rope go tight and halted his horse, turning slightly to see what was happening. As he turned, the lead rope slackened a tiny bit, and at that Clio sidestepped and sprung forward, heading for the far bank, wanting to be out of the water.

Gregor dropped the lead rope. I tightened my legs against Clio's belly and held on as she scrabbled across the stones, hooves sliding, water splashing, beyond my control. A front leg slipped. She stumbled, throwing me forward against her neck, my bad arm pushed against my body, shooting pain up to my shoulder. Somehow, she kept her footing, scrambling upward onto the far bank. She stopped, shaking herself like a dog, her sides heaving. I sat, hand still tight on the pommel, gasping with pain and relief. Gregor appeared beside me, reaching for Clio's bridle.

"Are you all right?" he asked. He led Clio—totally obedient now—further away from the bank.

I nodded, took a deep breath. "Yes," I managed. "Banged my arm, that's all."

"We'll need to strap it tighter," I heard Dagney say. "And you are wet, and will chill, and that will not be good for you or your arm." She brought her mare to beside me, reaching out to touch my wet breeches as she spoke.

"Can't get a horse across a ford without help," I heard Cillian mutter. "Needed a man now, didn't she?"

I bit my lip. *If I reply,* I thought, *I might cry, and I will not cry in front of Cillian.* But even as I looked mutely at Dagney, Donnalch spoke, his voice cold in rebuke.

"Hold your tongue, Cillian," he said, not raising his voice at all, but the anger and command still evident in his sharp, measured tone. "Her mare's fear of water is not a reflection on Lena's abilities, especially riding with one arm."

I reined Clio sideways and looked at Cillian. He was staring at Donnalch. "I think you make a heroine of this girl, *Teannasach*," he replied, his voice as cold and angry as his leader's. Suddenly, in the timbre of his voice, and the planes of his face in anger, I saw—and heard—the resemblance that had been plaguing me. I had a knack of seeing the overlay of one face on another, the way the women from Han could identify the bloodlines of their horses from their looks and the way they moved, a skill that had saved my cousin Garth's life during the Lestian invasion. But now I nearly spoke my shock out loud. He looked—and sounded—like Callan, cold and fierce in the aftermath of betrayal.

"I am of half a mind to send you home," the *Teannasach* said. "Mistake me not, Cillian; you are past insolence now, for all our tradition of free speech to our leaders. I brought you along to hear what our people have to say, and to give me your thoughts, but if you cannot keep from voicing your prejudices then you will be of no use to me at all. Less than no use; you will be dangerous, planting ideas in the minds of the people. So. You will not ride at the back with Ardan any longer, but beside me and Lena as we talk. And you will keep quiet, unless I ask you a direct question. But be prepared to speak with me in the evenings, in reasoned discourse. If you cannot do that, I will send you back to the *Ti'ach*."

I saw Cillian take a deep breath. Then he nodded. "Yes, *Teannasach*," he said, his voice flat.

Donnalch moved his head to look at me. "We will ride a bit ahead," he said. "The Lady Dagney will bind your arm again and help you to change into dry trews—you have such?" I nodded; the word was unfamiliar, but the meaning clear. "Be as quick as you can," he said to Dagney.

My mind spun. *How could Donnalch, who knew both the Emperor and Cillian, not see the likeness? What did it mean?* I thought of Turlo, seeing my father in me when I laughed. *How could he not have seen this?* He was too keen an observer, and he ignored nothing. Dagney had dismounted; I realized she was waiting for me to do the same. I slid off Clio.

Dagney helped me out of my boots and my wet breeches, and into the spare pair I had packed. Then she unbound, salved, and rebound my injured arm, tying it closer and more firmly to my body. I gritted my teeth and stayed still.

"Ready?" she said, packing away the salve.

"No," I said. "I need to check Clio's legs and feet." I bent to the task, running my good hand along her legs. *Should I say something about Cillian, about what I had seen? No,* I decided. *That was for Donnalch, if it were for anyone.* I straightened. "She seems fine," I said.

Dagney helped me mount, steadying me as I swung up onto Clio. The men had ridden ahead at a slow jog, keeping the horses moving against the chill of the river fording. We did the same. I was glad of Clio's smooth trot, and Dagney's tighter binding of my arm.

We caught up to the men after a few minutes. Donnalch slowed the group to a walk. "Ride by me, Lena," he said. I moved up beside him. The plateau we rode on was gravel and scrubby heath, the ground firm. The fog had lifted, revealing a cloudless blue sky. We rode a while without speaking. I had the impression Donnalch was gathering his thoughts. Cillian rode on his other side, silent, looking forward. I kept glancing at him, looking again for the likeness to Callan. If he noticed, he ignored me.

I decided to break the silence. I'd had enough of not talking. "Tell me more about the battle at the river," I said, "if you would, *Teannasach.*"

"It was the last battle between Linrathe and the Marai," he said, "fought in the autumn, after a summer of war. The Marai had been raiding since the spring, all along the coast and up the rivers. The *Teannasach* at the time, Neilan, had divided his men, sending some to the coast and some to defend the lands and people along the rivers. But most Linrathe's men were at the coast." His voice took on a rhythm, a thread of formality. I recognized the cadence of a tale told to instruct.

"Word came that the Marai were up the Tabha," Donnalch continued. "The summer had been wet, wetter than normal, and so the

104

boats of the Marai could be rowed up the river much further than usual, nearly to this spot. They found naught but sheep; the shepherd lads or lasses had fled at the sight of the boats. But one of those lads at least was fleet of foot, and so word reached his *torp* quickly, and from there a man and horse rode out across the hills, to find Neilan's army at the coast."

Gregor and Ardan had moved closer, Gregor's leg nearly brushing mine as he rode beside me. They would know this tale well, but I guessed they had not heard their *Teannasach* tell it; this would be a memory to tell their grandchildren, some day.

"That army marched and ran and climbed, across the mountains and the bogs, and came to the Tabha in two days, under cover of night. They hid in those hills." The *Teannasach* pointed, up to the hills to our left. "As the sun rose they saw the Marai on this plain below them. The weather had cleared, and the sun shone, and not knowing their enemy were in the hills, the Marai were at ease, eating and drinking, sleeping, playing games, in the sun on both sides of the Tabha.

"Neilan said to his men: a quarter of you stay here, in the hills; come only if the battle goes not our way. Then he signalled to the rest, and down they ran out of the hills, swords out, shouting, to take the Marai by surprise. For some time, it looked as if Neilan would take the day: they drove the Marai back across the Tabha, killing many, for they had been without their helms and shields, most able to put hands only to their axes and swords as the men of Linrathe raced down upon them."

Donnalch paused, clearing his throat. We had slowed to an amble. He glanced at us, and went on.

"But Halvar, the leader of the Marai, rallied his men and took them up the beginning of the hills, so that Neilan's men must come at them uphill. True and valiant as the men of Linrathe were, they had run for two days through deep bog and steep mountains to reach the battle, and exhaustion began to take them. The hidden men, seeing this, made their charge, and they were fresh and rested, and again the day looked to be Linrathe's.

"The Marai boats were moored some miles downstream, where the river became too steep to row up. Halvar had left men with the boats, and by some means the news of the battle had reached them." A wry smile crossed Donnalch's face; his eyes were distant. *He can see this battle in his mind,* I realized, *here on the land where it took place.*

"So again, just when the battle had turned to Linrathe, Marai reinforcements arrived, and these with armour and shields. In the end, the battle was not ours, but neither was it theirs. The men fought on and on, into the afternoon. Halvar died, an arrow piercing his throat, and his place was taken by his son-in-law Orri.

"But as the men fought the skies dimmed, the weather itself matching the darkness of that fight. Huge clouds rose over Beinn Seánfhear, and lightening flashed. The rain in the mountains must have been ferocious, for the river rose in spate, and water rushed down the hillside, breaking the Tabha's banks and flooding the plain. Men from both sides fell; many drowned. Marai clung to Linrathan; men who had been fighting to the death only a moment before helped each other to higher land. It is said that it was Neilan himself who led Orri to safety, at least," he added, with a glance to Dagney, "by our bards." He shrugged. "It may have been so. For Orri agreed to a peace, standing on a hillock with Neilan by his side, and by the time the waters had receded both sides had agreed on the Sterre as the boundary between Linrathe and Sorham, and Orri and Neilan took what remained of their armies away."

He was done. No-one spoke. I looked around me, at the plain and the mountains, and thought about what had happened here, the blood and bones lying beneath the soil.

"It was long, and bloody, but necessary," Donnalch said suddenly, in his normal voice. "They wanted our lands, to farm and to settle. To enslave us and displace us, neither of which we could allow."

"To impose their way of life," I said.

"Aye," Donnalch agreed. "But the flaw in your argument, Lena—for I can see where you are taking this—is that no-one in Linrathe asked the Marai to come. No more than your Empire asked Leste to invade. But the gates of the Wall were opened to us, do not forget."

"By a treasonous few," I replied. "They had no right to do so, no authority."

"They would have said they had a moral authority," Donnalch said. "For while it might not have reached your village, Lena, closer to the

Wall, where there is more congress between our peoples, authorized or not," he smiled slightly as he spoke those words, "there is more wish to see an end to the division of our lands."

"And so, you invaded, to free the Empire's women? Without knowing if that is what most of us wanted?"

"That was only one reason, as I have told you," he said calmly. "But, Lena, do you know what most of you want? Or do you think there is only one way to live?"

"What of your women?" I snapped back. "They lack the choice to live as I do, as the women of the Empire do. Surely, they should have that choice too? You sent only boys as hostages: were you afraid of what a girl, a woman, might learn?"

"That," Dagney said from just behind me, "is a very good question, *Teannasach.*"

"Aye, it is," Donnalch said finally. He fell silent. My own thoughts roiled. Change: it was what the Emperor had wanted as well, what I had been charged with speaking of, to women, as I rode south after the successful repulsion of Leste. I did know what most women wanted, at least those of the villages and inns I had visited. *But could I tell this to Donnalch? Could I trust him, this man who had led his men into our lands, and had suborned some of our soldiers to his way of thinking?*

In my mind, I heard a junior officer speaking, after the assassination attempt on Callan: *'Blaine wanted to be Emperor'.* Blaine's nephew had opened the gates to Donnalch. *Had Donnalch and Blaine made some sort of agreement, only to have Blaine fail in his attempt to become Emperor? Was opening the gates the contingency plan?*

I couldn't ask. But surely Callan had, in the long days of talk that had led to this truce of which I stood as surety. Callan, who wanted more choices for his people, men and women. *Free choices,* I reminded myself, *choices made by us, at Assembly, framed by our laws, not imposed by conquest, by the wishes of a few. But if Blaine had become Emperor, what would have happened? He would have acted within our laws too, surely?*

And if so, how many might not have died?

The thought horrified me. I could not bring myself to believe it. Blaine, who had colluded with not only Donnalch, but with the king of

Leste; Blaine, who had orchestrated—or at least made possible—the assassination attempt on Callan. I had no reason to believe he would have acted within the law.

My question—or Dagney's comment—had silenced Donnalch for the present. I dropped back slightly, trying to piece together understanding from surmise and rumour, partial explanations and memory, and failing utterly. "Only one reason," Donnalch had said. *What were the others?*

I felt like screaming, like kicking Clio hard and galloping away. I didn't understand these people, and I wasn't getting the chance to learn. I went where I was told, and tried to make sense of the bits and pieces of information I got, but I couldn't. The pieces didn't make a whole. 'Listen to what is said, about Donnalch's leadership, about the war, about what they wish to change. Exchange views on Partition, on your life as a woman of the Empire, our histories.' my Emperor had instructed me. *These were orders,* I reminded myself. *Calm down, listen, and eventually a story, a pattern, will emerge.*

Behind me, I heard the strings of Dagney's *ladhar* being plucked. I turned in my saddle. She was tuning the instrument, her horse led by Ardan to free her hands. Satisfied with the tuning, she began to sing.

The purple heath, the yellow broom,
Made glad the eye as out we rode,
To meet and fight at river's edge,
To hold our lands against the foe.

A river gleaming on the hill.

From down the ben the river splashed,
The Tabha bright in morning sun.
The Marai north and Linrathe south,
To fight until the day was done.

A river gleaming on the hill.

Ardan's voice, rough but true, joined Dagney's on the chorus.

A sword was raised, the arrows flew
Across the burn as thick as rain.
Below the hill, where field is flat,
The air was rent with cries of pain.

A shining river dulled by blood.

The battle raged, the sun rose high,
Knee-deep in water men fought on.
The Marai boats moored down the stream,
Linrathe's best men up on the ben.

A shining river dulled by blood.

By now all the men—even Cillian—were singing the refrain. I stayed silent, listening.

When bodies thick served as a bridge
And neither side could take the day,
The hidden men came forth to fight
Among the fallen where they lay.

A river red and thick with blood.

As evening fell and still they fought,
Both sides with numbers grievous few,
A shout came from the river's flow:
"Enough!" the cry, a voice none knew.

A river red and thick with blood.

Swords fell from hands; men stood as stone
As from the river words poured forth:
"I say enough. Go from this place,
And live in peace, both south and north."

An angry river flowing red.

"For red my waters flow today,
And silver only should they be.
Bury your dead here on my banks,
Forget not what you heard from me."

An angry river flowing red.

"For peace I want and peace I'll have
Or watch my waters rise and flow
To drown this land and all within,
Both north and south, both high and low."

A peace enforced by river's god.

Both sides obeyed, the cairns were raised
Against the raven, kite and crow.
The Tabha's peace has long remained,
No man would dare not keep it so.

A peace enforced by river's god.

A river gleaming on the hill.
A shining river dulled by blood.
An angry river flowing red.
A peace enforced by river's god.

No man would dare not keep it so.

The notes of the *ladhar* died away. The call of a curlew drifted over the moor, over our small and silent band, over the burial mounds I could now see on either side of the path, mournful, ancient, eternal.

CHAPTER NINE

"OF COURSE," CILLIAN SAID, AFTER WE HAD RIDDEN in silence for some minutes, "the river did not speak. The minds and voices of men spoke, seeing the futility of the battle and the loss, but better it be remembered that they obeyed a spirit of the waters than admit to conceding the day."

"Maybe," Gregor said. "But you were not there, Cillian, and I myself have heard voices in the wind and water more than once. I would not be too quick to doubt."

"Whether the voice was that of a river god, or that of the conscience of men," Dagney added, "the battle ended when the river rose, and we have kept the Tabha's peace." Her voice trailed off. She was looking ahead, her brow furrowed. I glanced at the men; they too stared ahead. Donnalch raised a hand. We halted. Across the plateau, I could see a pair of horsemen, galloping towards us.

"They are Marai," long-sighted Gregor said, "wearing the colours of King Herlief."

The men exchanged glances. "He is dead, then?" Donnalch murmured. No-one replied.

The horsemen galloped closer. We waited. When they were still some distance away, Gregor spoke again. "Their cloaks are bordered with black points. These are the Earl Fritjof's men, *Teannasach*, not the King's, and one of them is not Marai, but Linrathan."

"Fritjof sailed west two years ago," Ardan said, "looking for their promised land of grapes and honey. I had not heard he had returned."

"King Herlief forced him to go," Donnalch said quietly, "after he nearly killed his brother in a fight. Over what, I cannot recall."

I saw the men push their own cloaks back, making it easier to reach for their weapons. *What was happening?* I transferred Clio's reins to my left hand, holding them as best I could. I would need the right for my secca.

The approaching men slowed their horses to a trot. Hands on reins, they showed no sign of reaching for weapons. Both men were of medium height, with close-cropped light hair. Over a tunic and

111

breeches of brown they wore cloaks of blue and green, pinned with large circular brooches and edged, as Gregor had said, with a black border patterned into points.

The *Teannasach* walked his horse forward a few steps. "Niáll," he called, "what brings you into Linrathe, wearing the livery of Earl Fritjof?"

"*Teannasach*," one replied. He reined his horse in, inclining his head to Donnalch. "We came as messengers, not expecting to find you riding out in the land. We bring news: King Herlief is dead. Fritjof is king now. He asks that you make haste: he wishes your presence at the burial rites and his crowning, but neither can be delayed." His eyes flicked to Dagney and myself. The second rider reached for something. My muscles tensed, but he brought a rolled paper from the top his saddlebag, holding it out.

"The King himself wrote this," Niáll said. Donnalch rode forward to take it. Circling back, he returned to his place between Gregor and Ardan before unrolling it. He read quickly, then bent his head to say something to Ardan, who nodded.

"I am honoured that your King has asked me to be present at these ceremonies," Donnalch said, his voice formal. "But there is one of my party who is injured and cannot ride at speed; nor would I ask such of the Lady Dagney. We will need to make arrangements for them, before I ride north with you. Twenty minutes, and I will be ready."

Fritjof's two men glanced at each other. The one who had spoken nodded. "As you wish, *Teannasach*," he said. "We will wait for you at those trees ahead. There is a stream there, to water our horses." They reined their horses round and rode off at a trot.

When they were out of earshot, Ardan spoke. "Do you trust them, *Teannasach*?" he asked.

"Herleif's death was expected," Donnalch replied, "and the seal is Fritjof's. I would not recognize his hand, even if he did write the words himself. I believe the men are from Fritjof; I had heard that Niáll had taken Fritjof's coin. Whether I trust them—or Fritjof—is another question; not really, is the answer. The Earl was ever a plotter, subtle and fluid in his allegiances, but his eye was always on the throne. He has it now, over his brother, it appears. I wonder if Åsmund, too, is dead," he added quietly, as if to himself.

"Why should it matter if you are there for the rituals?" Ardan growled. Clearly, he was unhappy with this turn of events.

"It gives legitimacy," Cillian spoke. "If Fritjof is crowned in the presence of another country's leader, this will be seen to be wider acknowledgement of his right to rule."

"Aye," Donnalch said, nodding. "And therefore, his right to treat with me. I am guessing that not all Marai wanted Fritjof as their king. His brother would have had supporters. Personally, I, too, would have preferred Åsmund, but that," he warned, "cannot be said to anyone, mind."

"Now," he said briskly. "Gregor, you will stay with the Lady Dagney and Lena. Will you return to the *Ti'ach*, Lady?"

"Not immediately, unless Lena wishes to," Dagney replied. "Having started, I would like to continue with my plans to collect *danta*. There are three settlements I had hoped to stop at. If Lena and Gregor are willing, we could visit each for a day, and then return to the *Ti'ach*. The riding will not be strenuous, Lena; they are only an hour or two apart, and they will be generous to us, as travellers and a *scáeli*. And you will see a bit more of our land, and our people."

I considered. *Why not?* It would give me time alone with Dagney, and surely now we would be able to talk, if not while riding then when we stopped. "Yes," I said, "I would like that."

Donnalch nodded. "Good," he said briefly. "But when you return to the *Ti'ach*, ask Perras to spread the word of Fritjof's accession. It should be known, at least among the *Ti'acha*."

"Of course," Dagney said. *Should the Emperor know?* I wondered. *Would he care? Did he even know who ruled the Marai, or even of the Marai?* There was no mention of them, in Colm's history of the Empire.

"Cillian," Donnalch said. "You will come with me. You will keep your eyes open, to watch and listen and remember. Watch who speaks to whom, who is unhappy, who is angry. But give no opinion, even if asked, and above all put no words to paper. If something troubles you, find me. You understand?"

"I do, *Teannasach*," Cillian said. He looked, I noted, happier than I had seen him look before. Or if not happy, then interested. Intrigued. *That was the right word,* I thought. *Intrigued.*

Donnalch took Gregor aside, speaking to him quietly. Dagney and I waited. "Where do we go now?" I asked.

"Just a bit further north," she answered, "on the same path that the *Teannasach* will ride, for a little way. We take a track that branches off to the left, back up a bit into the hill. There is a *torp* there, the one these sheep belong to, and they will feed us and give us a place to sleep tonight, and we will sing and tell stories. But I was hoping that Cillian might stay with us, to write down the words of songs we will hear tonight. Otherwise, I must do it from memory." She smiled a bit ruefully. "And that was easier when I was twenty. But I will manage."

This was nothing I could help with: I barely recognized half-a-dozen words. "What's a *torp*?" I asked, remembering Donnalch had used the word earlier.

"A farm and its collection of cottages. Not a village, but not a lone house, either," she answered. "The farmer—the *eirën*—holds the land; the cottagers, or *torpari*, work for him, but have a bit of land for themselves. Much like the *Ti'acha*, in fact," she added.

Gregor rode back to us, his face grim. I wondered what Donnalch had said to him. Dagney, with the ease of authority and long acquaintance, simply asked. "What's wrong, Gregor?"

He shook his head. "Marai, riding bold as hoodie crows into Linrathe, with a Linrathan to guide them. I don't like it, Lady. The Sterre's been unguarded, or under-guarded, for too long."

"And is not the *Teannasach* sending you for more men to do so, now Fritjof has claimed the throne?" Dagney spoke in an undertone, not looking toward the small party of men.

"Aye, Lady, but I must see you safely back to the *Ti'ach* first, and you have places you wish to visit. So, it will be a ten-day before our men reach the Sterre, and that's too long."

Dagney made a gesture of impatience. "I have ridden these hills for thirty years. What do I need an escort for now?" Gregor looked uncomfortable.

"It's not you, Lady," I said. "It's me, the hostage. Gregor is charged with keeping me safe, and with ensuring I don't escape. When we are back at the *Ti'ach*, I am guessing Sorley will be asked to take on that role, so that Gregor can ride to the Wall. Am I right, Gregor?"

He looked even more uncomfortable, but nodded his head. "You are," he murmured.

"And if I give my word? Would that be enough?" Our eyes met. He assessed my words, his gaze level.

"It would be for me," he said finally. "But it's not my decision."

"*Teannasach*!" Dagney called. "A word, before you ride?"

Donnalch said something to the two Marai, reining his horse away from them. He trotted over to us. "Lady?" he asked.

Dagney kept her voice pitched low. "Let Gregor ride south," she said. "Lena will pledge her word to not try to escape. Surely that is enough?" He hesitated. "Fritjof's men riding freely in Linrathe, and one of them knowing every inch of this land?" Dagney echoed Gregor's words. "You need more men at the Sterre. Which is more important, Donnalch?"

The jangle of a bit caught my attention. I looked over to see the Marai riding towards us. Donnalch saw them too. "You are right," he whispered. "Gregor, as soon as you can, ride south. Ignore what I say, now," he finished. Raising his voice only slightly, he said, "and do not tire the women, Gregor. Keep the pace slow and the distances short. I will see you at the *Ti'ach* in a ten-day." He held a hand up to the messengers, who had stopped only a pace or two away from us, Ardan behind them. "Find some new songs, Lady," he said. He raised his voice. "And now I must ride to bid farewell to one king, and honour another." He swung his horse around, signalling it with heels and hands. It leapt forward, galloping across the heath, Fritjof's men, taken by surprise, lagging behind. We watched them for a minute, until Dagney spoke.

"Come," she said. "We should follow them; one might just look back. You will know where you can leave us, Gregor."

"Aye," he said. "There's more than one path from Bartolstorp to the Tabha. Greet my mother for me, will you, Lady, and my father and brother? I would have liked to have seen them, but this need is greater."

Half an hour later, in a fold of the hill, Gregor raised a hand in farewell and turned off the track we followed, onto what looked to me like a sheep trail along the side of the valley. "Ride safely," Dagney called to him, reining her mare to a stop. I followed suit. She looked at me. "Another half-hour to Bartolstorp," she said. "How are you feeling?"

"I'm fine," I said. She nodded, and we began to walk along the track again. After a minute, Dagney began to speak.

"Gregor's family have held this *torp* for many generations," she said, "long before the borders were set, and his *torpari* have been mostly the same families for all those years, as well. I will be asking them about a *danta* called '*Sostrae lys yn dhur*'; that is 'the dark and pale sisters', in your tongue. It tells, in its simplest meaning, of the drowning of the pale sister, the younger, by the older one, for the older one wants the younger's lover. The dark sister takes the younger one to the sea, where she drowns her, then tells her lover that the girl has run away with another. The body floats down a river, where it is found by a miller, who recognizes her and tells her lover, who in the meantime has wed the dark sister in despair. The grieving lover strings his *ladhar* with the pale sister's hair, but he will never again play the instrument for his dark wife, reserving it for when he is alone, to hear his true love sing to him."

"How horrible," I said. "Sisters, drowning each other over a man?"

Dagney laughed. "You forget," she said gently, "that here a man confers status and protection to his wife, and a dark mind might see that as a reason to commit murder. But I do not believe that is what the song is about at all, except on its surface."

"What, then?"

"I think it is about one people's conquering of another, probably in a sea battle, and how the conquered people keep their beliefs and ideas alive in secret, by song and story and custom, hidden from their overlords."

I considered. It made sense, in an obscure way.

"What peoples? What battle?" I asked, genuinely curious now.

Dagney shook her head. "That is what I am trying to find out. If I can transcribe different versions of the song, from here in the south to the

116

versions sung in the Rathe Hoys, I can look at the details, and perhaps work it out. It is very old, and I already know it varies greatly in the tellings: sometimes the girls are the daughters of a king, sometimes of a farmer. While both a king or a farmer represent the land, I think the versions with a king may be older, closer to the truth."

We rode on. I thought about what Dagney had said. Songs, for me, were just verses sung around a fire, stories set to music, but I had never thought about what they might mean. *Was the song I had learned from Tice anything more than a soldier's lament for leaving his lover? What was it Colm had said? Something about tax rolls and court records telling a story, if you knew how to hear it. If history lived in those dry documents, did it also live in songs?*

A shout from ahead of us brought me out of my reverie. I saw a shepherd hurrying towards us, his dog at his heels. "*Scáeli* Dagney," he said, and then much more, but I could understand none of it, the words soft and sibilant, running together like music. Dagney replied to him, gesturing. I heard my name. The shepherd looked up at me. I smiled a greeting. He nodded, and then, turning back to Dagney pointed down the track.

"*Meas*," Dagney said. She turned in her saddle to me. "Torunn— that's Gregor's mother—is at the house. Bartol and his older son, who is also named Bartol but is called Toli to distinguish him, are out on the hill with the men, mending walls. The shepherd will send his son to tell them we are here. Bartol has some words of your language, and Toli more, if I remember rightly, but I doubt Torunn has any; this will be awkward for you, Lena, but it cannot be helped. I will do my best to help you understand what is being said."

We rode into the *torp* a few minutes later. It was not dissimilar to the *Ti'ach*, as Dagney had said, with a largish farmhouse and a courtyard of outbuildings, but here there was no doubt that the concerns of sheep and cattle over-ruled all. It was not dirty, precisely, but the air echoed to the constant bleating from a pen of ewes and lambs, and the remains of a depleted stack of hay slumped to one side of the yard. Pigeons flew up from the muddy flagstones as we rode in, circling to land on the house roof. A sheepdog yipped from where it lay beside the sheepcote, but did not approach us.

A woman appeared at the open front door to the house, shading her eyes against the sun. "*Scáeli* Dagney," she said, and then a torrent of words I could not understand. Dagney dismounted, indicating to me to do the same. I did, fatigue suddenly washing through me.

A boy appeared to take our horses, leading them off somewhere. "Lena," Dagney said to me, "this is *Konë* Torunn, wife to Bartol, who heads this *torp*." I smiled at the tall woman, her dark hair braided and pinned over her head; her frame lean and wiry. Her sleeves were rolled up, and an apron covered the dark dress she wore: she had been working. Dagney said something to Torunn: I caught Gregor's name. Torunn smiled, her blue eyes crinkling, and said something, a question, I thought, from the inflection. Dagney laughed, and nodded. "She asks if he is well," she said to me.

Gesturing, Torunn led us into the house. Like the *Ti'ach*, it had a big central room, but unlike the *Ti'ach*, this was both kitchen and hall. A long table ran widthwise across the room; behind it were the hearth, where a pot hung over the flames, and the table itself was crowded with rising bread, a sack of grain, a platter of soup bones. A young woman was chopping root vegetables at one end of the table. From her build, and her face and eyes, I took her to be a close relation of Torunn— a daughter? I wondered, but she seemed too young. At Dagney's direction I sat, my arm throbbing. It had been improving, but this morning's accident had worsened it. I flexed my fingers, feeling pain shoot up the arm.

"Lena, this is Huld, Torunn's grand-daughter. Gregor's niece," Dagney added. Huld smiled at me. "Welcome," she said in strongly accented tones.

"*Meas*," I remembered to say, surprised that she spoke my language. My surprise must have shown, for she smiled again.

"I learn to speak your words," she said haltingly, "My *athir*...my father...he teach. My many-times mother's mother come from your land."

Gregor had alluded to that, I remembered.

"You learn our words?" Huld asked.

I spread my hands, shaking my head. "Only one or two," I said. "*Forla*," I added.

"We practice," she said. Torunn said something to her, and she ducked her head and went back to the vegetables, glancing at me occasionally. I wrapped my hands around the mug of tea Torunn had placed in front of me, welcoming the warmth, almost too tired to sip it.

Dagney and Torunn spoke at length. I let the sounds slip by, not trying to recognize anything, slowly drinking my tea. Through the open door, I heard the sheepdog whine, and footsteps, and a moment later two men entered the room. Gregor's father, Bartol, I thought, and his brother Toli.

Bartol strode forward to hug Dagney, an enveloping hug of real welcome. She was well-known here, I realized, as Toli also embraced her, if not as enthusiastically as his father. The room filled with talk and laughter. I finished my tea. Its warmth had revived me briefly, but now I felt tiredness overwhelming me again. It had been days since I slept well, the pain and awkwardness of my arm waking me every time I moved in my sleep. I shifted my stool, trying to find a more comfortable way to sit, the scrape of the wooden legs along the flagged floor sounding loudly and discordantly. Heads turned my way.

"Lena," Dagney said, "forgive me. Your arm needs tending and you need to rest." A word to Torunn had us being ushered up a flight of stone stairs to the sleeping chambers, where Torunn opened a door to a small room. One narrow bed, and a chest, was all the furniture it held.

I sat on the bed as Dagney unbound my arm and examined it. She tutted. "Give me a moment," she said, and left the room. A minute or two later she returned, carrying my saddlebags, followed by Huld carrying a bowl of water.

Dagney eased my tunic over my head and gently pulled it free of my arms, and then did the same with the linen undertunic I wore. I shivered slightly in the cool of the room, but the water Dagney bathed my arm in was warm, and the salve made my skin tingle. I felt Huld's eyes on me, but I did not look up. Dagney's ministrations were gentle, but I could feel tears threatening.

My arm salved and rebound, Dagney helped me dress again and sent Huld away with the bowl of cooling water. As soon as Huld closed the door behind her, I could not keep the tears away. Dagney, murmuring words of comfort, put an arm around me, and let me cry.

"I'm sorry," I said after a few minutes, snuffling. She handed me the cloth with which she had bathed my arm, and I found a dryer corner to wipe my eyes and blow my nose. "It's just..."

"All new. You are not here by choice, and you cannot understand what is being said. And in addition, you are in pain and tired. All very good reasons to cry," Dagney said. I forced a smile. "Now," she went on, "I think you should rest. Sleep, if you can. I will explain to Torunn, and we will not expect you at dinner, but someone will bring you soup and bread later. All right?"

I nodded. It was exactly what I needed. I lay down on the bed and let Dagney remove my boots and pull a blanket over me. She stroked my hair briefly before she left me. I did not sleep immediately, but lay, feeling the throbbing in my arm subsiding, thinking. I felt so alone. I had spent much time by myself before, riding between villages and inns, during watch-duty on the Wall, but at the end of the day there had almost always been someone to talk to, if I wished, or just to listen to others' conversations. Even if I had purposely remained on the periphery, I had still been part of what was happening. I had not realized what a barrier not understanding what was being said would be.

On top of this, I was frustrated. There was so much I wanted to know, both for myself and to take back to the Empire, and every time an opportunity presented itself to learn more it was thwarted. I was failing in my task. I shifted on the bed, rolling over on one side. *I will just have to get Dagney to talk to me*, I thought, as I drifted into sleep.

The sound of a *ladhar* drifting up from below woke me some time later. No light came in through the small window. The sun had set. I sat up. My bladder twinged. Reaching under the bed with my good hand, I felt around for the chamber pot; finding it, I crouched beside the bed to relieve myself.

A soft knock at the door came just as I adjusted my breeches. I pushed the chamber pot under the bed. "Yes?" I called. The door opened. Huld came in carrying a tray. She pushed the door closed again with her hip, putting the tray on the chest.

"Food," she said, gesturing.

"*Meas*, Huld," I replied. The soup smelled good: lamb and barley, I thought, and the bread looked fresh-baked. There was nowhere except the bed on which to sit, so I sat on the edge. Huld put the tray on my knees, and I picked up the spoon. One spoonful reminded me how hungry I was. I ate with appetite, trying to not gulp my food. Huld perched on the side of the chest, watching me.

When I was done, she took the tray from me. "Come for music?" she asked. I hesitated. I felt grubby, travel-stained, not fit for company.

"*Allech'i*, Huld, *vann*?" I asked. "To wash," I added in my own language, pointing to the washbowl on the end of the chest.

"Ahh, *ja*," she replied, jumping up. Taking the tray, she went back downstairs, to return five minutes later with a jug of steaming water, a towel, and a chunk of soap.

"I help?" she asked, as I struggled with my tunic.

"*Ja*," I replied gratefully. I could handle my breeches, but pulling a tunic over my head one-handed was a challenge. She lifted the outer tunic, and then the under, over my head carefully. "*Meas*," I said, and bent to my washing.

After a few minutes, she took the soap from me. I looked at her questioningly. She smiled, and began to wash my back. Her hands on me were firm, and after the first surprise I let myself enjoy the feeling. I had last had a bath at the *Ti'ach*, some days ago now. While I had grown accustomed to brief washes and long gaps between baths on the Wall, I preferred to be clean.

When Huld had dried my back, I reached for the drawstring on my breeches. Huld took a step back. "I go," she said. "I come back, help you dress, *ja*?"

At Tirvan, like all the women's villages of the Empire, and on the Wall, there were no nudity taboos among women. I had bathed and swam and washed among girls and women of all ages since I was a toddler. Huld's modesty startled me, especially as she had had no problem with either seeing or touching my naked upper body. "You can stay," I said. "I don't mind."

She blushed. "*Ja?*" I nodded, stepping out of my breeches and under-breeches. I washed, feeling Huld's eyes on me. I glanced over at her as I dried myself. Music floated up from the hall. Her lips were slightly parted, her eyes wide. I felt an answering tug, deep and low, and looked away. *Did she even know what it was she was feeling?*

I dressed again, in cleaner clothes, and followed Huld downstairs to the hall. The meal was clearly over; Dagney and Tori sat on tall stools in front of the table, *ladhars* on their laps; around the periphery of the room men and women sat or stood; children sprawled on the floor. The fire in the huge fireplace glowed, giving off the same smell I remembered from Perras's room. Wall-sconces lit the rest of the hall. We found a space, and a stool for me, on the outer wall. I saw eyes turn my way: I guessed my presence and my role as a hostage to the peace had spread among the folk of this *torp*. Or perhaps, I reflected, it was simply that I wore breeches. Most folk, I saw, had on what looked like their best clothes. *To honour Dagney*, I realized.

Tori said something to Dagney, and they began a song, the melody jaunty, quickly repeated. The smallest children began to dance to it, jumping up and down, twirling, slightly older ones attempting a few more complex steps. My foot began to tap. Hands started to clap, and then one or two couples stood to dance, hands and feet in rapid motion.

After a few bars Dagney began to sing, the words, like the music, simple and repetitious. Voices from the room began to sing the chorus. The music gained in speed; hands clapped faster, feet moved rhythmically and rapidly. Voices sung louder. The music reached a climax of beats, and ended.

I realized I was grinning. It did not matter here that I couldn't understand the words. Music was its own language, not needing translation. After another song, not dissimilar to the last, Dagney changed the tuning on her *ladhar*, and began a slower melody.

"Women's dance," Huld said in my ear. "You try?" I hesitated. "Is slow," she added.

Why not? I thought. I liked to dance. I followed Huld out onto the floor, joining maybe a dozen other women. We lined up in two rows, facing each other. The women began a slow clap, matching the beat of the music, advancing to meet each other. I followed suit, clapping my good hand against my thigh. When we met, we held our hands high to clap against our partner's, then linked arms to circle around each other. A few steps backward, still clapping, and we repeated the moves. I was awkward at first, with only one free hand and arm, but as the *ladhar*'s melody became a little faster, we met its challenge, our feet and hands moving more quickly. On the third time our hands met, we held them up to allow the furthest right couple to move under our linked hands.

When it was our turn to duck under the canopy of hands, Huld kept my right hand firmly in her left, her skin warm against mine. Our hips brushed as we ran to the end of the line. As we took our places she caught my eye: her face was flushed, her eyes dark, and she smiled in delight. I smiled back, unable not to, feeling the beat of the music reverberating through me.

The dance was done. Huld kept my hand in hers, leading me outside into the cool night. Stars whitewashed the sky, the night cloudless. Huld led me behind an outbuilding. In the shelter of its walls she turned and kissed me, hard and urgent. I felt desire shoot through me. How long since I had taken comfort in love-making? Weeks, now, maybe months, brief interludes with other Guards, affirmations of life amongst the deaths. Huld's hands had begun to move. I pulled away. "No?" she said. I could hear the puzzlement in her voice.

"How old are you?" I whispered.

In the starlight, I saw her smile. "Eighteen years," she said. "A woman. I choose this, yes?" She paused. "And you not first," she added.

Her kisses had told me that. "Is this accepted?" I whispered.

"No," she said. "But no-one sees; they all dance, or if out in night like us, what they do is secret too." She drew a finger down from my lips, along my neck, and lower. I shuddered.

"Then, yes," I said, sliding my hands down her back, drawing her to me, my lips finding hers. This time she pulled away.

"Come," she said. I let her lead me again, through a door and up, by feel, a wooden ladder, into the loft of a byre. Below us cattle slept, warming the shed. I felt hay beneath my feet, and sank to my knees, pulling Huld down beside me. Faint music drifted in from the hall. We fell into the hay, lips joined, hands exploring, touch and scent and sensation our only guides in the utter blackness of the night.

CHAPTER TEN

IN THE MORNING, HULD WAS NOT AMONG THOSE gathered in the hall to bid us farewell. Late in the night we had slipped back, separately, to our own rooms, when voices outside told us the *torpari* were returning to their cottages. Finding hay still in my hair this morning, I hoped we had been unseen.

After the love-making Huld had curved herself against me, one finger stroking my cheek. "Tell me of her," she murmured.

"Who?" I asked, already drifting into sleep.

"The woman who hurt you. You make love for the body, for pleasure, yes? Not for heart. You hold back what inside you."

I rolled away from her, staring into the darkness. Huld put out a hand to touch me. "I not upset," she said. "Just say what think. I wrong?"

"No," I said slowly. "You are not."

"Tell me," she urged. "Talk is good."

Was it? "Her name is Maya," I said. "When Tirvan—my village—voted to fight against the invasion from Leste, she chose exile from Tirvan rather than fight. I stayed to fight, but when it was over, I went to find her."

"And she not want you?"

"No," I answered, "She didn't, because she had found like-minded women and they were going to start a new village, one open only to those who had been exiled from their home villages. There would have been no place for me."

"Is sad," Huld said.

"I understood that, though," I said into the night. "It was the second time, later, that I could not understand."

"You join up again, then?"

"Not quite," I said, hesitating, looking for a simple way to explain. "After Linrathe invaded, I stayed in the south. I had a male lover for a while, and he had a son in a village that grew grapes and made wine, and so I went there, to help raise his son."

"So, you not fight again?"

"Not at first, no. The woman who was raising Valle—the boy—decided to go to Casilla, our one city, to live with a friend, who had a child of about the same age. I went with her. We weren't lovers, but I didn't have anywhere else to go. I found work on the fishing boats—Casilla is on the coast—and helped support us. And then Maya came looking for Valle, too, because his father was her brother. She moved in, and after a while, she asked me to leave. She told me I had no reason to be there, and she wanted me to go."

"So, your man, he your Maya's brother?"

"Yes," I said.

"She know?"

"No," I said. "I never told her."

"Then why send you away?"

"I don't know," I said. "I don't know." I felt the mix of anger and humiliation I always did, when I thought of that time. Huld lay silent for some minutes.

"Was only pleasure with this man, too?" she asked.

It was easy to speak the truth in the dark. "No," I said. "It started as comfort, but by the end, when he had to leave for his ship, I loved him."

"Then we try for comfort, again," she whispered, running her hand down my arm. I turned back to her, to the taste of her lips and the heat of her skin against mine.

At breakfast, Dagney had not asked where I had disappeared to the night before. Dressed for riding, she ate hungrily, speaking only of the *danta* versions Toli had transcribed for her, and where we would ride to tonight: another *torp*, the *eirën* named Sinarr. Sinarrstorp, she said, was a good day's ride to the east, across the hills, but Bartol had sent a boy on a pony at dawn, to tell them we were coming.

I also ate with hunger. My arm pained me less, and I could move my fingers and wrist more easily. Free of intense pain, and buoyed by last night's love-making, I had an appetite. We ate porridge and bacon, and barley bread with honey, all tasting wonderful to me. What sky I could see through the narrow windows was blue. I looked forward to the day's ride with only Dagney. Perhaps I would get some of my questions answered.

I smiled and said *meas* to Bartol and Torunn and Toli, and to anyone who spoke to me. I did not look for Huld. She had told me early this morning when she had come to help me dress that she would not be here. "I go red," she had said, as she salved and bound my arm, "and others see, maybe remember we gone from dance. It not shame, *leannan*; but for me and you only. You understand?" I had assured her I did. I felt much the same. At the Wall and throughout the Empire, all pairings were accepted and unremarkable, unless the age difference was too great, but I did not understand the structures and mores of Linrathe. *I too,* I thought, *would 'go red', if anyone were to guess what Huld and I had been doing in the hayloft.* Or even in my room this morning, although we had had time for little more than a few kisses.

The thought must have made me smile, because Dagney suddenly spoke. "You are looking much better this morning, Lena. I was glad to see you dancing last night; it has done you good. You slept well?"

"Very well," I said truthfully. "And my arm hurts much less this morning. Look," I added, wiggling my fingers.

"Pleasure helps the body heal," Dagney said. I felt my face grow hot. She continued, either not noticing or choosing to ignore my flush. "Now, are you finished? We have a long way to go today, and should get started."

We rode through the early morning sunshine along a reasonable track, the route, Dagney told me, that traders took with their pack animals between the *torps*. The boy who had ridden to Sinarrstorp at dawn on a sure-footed hill pony would have taken a different route through the hills, faster, but also easy to lose, or be lost on.

"If Sinarrstorp is so close," I asked, "won't their *danta* be the same as Bartolstorp?"

"Not necessarily," she answered, turning her head to talk to me; the track, while good, was not quite wide enough for us to ride abreast. "It will depend, in part, on where the families came from, originally; if most share an ancestral village with Bartolstorp, then, yes, the *danta* will be much the same. But if not, and I do not know if they did or didn't, then the *danta* may be very different."

Where they came from originally? "Haven't these people been here, well, forever?" I asked, genuinely curious. "Where would these ancestral villages be?"

"In the north," she said. "When we spoke of this, when you first came to the *Ti'ach*, perhaps we made it too simple. The Sterre is the boundary between Sorham and Linrathe, and Linrathe pays tribute to Varsland for Sorham, but by the time of the battle of the Tabha, many with northern blood had settled in these lands as well. They chose to stay, when the Marai withdrew for the last time, and it is those people who farm the torplands hereabout."

"And everyone lives peacefully?" I asked.

Dagney laughed. "Yes," she answered. "It was all so long ago. Bartol and Toli and Sinarr, and their *torpari*, if you asked them, would tell you they are Linrathan, not Marai, or even Sorhaman, although they likely have distant family there. There is trade between us, and people do move back and forth, but their allegiance is to the *Teannasach*, not to King Herlief, or rather, Fritjof, now."

I thought of Gregor's reaction to the Marai soldiers; certainly, he had not been pleased to see them in Linrathe. *And why should Dagney not know how her own people thought?* But even those who appeared most loyal could have secret sympathies, or else Linrathe would not have found the Wall open to them two years past. I kept my thoughts to myself.

"Well," Dagney said after a minute. "We have a long ride, the weather is good, and so we have the time and opportunity to talk. What would you like to know, Lena?"

I had so many questions. Part of me wanted Dagney to explain how relationships—between men and women, or otherwise—worked here in Linrathe, enlarging on the conversation we had started. On the other hand, I might find myself flushing again, and Huld had asked for privacy. Our brief liaison could not be known; I had no idea what the punishment—for her or me—might be. My thoughts went back to my last conversation with Perras.

"The Eastern Fever," I said. "Perras told me the Eastern Empire fell because of it, but we did not have time for him to fully explain. He said you could, on the ride."

She said nothing for a moment, and then, unexpectedly, began to sing.

A ring around, a ring around
A ring of blossom hiding thorn,
We dance and dance but only one
Will stand alone now all forlorn.

"Do you know that song, Lena?" she asked.

"Yes, of course," I said, puzzled. "It's the ring-game song; I played it as a child. But what has that to do with the Eastern Fever?"

"That is what it is about," she said. "Like the *danta*, it is more than a child's game-song. It is a memory of how the red rash of the fever killed almost everyone. When you chose the one who would stay standing at the word 'now', you were playing at being the lone survivor of ten or a dozen or even more in a village or farmstead."

"That's horrible," I said, grimacing. "But I never liked the game. I hated to be the one left standing, fingers pointed at me, and the others going on without me."

"On to death, and to whatever lies beyond," she said. "but that is how it was supposed to make you feel, bereft and terrified, as the lone survivor at a *torp* might."

"Where did this fever come from?" I asked, "And why did it go away?"

"I can answer the first to some extent," Dagney said. The path had widened slightly, and I could ride beside her now. "It began in Casil, the capital of the Eastern Empire, and then its outposts and colonies. It was probably spread by those who were sent as messengers, or perhaps by people fleeing Casil. In either case, it killed almost everyone, including, we must assume, the Emperor and his heirs. But how it got to Casil is not known to us, although some writings suggest it came with traders from countries even further east. And why it disappeared? That I do not know, although perhaps it has something to do with the cold. For while there were deaths, in Linrathe and in the Empire—and more in the Empire than in Linrathe—north and east of the Durrains only a comparative few died."

I thought about something she had said. "Deaths in the Empire, and Linrathe, but not further north?"

She shook her head. "No. Or if there were, they were negligible. That is why the Marai rebuilt the Sterre, to keep us out, to keep the fever from their lands. It is also why they have never travelled south to your lands, because, as I said, the fever was worse there than it was here in Linrathe. Did Perras tell you of their prophecy? They were to explore to the west, to find there a land of grapevines and honey and mild weather. They believe they were spared from the fever to fulfill that prophecy, but only if they never go east or south?" I nodded. "So," she went on, "even though they are great sea and river-farers, they have not ventured south or east, but only west, for all these years."

"So, no-one knows," I said, after a minute or two of contemplation, "what might be left now, over the mountains?"

"None who have travelled that way have returned to tell us," she said. *That meant,* I realized, *that people had travelled east, beyond the Durrains.* I wondered if any of the Empire's men had done so; I knew of soldiers who had scouted into the mountain range, but beyond it? I opened my mouth to ask Dagney more about these travellers, when I saw, riding rapidly towards us on the path, two mounted men, wearing the colours of Fritjof. I also saw their drawn swords.

I reined Clio to a halt. Beside me, Dagney did the same with her mare. Metal clinked behind me. I turned in the saddle to see two more riders approaching. The same livery, the same drawn weapons. *This was an ambush.*

How had they known where we were? Thoughts of Gregor's loyalty, and then of Bartolstorp, flitted through my mind. *But no: more likely they had simply followed us, waiting until we were in a good spot to be taken easily. No betrayals.* I met Dagney's eyes. She shook her head, made a small gesture of resignation with her hands, both almost imperceptible. My secca was on my waist. I pulled my tunic over it.

The men surrounded us, blocking the path from all directions. One spoke to Dagney, in a tongue more guttural than that of Linrathe; the language of the Marai, I assumed. She replied. I caught nothing in the flow of words, but another man spoke again, this time addressing me.

"You will come with us, my ladies. King Fritjof wishes to extend his hospitality to include you both, and we are to escort you at all haste to his crowning." Polite as the words were, I knew we had no choice. *Had the boy sent to ride to Sinarrstorp made it,* I wondered, *or had he been intercepted? If he had reached his destination, then we would be missed this evening. If not...*

"We will come," Dagney said, as politely as if the invitation had been real, although I could see a tiny flutter in her cheek. "I am honoured to be invited, as I am sure Lena is too." She looked toward me. I could see the warning in her eyes.

"I am honoured," I said, hoping my voice was steady.

"That is good," the leader said. I thought I recognized him: he had presented Fritjof's letter to Donnalch, yesterday morning. *Niáll,* I remembered, *the Linrathan. Who escorted Donnalch now?* Two of the men rode forward, grasping the bridles of our mares and attaching a lead rein to each. All pretense of an invitation accepted vanished. Clio tossed her head, protesting. I soothed her with voice and hands, inwardly matching her protest.

We rode north at pace, stopping occasionally to relieve ourselves, and for food and water for us and the horses. The men were courteous but firm. The sun sank behind the hills, forcing us to ride more slowly, and eventually to stop, in the shelter of boulders beside a small stream. My arm ached steadily, and I could see the fatigue on Dagney's face.

We were allowed to go a distance off to empty our bladders. At the campsite, one man guarded us as the others built a fire and saw to the horses. Niáll walked off beyond the campfire. He returned a few minutes later.

"There are many stars, and no sign of rain," he said. "No tents are needed tonight."

"We have no blankets," Dagney protested. Whatever was in the pot over the flames was beginning to simmer, the scent of broth rising.

"We have blankets for you," he said. "You will be warm enough, beside the fire, if you sleep side-by-side." I knew, from my days and nights on the road and on patrol, that he was right. I wondered where we were, in relation to Sinarrstorp, and whether the *eirën* would send out men to search for us. Frustration rose. I could not even ask Dagney, because Niáll spoke the language I would have to use. I realized, suddenly, that that was why Dagney had requested we speak my language, to let me know that anything I said would be understood by our captors.

Later we were given bowls of broth, thick with barley and beans, and chunks of a dark bread. Fair trail food, and tasty enough; the hard-cooked eggs and cold mutton of lunch had been hours ago, and the porridge of breakfast even longer. We ate, and then went briefly out into the night again, returning to blankets spread by the fire, with rolled sheepskins for pillows. Dagney helped me pull off my riding boots, and I hers, and we settled onto the ground, wrapping the blankets around us, Dagney closest to the fire at my insistence. Under the cover of the blanket, I moved my secca to where I could easily reach it. We had not been searched for weapons. I guessed they would not think to: we were women. From beyond the firelight an owl called, a long, wavering cry. Fatigue seeped into my bones and my mind. I slept.

For the next three days, we rode north and west at a steady but not gruelling pace. The weather, thankfully, held, although it grew colder as we moved north. Ice edged small ponds in the mornings. The men were generous with the night-time fires, and with food; it was clear we were not to suffer privation.

Behind a boulder on the second morning, crouched to urinate, I whispered to Dagney. "What do they want from us?"

"You, I think," she whispered back. "I cannot think what value I might have to them, so it must be you."

But why? I turned that question around and around in my head as we rode, reaching only one answer: King Fritjof wanted me for what I knew of the Empire. He had no faith in prophecy, and no fear of fever: he planned to invade. I grew more sure as I thought it out. *But if that was why he wanted me, why did he want Donnalch? To ask him to join in this attack? And if he said no—then what? Donnalch's life would be forfeit,* I thought, *and the Marai would sweep down through Linrathe, its army scattered by our truce, and into the Empire.*

132

I murmured this to Dagney, again as we emptied our bladders, the only time we had to exchange thoughts out of hearing of the men. Her face paled, but she whispered calmly, "I had the same thought. I think you are right; it fits with what I have heard of Fritjof. But the Marai will not send all their men through Linrathe to the Wall. Some, yes, but it will be boats, along the coast and up the rivers, that make up their greatest force."

I straightened, hands automatically tying my breeches, tucking the secca into its hidden position along my groin. My mind focused on what Dagney had just said.

"Come, Lady Dagney, Lena!" Niáll shouted, closer than I had thought him. *But not close enough to hear,* I reassured myself. Whatever orders the men had been given, they must have included giving us no chance to complain of any indignity to our bodies or our privacy. They were scrupulous in leaving us alone. But I said no more.

We had repelled an invasion just two years ago. Could we do it again? But that time we had had six months' warning, six months of preparation and planning. If there were any chance, then word had to get to the Wall. Gregor would bring the story of Marai riding freely south of the Sterre to the Linrathan commanders at the Wall, but would they tell the Empire's Wall commanders? And even if they did, what would those men make of it, knowing nothing of these people, of their command of boats and the sea?

At the camp that night, after we had eaten, Niáll stood over us by the fire. "Play for us, if you would, Lady?" he asked Dagney. I saw the quick look of surprise on her face, followed by acquiescence.

"If you like," she said. "I will need a minute to tune my *ladhar*, though." She fetched the instrument, plucking the strings and adjusting the tension on the pegs until she was satisfied. Then, quietly, she began to play.

After a few minutes of the *ladhar* only, she started to sing, in a language I thought must be Marai. Sometimes the men joined in, sometimes they simply listened. After an hour or so, she began a song I thought I recognized, the preliminary notes she played bringing back the words of the chorus to me: 'A shining river dulled by blood'. Niáll stiffened.

"Not that one," he said sharply. "That's enough music. We should sleep now."

†††††

I could smell the sea long before I could see it. We rode to the top of a ridge, and there before us was the ebb and swell of waves, and the scream of gulls. An archipelago of islands dotted the sea, separated from the mainland by a tidal channel. On the largest of these islands a long, low building dominated.

The tide was going out, revealing with each ebb a causeway linking the mainland with the largest island. *An hour,* I estimated, *before we could ride across safely.* My thought was echoed by Niáll. "We wait," he said, "but not long. Dismount."

Four days earlier we had crossed the Sterre. The building on the island reminded me of that boundary wall: not stone, like the southern Wall, but primarily timber and sod, reinforced with stone buttresses. The hall, from what I could see, echoed this construction. It looked new, the wood not yet weathered grey, standing on the highest land on the island. Below it, straggling down to the tideline, were other buildings, workshops and houses, I guessed, all sharing the yellow gleam of new wood.

I swung down off Clio. I could use both arms now, and wore no bandage nor sling. Loosening her girth, I looked over to Niáll.

"I'll have to walk my mare across," I said. "She doesn't like water."

He nodded in acknowledgement. A shout came from over the water. We had been seen. Words were exchanged, with much gesturing. I saw a man running up to the hall. *Delivering the news of our arrival, no doubt.*

I watched the tide receding, and the red bills of the big black-and-white sea-pies probing for food along the exposed rocks, just as they did at Tirvan. Smaller brown plovers ran on the shingle, picking up things too small to see. Home-sickness flowed into me, an almost physical pain. I turned to look along the headland to hide the welling tears. Just south of where we stood, a small jetty nosed out into the sea. Moored to it, listing into the shingle with the retreating tide, were two small rowboats. Somewhere over on the island would be another jetty, and more boats, for crossing when the tide was high. I heard my name, and looked back at the group. Dagney and Niáll were talking.

Dagney left his side and came over to me. "Walk a bit along the shingle with me," she said. "There are things you need to know, before we cross, and Niáll feels I should tell you now, and beyond the hearing of the other men."

I frowned. I handed Clio's reins to one of the escort and followed Dagney. *What could the men not hear?* At the jetty, she stopped. "Here will do," she said.

"What is it you need to tell me?"

"Wherever it is Fritjof has been for the last two years, he has brought back customs new to the Marai, ones that concern us. He houses his women in a separate hall now, and rarely, and only at his command, are they allowed into the men's presence, to dine, or in my case, to entertain. Your clothes will be taken: women are forbidden breeches, so if you can find a way to hide your secca, do it, although I think our belongings will be searched. And if it is your time to bleed, Lena, you may not come into the presence of the men at all, but stay in the women's hall."

What did it matter if I bled or not? But Dagney was not done. "If Fritjof were to take an interest in you," she hesitated, "he is giving women no choice, if he decides he wants them."

"But I am not a Marai woman!"

"True. That may work in your favour. And the *Teannasach* is pledged to your safety, for whatever that is worth here. But you needed to know."

I saw her point. I wondered if our captors' scrupulous respect of our privacy and our bodies on the ride here meant that I was already seen as belonging to soon-to-be-king Fritjof. The thought made me shudder. I swallowed. "Is there anything else?"

"Yes." Her voice dropped to a whisper. "We are still in Sorham. Fritjof is choosing to be crowned in lands ceded to Linrathe in exchange for tribute long years past. He is making a statement that all can understand. And perhaps equally as frightening, no-one from Sorham has told the *Teannasach* that he has built a hall here." *So perhaps my earlier fears of treachery were not far off,* I thought. Dagney continued, her voice at a natural pitch again. "Follow my lead in all things; I doubt they will separate us, as they will need me to translate for you. Now come, Niáll is signalling. It's time to cross."

I led Clio across without incident, the occasional wave lapping over the cobbled causeway. Probably I could have ridden, but I wasn't willing to take the chance. Niáll rode ahead of us, the other men following Dagney and myself. On the island shore I remounted, riding at a walk to the open area at one end of the hall.

A tall man waited for us, flanked by two guards. He towered over them both by at least a head, his pale hair tied back from his bearded face. We dismounted. Niáll said something; the tall man made a gesture of acknowledgement. His eyes travelled to Dagney.

"*Scáeli* Dagney, *Härskaran,*" Niáll said. Dagney bent her knee, her eyes down. *So this was Fritjof. He has cold eyes.*

"*En mathúyr?*" Fritjof said. "*Mer heithra, scáeli.*[1]" He said something else, and Dagney stood. Fritjof's gaze turned to me. I saw his eyes narrow. He glanced at Niáll.

"Lena," he explained, "*Gistel te Teannasach, fo handa marren, Härskaran.*[2]"

I inclined my head, but did nothing more. Fritjof frowned. He snapped an order, jerking his head to the left.

"*Härskaran,*" Niáll replied. "Come with me," he said. "I will take you to the women's hall. There you can wash, and proper clothes will be found for you. Take your saddlebags, but leave your horses."

---

[1] "A musician? I am honoured, bard."
[2] "Hostage to the *Teannasach,* from the south, King."

CHAPTER ELEVEN

THE WOMEN'S HALL STOOD DOWN THE HILLSIDE, in a flat area sheltered by cliffs on two sides. At a doorway Niáll halted. He knocked and called out, but did not open the door. A moment later it swung open, and a girl of perhaps twelve looked out at us. She gasped when she saw Dagney and I, and ran back in, calling.

A woman, perhaps in her thirties, came to the door, dressed in a rich embroidered tunic and skirt. She looked at us both, and then at Niáll, questioningly. I caught our names in the exchange, and I thought the word *Härskaran*. Dagney added something, and the woman beckoned us into the hall.

"Just follow my lead," Dagney said to me. "They will make us welcome here, and I have told them you do not speak the language, so they will not expect you to understand them. I will translate."

We were shown to seats on a bench covered with furs, and wooden cups filled with a hot tea brought to us. The women crowded around while Dagney and the headwoman, as I thought of her, spoke. I sipped the tea, looking around.

One long room made up the central portion of the hall, its roof supported by tall pillars and arches of wood, not dissimilar in structure to the meeting hall in Tirvan, although that had eight sides, whereas this was a rectangular building. Beyond the pillars, where the roof dropped lower to meet the walls, the space had been partitioned, and divided from the hall by curtains, mostly of woven wool, although I saw one or two that were fur. Private spaces. Underfoot, the floor was of wide boards, covered with woven rugs. Hearths burned along the central space, warming and lighting the hall.

"Lena," Dagney said, putting an end to my observations, "this is Rothny, wife to Fritjof and the highest-ranking woman of the Marai. I have explained who you are, and why you are with us. Be respectful, be friendly, but do not trust too much." A smile never left her face as she spoke. "Greet Rothny, if you will; the words are *'Mer heithra, Fräskaran Rothny'*."[3]

I turned to face Rothny. Inclining my head as I had for Fritjof, I repeated the words as best I could. Rothny smiled. "*Glaéder min halla.*"[4]

Dagney stood. "Come now," she said to me. "The women have prepared baths for us, and fresh clothes, and I for one will welcome both." I followed her again. Behind one of the woven curtains two baths, looking like oval half-barrels, waited, steaming slightly. I put my saddlebag down, waiting to see what Dagney did. The women who had led us to the baths left the space, pulling the curtain closed, and in the dim light we undressed and climbed into the baths.

The water's heat penetrated my limbs, easing aches I had grown accustomed to on the ride. I heard Dagney sigh with relief. We soaked for some time without speaking. I found soap on a small shelf near my head and washed, submersing myself completely to rinse off, and to wash my hair. Two women slipped in, each with a bucket of steaming water to add to the baths, disappeared again, and returned with clothes and towels. I lay in the water until it began to cool, then stepped out, reaching for the towel that had been left on a small stool, folded on top of the clothes.

"What happens now?" I said to Dagney, who was also drying herself.

"We go to the hall to eat the mid-day meal with the men; the *Härskaran*—Fritjof—has asked for us. The *Fräskaran* will accompany us," she answered, the last muffled as she pulled a tunic over her head. I picked up the clothes left for me from the stool. A woollen tunic, and a skirt of the same fabric. I dressed. The skirt, falling nearly to my ankles, felt confining, for all it was loose enough.

I looked around for my saddlebag, which held my light shoes. I could not see it, nor the clothes I had so recently taken off. "Where are our things?" I asked.

"Probably at our sleeping quarters," Dagney said. "Did you hide your secca?"

"It's in the boot sheath," I answered. "But that won't fool a determined searcher for long."

---

[3] "I am honoured, Queen Rothny."
[4] "Welcome to my hall."

"I don't think the *Fräskaran's* women will be looking for a weapon," Dagney said. "Unless Niáll has let it be known you may be armed, and there is no reason he would know that; he has been serving Fritjof since before Leste attempted its invasion of your country. So, hope that Rothny's serving women don't decide to clean your riding boots." She ran a bone comb through her hair, wincing at a tangle.

The curtain slid back, and one of the serving women beckoned to us. We followed her along the central space to another curtain. The woman pulled it back, showing us two beds with a table between them. The contents of our saddlebags had been neatly arranged on shelves over the beds. My boots and my slippers stood at the end of the left-hand bed, Dagney's at the right.

"*Takkë*," Dagney said. She sat on her bed, combing her hair dry. The serving woman spoke, gesturing at the comb; Dagney shook her head. "*Takkë*," she said again, this time with clear dismissal in her voice. *I had no trouble understanding that exchange,* I thought.

"I should have insisted you learn the language of the Marai," she said. "At least you'd have a few words. *Takkë* is thank you; *vaëre*, please. Have you looked at your boots?" Her tone remained conversational.

I bent to check the hidden sheath. My secca remained in place. "Should I leave it there?"

She shook her head. "No. Somewhere safer, if you can think of a place."

I looked around the room, and then at the items on the shelves. A small bundle caught my eye, beside my journal and Colm's history. "Dagney," I asked, "what is the custom here, for blood cloths? Would I wash them myself?"

She followed my eyes. "A good thought," she said. "Yes, custom here too says each woman washes her own, unless she is very ill; even the *Fräskaran* would not usually ask that of her serving women. No-one will touch them. I am a bit surprised they were even unpacked, but I suppose they had orders to completely empty the saddlebags, and they are in a case."

"Good." I untied the soft leather case, then wrapped my secca in the stained cloths it held. Once the package was returned to the shelves I slipped my feet into my indoor slippers. The skirt caught at them, irritating me. I couldn't remember the last time I had worn skirts. *At the ceremony binding me to my apprenticeship?* I wondered. It seemed unlikely.

I heard soft footsteps approaching. A question, in Rothny's clear voice. *"Ja,"* Dagney said, tying back her hair. A hand moved the curtain aside. "Time to eat," Dagney said to me, standing. The *Fräskaran* waited for us, in the same embroidered tunic as earlier, but now with bracelets on both arms and several rings on her fingers. Braids encircled her head like a crown. She gestured.

"Vaëre." As we moved toward the centre of the hall, she held up a hand. *"Din ladhar, scáeli,"* she said, *"vaëre."* Regardless of the 'please', I didn't think this was a request. Dagney nodded, and retrieved her instrument.

Fritjof's hall rang with voices as we entered. As my eyes adjusted to the gloom, I saw a long table set crossways to the length of the room, raised on a wooden platform about two-thirds of the distance down the hall. Fritjof sat in a tall chair, facing the lower tables and benches, an empty chair to his right. Donnalch sat to his left. His face lit when he saw us, but as I met his eyes across the space I saw warning in them, after the relief.

I could not see Cillian, nor Ardan. We walked toward the high table; nearly at the platform, Rothny stopped, pointing at two empty spots on the bench. *"Takkë, Fräskaran,"* Dagney said. I echoed the *'takkë'* and slid into the spot furthest from the high table, allowing Dagney the end spot; she would have to stand to play at some point. Rothny walked on, mounting the platform to take the chair beside her husband.

The hall had fallen silent as we—or rather the *Fräskaran*—approached the high table. Fritjof stood as his wife joined him, remaining standing after she had taken her chair. He waited a moment, then began to speak. His words sounded to me precise, brooking no argument or dissension. I felt my skin prickle. Dagney turned to me.

"He says," she murmured, "that now all witnesses he required are present—he means us, or at least you, by that—then his coronation can proceed, tomorrow. And then he bade us to eat, and enjoy ourselves."

Servers began to bring platters of meat and bread to the tables. "Who are the other men at the high table?" I whispered to Dagney.

"Two are *Harr* of Sorham, landholders and leaders; the others I do not know. Marai, I presume. Fritjof's brother, Åsmund, is not among them. I wonder what that means."

The man across from us looked up, catching Åsmund's name. He frowned. Dagney, seeing his reaction, said a few words to him. He nodded, and made a gesture of dismissal with his hand.

"I told him I was only explaining Fritjof's lineage to you," Dagney murmured. "There is tension here, about the brother."

The server reached between us to place a platter on the table. When I looked up, he handed me a short knife, set into a wooden handle, a tool for cutting meat. I realized there were no other implements on the table, save for an intricately carved wooden spoon at each place. "*Takkë*," I said, glancing at Dagney.

"Every Marai carries his or her own table knife," she explained. "These are ours to keep, and to bring to each meal. They are used by women to cut spun wool, and small hides, to skin rabbits and gut fish, and whenever a small blade is needed. There is a pocket in your sleeve—see?—to carry it. Use it, and not the pockets in the skirt; otherwise you will cut yourself. Now, Fritjof's table has been served, so we may eat."

She reached over to spear a piece of meat from the platter, transferring it to her own plate and reaching for bread. A dish of stewed berries sat beside the platter. Dagney spooned it liberally over the mutton. I followed suit. The berry sauce was tangy, almost astringent, but it balanced the strong, salty flavour of the sheep's flesh.

Ale splashed into the earthenware beaker above my plate. At the parallel table, I saw the servers moving along the rows of men, pouring the drink. One caught my eye: Cillian. I schooled my face to impassivity, barely moving my head. He poured wine for Niáll, who barked something at him. Cillian nodded. Putting down his jug, he went away, returning in a minute with a bowl. I saw Niáll spoon sauce over his meat.

Cillian moved along the table, not looking at me. I concentrated on my food. After the mutton and bread a sweeter bread, rich with dried fruit, was brought. For the lower tables, at least, that was the end of the meal.

I looked around the room, catching several people staring at me. *Well,* I thought, *I am a stranger, and hair is short, not like these women's.* I sipped the last of my ale, moving my gaze to the head table. Donnalch looked our way occasionally, but when his eyes caught mine they did not linger; he watched the room constantly, I noted. The others paid us no attention at all.

A server bent to speak to Dagney. She nodded, standing, picking up her *ladhar.* "I must play," she said to me. A stool had been placed for her on the platform; she sat on it, tuning her instrument. The servers brought more ale. Benches scraped as men pushed back from the tables, making themselves comfortable.

Niáll took Dagney's place beside me. "I am here to translate, should it be needed," he explained. I nodded. Dagney began to sing, a melody I had heard played before. After a moment, I leant towards Niáll. "What song is this?" I asked.

"In your tongue," he said, "something like 'Sisters Dark and Light'."

"*Forla,*" I answered, thinking about what Dagney had said about this song. *Was she taking a chance playing it, sending a message? Or was it just a familiar song to please the crowd?*

Dagney played three songs. Niáll told me the names of each, but said nothing else. Occasionally, from the corner of my eye, I glimpsed Cillian clearing tables and pouring ale, but he stayed away from our table. I did not look at him. During the last song, Niáll shifted in his seat as if he were uncomfortable, distracting me. Glancing at him, I saw beads of sweat on his face. Suddenly he got up, walking rapidly out of the hall. *Too much ale,* I decided.

When Dagney finished her last song, to much stamping and cheering, Fritjof stood. Whatever he said resulted in more stamping and cheering. He turned on the dais and bowed to Rothny, extending a hand to help her rise. I watched as she smiled at the other men at the high table before descending. *Were we to go with her?* I looked at

Dagney; 'stay there', she gestured. I waited. After a moment, she beckoned to me. I slid along the bench, inwardly cursing my skirts, and stood. A tug on my sleeve made me turn. The man who had been sitting on my far side held my eating knife out to me. "*Takkë*," I said, smiling at him. I found the sleeve-sheath, and slid it in.

I climbed onto the platform. Donnalch stood. "Lena," he said, "I am glad to see you well; your arm is better?" His voice was formal.

"*Teannasach*," I replied. "It is much better, thank you."

"I am glad to hear it," he said. "King Fritjof wishes to speak to you, to learn more about the Empire. I will translate, and my clerk will transcribe, so that there is a record."

His clerk? That had to be Cillian. Fritjof, I guessed, would have little regard for those whose work was to read and write, except to use them as needed. "Of course." *How truthful should I be?*

We followed Fritjof towards the back of the hall, partitioned off with walls of wood to make a private room. Inside, a fire took the chill off the room, and several chairs faced the hearth. Sheepskins lay in front of each chair. Unshuttered windows set in the end wall let light into the room, far more comfortable than anything I had yet seen in the women's hall.

Cillian, summoned from his serving duties, caught up with us just as we entered the room. The door shut behind us. Fritjof gestured us to the chairs, choosing one closest to the fire for himself. Donnalch sat opposite to him; Dagney and I in-between. Cillian did not sit, but prepared to write at a tall desk near the windows.

Fritjof asked a question. Dagney shook her head, as did Cillian. Dagney turned to me. "Lena, where is Niáll? He came to translate for you, when I was singing."

"He left in a hurry," I said. "I thought perhaps he felt sick, too much ale? He did not look well." She translated this for Fritjof, who scowled. *He had wanted him here,* I thought, *to verify that what I said was correctly translated.*

Fritjof began to speak. Donnalch explained rather than translated his first sentences, welcoming me to his lands and his coronation, the first person of the Empire to have witnessed this. I saw a small muscle twitch beside Donnalch's eye when he spoke the words 'his lands'. Then the questioning began.

"How large is the Empire?"

"About the size of Sorham," I answered, "if my understanding of that is correct." Fritjof nodded when this was relayed to him. *Had he known that, and was only testing me?*

"How many boats does the Emperor command? How big are they?"

"I do not know the answer to the first question," I said. Donnalch relayed this. Fritjof frowned. "As to how large—maybe fifteen paces long?" I said, purposely underestimating, looking at Donnalch as I did. He moved his head slightly, a tiny negative gesture. "No, wait," I said, as if I had reconsidered, "maybe longer, maybe twenty, twenty-five paces. Thirty men, and their officers." I had been warned; I was to speak the truth. *Or,* I thought, *at least I should be truthful, if Donnalch will know if I'm not.*

The questioning continued. I was asked about rivers, about harbours, about towns and roads. I pleaded ignorance when I could, and carefully minimized what I said about Casilla. I was not asked about the Wall; Fritjof had other sources for that information. Nor, I noted, was I asked about the women's villages, other than to confirm that was how we lived.

I had no doubt that Fritjof planned an invasion. I was also certain he had reclaimed Sorham for Varsland, and that Donnalch was a guest in name only.

Finally, Fritjof leaned back in his chair with a grunt. He looked over at Cillian, who still wrote. When Cillian put down his pen, Fritjof said something, clearly a command. Cillian walked over to a sideboard to pour wine for us all.

I took the cup. I was thirsty from all the talking. As Cillian handed it to me, he murmured something: *'tonight'*, I thought. "*Forla,*" I replied, hoping he would know I had heard him.

Dagney and Donnalch began to talk, in the language of the Marai. Fritjof did not react, but sipped his wine, listening, his eyes sometimes straying to me. Suddenly, Dagney switched languages. "And I bring you greetings, *Teannasach,* from Einar and Bartol, and also from Ingold; he asked to be remembered."

"*Marái'sta!*" Fritjof barked. Dagney turned to him and bowed, speaking words in a contrite tone. He stared at her, then turned again to Cillian, who repeated the words in Fritjof's language, or so I guessed: I could only pick out the names. *Was she telling him where we had been, or planned to go? Why had she spoken so that I could understand?*

After another minute of scrutiny Fritjof dismissed us. I put down my wine cup, standing. In one swift movement, Fritjof stood beside me. He took my chin in his hand, firmly, as I instinctively pulled away. He tilted my head upward, studying my face. After the first glance, I kept my eyes downcast. I felt his eyes travel up and down my body, his hand moving from my face to my arm. I willed myself not to flinch. "Hm," he grunted. He let me go.

Trying not to tremble, I followed Dagney out of the room and the hall. The sun shone. I blinked, adjusting my eyes. "Are you all right?" she asked.

I took a deep breath. "Yes," I said. "I think so." *Was I? I had never been looked like that in my life, assessed as if I were a pig at market.* "The last time," I said to Dagney, "a man attempted to make me pay attention to him against my will, I punched him until he was sick."

She raised her eyebrows. "Good for you. But punching Fritjof might not be diplomatic."

I stared at her for a moment. Her mouth quirked. I started to laugh. I covered my mouth with my hands, knowing the laughter was a release of tension, not wanting to draw attention to myself. I focused on what I had sensed in the room.

"Dagney, is the *Teannasach* a prisoner?"

She looked around. We were alone. "I think so. Cillian, if he can keep calm, and not go off hot-headed, should be safe. Fritjof thinks he is just a clerk. As for Arden..." She shook her head. "I am afraid of what Fritjof is planning for Donnalch."

I thought about what she had said to the *Teannasach*. "Who is Ingold?" I asked. "Was it his *torp* we were to visit, after Sinarrstorp?"

She smiled. "No, although it is not an uncommon name, and there is an Ingoldstorp, much further east. Ingold—or Ingjald, to give it its proper pronunciation—is a character in a *danta*, a king who invites other kings to a feast in his new hall, and then, as they sleep that night, burns it down, killing them all."

I had heard this before somewhere. "A warning, then."

"A warning," she agreed, beginning to walk towards the women's hall. "Donnalch would know which *torps* I could reasonably visit, and Ingoldstorp is not one of them. And he knows the *danta* well."

We returned to the women's hall, to spend the afternoon outdoors, on benches along the western face of the building, overlooking the sea. The Marai women spun wool, their drop spindles in constant motion. They had offered me a spindle, but I did not know how to spin, a fact which led to much chatter. Dagney played her *ladhar*, singing occasionally, but mostly allowing the notes of the melodies to weave among the women's talk. A few women rocked cradles with one foot, and small children played around the benches. Seabirds circled and cried, wheeling and gliding in constant motion.

I wondered where Clio was, and if I would be allowed to see her. I wondered if Ardan were safe, if any of us were. I played clapping games with the children, and gave in to encouragement to use a spindle, resulting in uneven, lumpy yarn and much laughter; even the little girls could spin better than I. The waves swelled and retreated. I watched the flow and eddies, how the rocks were exposed and covered, where the weed grew thickest, thinking about how to fish these waters, how to navigate them, my years of training guiding my thoughts. It was something to do.

CHAPTER TWELVE

BEFORE WE WENT BACK TO THE HALL FOR DINNER that night, one of the women brought me two silver bracelets, and a pendant of a clear, honey-coloured stone. She touched my hair, making a 'tsk' sound, but there was nothing to be done with it. Dagney refused bracelets, explaining (I thought, from her gestures) that she could not play the *ladhar* with them on, but accepted an enamelled comb for her hair, and a brooch.

"I will not sit with you tonight," she told me as we waited for the rest of the women, "I am directed to play during the meal." For this occasion, several of the other women would be joining us in the hall. They had been busy dressing hair and comparing jewellery for the last hour. I remembered what Dagney had said: that here a woman's status came, usually, from her husband. *Whose wives were these, to be invited tonight? Or did they all 'belong' to Fritjof?*

"Dagney," I said, quietly, "are these women accepting of this new way of life? Surely they find it restrictive, if they used to live and work with their men?"

"I do not know," she replied. "I have not heard any complaints: the *Fräskaran* seems to accept it, and the others take their cue from her. But I wonder where his brother's wife is, and her women: I fear for them."

"You think they are dead?"

"Or perhaps held captive elsewhere. In either case, it appears to be enough to keep these women silent, even if they dislike the changes in their freedom."

Her answer left me unsatisfied. I tried to imagine Huld in this setting. Could she submit to this isolation, this reduction in her freedom, her life? *Perhaps,* I thought, *when the alternative is death.* But I thought too that she would find a way to resist.

The hall glowed with lantern light; I recognized the odour of burning whale oil. Candles gave further light to the head table. I followed the other women to a table near the side of the hall, but not too far from the head table. As we sat, Cillian slipped into the seat beside me.

"I am here as your translator," he said. "There will be speeches tonight."

"Niáll is still unwell?"

"He should be, "he said, his voice conversational. "I put enough holly berries in his sauce to make him sick for several days. The other men who shared that bowl are also ill, but not as severely. He took most of the holly, as I intended. It shouldn't kill him, but he won't be going far from the latrines for a day or so."

I smothered a laugh. "That was well done," I said. I noticed a glance or two towards us.

"We shouldn't talk," Cillian said. "When I translate, I will add a sentence, or two, to the end of each translation. If you must respond, make it sound like a question; both languages use an upward inflection for questions, so those around us will think you are asking only for explanation. Now, I am going to make some signs of worship, as if we had been praying. Repeat them after me."

He touched his forehead, lips, and breast. I did the same. I wondered whose god this honoured.

A few minutes later we all rose, as Fritjof and Rothny entered to make their way to the high table. Both, tonight, wore robes of fur, Fritjof's trimmed with the pelts of winter weasels, pure white except for the black-tipped tails; Rothny's with the feathers of the snow owl, white with black barring. Behind them came a boy of fourteen or fifteen—Fritjof's son?—and then the same men, the Sorham *harrs*, who had sat with them at the mid-day meal, and finally by Donnalch. Two guards followed the procession. When all were seated, they took their places, each at one end of the dais.

Fritjof stood again, gesturing to us to stay seated. He spoke briefly, sounding cheerful and relaxed.

"Enjoy the meal," he says, Cillian translated. "Drink heartily. *Did you note how he is treating our leader?*"

I smiled and nodded. Fritjof had given the Sorham *harrs*, mere landholders, precedence over the *Teannasach* of Linrathe. It was a subtle but clear insult, *and*, I thought, *a message: he is sure of Sorham, or at least where these men hold sway.*

The meal was impressive, especially for early spring. The high table ate fish, followed by platters of small birds—the shore plovers, I guessed—and then a haunch of venison. The lower tables fared nearly as well. We too ate fish, and then deep pies made from the lesser meats and organs of the deer, rich with gravy. Where the head table had wine, we had ale, and we were given only dried fruits to nibble on after the pies, but it was by far the best meal I had eaten in a very long time.

When the platters had been cleared and the cups refilled, Fritjof stood again. Benches scraped as we stood for the *Härskaran*. Fritjof raised his glass and shouted a toast. The room shouted back.

"To the Marai kingdom restored," Cillian said. "*He is claiming this land.*"

I watched the two *harrs*. Their pleasure in toasting Fritjof looked real to me. *What will Sorley think?* I wondered, remembering him telling me that he would be coming home soon, to this province, to learn to be the head of his holding. *Was either of these two men his father?* I slid my eyes to Donnalch. He held his cup high, his face impassive.

At a word and gesture from Fritjof, we sat. Fritjof began to speak.

"Tomorrow, I will be crowned," Cillian translated. "*He has killed his brother, and many of those loyal to his brother.* A new day dawns, one that will see the Marai returned to their rightful place as lords of sea and land, not just in the north, but south as well. *Our leader is a prisoner, a guest in name only, and his guard is dead.*" The room had begun to murmur at Fritjof's mention of the south.

He held up a hand for silence. Cillian followed his words in a quiet undertone. "Yes, the south. We know the stories are no more than old wives' tales and meaningless prophecies. We sailed west for many years, many generations, and found nothing, until only I had the courage to sail east. Rich lands lie close at hand. *I am going to plead illness tomorrow morning, and escape while all eyes are on the crowning.*"

"I will come with you?" I said, remembering to make my statement sound like a question. "Did he say he sailed east?"

"Linrathe we have, or at least we have their leader, and without him they will turn from the fight easily," Cillian translated, his eyes on Fritjof. "*He did, although I do not know what he means by that. And I will be better alone.*"

"Not necessarily."

He frowned. "He is speaking of you," he whispered. "Listen. And for the lands south of Linrathe, south of the Wall, lands we know only from stories, I will hold as hostage the woman Lena, sent to Linrathe from the southern Empire to ensure the peace between them. More than hostage; on his birthday, when he becomes adult, I will give her to my son Leik as his wife."

What? Heads turned to look at me. I looked up at Fritjof, hatred and fear welling. I glanced once at Donnalch, whose eyes told me nothing. *Had he agreed to this?* I looked at Leik. He gazed back, interest on his face. Then, slowly, I turned my gaze back to Fritjof, and bowed my head. *Let him think I accepted it.* "When is the boy's birthday?" I whispered to Cillian.

"In a few days," he said. Fritjof was speaking again. Cillian translated, the explosion of cheers and shouting in the room almost obscuring the last sentences. "Tomorrow I am crowned. Three days after that, Leik reaches his manhood. We will celebrate that, and give him time to enjoy his bride, and then we will take to our boats and sail south, Marai once again, masters of the sea, conquerors. Now, bards, music! *I will take a rowboat when all eyes are on the crowning, and cross to the mainland. I will try to steal a horse somewhere.*" The music began, a fast, bright tune.

"Steal a fishing boat from a harbour. You can sail faster than riding," I said.

"I can't sail a boat."

"Then you need me; I can. I will find a way to stay back. And I will not be that boy's wife." Cillian said nothing. I glanced at him, to see him staring at Donnalch, indecision on his face.

"If you are at the jetty soon after the crowning begins, then, yes," he said finally. "But I will not wait."

"I will be there." *But how?*

After that, the night was music and drinking. The women talked, ignoring me. Men drank and gamed. A server bent to speak to Cillian. "I am summoned," he said to me. "I must go." I watched him leave the hall. *Who had asked for him? Why?* A thread of fear tightened around my thoughts.

One of the musicians—a man—stood, calling something. The room quietened. The three musicians, Dagney among them, I knew, although I could not see her—were seated at the far side of the high table. This man had stepped up onto the dais to make himself heard. Once the room was close to silent, he began to sing.

The tune rollicked, and the audience sang along. At the end of every verse, they thumped the tables and drank. A drinking song. We had those, too. I could not sing the words, but I joined in the drinking, although I swallowed very little. I wanted to look as if I were trying to fit in. But sips of ale and table-thumping did not keep the fear at bay. To distract myself, I thought about what Fritjof had said. He had sailed east, and returned to tell his tale. No fever had ravaged his men, and he had found a people whose customs he liked enough to copy. *What did this mean?*

At the end of the song, men left the room singly and in pairs, a few from each table. One of the women tapped me on the shoulder. I looked around. She stood beside me. She cocked her head, and mimed squatting slightly, then pointed at me. "*Ja,*" I answered. I followed her out into the night.

Our bladders relieved, I lingered, looking up at the stars and the sliver of the moon, the cool breeze off the sea welcome. No hint of poor weather on its way, although I knew as well as any coastal dweller how quickly that could change. *There might be fog in the morning,* I thought; the breeze was slight, and dying.

My companion tugged on my arm. I followed her again, back into the light and heat and noise of the hall. When we got back to our table, Leik sat on the bench, talking to the other women. He stood at our arrival, politely gesturing for me to sit. I did my best to smile at him, and took my place. He sat beside me, offering me a cup of wine.

He looked more like Rothny than Fritjof, except for his eyes. Those were Fritjof's, and they looked at me the same way, assessing, the undercurrent of desire evident in the heaviness of his eyelids and the set of his lips. *Manhood might be official in three days,* I thought, *but he had experience of women.* He took my hand, running a finger over my wrist and along the vein. I pulled my hand back, unthinking. He frowned, and grabbed it, holding it tightly. I forced a smile, and dropped my eyes, playing the shy maiden, anger coursing along every nerve of my body.

Leik laughed, and stood. He put his fingers under my chin, forcing my head up. I kept my eyes down. He ran a finger along my neck, to where the tunic began. He said something, holding up three fingers. *Three days,* he was telling me. I nodded. "*Ja,*" I whispered.

He walked away. The other women chattered at me. I drank the wine, willing the trembling to stop. I wanted to talk to Dagney. I wanted to not be here at all. I had agreed to be hostage to the Empire's truce, but this had gone beyond what I thought was expected of me. *I must escape.*

The men were getting louder, the laughter more raucous. At the tables where dice were thrown, tempers flared. I could feel sweat between my breasts and on the nape of my neck. On the far side of the hall, a man stood suddenly, shouting, clearing the table in front of him with one sweep of his arm. The women beside me said something, my earlier companion grasping my arm. When I looked at her, she swept her head towards the doors. Time to leave.

No-one blocked our departure, or bothered us on the path back to the women's hall. No-one took any notice of us at all, I thought, although men were coming and going from the feast. The breeze had dropped, the still air cool on my skin. Wisps of mist or low cloud floated over the stars. I could hear the lap of waves on the shore, and the faint bump of a boat against a jetty. Just as we reached the hall, I took a last look out across the water, along the mainland. A light flickered, very faintly, somewhere south along the coast. *A house?* On the coast like that, they were likely to be fisher-folk.

Inside the women's hall the fire was banked and glowing. Women who had not attended the feast sat around it, drinking tea. When we came in, they jumped up, clearly asking questions. Someone pointed me towards the fire, handing me a mug. I sat, glad of the tea, but as I sipped it, fatigue dragged through me. The women chattered. I noticed eyes turning my way. Finishing the drink, I stood, pointing towards my sleeping chamber and miming sleep. Heads nodded; one word— probably good night, or the equivalent—was repeated. "*Takkë,*" I said, "*takkë.*"

They are talking about me and my 'betrothal' to Leik, I thought as I undressed in the small space, lit by one candle. *If women here take their status from their husbands, then I will be more important than any of them but Rothny. They won't like that.*

And perhaps no-one would be upset if I couldn't attend the coronation. But how to get out of it? My eyes roamed around my sleeping area. A glimmer of an idea came to me. *I would sleep on it,* I thought, *and see if it still seemed a good idea in the morning.*

Dagney came in, very late, barely disturbing me. Just before dawn, the seabirds already calling, I opened my eyes, wide awake. I lay, listening, hearing the first stirrings of other people. There were fires to tend, food to prepare, and much else to do, on this momentous day.

When the voices in the hall grew louder and more numerous, I got up. I went out to the latrines, came back in, accepted a mug of tea. Dagney yawned her way into the room, cupping both hands around her mug as if in need of the warmth. Her face sagged with tiredness.

"Did you hear what the king said last night?" I asked, as soon as I could. "About sailing east?"

"I did," she said. "If he speaks the truth, it changes so much."

"Do you doubt him?"

She shook her head. "Not really. But who are the people he found? Will they follow him here, to be yet another threat, either from disease or by arms? What does it mean, for us, for the Marai, for your Empire? There is no-one I can ask," she finished, and then brightened slightly, "unless I couch it in terms of *danta,* of songs...maybe that would work, if they thought my interest was only that of the *scáeli,* wanting to write a song in honour of the voyage. Perhaps I will mention it to Fritjof later."

"Do you play again today?" I asked.

"Yes," she said. "Lena, I must tell you this: I spoke to our leader briefly last night; we had only a minute. He wants you to know he did not betray your presence in our lands to Fritjof purposely; he and Ardan were overheard, when they thought themselves alone and free to speak. A mistake, and one he regrets deeply."

"Had he any words of advice?"

She shook her head. "None. Or perhaps no time to speak them; Fritjof called him away."

"And Ardan is dead," I said. She looked startled. "Cillian told me."

She closed her eyes. "Dear gods," she said.

"And you are caught in this too," I pointed out. She made a gesture of negation.

"I may have been anyhow," she said. "Fritjof knows me as a bard, a *scáeli*, and might well have demanded my presence here." I thought she was making excuses, but I let it go; I couldn't carry that guilt right now. I needed to be focused.

"What will you do?" she murmured.

"Better you don't know," I answered. She held my gaze a moment, then nodded slightly and turned away to pour more tea.

"By tradition," she said, "there is no food served until after the crowning. And do not drink too much: the ceremony is long, and no-one can leave. I am glad it is spring, and the sun not too hot."

"Where is the crowning?" I asked, keeping my voice casual.

"On the highest point of the island. Fritjof will face north, towards the lands of the Marai; the witnesses—which will be everyone on the island—also face north. During the ceremony, we see only his back. The priest who crowns him is the only one to see his face until the crown is on his head. Only then will he turn to greet his people."

"Thank you." Information I needed; the chance of me being seen slipping away towards the mainland, to the east, were negligible, if I kept to the cliffside. I took my mug to the table, then stopped, frowning slightly. I rubbed my lower belly. The girl serving the tea held up the mug, asking a question. I shook my head. "*Na, takkë.*"

We dressed and donned ornaments, more than for last night's feast. I, Dagney explained, was to walk just behind Rothny, as befitted my

154

status as Leik's betrothed. She and I, and her serving girls, would come last, after everyone else had gone to the ritual grounds.

I slipped the eating-knife into its pocket in my sleeve. We would go from the ritual to yet another meal, a simple one of smoked fish and bread, so that the kitchen-folk could be at the crowning. The feast tonight would make up for it, Dagney assured me. Then it was time for her to go, to play as the people gathered. She touched my arm, gently, and left.

I sat, waiting. Women began to leave in groups. When only a few remained, I slipped out to the latrines. Very carefully, I drew the long skirt of my gown up, and with my woman's knife I made a small and shallow cut, high on my thigh, wincing at the pain. I hoped I had judged the cut right: deep enough to bleed, but not too quickly. I wiped the knife, returning it to its pocket.

When I returned to the hall Rothny stood alone, except for her two servants. She gestured to me; we needed to go. I nodded, and followed her out of the hall.

We walked up the path, past the feasting hall, climbing towards the broad summit of the island. When we about half-way, I stopped, clutching my belly, moaning. Rothny frowned. I looked up at her, trying to look regretful. I pulled up my skirt just enough for her to see the blood trickling down my leg.

She said something, sharp and angry, shaking her head. She turned to the youngest servant, giving orders; the girl looked stunned, bursting into tears. Rothny gave her a push, looking at me, pointing back to the women's hall. The message was clear. The girl was to accompany me back to the women's hall, missing the coronation. She was small, and young, no match for my skills. And by sheerest luck, no other woman was at her bleeding time, or if she was, she was watching the crowning from some hidden place on the island. The hall was empty. I could make my escape.

The girl grabbed my arm, pulling me along the path back to the women's hall. I let it happen, allowing her to think she was in charge. At the hall, she shoved me towards my sleeping chamber. I took one stumbling step forward, then pivoted, keeping my body crouched, and lunged upwards at her, punching her in the stomach. She gasped, doubling over, but she had no air in her lungs with which to scream. I had her on the ground, my hand over her mouth, before she could take a breath.

She stared up at me with frightened eyes. I pulled a strip of cloth from the pocket of my skirt, a strip cut from my lighter riding tunic early this morning, and gagged her. Then I rolled her over, and with more cloth strips I tied her hands and feet. I dragged her into the sleeping chamber, put her on the bed, and tied her to it. She would come to no harm.

I felt her eyes on me as I stripped off the skirt and pulled on my riding breeches and boots. I reached up to the shelf for my few things: the wrapped blood cloths, my comb, my books. The books were gone. *When had I seen them last?* There was no time to think about it. I pushed things into my saddlebags, slung them over my shoulder, and started for the door.

CHAPTER THIRTEEN

I SCRAMBLED DOWNHILL, KEEPING BEHIND boulders and in dips of the ground whenever I could. The breeze was in my face; it would carry any sound I made towards the crowd watching the crowning, but they would be, I hoped, too engrossed in the ceremony to care.

Cillian waited at the jetty. He had untied the small rowboat, his small pack already stowed under the seat. Wordlessly I slipped onto the boat, pushing my saddlebags against Cillian's pack, steadying the boat against the dock with one hand. Cillian climbed in, the boat rocking as he took his seat. I pushed off, and began to row.

The oarlocks squealed. Cursing—Cillian had had time to remedy this, had he known to—I stopped rowing to dig in my bag. I found my blood cloths, pulled the oars up, and wrapped and tied cloths around the shafts. Cillian offered no help. I shoved the empty case back into the bag and picked up the oars again. The tide was rising. We reached the other jetty in a matter of minutes. Cillian clambered out to tie the boat. I unwrapped the cloths from the oars and stuffed them in my bag, not bothering with the case. I pulled Cillian's pack out from beneath the seat, handed it to him, and stepped up to the jetty. Without speaking, we climbed the angled path to the top of the cliff. At the top, Cillian broke into a run. I kept pace, the leather saddlebags bouncing on my shoulder, following him east and south until my side stabbed me with every breath. Only when we reached a small stand of pines did he stop.

"We need to find a *torp*," he panted. "We need horses."

I shook my head. *Hadn't he listened?* "Too risky. Too slow. We steal a boat. We can sail faster than riding. A lot faster."

He stared at me, a muscle working in his jaw. "Where should we go?" he said finally.

I had thought about this. "Berge. Or, not Berge, but the fort just north of it, at the Wall. There will be ships there, almost certainly, and it will be easy to get word to the White Fort, if that is where our leaders are."

"Gregor should have reached the White Fort by now," Cillian argued. "Miach will be leading men north already."

"But not fast enough, and Fritjof will be sailing south, not marching. We need the Empire's ships to be waiting, and the Emperor must command that. He will believe me, Cillian, but we need to get to him as quickly as we can. And we are not doing that if we stand here arguing!"

I saw the flicker in his eyes as he acknowledged the truth of what I said. We began to run again, angling west, back toward the coast.

In mid-afternoon Cillian spotted a small cluster of buildings in a cove ahead of us. My eyes found ropes and floats, a pile of traps, the paraphernalia of fishing. I glanced to the sea; the tide was out, which meant the boat would be too. We would have to wait. Cillian scowled when I told him this, but said nothing. We found a group of boulders, warmed by the sun, and sat against them. Cillian dug in his pack, handing me a piece of bread. "There isn't much," he said, "but we should eat a little."

I chewed it, calculating. The tide would turn soon. I expected the boat back in late afternoon, although it could be later, if the fishing had been good; there were still five or six hours of light. If we waited until a couple of hours after dark, we stood little chance of detection, and the tide would be nearly high again. But we would need to hide until then. I looked around.

"What are you looking for?" Cillian asked. I explained. He frowned again. "Why don't we just keep going? This can't be the only fisherman's hut on this shore. And if they've sent men after us, they'll find us in that time."

He had a point. I glanced again at the buildings. The shed at the shore stood open, back and front, no boat inside. No boat pulled up on the beach. Cillian spoke the truth: we needed to keep going. I finished the bread. "You're right," I said. "Let's go."

We circled wide of the cottage, but even so a dog yipped from the buildings, shouted down by a woman's voice. I hadn't expected a dog at a tiny fishing settlement; in Tirvan, all the dogs were for the sheep and for hunting. They had no place around the boats. Perhaps this one was a pet. We would need to be careful.

We passed by another fishing settlement, and another: they seemed to be evenly spaced along the shore, sharing the waters. *If they were*, I estimated, *we should reach the next just about at dusk.* We continued, alternately walking and running, keeping close to trees and rocks where-ever we could. The land underfoot was a sandy heath, sometimes soft enough to make movement difficult, sometimes firm. We saw no-one. What sheep we saw were gathered along the tideline, eating seaweed, no shepherd or sheepdog guarding them.

The light began to fade. Ahead of us, the land rose, the curve of the beach below us giving way to cliffs where seabirds circled and screamed, landing on narrow ledges in the rock. I cursed. There would be no fishing huts here; we would need to clear this headland. My stomach growled. "Cillian," I said, "we need to stop."

"It's getting dark," he objected.

"I know. But we need a bit more food, and water. Then we cross this headland, and hope there are fisher-folk in the next cove."

He handed me another small piece of bread, and the water-skin. *We would need to find fresh water again,* I thought: it was at least a three-day sail to Berge, and that would be with favourable winds. Food we could do without, if we must, and we could always trail a baited line, but water we would need. I took a scant mouthful to wash down the bread, and then another, and handed it back to Cillian. "Drink sparingly," I warned.

We started off again. There was no track to follow; whatever dealings these fisher-folk had with each other, it was by boat, not by land. There had been tracks leading inland from each settlement, probably to the *torps* that each served, but nothing between them. The land rose. We climbed, the coarse heath scratching against our boots. A huge bird, white-tailed and pale-headed, soared up from the cliffs and over our heads. I ducked, reflexively, then stared up at it. It was enormous, larger even than the golden eagles that hunted the hills above Tirvan. "What is it?" I asked.

"Sea-eagle," Cillian said. "Keep going."

We reached the crest of the headland. Beyond us I could see the curve of another cove, and another cluster of huts. I closed my eyes in relief. Every inch of me ached, fatigue was sapping every muscle, but I could make it to that settlement.

Half an hour later we crouched in the heather and bracken, watching and listening. The boat—a small fishing boat, single-sailed—lay anchored just off-shore, its sail lashed to the mast, rocking gently on the swells. In the larger hut, the flicker of firelight and the smell of frying fish told of the family preparing for the evening meal.

"Pull your breeches' legs out of your boots and then down over them," I murmured to Cillian. "It helps keep the water out of your boots," I explained, at his puzzled look. I pulled my secca out of its boot sheath, tucking it into my belt, and adjusted my breeches. "Now," I continued, "we wade out to the boat. It won't be deep: the moon is nearly dark, so the tide is low, but be prepared to get wet. When we get there, throw your pack in, then lean over it and grab something as close to the far side of the thwart as you can—the far edge of the seat," I clarified, seeing his frown, "and then step in. I'll keep her steady. Stay close to the far side to let me climb in. Then haul up the anchor, but stay near the centre of the boat. I'll start rowing. We won't put the sail up until we're out a bit." He exhaled, loudly. "A problem?" I asked.

"At least we could both ride," he said.

We crept along the shore. The waves were gentle, not making enough noise to muffle our steps. I rolled my weight on my feet as Tice had taught me, all those months ago, but Cillian had no skill in walking quietly. The cot was almost dark now, just the soft light of a banked fire glimmering through the shutters; they'd be up early to sail as soon as the tide allowed in the morning. With luck, the inhabitants had eaten their supper and were soundly asleep.

We were approaching the water when Cillian stepped on a something—driftwood, I guessed—that snapped loudly. We froze. A dog barked, sharply, from the cot. I took a step back and sideways, avoiding the wood, cursing. A voice called a challenge. "Go," I hissed at

Cillian. "Get on, and get that anchor up." We both began to run, heedless now of sound. A shape emerged from the cottage, silhouetted against the faint glow, and then another, the dog growling nearly at our heels. *We would make the boat before them,* I estimated, trying to angle my direction to reach the boat as quickly as possible. Waves slapped against my legs. The dog barked from the waterline. Cillian was at the boat, reaching over, climbing on—and my left ankle caught the anchor rope. I fell, heavily, the water over my body and my head, flooding my mouth and nose. My bags slipped from my shoulder. I blew out, pushing up with my arms, trying to stand, when arms caught me from behind.

I struggled, but the man's arms were strong from fishing and he held me tightly. I heard the splash of another person's strides behind him. He was shouting something, angrily, pulling me around to face him. One clutching hand fell on my left breast. He stopped. His hand groped. He called something to the other man, and then shoved me around, ripping at my tunic.

His hand was rough against my skin, and he stank. There in the waves, he caught a nipple between thumb and finger, squeezing. He raked his fingernails, ragged and sharp, across my breast; I gasped. He laughed. His other arm was tight around my waist, but one of my arms was free. He brought his head down to my neck, half-biting, half-sucking, the one hand kneading my breast, the other dropping lower to my buttocks, pushing me against him. He was hard, even in the cold water. I willed myself to become limp. I let my free arm drop slowly, to take the secca from my belt. Raising it, I stabbed him in his exposed neck, once, twice, rage powering the thrusts. He gurgled, moving his hand from my breast to his neck, and then he fell into the sea.

I looked up. The other man was no man at all, but a boy of perhaps twelve years. He stood in the sea, staring at the body. *His father, probably.* Behind him, the dog whined. I pushed the secca back into my belt, turned, and pulled myself onto the boat. "Go," I said to Cillian. "Go!" I screamed, as he hesitated, looking at me. He turned, pulling the anchor up as I pushed oars into their locks. As soon as the anchor-stone was out of the water I was rowing, all my fear and anger channelled into the action, taking us away from that place.

When we were out deep enough, I pointed the boat into the wind and stopped rowing. Cillian had hunkered down in the stern. I shipped the oars and stood. "Need to get this sail up," I panted. "Stay there. You'll only be in my way." I glanced back shoreward. In the last vestiges of light, I thought I could make out the shape of the boy, crouched over his father's body at the sea's edge. *No-one else.*

I unfurled the sail, a simple square, clipped the lines in place, and hoisted the yard. There was no moon. The breeze was mild, but enough for us to sail. But I did not know this coast. If the man had done any night fishing, there might be a lantern. I could see a shape under the thwarts that could be a chest. I pushed it out. It held a lantern and candles, a loop of rope tied to the top of the lantern. I ducked under the sail and hooked the lantern in place at the bow; it hung above the water, giving me a chance of seeing rocks, or the change in wave pattern that told of submerged rocks. But even as I hung the lantern, I debated my choices. Night sailing was risky, and I had never done it alone. Cillian would be of no help, more likely a hindrance. We had a long way to go, and haste was needed, but if we lost the boat—and ourselves—to rocks, then word would never reach Berge. The boat was still headed into the wind, and we were drifting slowly backwards. I needed to decide, but my mind was fogged with exhaustion.

"Cillian," I said, "do you know this coastline at all? Can you tell me about rocks, small islands, anything?"

"There are a lot of islands," he said, "big and small. Further south there are fewer, except in one place; the coast is flatter there, with long beaches of sand, but not here."

"I don't know what to do," I admitted. "We need to get away from this cove, at the very least, but there could be another settlement in the next. We should get out into the deeper water and anchor, so we can start sailing at first light, before other boats come out, but we risk hitting rocks in the dark."

"Wouldn't it be safer to row?"

"It would be," I said. "But I don't think I can." The spurt of energy engendered by the attack had gone, leaving me drained. And my arm was aching, a deep, nauseating ache, adding to my fatigue and confusion.

"Show me how," he said. I hesitated.

"It's not that simple," I started.

"Show me," he insisted. I nodded, then realized he couldn't see my acquiescence.

"All right," I said. "Come up to the thwart. Keep your body low as you move."

The boat rocked as he made his way to the rough seat. When he was seated, I moved behind him and helped him place the oars in the locks. "Hold the oars here," I said, indicating the grips, "with your hands on top, right, good," I added, as he grasped the oars in a serviceable manner. "Don't let the oars go too deep," I said, as he moved them down toward the water. "Right now, just hold them, while I drop the sail."

When I had the sail down and furled, I came back to the thwart. "Now, lift the oars out of the water and bring them forward." Cillian did as I said. "Keep the angle shallow as you drop them and pull back evenly and steadily." The boat moved forward. "Not too far back," I instructed, as I tried to see his movements in the dark. "Now lift them, bring them up and forward, back in, good." We slid through the water, not smoothly, but it would do.

"Can you keep that up?" I asked.

"For a while," he said.

"Don't grip too hard, or pull too hard, you'll tire yourself too quickly," I said. "Just row steadily. We don't want speed, anyhow. I'm going back up to the bow, to watch for rocks."

The oars splashed too much, but there was no-one to hear. Cillian kept the boat to a straight line while I peered forward into the pool of light the lantern created. The sea to all sides was black, no other lights on the water, no lights on land, only the stars to differentiate sea from sky. We moved forward. Suddenly I saw, or felt, rocks looming up ahead. "To larboard!" I shouted.

"What? How? Tell me!" Cillian screamed.

"Dig in hard with your left oar!" I shouted, cursing Cillian's ignorance and my own stupidity. "Get the right out of the water, now. Keep rowing with the left, hard." I felt around for something to push off the rocks with, finding nothing. The little boat swung left. I scrambled to the stern, just as the boat bounced off the rocks. Ignoring its roll, I reached out and pushed, hard. We moved away from the rock. I slid forward to balance the boat, hoping the side of this rock was straight and clean, with no sharp angles below the waterline waiting to hole us.

We were swinging too far larboard, spinning round towards the rocks again. Cillian had not steadied the course; the starboard oar was still out of the water. I pushed in beside him, picking up the oar. "On my count," I panted. "One, two, three..." Our oars splashed into the water nearly in unison. We surged forward, almost straight. I said a silent prayer to any god listening and kept rowing, away from the rock.

Nothing holed us. After a minute or two I told Cillian to stop rowing. We drifted, rocking gently, while I studied the sky. In the effort to get away from the rocks, I had lost track of our direction. I found the twin stars, high above the hunter: south. The bow of the boat was pointing west, towards the land.

"Drop the anchor," I said. "We need sleep. We will sail at first light." Cillian said nothing, but he pulled up his oar and laid it along the boards before lowering the anchor-stone overboard. I steadied the boat against the pull of the anchor until the stone hit bottom. Cold seeped into me. I was wet and exhausted, and all my spare clothes had been in my saddlebag.

I slid off the seat and onto the boards. "Come here," I said to Cillian. "We need to share body heat."

"I'm all right," he said.

"No, you're not," I answered. "You're wet, and now you've stopped rowing, you're going to get cold. Did you bring any dry clothes, anything we can put over us?"

"My riding cloak," he said. "It's in my bag." He fumbled at the ties of his bag, cursing at his clumsiness, but after a minute he freed the knot to pull out the woollen cloak.

"You have it," he said. "I don't need it."

"Cillian," I said, exhaustion blunting my voice. "Don't be stupid. Get down here. I need your heat, even if you don't think you need mine. If I die of exposure, what are you going to do?"

That silenced him. He crawled down beside me; we spread the cloak. It didn't quite cover us, but Cillian was still a hand's-breadth away from me.

"Closer," I said, feeling the first shivers beginning. He edged closer, still not touching me. I sighed. "Roll over." He did as I asked, dislodging the cloak. I wrapped it around us again, and then put my arm over him, pulling my body against his until there was no space along our lengths. He tensed, but as the cloak and our proximity began to warm us, he began to relax. I slowly stopped shivering. I tucked my head in against his neck, and fell asleep.

Chapter Fourteen

I WOKE, STIFF AND SORE, TO A FAINT PALENESS in the eastern sky. I had roused several times in the night to pull the cloak back over us, and once to make my way to the gunwales to relieve myself, falling back into a shallow and fitful sleep again each time. But now I was fully awake, and it was time to sail.

"Cillian," I said, "wake up." He grunted, and stretched, rolling onto his back.

"Lena," he muttered.

"Time to get moving," I said, sitting up. I looked around. The stars were clearly visible, and already seabirds were skimming the waves, hunting. No fog, but a stronger breeze, blowing from the north-west. Exactly what we needed.

Cillian got up, uncertainly moving toward the stern. I glanced at him; he was undoing his breeches. "Pay attention to the wind direction," I told him. I turned my back on him—there were basic courtesies on a small boat—and opened the lid of the chest again, looking for water. An earthenware pot, stoppered with a woollen rag, looked promising. I picked it up. It sloshed, but it sounded and felt half-empty. I removed the rag, sniffed, and sipped. The water tasted of the pot. I allowed myself two small swallows, before passing the pot to Cillian, who had come forward again, tying his breeches.

"A couple of mouthfuls, no more," I warned. "We will have to find more water somewhere."

With the water re-stoppered and stowed, I used an oar to swing the boat into the wind again. "Hold it there," I said to Cillian, and raised the sail. He pulled up the anchor-stone, and we began to move south slowly, the light wind just sufficient to propel the heavy boat. But until it was fully light, this was enough.

As the day brightened, I could see we were among a line of islands, creating a wide channel between the open sea and the mainland. Other boats would be on their way out soon. We needed to stay as far out from the mainland as was safe, and even that course was predicated on none of the islands being inhabited. And somewhere, we needed to go to shore for water. I would worry about that later. The wind was freshening, promising a long reach. I adjusted the sail for the increased wind. "Sit there," I directed Cillian, pointing to the opposite gunwale. He complied, although a glance over showed me his face was set and his knuckles white.

The little boat ran with the wind for some time, needing little adjustment of sail or tiller. But looking ahead, I could see the line of offshore islands was ending; we would lose our shelter from stronger winds. Dark patches in the water beyond the last island told of stronger waves. "Cillian," I said, as I shortened the sail, "be prepared for some rougher water, and move as quickly as you can if I tell you to." I reminded myself to use terms he would understand.

The wind hit the sail with more force than I had expected, the boat heeling sharply. I reefed the sail, shouting at Cillian to move to the other side of the boat as I did. I felt the boat settle. A few more adjustments to sail and lines, and we were sailing at a fair clip, the little boat taking the waves remarkably well. I rested one hand lightly on the tiller, and glanced over at Cillian. He held on to the boat with both hands, his shoulders tense, his eyes moving from the land to the waters behind us, and back again.

All the rest of that first day we sailed with a favourable wind. I showed Cillian how to steer, and how to make small adjustments to the sail, having him take over when I needed to relieve myself, or to move to stop my muscles cramping. I had seen line and hooks in the chest, so when we switched places again, I set up a line, baiting the hook with dry bread, and gave it to Cillian, explaining as best I could the difference between how a nibbling fish and a hooked fish would feel. He lost the first fish, but hooked the second with a firm tug. I filleted it with my secca and we ate the firm, wet flesh, me hungrily, Cillian doubtfully. He kept it down, though, even with the swells, although I saw him swallow hard a time or two.

Hunger had been satisfied, and the boat ran fair with the wind, needing little attention. "Cillian," I said, "what of these lands to the east, where Fritjof claims he sailed? Could he be telling the truth? Did he talk about his travels to the *Teannasach*?"

"Not when I was there," Cillian said, 'but, yes, he could have travelled east, I think. I have been trying to recall the maps. There are rivers that reach down into the eastern lands, and the Marai boats are shallow. It is possible he could have rowed down those rivers."

"He would go against the prophecy, and convince others to go with him?"

Cillian snorted. "In a moment. The *Teannasach* and Fritjof's older brother, Åsmund, were friends; King Herlief sent Åsmund to Linrathe as a boy for a time, to the *Ti'ach na Perras*, and he and Donnalch would hunt and hawk together, as well as have lessons. It was why Donnalch thought he could renegotiate the terms of our treaty with the Marai, once Herlief was dead. But from what I have heard, Fritjof was wild even then, wanting what Åsmund had—not the schooling, for that was never Fritjof's interest—but his hawk, his horse, even when the animal was too large and strong for him. He could never wait, or be counselled by wise words. The King sent him away, finally, after he tried to force himself on the girl being considered for Åsmund's bride, and then nearly killed his brother in a fight when he intervened."

I shuddered. "And his men?"

"If you had been at the *Ti'ach* longer," Cillian said, "you might have heard some of the *danta* that concern themselves with the exploits of the Marai, of their raids and battles and the glory those brought. There were—are, no doubt—those among the Marai who thought they had grown soft and land-bound under Herlief, weak. Fritjof would have had little trouble in convincing that faction to support him."

"And now they all must support him, or die," I said.

We saw the occasional other fishing boat, but they were well in from our position, fishing the more sheltered waters. In mid-afternoon, a headland reached out towards us; as we passed it, I saw the half-moon curve of a long cove, and the sparkle of a stream running down the cliffside. I could see no buildings, and no boats. "We're going in," I said, through lips chapped now from the salt air, the wind, and thirst. I gybed the sail. "Prepare to row," I ordered Cillian, bringing the sail down as we reached the beach. He rowed us in fairly smoothly; when I could see the bottom close, I jumped off, to haul her up to the beach. As I did, I felt a sharp pain in my upper chest.

"Be quick," I said to Cillian. "Drink your fill, fill the water-pot, and we'll get off this beach before someone sees us." While he knelt at the stream, I untied the top of my tunic and felt my chest where my attacker had scratched me last night. The skin was tender, and felt puffy. I cursed. I had, in my haste and fear, forgotten a basic principle: I had not soaked the ragged cuts in sea water. Over the years, I had escaped infection from hooks and spines, rock scrapes and knife-slips, by immersing the injury in the ocean for several minutes. There was only one thing to do.

"Cillian," I called. He looked up from filling the water jug. "Come here, will you, when you're finished that?" I walked to the sea edge, bending to wash my secca thoroughly, holding it in the waves. Cillian approached me. "Put the water-pot in the boat," I directed. "Then I need you to do something for me."

When he stood before me, I said, "Look." I pulled open my tunic, pushing aside the torn pieces to expose my breast. He looked away, his face reddening. "I'm injured," I said bluntly. "The man last night scratched me, and the scratches are infected. Don't look away." He brought his eyes to my breast.

"There is pus, here," he said, reaching a finger out and then pulling it back.

"I thought so," I answered. "Take my secca, and cut the scratches deeper." I saw the look of horror on his face. "I can't do it myself," I said, "and it has to be done, or the infection will spread. The secca is clean. I will hold my breast taut, but you must make the cuts. And if you must touch my breast to do so, then do it. Can you do this?"

He looked at me for a long moment. "I can," he said. I flattened my breast down with my hands, feeling the tug and stab of the infection as I did. He brought the knife tip down. I closed my eyes, biting my lip against the sharp, exquisite pain of the blade. He made three cuts. I did not cry out.

"Thank you," I said, when he was done. Blood dripped down my breast, staining the tunic. He handed me back the secca. "I will soak it now, in the sea." I told him. "Then I will get a drink, and we will go back out."

I waded out into the water, crouching down so the sea would cover my chest. I steadied myself with one hand, and with the other massaged the cuts, pushing pus and blood out, letting the sea-water in. It stung, worse than the initial cuts. Involuntary tears sprung to my eyes.

When I felt I had soaked long enough, I stood and walked back out of the water. At the stream, I knelt and drank deeply, resisting the desire to rinse the cuts in fresh water. I retied my tunic as best I could, and we pushed off, rowing back out to deep water.

The sun and wind dried my clothes, and as I sat by the tiller I wrapped Cillian's cloak around me until I was warm again. Cillian caught more fish for supper. As the sun set in the west, I saw him gazing out at the mainland. The breeze was dropping with the sun; we sailed slowly now.

"I know where we are," he said. "That is Linrathe, now. You were right, Lena. Even on horseback we would not have got this far, so fast."

"If that is Linrathe," I said, "we could make land, find a cove or even a settlement."

"Not tonight," he answered. "These waters are called the Maw: along these cliffs there are submerged rocks, sharp and frequent as teeth, for many miles; a barrier to landing. Some say that is why the Sterre is built where it is, to extend the sea barrier on the land. But tomorrow, yes, further south, we can get water and food, and send word overland, perhaps."

"I see," I said, feeling the disappointment. "We should anchor soon. If this is the Maw, then we cannot afford to be caught amongst the rocks in the dark."

We dropped the anchor stone, and ate the fish Cillian had caught. The little boat rocked gently on the waves. The evening star appeared on the horizon, and streams of gulls headed back towards land, over our heads. The approaching night felt peaceful, but my thoughts were not. All afternoon I had considered what Cillian had told me about Fritjof, and the threat to both Linrathe and the Empire. Our two countries must work together, if were we to defeat the Marai. Cillian knew this better than anyone else, but he hated the Empire. He needed to hear what I had to tell him.

"Cillian," I said, "I have something to say, and I think it will make you angry. Will you hear me out?"

In the fading light, I could not read the expression on his face. "I suppose," he said flatly.

"My first night at the *Ti'ach*," I said, "I asked Sorley why you seemed to resent me." That wasn't quite true, but I wanted to deflect any reaction away from Sorley. "He told me about your mother." I paused.

"He shouldn't have," Cillian said. "It was not his story to tell."

"Nonetheless," I said. "It is done. I have a question, and it might be important. Do you know nothing of your father?"

He did not reply at first. Overhead, gulls continued their arrowed flight back to land, silhouettes now against the darkening sky. "Nothing," he said finally, "except that he was a soldier of the southern Empire. My mother was sixteen. She lived just north of the Wall, on a small steading. Whoever he was, he took advantage of a young girl, and then deserted her."

I had one more question. "How old are you, Cillian?"

"Thirty-three. Why?"

A fish jumped, splashing back into the water off the bow. I did the calculation: thirty-four years ago, Callan would have been seventeen. "I think," I said slowly, "that the Emperor, Callan—he might be your father. You have a strong look of him."

I saw his head turn to look at me. "You know the Emperor well enough to say this?" It was not the response I had expected.

"I think I do," I answered. "I have spent some hours in his company. I have seen him when he is pleased, and when he is angry, and it is when you are angry you look most like him. But even that first night—I thought I knew you, but it is your likeness to Callan I was seeing."

"More proof of the malevolence of Empires, then," he said.

"That isn't fair!" I said. "Callan would have been a soldier then, a cadet, actually, nothing more. He may have been posted away from the Wall, without ever knowing your mother was with child."

171

"But he never came back," he said into the night. I had no answer for that.

"Cillian," I said after a moment, "this goes beyond you. The *Teannasach* and the Emperor together paid homage to the Eastern Empire, to what it once was. Many of my people crossed into your land at Partition; we share blood and history, and you more recently than most, perhaps. We must remember that, and work together, if we are to defeat Fritjof." I waited. There was no answer, only the steady slap of the waves, and the beating of wings overhead, in the dark sky.

He tucked up against me more willingly that night, under the heavy cloak, although he kept his back to me, afraid, I surmised, of his body's involuntary response to mine. He held no attraction for me, and I doubted I truly did for him, but we are not always captains of our bodies' reactions. I woke heavy-headed and aching, to a grey morning; a light fog hung over the sea, beneath a clouded sky. "We will have to sail with the land in sight," I told Cillian as we prepared the boat. "If we lose the land, we can lose all sense of direction, and the wind is no help; it can change in a moment." The wind, in fact, still blew from the north-east, but it was gustier, possibly presaging a storm. I would be busier with the sails today.

As I reached up to adjust the sail, pain shot through my breast. The area had been throbbing when I awoke, but I had ignored it, telling myself it was just the throb of any cut. But the pain said otherwise. When I had the sail set and the lines fixed, I touched my breast, feeling beneath the fabric of my tunic the inflammation of infection. I shivered. If draining and soaking the scratches yesterday hadn't cleared the infection, doing it again would not likely help. The salve which might have had been in my saddlebag. I pushed the fabric aside, looking down. Red streaks extended from the cuts, too far to be just the usual redness of healing. I closed my eyes. "Cillian," I said. Something in my voice alerted him.

"What's wrong?" he asked.

"My scratches are infected," I said, as calmly as I could. "Badly. The seawater did not help; I did it too late. I must show you how to sail, alone, because you may need to do so. We'll head for land as soon as it's safe, and I should be able to sail until then, but you need to know how. So, come, sit beside me."

He came forward. As the sun rose behind the clouds, and the fog slowly dissipated, I taught him the basic theory of sailing. I showed him how to judge the wind by the thin tell-tale strip tied to the mast; I explained how to trim and let out sail, how to tack, how to gybe, and when, how to furl and tie the sail before taking to the oars. Then I sat back and let him do it, watching, suggesting, correcting, feeling the throb in my breast deepen as the first signs of fever invaded my body.

Sweat beaded my brow and I was wrapped in the cloak against deep shivers by mid-day. "We must be past the Maw by now," I said. "We should find a harbour." The wind was strengthening, the gusts coming more frequently, and I was afraid for the boat under Cillian's hand if we had to run in front of a gale. One misjudgment and we would capsize, and that would be the end.

I turned my head to look at the sky behind us, and caught my breath. On the horizon, further out than us and still a good distance behind was a boat, a ship, much larger than us, square-rigged and moving fast.

"Cillian," I croaked. He looked at me; I raised an arm to point, ignoring the pain that shot through my breast as I did.

"That's a Marai ship," he said.

"After us," I said.

"Can they see us?" he asked.

"Doubt it," I said. Talking took effort. "Maybe in the sun, but everything is too grey today."

"What do we do?" His mind was off the sails. A gust hit, swelling the sail, pushing the boat forward and sideways, rocking it violently.

"Trim the sails," I gasped. "Quickly!"

He leapt to the lines. As he did, another gust hit, this time on the opposite side of the sail. The wind swirled. The boat swung, sails flapping. A wave broke over the bow, soaking us. I pushed myself up, shedding the cloak, reaching for the lines, ignoring pain, ignoring weakness. Cillian stumbled, falling against the gunwale, grabbing desperately for something to hang on to. He scrabbled against the boards, found his feet, reached for the sail. I crawled forward, and together we furled and tied the sail, leaving the little boat drifting on the growing swells.

I fell against the gunwale. "You'll have to row in," I said. My head spun. I crept to the centre of the boat, where a dead weight would best lessen pitch. "Give me the cloak," I muttered. I felt the weight of the cloth cover me; I heard the creaking of the oars in their locks, and then I knew nothing at all.

Chapter Fifteen

OR ALMOST NOTHING. I HAVE CONFUSED MEMORIES of being moved, of voices and pain, and then truly nothing until I woke—*when? where?*—in a bed, under warm blankets, in a dim and quiet room. I blinked, even the muted light causing my eyes to hurt. My mouth felt parched, tasting foul. I moved my head, looking for water.

"Lena?" My mother's voice. *What was she doing in Linrathe? I'm dreaming*, I thought, but then she was bending over me, her hand on my cheek.

"Lena," she said again. "Can you hear me?"

I focused on her face. She looked worried. "Yes," I whispered. "Thirsty."

She smiled. "Let me help you up," she said. She put one hand behind my shoulders and pushed me up, propping me on pillows. I tried to help her, but I was as weak as a newborn mouse, and sitting up brought a spasm of coughing, deep and painful. When the coughing stopped, I was exhausted. The room spun. My mother held a cup to my lips. "Slowly," she warned. I took a sip, and another, the water cool on my raw throat.

"What happened?" I croaked. She shook her head.

"Later," she said. "A sip or two more, and then you should sleep again." I took another tiny bit of water. Then I closed my eyes to let sleep take me again.

When I woke the second time, I felt stronger, and the room stayed in one place. My mother was at my bedside in an instant—*she must be watching me constantly*, I thought—this time with a bowl of warm water, with which she washed me, as if I were a baby, before dressing me again in a clean, warmed nightgown, rubbing my back when the change in position brought on the coughing again. She still wouldn't let me ask questions, but this time, even in my weakness, I felt myself getting annoyed.

I let her brush my hair and feed me some broth, but when I felt myself slipping back towards sleep, I pushed the spoon away and said as firmly as I could, "Where am I?"

"Berge," my mother said.

"How?"

"Cillian brought you," she answered.

I tried to shake my head, but the movement hurt. "No," I said. "He can't sail."

"He didn't," she said, smiling. "He rowed the boat you took into a cove, and by blind luck it had a fishing settlement. Cillian convinced the fisherman to bring you both to Berge. How, I am not sure."

"Why are you here?"

The smile disappeared. "Oh, Lena," she said. "Casyn sent for me. He thought you were dying, and in truth so did I, when I arrived. You had an infection raging in your blood, from the scratches on your chest, and another in your lungs. You have been very ill, Lena, so ill it took all my knowledge to keep you alive." Tears shone in her eyes.

"But you did it," I whispered.

"Only because you are so strong," she answered. Something she had said came back into focus.

"Casyn is here?"

"Not right now," she replied. "He'll be back soon. That's enough talking, Lena. Rest again. The Empire is safe, and Linrathe, and that is all you need to know."

My mother was right. It was all I needed to know then. For the next few days I slept, waking to eat a bit, be washed, and after the first day, be taken to the latrine and made to walk a few steps. This took all my strength, of body and of mind. Anything else seemed unimportant, and very far away. But I coughed less every day; soon I could sit up on my own, and eat porridge and soft-cooked eggs by myself, and as my body grew in strength, my mind moved away from self-absorption. I was allowed no visitors, and this made me wonder.

"Mother, why can't I see Cillian?" I demanded one morning. "Or is he hurt, or sick, too?"

"No," she said. "Cillian is well. But right now, Lena, your body is still weak, and you could catch any illness very quickly. Until I am sure you are strong enough, you cannot risk visitors." Her voice was firm, the healer, not the mother, speaking, but she *was* my mother, and watching her hands automatically retying her hair, and the small lines between her eyes, I knew there was something she was not telling me.

"How is Kira?" I realized I had not asked about my sister yet. *Was that what she was keeping from me?*

Her face cleared. "Kira is well, very well," she said. "I have left Tirvan in competent hands, that I know. She will have four deliveries to cope with this spring, and Casse is failing, I'm afraid, but I think she will live through this summer, and perhaps see one more autumn hunt."

"Kira is seventeen now," I said slowly. "A woman."

"She is," my mother said. I could hear the pride in her voice, for the daughter that had been her apprentice and was now her equal.

"She will stay in Tirvan?" I asked. She would have the choice, now, to leave for another village, to be their healer and midwife, if she so wished.

My mother laughed. "What do you think?" she asked.

I smiled, thinking of my sister. "She'll stay," I agreed. "What else has happened in Tirvan? I've been gone so long now. Tell me what everyone is doing."

For the next hour, my mother recounted the doings of my home village in the nearly two years I had been gone. My small cousin Pel was gone, now, of course; the men had come for him last autumn, a year late, but the need to concentrate the Empire's forces on the Wall had kept the soldiers from Festival and from claiming their sons. Even last autumn, my mother told me, only a few men had come, and all the boys, the village had been told, were to be taken to the Eastern Fort, as far away from the fighting as possible.

"Your aunt was glad, in a way, to see him go. He was growing headstrong, and we have no experience with raising boys over seven. He needed the discipline of cadet school," my mother said. "And he— well, not just Pel, but all the boys of age—were wild to be gone. They threatened to take the ponies and find the army themselves, when no men came in the spring," she added.

"Pel would have done it, too," I said, contemplating. "Especially after Garth taught them to ride. How did you stop them?"

She laughed. "It was Casse. She rounded them up and told them, in no uncertain terms, that the ponies belonged to Tirvan, they were needed for the hunt, and if they took them, they would be guilty of theft. And thieves, she pointed out, were punished severely in the army; not only would they have disappointed their fathers, they would have robbed themselves of any chance of advancement. I am not sure if it was those reasons, or when she told them bluntly that their only work in the army would be digging latrines and cleaning them, too, that convinced them, but convince them she did."

I laughed. "Good for Casse," I said. "And Dessa? How is she?" Dessa had been my apprentice-master on the boats. Her partner, Siane, had been killed in the failed invasion by Leste, leaving Dessa to raise Siane's daughter.

"She is better," my mother said. "And Lara," she added, brightening, "is apprenticed to me, or to me and Kira, I suppose, as of last autumn."

I raised an eyebrow. "I can see Lara as a healer," I said, "but I did not think she would leave Dessa. Before I left, she was like her shadow."

My mother nodded. "She was. But in the spring after the invasion, when Dessa began fishing again, Lara was sick with worry every time she took the boat out. It was Kira who began to spend time with her, taking her to pick herbs, talking to her, reassuring her. So, when she turned twelve, and asked the council to let her apprentice with us, well, we could not say no. And Dessa approved. Lara is slight, as you know. The boats would not have been a wise choice."

"I'm glad," I said. I was suddenly homesick, the stab of longing a physical pain. I wanted to see Tirvan again, the unpainted clapboard houses on the hill, the jetty and the boats, my upstairs bedroom in my aunt Tali's house. I wanted my boat back, my *Dovekie*, built for a crew of two. I wanted to soak in the baths and watch the golden eagles hunting over the high fields where the sheep grazed. *But I could,* I realized. *I could go home now, when I was well enough, surely?*

The next morning my mother came in with something in her hands. I was standing, restless and unsettled, looking out the window at the glimpse of the sea beyond the roofs and streets of Berge. I turned as my mother came in.

"I have something for you," she said. I looked at what she held out.

"Colm's history!" I gasped. "How...? It was taken, at Fritjof's hall." I recognized the other book, too: my journal. I took them from her, turning them over in my hands.

"Cillian had them," she said. "They had been given to him to begin translating. He knew they were precious to you—and to Perras, he said—so he took them. I thought it was time you had them back."

I stared at the books. Even if they had not been taken from me, they would have been lost with my saddlebag, the night we stole the boat. Cillian had saved them. My hands trembled. Tears stung my eyes, and then I was sobbing, deep, racking sobs that brought back my cough. My mother put her arm around me, and guided me to the bed, sitting with me, holding me, as I cried, and coughed, and cried some more.

"Clio," I said, or rather wailed, when I could speak at all again. "I left her there. I had to, but I miss her...and what will they do with her?" I said between sobs. "They will have ridden her to war, and she could have been killed."

"Shhh," my mother soothed. "You had no choice, Lena. You did the best you could, and you did well."

Anger took the place of grief, suddenly and violently. I pulled away from my mother. "You are right," I shouted. "I had no choice. I was a hostage. I was meant to be at a house of learning, not forced into marriage with a prince of a people I didn't know existed. I said I would go, I would be the hostage, because I didn't...I couldn't disappoint Casyn again. I owed him that. He said I was like a daughter to him...how could I say no? But I went to learn..." I stopped. Even through my flaring anger I knew what I was saying was wrong. I had not known what being a hostage entailed when I agreed. *And how could Casyn have known what he was sending me to?* I shook my head, my anger turning against myself. My mother was murmuring something.

"Don't listen to me, Mother," I said wearily. "I know it's not Casyn's fault, or the Emperor's. It's just how things turned out. They couldn't have known."

"You are allowed to be angry," she said. "None of this—none of the last two years—is what you thought your life would be: there have

179

been forces beyond your control, as well as the consequences of your own choices." I swallowed, nodding. She went on. "And when we doubt our own choices," she said gently, "it can be easier to let others make the next decisions for us, or do what we think they would want us to do. It's why there are three council leaders in the women's villages, Lena, so our decisions are never made alone, and two of us must agree."

"But how do you know your choices are right?" Even to my own ears, I sounded about ten. But my mother just put her arm around my shoulders, and pulled me to her.

"We often don't," she answered. "Lena, do you want to tell me what happened with Maya?

I shook my head, tears leaking from my eyes. My mother rocked me gently. "Your letter reached me, although it took a very long time," she said. "You sounded so hopeful, when you wrote: Maya had come to Casilla, and you had found work on the fishing boats, and there was Valle to raise. I thought you were still there, you know, until Casyn's first message came to tell me you had been sent north, as a hostage to the peace. Why did you leave Casilla, Lena?"

"She sent me away," I whispered.

"Maya sent you away?" I heard the surprise in my mother's voice.

The tears rolled down my cheeks. I did not try to check them. "She wanted Valle to herself, because he was Garth's. She could accept Ianthe; she was Valle's aunt, too. But I didn't have a claim, she told me, so I didn't need to stay. She and Ianthe could raise him, without me."

"Did she know about you and Garth?"

"I don't know," I admitted. "I never told her, but maybe she guessed, from all the time we spent together on the road. Or maybe Garth told Ianthe, and she told Maya. I don't know," I repeated.

"Oh, Lena," my mother said. "Why didn't you just come home?"

I sat up, wiping my eyes. "I was going to," I admitted. "And then Dian came, looking for supplies and recruits, and she told me how hard the fight was on the Wall. And Casyn had asked me to come north, and I hadn't. I thought about how I had had a choice, but Garth and Daryl and Finn and all the other young men didn't...and I could be useful. So I went."

"To where you were wanted, and where you didn't have to make choices," my mother said gently.

I pulled away from her slightly. "Yes," I admitted slowly. "But it was more than that, Mother. Casyn had trusted me to be a leader at Tirvan, and a messenger on the road, and had made me privy to some of the inner thoughts of the Emperor. The Emperor himself had trusted me. Even when I was working in Casilla, helping to raise Valle, the thought was at the back of my mind that I had betrayed their trust. So, I went to the Wall."

"Did you never think that we needed you in Tirvan?" The question was asked gently, without accusation.

"No," I said. "Tirvan was fine without me." She sighed.

"You are so like your father," she said, surprising me.

"My father?" I said.

"Yes," she answered. "The Festival you were conceived, he told me right from the start he wouldn't be back to Tirvan. If I birthed a boy-child, he'd come back to claim him at the appropriate time, but otherwise, no. He liked seeing new places, he said. In reply to my letter telling him of your birth, he sent a doll—do you remember it?" I nodded. "And I never heard from Galen again."

"I met him," I said.

"Did you?" She sounded surprised. "So he's still alive."

"Well, he was around midwinter," I clarified. "He'd ridden in from the eastern end of the Wall, where it meets the Durrains, for supplies and probably with information. Turlo introduced us. He seemed likeable. We talked for a few minutes; he asked about you," I remembered. "I have a sister, he told me, in Rigg, and two brothers at the cadet school at the Eastern Fort. Then he wished me luck, and rode away." I shrugged. "But why do you say I'm like him?"

"Oh, Lena," she said, a trace of amusement threading her voice, "adventure. Do you remember asking me why you couldn't ride away with the men, when you turned seven?"

"Did I?" I said. "I don't remember that." But her words brought back, not a memory, but a feeling, an inchoate longing, mixed with a vague sense of failure.

"And then later you always wanted new coves to fish, new directions to sail. And you certainly didn't get that from me! I've never been out of Tirvan in my life, until now."

"But I wanted to come home," I protested. "I was going to, until the Wall was breached, and Casyn needed me to ride south to ask for help. And I'm coming home with you now, when I'm well enough."

"If the Emperor will let you," she said gently.

I frowned. "What do you mean?"

"You are still sworn to his service, you know, and bound by the terms of the truce between him and Linrathe. For which you stood hostage, Lena. Just because we gave—are giving—aid to Linrathe against a common enemy does not mean the truce is superseded. The Emperor may choose to send you back to the house of learning you first were at, and is within his rights to do so."

"I don't think he would, though." I answered. "Callan is a just man."

"He is also an Emperor at war," my mother said. She sighed. "Try not to worry about it, Lena. Do you want to read now? Or write in your journal? I'll leave you in peace, if so."

"Maybe I'll try to write a bit," I said. "A lot has happened. I'm not sure I can remember it all."

"It may come back, as you write. I often found that, when I wrote notes about childbirths." She stood. "Tomorrow, if the day is dry, I will take you outside. You need to begin to walk, to build up your strength."

I smiled at the thought. "Then I hope the day is dry," I said. "I'm feeling like a newly-sheared sheep. I just want to get out of this pen and back to my fields."

She laughed. "Good. One more day, and you can be out in the air again."

When my mother had left, I opened my journal. I had written nothing since my arm had been injured the first time, saving Donnalch's hawk. So much to remember. *I would make a list,* I decided, *to begin with, and then fill in the details.* I picked up the pen, dipped it in the inkpot, and began.

CHAPTER SIXTEEN

THREE MORE DAYS PASSED. TRUE TO HER WORD, my mother took me out, first into a walled courtyard that caught the sun, and then for longer walks, into Berge itself. We stopped a lot, sitting on whatever was at hand: sometime the steps of a house, sometimes a low wall. But by the third day, I could walk to the harbour overlook, although my mother would not allow me to attempt the long descent down to the sea itself.

Berge itself felt both familiar and unfamiliar. The village was perhaps twice the size of Tirvan, and unlike my home village, which straggled down a reasonably gentle slope to the harbour, Berge had two sections: the houses and workshops on the top of the cliff, and those at the harbour. A track angled down steeply between the two halves of the village, with a few buildings along it. More stone had been used in building here, especially at the harbour level, perhaps for strength against the wind and tide. The Wall could be seen easily from Berge, its line along the northern horizon following the contours of the land, extending from the fort at the land's end, down the cliff, to end at the military harbour. From my vantage point at the top of the cliff, I could see several ships at anchor. *One of them,* I thought, *might be* Skua.

The on-shore breeze brought with it the smell of fish, and I could hear voices from the harbour and the occasional jangle of rigging. Seabirds soared along the cliffs, their grace in the air changing to clumsiness when they landed at their ledge nests. Out to sea, I watched the gannets fishing, their black-tipped wings folded as they dove vertically into the water, almost always coming up with a fish in their beaks. Some fisherwomen hated them, thinking they competed for fish, but I loved watching their precision and skill.

But as much as I wanted to watch the birds and the sea, my eyes kept returning north, to the ships and the fort and the Wall. I thought of the conversation my mother and I had had, sitting on a stone wall in the morning sunshine the day before.

"Why hasn't Cillian come to see me?" I had asked again.

"Lena, think," she had answered. "This is a women's village of the Empire. Cillian is a man of the north. How could he come?"

"Oh," I had said, feeling stupid. "Of course. I wasn't thinking." But the exchange had reminded me of something else. "Why was I brought to Berge, and not treated by the Empire's medics, anyhow?" I had asked. "At the White Fort, Guards weren't sent to the nearest woman's village if they were injured or ill."

"Who nursed them? Not the actual treatment, but who dealt with their personal needs, if they were unable to take care of themselves?"

"Women," I had admitted. "So here, with Berge so close..."

"Exactly," she had said. "The medic had drained your cuts, and poulticed them, exactly as Marta or I would have done, but you needed constant care, and the women of Berge could do that better than the army could. Remember, you had brought word of imminent invasion, and all hands were needed to respond to that." She had sighed, then. "I know you are restless, Lena, and you have questions that I cannot answer. But you must be patient."

I was not good at patience. I felt almost as much a hostage here in Berge as I had at the *Ti'ach*: I had little choice in what I could do, and my future depended on what Callan—or more likely Casyn or Turlo— determined. I needed something to do, and I knew I lacked the strength to make the walk down the cliff to the harbour and back, even if I could have been useful once I was there. I was writing my journal, slowly, but I could not do that all day. I looked north, one last time, and stood to begin my slow walk back to Marta's house.

This was the first day my mother had allowed me out alone. I was grateful for that: I needed space and solitude, and while I was surrounded by houses and other people out about their business, their brief greetings did not intrude on my thoughts, and the long views sufficed to make me feel less cooped up. As I walked back through the upper village, I resolved to ask for some light work, something that would occupy my hands for a few hours a day, at least.

The mid-day meal was ready when I arrived, bread and smoked fish, and some spring greens, served at a table on the broad porch of Marta's house. I had my appetite back, and I ate hungrily. When the meal was over, I stood to carry dishes to the kitchen.

"Lena, you don't need to do that," Marta, Berge's midwife and healer, said. "Kyreth can do it." Kyreth was her apprentice, a girl of fourteen, who had brought me drinks and food when I was still bedridden, and listened while my mother and Marta had discussed my progress.

"No," I said firmly. "I need something to do. Let me clean up, so Kyreth can do other work. I have caused you enough extra work, these past weeks. Let me start to make up for it."

"All right," Marta said, with a glance at my mother. "But let Kyreth bring the water from the well. You should not be carrying the bucket yet."

I conceded this point. While I moved from porch to kitchen with the plates, Kyreth fetched water to fill the kettle simmering over the banked fire. Then, with a brief "Thank you, Lena," she disappeared, leaving me alone in the kitchen.

When the kettle steamed again, I swung it away from the fire, carefully lifting it off its hook. It was the smaller kettle, the one used to heat water for tea, but even so the weight of it tugged at the scars on my chest. I rested it on the kitchen table before I took the last steps over to the counter where the basin awaited, put it down again, and counted to twenty before I lifted it again to tip the water into the basin.

Washing dishes had never been such hard work. Four plates, knives and forks, and a few serving bowls, and by the time they were washed, dried, the wash-water poured away and the kettle returned to the fire, I needed to sit. I had done little that used my upper body in the last weeks. My chest ached. I explored the area with my fingers: no bleeding, just the tenderness of healing tissue after use.

I rested, looking out the kitchen window to where Kyreth worked in the herb garden. I wondered what else I could do. Washing hung on a clothesline, moving slightly in the gentle breeze. *I would fetch that in, when the warmth of the day began to fade,* I decided. I got up and went outside, to tell Kyreth.

And so it went, for a week, ten days: I did household chores, more each day, and began to run errands for Marta, delivering salves and teas, finding my way around Berge. The scars hurt less, and I grew stronger. When it was sunny and dry, I would linger at the top of the cliff, watching the sea, breathing in the familiar smells. I thought about returning to Tirvan. The thought made me oddly uncomfortable, and I tried to analyse what it was. *Surely I wanted to go home?* It was all I had thought about, many times, on the Wall, and as a hostage. But when I turned my mind to my village, to my little boat *Dovekie,* to the work out on the sea and at the jetty, I felt the inertia of reluctance underneath the pull of the familiar.

On a clear afternoon, I sat on the wall above the harbour watching a small boat, in design and size almost identical to *Dovekie,* sailing in to the jetty, crewed by two women, working together with the competence of long practice. Observing them, I realized the source of my vacillation about going home. *Who would I fish with? Or live with?* As I analysed this thought, I saw it was deeper than that. My life in Tirvan had been, since earliest childhood, shared with Maya. We had been friends, then lovers, then partners in life and work. In the weeks between her exile and when I had left Tirvan to search for her, invasion, and aftermath had distracted me. While I had missed her, deeply and intensely, there had been too much else to think about and do. I had not considered what my life there would look like without her, forever. Now, confronting that truth, I wondered if it was truly the life I wanted. There would be a thousand reminders of her at Tirvan. *But if I did not go home, then where? What would I do? Stay a Guard on the Wall? Go to Han, and learn to breed and train horses? Go back to Casilla and the fishing fleet there?*

"Lena!"

I turned to see Kyreth running towards me. "What is it?" I called, standing.

"There is a soldier, come to see you," she said breathlessly. "An older man, with a beard."

Casyn. I followed her through the village, walking quickly, resisting the impulse to run. He was standing outside Marta's house, by its low wall, looking down the track towards us.

"Lena," he said, and opened his arms. I went into them, hugging him tighter than the soldier's embrace called for, resting against his strength. It was he who pulled back, just slightly, and I took the cue and stepped away, looking up into his lined face.

"I hoped I would see you," I said. He smiled.

"You look well," he said. "Very well. Your mother is skilled in healing. When Cillian brought you to the harbour, we thought you were dying."

"I know," I said. "I think I was. Casyn, thank you for sending for her." The words were inadequate, but he understood.

"It was Marta's idea. She said if anyone on this side of the Wall could save you it would be Gwen of Tirvan, and the fact she was your mother was even better. One of the fisherwomen here went, by boat, to save us sending a fighting man. Or woman," he added.

How did Marta know of my mother? But there was a more pressing question. "What happened, Casyn? You turned Fritjof back, I know, but how? Where?"

He smiled again. "Shall we sit?" he said, indicating the steps leading down to the road. Kyreth had disappeared. We sat side by side. The stones were warm from the afternoon sun, now beginning to wester over the sea. Casyn said nothing for a minute, collecting his thoughts.

"When Cillian—or rather Piet, the fisherman, with Cillian and you on board—reached the military harbour, we had three ships at anchor: *Skua*, *Osprey* and *Petrel*, with crews totalling just under a hundred men. Cillian told us there was one Marai ship in pursuit, possibly, if they had not turned back, believing you dead; he guessed that ship was lightly crewed, perhaps no more than ten men."

"Wait," I said. "Why would they have believed us dead?"

"Ah, of course," he answered, "you wouldn't know. Cillian persuaded Piet to bring you here in his own boat. The one you took was towed out behind until the waters were deep, and then overturned, in the hope the pursuing ship would find it and think you drowned. As far as we know, it worked."

"That was good thinking," I admitted.

"It was," Casyn agreed.

"Fritjof had said he would sail south three days after his crowning," I said. "We must have been three days getting here, and the winds were with us. So you must have met him off the coast of Linrathe."

Casyn shook his head. "Do you not remember? The weather was changing, the night you fell ill. The winds switched to the south. Cillian and Piet rowed here as much as they sailed. It gave us the advantage.

We met them further north, and we took them almost entirely by surprise. They turned inland, rowing up a river to escape our larger ships, and were caught by Linrathe's men: Lorcann, Donnalch's brother, had been riding north at all speed, once he had gathered his troops. By pure chance, we came together nearly at the same place."

"Is Fritjof dead?"

"No. He escaped north, back into Varsland. Lorcann tells me there are a hundred islands and inlets where he could have hidden. We chose not to pursue him."

By Lorcann. A chill arose inside me. "Casyn," I said. "What has happened to Donnalch?"

I saw the flash of pain on his face. "He is dead," he said gently. "Fritjof killed him."

I put up a hand to my mouth. *The* Teannasach, *dead.* "Dagney said he would," I said after a moment.

Casyn raised an eyebrow. "Did she?"

"She tried to warn him, with a song she sung." Casyn's face showed doubt. I frowned. "Did you think it was because of *me*? Because I escaped?"

He spread his hands. "You and Cillian. It may have been part of the reason."

"Dagney tried to warn him." I repeated, my voice rising. "Did Fritjof kill Dagney too?"

"No. She is safe. Lorcann said that Fritjof would not kill a...a singer— although he used another word, or he would bring down the wrath of all their gods on his people."

"A *scáeli*," I said. "More than a singer. They keep the history of their people, in the songs and stories." Emotions battled in me; relief for Dagney, sorrow for Donnalch. *And Ardan,* I remembered, *who Fritjof had had killed earlier. Who else, either on the island or in the battle?*

"Lena," Casyn's voice was solemn. "There is more, and this will be even harder to hear. Should I call your mother, to be with you?"

I stared at him. *Was Callan dead? Or Garth? Skua* had been among the ships in battle. I searched Casyn's face: it was grave, and I could see sorrow in his eyes, but not, I thought, what I would see if his brother had been killed, or if he had to tell me that Garth was dead. I shook my head. "Tell me," I said.

He sighed. "Fritjof taunted the men of Linrathe with Donnalch's death. He had beheaded him, and carried his head with him on his ship." I swallowed, hard. "He told them Donnalch was dead because he, Fritjof, had claimed you as hostage and bride for his son, and you had broken that treaty." I must have made a sound, because he put out a hand to touch my shoulder. "He was trying to turn them, Lena, by telling them that you were untrustworthy, and by extension all the Empire as well. He failed: for the greatest part, the men of Linrathe stood with their leader and with us, and we prevailed against the Marai." He fell silent. Cold emanated out from my core.

I forced the words through my lips. "For the greatest part?"

"There were some who believed him." He took a breath. "Lena, do you remember the terms of the truce signed on the Wall? That your life was forfeit, were the truce to be broken?"

I nodded. "But the truce was not broken, not by us."

He hesitated. "You killed a man," he said finally.

"A man who tried to rape me! And that was not in Linrathe!"

"But it was in Sorham, which is Linrathe's. But even without that, Lena, even if that killing could be explained and excused—which it is, in my mind—Fritjof claimed he killed the *Teannasach* as a direct response to your escape. Yours and Cillian's." He looked away.

"And?" I whispered. "What is it you aren't telling me, Casyn?"

"Two men left the fight after hearing Fritjof's words," Casyn said, his voice almost a monotone. "They rode east, and south, to where Darel was."

"No. Not Darel. No..." I started to weep. "How could I have foreseen this?" I said between sobs. "I was trying to save Donnalch, Casyn...oh, Darel..."

"By the terms of the truce Linrathe had the right," Casyn said bleakly. "Although the right did not reside in those two men, and Lorcann has had them killed."

"That will be little comfort to Turlo," I sobbed. Casyn took my hand. We sat on the cooling steps as the sun dipped further into the sea and the light dimmed. Slowly, a cold truth crept into my battered and grieving mind. I took a deep breath, and another, and wiped my eyes and face with my free hand. "General." My voice rasped with weeping, and a bout of coughing kept me from speaking for some minutes. Casyn took his hand away, straightening. I stood. He too brought himself to his feet. I looked up at him, controlling the coughs. "By the terms of the truce," I said, "my life is forfeit too."

His grey eyes never left mine. In them I saw regret, and deep pain, and the clear honesty I had always seen. "Yes, Guardswoman," he answered.

I forced myself not to look away. "Better that I had died, then," I said. "Does my mother know?"

He shook his head, a tiny motion. "No."

No-one has told her, I thought, *but she is a council-leader, and she will know what the truce said. She can work it out.* "Will you send her away, before...before it is done?"

"There will be a trial," he said. "For you, and for Cillian, although he will be tried by his own people, of course. Do you not want her here, for that? I cannot force her to go, Lena. She is a guest of Marta, and of Berge."

He was right, of course. It was only my life he could order. "The trial is a formality," I said. A shadow of indecision passed over his face.

"Much rests on it," he answered. "Lorcann—he will be *Teannasach* soon, and is now save for the ceremony—thinks more in black and white than his brother did. He will, we are nearly sure, sign a permanent truce with the Empire, for we are not the enemy snapping at Linrathe's heels, but rather an ally, now. And we too need Linrathe, as a buffer between us and the Marai. But before that, we—Callan— must prove he is a man of his word."

I was a piece in the game, I thought, not for the first time, *a piece of little worth, to be sacrificed to the greater plan.* I remembered accusing Callan of treating the women's villages that way, all those months ago at his winter camp, after the Lestian invasion. He had not denied it then, not entirely. I should have remembered that, when I agreed to be a hostage.

I took a deep breath against the welling anger and fear. "Thank you, General. Will I be told when the trial is?"

"Of course, Guardswoman. Expect it to be another week; I was here in part to judge if you were strong enough to be tried. My judgement is you need a little more time."

"I am not strong enough to be executed?" I shot back.

He sighed. "Not that. But do you not want time with your mother, time to write letters?"

"No!" I snapped. "I do not want my mother to know. Better she thinks I died another way, a relapse perhaps. Can you grant me that, General?"

He spread his hands. "I could...but if she is still here, in Berge?"

"She won't be," I said. "I will find a way to send her home. Cannot I be tried at the White Fort?"

"Perhaps," he answered. "I will suggest it." His face softened. "Lena..."

"No, General," I said, as coldly as I could. "We must be Guardswoman and General, now." He held me in that grave, assessing gaze, for a heartbeat, and another. Then he nodded.

"Farewell, Guardswoman," he said. "I will make my recommendations. Please let me know your mother's plans."

"I will, General," I answered. "Farewell."

I watched him walk away to the north. Suddenly my legs gave out. I sat, hard, on the steps, cold now in the dusk, and took several deep and unsteady breaths. *Darel,* I thought, tears starting again. *Brave, funny, irreverent Darel. I hope it was a quick death.* He was only fourteen, and so like his father. *So like his father...*the thought reverberated in my fogged mine. *I must tell Casyn about Cillian, about his likeness to Callan.* In the horror of what he had told me, I had not thought of it. *Perhaps it could save his life.*

"Lena?" My mother spoke from the porch. "Come in. It's getting cold."

I stood, wiping my eyes, wondering how to face her. But she had seen my hand go to my face, and came towards me. "What's wrong? What did Casyn say to you?"

"Just...deaths," I said. "He came to tell me of deaths. The *Teannasach* of Linrathe, and Turlo's son, Darel. The other hostage."

"Oh, Lena," She put her arms around me, holding me. I took a deep breath, and started to cough again. I pulled away to cover my mouth, unable to stop the deep racking spasms. "Into the house," she ordered, "and into bed. Now, Lena."

She helped me up to the porch and up the stairs to my room. I undressed. She pulled a thick nightdress over my head and pulled back the covers for me. I climbed in, letting her tuck the blankets around me as if I were a child, piling pillows behind me so I was half-upright. "Tea, soup, and sleep," she said. "Tea first, and a salve for your chest. I will be back in a few minutes."

But it was Kyreth who brought me the tea, tasting of honey and herbs, warm and soothing for my raw throat. The coughing subsided. The salve my mother brought smelt of the same herbs, and it too warmed me where it was rubbed into the skin of my chest. I submitted to all these ministrations calmly, glad at some level of the distraction. But after I had drunk my soup, and another cup of tea, had had a heated stone tucked into the bedcovers at my feet, and the curtains closed against the night, I was left alone with the stark truths Casyn had told me. I was responsible for two deaths, of people I had known and liked. For that, I too would have to die.

CHAPTER SEVENTEEN

I SHOULD NOT HAVE SLEPT, BUT THERE MUST have been poppy in that last cup of tea, for I did, for some hours. It was past midnight when I woke. I got up to use the chamberpot, afterwards pushing the curtains aside to look out into the night. Stars gleamed from between clouds, but there was no moon.

I would be sentenced to death, in a week or so. Cold words, to match the cold inside me. Oddly detached, I thought about what that would mean. *How was it done? A knife to the throat? Hanging?* I shivered. *I would prefer the knife,* I thought. *Something quick.* I remembered the gurgling, coughing death of the boy whose throat I had cut, when Leste had invaded, and that of the fisherman in the water. *Maybe not. Although it would be only fair, somehow.*

Only fair. *What was fair about this?* The cold in me coalesced into the ice of anger. I had risked my life to bring word of the Marai plans to the Emperor, and this was how I was rewarded? *Should I have just allowed them to invade, while I myself became an unwilling bride?*

The anger grew. I wanted to smash something, or scream, or both, but some vestige of civility, here in Marta's house where I was a guest, kept me from doing so. I paced the room, the word *'unfair'* pulsing in my mind.

Finally, I sat on the bed, drained and numb. I looked up at the window again, and as I did so my eyes fell on my books: my journal and Colm's history.

I went to the shelf, took the history, lit a candle. In its flickering light, I leafed through the opening pages. I thought I knew these words by heart. I read, once again, the description of Lucian's reign. In the third paragraph, a line caught my attention:

'But the decree from the Emperor after the Partition vote was not to the liking of many men and women, not even some men senior in the army and long trusted by Lucian, even though that disagreement meant their death by the laws of the Empire.'

I read quickly.

> 'The northern people, beset by the same conditions unsuited to crop or cattle, began a series of skirmishes south, raiding for whatever food could be taken. As the days shortened the Emperor gathered his troops and rode north to meet the enemy, but three things were against him: the cold and snow of an early winter; the lack of adequate rations for his men, and the presence, in the enemy's bands, of men of the Empire, who had trained and fought with Lucian and knew his tactics. Among these men may have been the generals who had disagreed with Lucian, for he had commuted their sentences of death to banishment, outcast beyond the Empire's borders, as was his right as Emperor.'

I stopped reading. *Was there a chance for me, here?* I thought back to Callan, pronouncing summary justice on Blaine and Nevin, after their betrayal, the cold steel in his voice. He had shown his rogue commanders no pity, no generosity. *Would he deal with me in the same way?*

Part of me could not believe it. Blaine and Nevin had been complicit in a plan to kill the Emperor, an act of treason. I had broken a truce and a promise to bring word of a planned attack. *Surely these would not have the same punishment? But I had violated an oath given in the Emperor's name. Was that not also treason?*

I slept a bit more, fitful dozing rather than deep sleep, but when the sun rose I was awake, a few decisions made. I would use Colm's history to plan my defense, and I would tell my mother as little as possible. I would try to get her to leave, even if it meant telling her lies. The anger remained, coiled and cold inside me, and beyond that, deeper and even colder, the terror of what was to come, but I would ignore them both, for now. I dressed and went downstairs. The day was damp, a fine misty rain falling. I took a shawl from a peg in the kitchen to cover my head and shoulders as I went out to the privy to empty the chamberpot, shivering slightly in the cool air.

Back inside I met my mother on the stairs. "Lena," she said. "Why aren't you in bed?"

"Because I am awake, and feeling fine," I said. "I'm not even coughing." Which was true, apart from a few shallow coughs when I first got out of bed. "And I'm hungry. All I had for supper was the broth."

She regarded me, her hands moving to re-pin the knot of her hair. "All right," she said. "But stay indoors, near the fire, and rest this afternoon. And tell me if you start to cough again."

"I will," I promised.

I washed and dressed and went back downstairs, to find Marta in the kitchen. "There's tea," she said, indicating the pot keeping warm on the stove. I poured myself a cup, sliced some bread, and sat at the table to eat.

"Marta," I said, "did you know of my mother, before she came here to tend me?"

"Of course," she said. "Gwen of Tirvan is an honoured name among midwives and healers, did you not know? We have exchanged letters over the years, sharing what we know of the uses of healing herbs, and other ways of treating illness and injury. Her knowledge of the uses of anash, for example, goes far beyond what many others know, myself included. We have had some long talks while she has been here."

I shook my head. "I had no idea," I said. "She is just my mother, and our healer and midwife."

Marta laughed. "It is always so," she said. "What made you ask?"

"Something the General said, when he came to see me yesterday," I answered. "Shall I do these dishes, Marta, and then chop vegetables for soup?"

I spent the morning doing kitchen chores. These tasks seemed unreal, but they were something for my hands to do, and my mind. If I did not focus hard on the steps, I forgot things, forgot even what I was doing, sometimes. When the bread was rising and the mid-day soup simmering, I poured myself tea and sat at the kitchen table. I leafed through Colm's history, looking for other instances of Emperors choosing to banish a wrong-doer, rather than execute them. If I were given a chance to speak in my defense, I needed to know this history.

I found a brief reference to the exile of a murderer in Mathon's reign, clemency granted because the Emperor thought the killing, retribution for a physical attack, a form of self-defence. *Had I not killed the fisherman for the same reasons?* I read the passage again, committing it to memory.

In the late morning, the skies cleared a bit, the fine rain giving way to a weak and watery sunshine. I took the book back to my room and went outside to gather greens and radishes for the meal. When I came back in, my mother was in the kitchen, setting the table.

"What else did Casyn say yesterday?" she asked. "Something has upset you. Will you be allowed to go home?"

I hesitated. I had planned what to say, when she asked this. "No," I said, and saw her face fall. "Not yet. There will be a hearing, for me and Cillian, a formality, Casyn says, and then I will either be sent back to the *Ti'ach*, if the peace still requires hostages, or allowed to leave the Emperor's service." *Half a lie.*

"I see," she said. "You must be disappointed, Lena. You wanted to come back to Tirvan."

"I did. Or I thought I did, when I was first recovering. But I'm not sure, now."

"Why not?"

What would she believe? "I'd like to see everyone," I said. "But I don't know how to live there without Maya. Everything we did, apprenticing, fishing from *Dovekie*, we did together. I don't know if I can go back to that life." *And I never will,* I thought, glad of the cold that numbed me, keeping tears from my eyes.

"Had you not left Tirvan, you might have found a way," she said thoughtfully. "And you may yet, but I think I understand." She held out her arms, and I let her hug me, and did my best to hug her back.

"Mother," I said, when we had stepped apart, "should you not be going home, yourself? I am well, or nearly so, and I think you are worrying about Tirvan, regardless of how competent you know Kira to be."

She laughed. "You are right. But I was more worried about you. And I still am."

"But I am fine," I insisted, hoping she could not see the lie in my eyes. "And the fishing boats will be growing busier as the weather warms; if anyone is going to make time to sail you home, it needs to be soon. I will be going back to the Wall, to the White Fort, for the hearing and the decision." If she thought the hearing would not be here, at the coastal fort, she would have no reason to stay.

"Perhaps you are right," she admitted. "You are past danger. I will stay, though, if the fisherwomen will bear with me, until you leave for the Wall. And you will send word?"

"Of course," I promised.

"Oh, my dear," she said. "I hope you find what you want, wherever you go."

I tried to smile. "So do I," I said.

How, I wondered, *could I get a note to Casyn, once my mother's plans were made?* I could ask my mother how she had sent word of my health, if I told her I wanted to send greetings to Cillian. But I did not need to: after the mid-day meal, Casyn's soldier-servant, Birel, arrived, leading a compact chestnut gelding behind his own horse.

"Guardswoman," he greeted me, swinging down off his bay. "The General has sent you this horse and its tack, as compensation for the loss of your mare. He's newly-shoed, and a good steady horse. I've ridden him myself, at times."

"Hello, Sergeant," I said. "This is unexpected." *Did this mean I would be riding to the White Fort?* I stepped off the porch to go to the horse's head. I let him smell me, rubbing his neck. He snuffled my hand, blew out, and stood quietly. "What's his name?" I asked. He was slightly taller than my Clio, with heavier legs.

"Suran. He'll serve you well, I've no doubt. I was also to tell you: his food and stabling will be paid by the General, while you are in Berge. And now I should be getting back."

"Wait," I said, adding quickly "if you would. I'd like to send a note to the General. I won't be five minutes."

"Of course," he replied. He stood at ease, holding the two horses. I ran inside and up the stairs to my room. Writing as quickly as I could, I thanked Casyn for the horse and then made my request: could he, somehow, call me back to the fort some days before the trial? My mother would leave Berge then, I wrote. I signed the note, folded it, sealing it with wax from my candle.

Back outside I handed it to Birel. He slipped it into his tunic pocket. "I'll see he gets it, Guardswoman," he said. Then he held out his hand to me. Surprised, I took it. "You're a brave soldier, Lena," he said roughly. "There'll be many who'll speak for you, if necessary. Don't lose heart."

*So he knew...*but of course he did. Men like him, who served the senior officers, were privy to many secrets. The unexpected kindness touched me. "Thank you, Birel," I said. He nodded, mounting his bay to ride back to the fort. I watched him leave, then turned to the horse whose reins I held. "Well," I said, "what to do with you?" I looped the reins around the gate-post, and went in search of Marta.

She was mixing a salve in the still-room, instructing Kyreth. "Keep stirring," she said to her apprentice. "What can I do for you, Lena?"

I explained about the horse. "Where can I stable him? The army will pay; I am still a soldier."

She nodded. "They sent money for your care and food here, too. Our own ponies are pastured at the top of the village, and there is a barn for poor weather, but it won't be an army stable."

"It will be fine," I said. "Army horses are adaptable; they are often picketed outside, in all weathers. Who do I see about it?"

"Risa. She's probably up with the sheep, in the fields. If not, her apprentices will know where she is."

"Thank you," I replied. I went back out, looking east; there were sheep grazing on the uplands. I untied Suran, adjusted the stirrups, and using the steps as a mounting block, swung up into the saddle. He stood steady as I mounted, and obeyed the reins without hesitation.

I tested his paces as we rode towards the pasture, finding he had a comfortable trot and a rolling, easy canter. My own muscles ached even from this brief test, so I brought him back to a walk as I approached the lower fields where a group of ponies grazed. The breeze was off-shore, and their heads went up as we came closer, the wind carrying the smell of a strange horse to them. They trotted up to the wall. Three of them were heavily in foal. I brought Suran closer, letting them smell each other; if he was to share a field with them, the sooner they got to know each other, the better.

No-one seemed to be around. I surveyed the higher fields, and there I could see two figures and a dog, working the sheep. I followed a track up between the walls.

"Are you Risa?" I called, as I approached them.

"I am," she called back. "Give me a minute; we're nearly done with this group." I watched, recognizing the task she was at: dagging, clipping dried dung off the flanks of the sheep. Now the weather was warming, the dung attracted flies, which would lay their eggs in the dung; when the larvae hatched, they would burrow into the sheep's flesh. I remembered why I hated sheep.

I dismounted, letting Suran drop his head to graze. Risa finished her work and, after a word to her apprentice, came over to me. "Lena, isn't it?" she asked.

"Yes," I said. "I've just been assigned a horse, to get me back into riding shape before I return to duty. I'll need a place to pasture him and store his tack, for a week or so. The army will pay. Can I turn him loose with the ponies?"

"He'll need some hay, too, if you are going to be riding him daily," she said. "But it's there in the barn. There's a tack room. Will you be taking care of him?"

"Yes."

"Good; we're busy right now, as you can see. There's a small paddock just by the barn; put him there for a day or so. It adjoins the geldings' field. I don't want him in with the mares; they're too close to foaling. Does that suit?"

She reminded me of Daria, from Karst: plain-spoken, practical, and good-hearted. "Yes, of course," I said. "Can I ride around here for a bit, before I turn him out?"

She shrugged. "It won't bother the sheep."

"Thanks," I said, and with a wave to the apprentice, I kept riding. The track curved up to the higher pastures. Near the top, I stopped. North of us, I could see the line of the Wall, following the landscape. I was high enough to see a couple of the watch-towers, spaced along its length. The coastal fort spread out southward from its line, itself walled and towered, and below both, ships stood at anchor in the harbour. One of them could be *Skua*. I hoped not. I did not want Garth, or Dern, to witness my trial. *But maybe it would be at the White Fort. Why else would Casyn have sent me a horse?*

I had tried to be a good soldier. From the first day Casyn had ridden into Tirvan, I had done what he asked. *Except once*, I reminded myself. 'Will you come north?' he had asked, in the hours after word of the Wall's breaching had arrived. And I had not, not for long months. *But when I did*, I thought, *I served the Emperor well, on the Wall and then as hostage.* The anger in me twisted. *Why had I done what Casyn had asked, and Callan, so blindly, so trustingly?* Tears rose in my eyes. *From the wind*, I told myself. *What a fool I had been, seeing only the adventure, and not the cost.*

I rode back down to the barn and paddock. I unsaddled and curried Suran, turning him out into the paddock with a biscuit of hay. The geldings in the next field trotted over to examine him; nothing untoward happened, so I went back into the dim barn to put away his tack. My back and legs ached from the riding, and my thigh muscles trembled. I was glad the walk back to Marta's house was downhill.

"The army has sent me a horse," I told my mother at supper that evening, "so that I can re-accustom my body to riding. I would think I will be called back to the Wall in about a week, and then on to the White Fort."

"I hope they do not ask you to ride all day," she said, frowning.

I shrugged. "They know I have been very ill. I am to tell them when I can ride for half a day," I lied, "so that is what they expect." I concentrated on the fish on my plate. I had no interest in food, but I knew my body needed fuel.

"Don't push yourself," she warned. "I spoke with the fisherwomen today. Elga, who fetched me from Tirvan, is willing to take me back in a few days. While she was waiting for me to pack my things when she came to find me, she spoke with Dessa, and there are some ideas about boat design she'd like to discuss with her. So, she is happy to take me back, but as you guessed she wants to do it soon. I will tell her tomorrow to choose a day."

"If the seas allow," I said, the fisherwoman's caution coming automatically to my lips.

The weather held, only small showers of rain blowing through, not enough to keep the boats off the water. I rode Suran daily, rain or no, testing his trot and his canter, strengthening my muscles and building my endurance. I wanted no weakness to prevent me from riding to the White Fort. I ached from the effort, and part of me wished Berge had baths like Tirvan's, to soak my tired body in at the end of the day, but no hot springs bubbled out of the ground here. There was a bath house, but using it meant building fires to heat water, and I couldn't be bothered to go to that effort.

I found no more mention of banishment in Colm's history. I thought of the books on Perras's shelves, at the *Ti'ach*, and wondered what the punishment for treason would be in Linrathe. I knew what it was in Varsland, under Fritjof. *Was there an argument there, that we were better than the Marai?* I turned that around in my mind, examining it from every side. I could not decide. *Who could I ask?* The only possibility was Cillian, were I allowed to talk to him. *Where was he?*

I needed to get to the Wall, I thought, frustrated. I was well, and the advice I needed now could come neither from my mother, nor the women of Berge. That afternoon, I turned Suran's head north. A tower stood where the fort's wall turned back toward the Wall. A lone soldier looked north, his eyes moving from the sea to the lands beyond the fort, and back again. He did not look south: what threat could be expected, from Berge?

"Soldier!" I called. He turned rapidly.

"What do you want?" he called down.

"I am Guardswoman Lena, lately of the White Fort garrison. I have been recuperating from injuries at Berge. I need to send a message to the General Casyn that I am well and can return to my duties. Can you take this message?"

"At the end of my watch," he said. It would do.

"Thank you," I called back. I saw him nod, his eyes returning to the sea. I reined Suran south, and gave him a gentle kick. He broke into a canter, and then with further encouragement from me a gallop. I turned him east, along the track that ran up into the hills, climbing higher, until we reached the highest ridge. From here the land unrolled before me in all directions, and just to the east I could see the road, the road that ran from the Wall south to the Four-Ways Inn, before turning east to Casilla; the road I had ridden almost every mile of, save this most northern section.

What if I just kept riding? The idea shimmered in my mind like a sea-mirage, beckoning, but like those false visions of islands on the horizon, I knew it had no substance. I would be followed, caught, to stand trial not only for treason but also for desertion. I sat on my horse, feeling the wind in my hair, my eyes taking in the space and distance that had always been my deepest solace.

A flash of movement, high in the hazy sky, caught my attention. I searched the sky. *What had I seen?* There it was, again: a tiny speck, blinking in and out of the high clouds to the west, circling, until it suddenly dropped, straight down, plunging arrow-fast toward the sea. A *fuádain*, I realized, the wandering falcon, remembering the bird I had seen hunt from Donnalch's hand so few weeks earlier. But this one flew free.

Birel came for me the next morning. I had packed my bag in expectation, and given my thanks to Marta and Kyreth. Suran stood, saddled and bridled, at the gate. I sat on the porch of Marta's house with my mother, waiting. I had to keep our speech light, or I would break.

"Mother," I began, "I didn't realize you were such an honoured healer. But both Marta and Casyn say you are. Shouldn't I have known that?"

"Why would you?" she said simply. "And I don't know that I'm all that honoured. Tirvan has a few more books on healing and midwifery than some other villages, and I have spent time reading them. I have shared some of what I have learned with other healers, by letters. That's all." She smiled. "And Marta is twenty years younger than I am, so she sees me as vastly more experienced. Although she knows things I don't, such as different methods to treat frost-burn."

"If there were somewhere you could go, to learn more, somewhere with more books, would you?"

"What do you mean?"

"Sorley—he was another student at the *Ti'ach*, the house of learning that I was at—told me there is one *Ti'ach* that specializes in healing. He said you could go there, for a season, if there was a peace. Would you, if you could?"

"Oh," she said. "I don't know. North of the Wall?" Her hands went to her hair.

"Yes," I said, "north of the Wall. The *Ti'acha* are unlike anything we have in the Empire: communities of men and women, dedicated to learning and teaching. I would have enjoyed my time at *Ti'ach na Perras*, I think, learning more history, and about peoples we didn't even know existed." I sighed. "But other events took over."

"Well," she said. "It's tempting, now Kira is qualified."

"And you might have things to teach them," I suggested. "Perras—he was the head of the *Ti'ach* where I was sent—was shocked to learn you knew of the Eastern Fever. He said he wished he could talk to you about it."

"But there would need to be a peace," she said.

"I think there will be," I answered. "Casyn told me that Lorcann—he will be the new *Teannasach* of Linrathe—will sign a treaty; we need to be allies, if the Marai are to be held back." *And if the Emperor assuaged his anger with my punishment, and Cillian's,* I thought.

I looked away, hiding my face from my mother, to see Birel riding towards the house. "It's time," I said, standing. Fear and relief battled inside me. I glanced up at the sky. "The weather will hold," I said, "for your sailing." My mother had gone to see Elga yesterday evening, after I had told her I would be leaving in the morning. They would sail on the afternoon's tide.

I let my mother hold me, but only briefly. She kissed me on the forehead. "Say hello to Kira, and everyone," I said. "I will write, when I know where I am posted." My mouth felt stiff, the words forced out, hoarse to my own ears. I thought I was trembling, but my hands on Suran's reins were steady. I swung up into the saddle.

203

"Farewell, my daughter," my mother said. I could hear the tears in her voice. *Did she know, or suspect, more than she was saying?* I raised a hand, willed a smile, and walked Suran forward to meet Birel.

"Ready, Guardswoman?" he asked.

"I am, Sergeant," I lied.

CHAPTER EIGHTEEN

WHEN WE WERE FREE OF THE VILLAGE, I moved up to ride beside Birel. "Where will I be taken, Sergeant?" I asked.

"First, to the General," he said.

"And then?" He did not answer, simply shaking his head. I realized it was unfair to ask him. "Where is Cillian?" I asked. "Do you know?"

"In the fort's prison," he said. "The northmen asked us to hold him."

Why? I did not ask. We rode to the gate-tower that faced Berge. On the flat ground bordering the fort, men were practicing swordplay. No-one looked our way. The wooden gates swung open at Birel's command, moving noiselessly on their huge iron hinges. The street beyond was cobbled and ditched. Buildings lay on either side. I recognized them from the White Fort: barracks and stables, workshops and the baths, and in the centre, where the two major streets crossed, the headquarters. The shouts of officers, the ring of hammer on anvil, the smell of roasting meat from the kitchens; all were familiar.

Outside the headquarters Birel halted. We dismounted. A cadet appeared to take our horses. *Would I see Suran again?* I followed Birel through a courtyard, where a cracked bowl as wide as I was tall sat in the centre, an incomplete border of blue tiles around its rim. I wondered what it was for. The walls of the courtyard were pillared and arched; every second arch was a window, some shuttered, some open. The centre archway on each wall held a door. Birel stopped. "Give me your bag," he said. I complied. He opened the door on the eastern wall, but did not cross the threshold. "General," he said. "Guardswoman Lena, as you requested." He gestured to me to enter.

Casyn sat beneath the window, writing. I blinked in the dimmer light of the room. He held up a hand, telling me to wait, as he finished what he wrote. I looked around. On the plastered walls, I could just make out a faint pattern in places, diamond shapes under the whitewash. I glanced down at the floor, remembering the pictures in the floor at the White Fort, but here the tiles were dull and worn. Casyn turned to me.

"Guardswoman," he said. "You are well?"

"I am, General," I said. "And I thank you for the horse. I have been riding daily, and can spend several hours in the saddle without discomfort."

"Good. Let me tell you what will happen now," he said bluntly. "I have been in correspondence with the Emperor. He wishes to oversee your trial himself, so we will be riding to the White Fort tomorrow, along with Cillian of Linrathe. Lorcann and our Emperor have chosen to hear your trials together: one trial, one consequence. A united voice."

"To send a message to the Marai, and to those who might support them," I said.

He nodded. "Exactly. And I must ensure that there is no difference in how you and Cillian are treated, now you are here at the Wall's End fort, so when our interview is done you will be taken to the prison, Guardswoman, for this night. And you will both ride shackled. We must be seen to be punitive." He frowned. "Is your mother gone?"

"She sails this afternoon," I said.

"Good. Have you anything to say to me, Guardswoman, before the sergeant escorts you to the prison? We will debrief on the ride, but is there anything you would wish others not to hear?" His voice was formal, brusque, but his eyes were not.

"Yes," I said, relieved I had this chance. I owed it to Cillian; he had saved my life. Perhaps I could save his. "General, you know I am good at seeing likenesses; it was how I recognized Garth." He nodded. "I think..." I hesitated, looking for a way to say this, "Is it possible that Cillian could be the Emperor's son?"

His eyes widened. He said nothing for some moments, thinking. "How old is he?"

He had not dismissed the idea. "Thirty-three."

"What do you know of his mother?"

"Only that she was very young; she lived just north of the Wall, and he has always been told his father was a soldier of our Empire. As far as I know, his mother died very soon after his birth."

"Do you know her name?"

I shook my head. "No."

"What did you see in Cillian, Lena, to make you think this?" he asked.

"The first time I saw him, I thought I knew him. Then I decided I was wrong, but every so often I would see a glimpse of something, a reminder...and then one day he was very angry, and he was exactly like the Emperor, on Midwinter's Day, after Colm was killed. And since then, I can't not see the likeness."

He leant back in his chair, thinking. "Have you said this to anyone else?"

"Only Cillian himself," I answered.

"Cillian? Why?"

"Because he hates the Empire, General," I said, a flash of anger heating my words, "and I needed him on my side, on our side, to bring you word of the Marai, to not see us as another enemy."

"Well," he said, "I may wish you had not done so, but I follow your reasoning. But did Cillian?"

I shook my head. "I don't know. I fell ill too soon after the conversation to be sure. But he saw that an alliance with our Empire was better than being conquered by the Marai, although reluctantly, I believe."

"It is likely of little importance," Casyn said, "except that it might affect how he comports himself, at the trial. Do you have any influence with him?"

"Probably not," I said. "And what will it matter, General, if execution is to be the consequence, and the trial only a formality, a sham?"

His grave eyes studied me. "I did not say that, Lena," he said. "I said much depended on it. The Emperor has the right to determine another punishment, another consequence, but both he and Lorcann must agree."

"Banishment," I said.

"A possibility," he agreed. "Do you see, then, why it is important for Cillian to be co-operative, at the trial?"

I damped down the leap of hope that had arisen at Casyn's words. It was a chance, but a chance dependent on three men: one stranger, angry at the death of his brother; one little better than a stranger, angry at the world, and one the Emperor of a nation at war once again, who had to balance his new and fragile alliance with Linrathe against one life. *But still....*

"I do, General," I said. "I will do my best." I would do as Casyn requested, *but this time it was for me*, I thought. "I will be allowed to speak with him?"

"I will ensure it," he said. He stood. "Now, Guardswoman, I will have Sergeant Birel escort you to the prison." He went to the door. Birel entered promptly: he must have been just outside, I thought. *How much had he heard?*

Casyn returned to his desk to scribble a note. "Give this to Cormaic," he said to the sergeant. "We ride to the White Fort the day after tomorrow. Tell that to Cillian, please."

"Yes, sir," Birel replied.

"General," I acknowledged.

"Dismissed," he said, already turning to his papers. I followed Birel out through the courtyard and along a cobbled street, past barracks and workshops, to a small building adjoining the western wall of the fort. Built of stone blocks, it had been lime-washed once, but now only flakes of a whitish-grey remained; along with the lichens that grew on the bare stones, it gave the building a motley look. Small windows just below the roof were barred, and the door was guarded.

The guard saluted Birel. "Sergeant?"

"Place Guardswoman Lena in a cell adjoining the Linrathan's," Birel instructed. "They are to be allowed free conversation, and she is to have the same exercise daily as the man." He turned to me. "I will return the contents of your bag, Guardswoman, once I have searched it." I was led to my cell; a tiny room, big enough to hold a pallet on the floor, and a bucket, and nothing more. The door was an iron grate, allowing me no privacy. Cillian's cell was directly opposite. I had seen him stand as we came in, hands on the grate of his door.

"Lena," he said. "You are well?" He was pale, thin, his hair longer and unkempt.

"I am," I said. I walked into the cell, hearing the door locked behind me. "And you?"

"Well enough," he said.

"I am to tell you we ride for the White Fort the day after tomorrow," Birel said to Cillian, forestalling anything further he was about to say.

Cillian only nodded. We watched the two men leave, hearing the outside door close and the key turn.

"We have leave to talk," I said to Cillian. "Talk freely, I mean. I have just come from the General Casyn."

"How kind of him," Cillian said, sinking down onto his pallet. "Having saved the Empire, and Linrathe, we are rewarded with prison cells, but are allowed to talk freely to each other. So very generous."

"Be reasonable..." I started to say. I stopped. *Why was I defending the actions of our leaders?* "You're right," I said, letting my banked anger flare. "It's minging unfair. Have you been locked up here the whole time I was sick?"

"Not quite," he said. "At first, I was given a decent room in one of the barracks, and consulted for hours on what I knew about the Marai, and their boats, and where Linrathe's forces might be, all reasonable questions, given the threat. I drew maps and estimated distances and was useful, Lena, useful to Linrathe and the Empire. But then word came back that the *Teannasach* was dead, and suddenly I was here, by the direction of Lorcann, to be tried for treason. Treason! After we saved them, you and me."

"Did you know they are trying us together, the Emperor and your new *Teannasach*, to show a united front to both our peoples? We are game pieces, Cillian, nothing more."

He looked up at that. "That's a different song you're singing," he said quietly.

"Ah, gods," I said, "I'm minging angry, Cillian. I feel like I've been lulled by reasonable words and gently-phrased requests ever since Casyn first came to Tirvan." I moved restlessly in the cell, wanting to pace, but there was not the space.

He laughed, a dry, mirthless sound. "Now you know why I have no love for the machinations of power, whether they are practiced by Emperors or *Teannasachs*."

"What do you know of Lorcann?"

He straightened on his pallet. "Older than Donnalch, by a year or two. Hotter-headed, quicker to anger, holds a grudge. That was why Donnalch was chosen *Teannasach* over him."

Not good, I thought. "Callan is calm, thoughtful, even reasonable—or so I used to think," I amended. "But if he is angered, then he is cold, ruthless even."

For all his bitterness, Cillian was clever. He smiled. "So, we must be careful not to anger either of them. That is what you are saying, isn't it, Lena? And 'we' really means 'me', does it not? But what is the point? The punishment for treason is death."

"Not necessarily," I said. "I read through the history of the Empire again. There are a couple of instances when Emperors banished those who had committed treason, or murder, rather than executing them. If Birel returns my books I will show you the passages."

"Emperors, maybe," he countered, "but in Linrathe's law the punishment is death. So perhaps you will be spared, but not I."

He had answered my question. *Treason,* I thought, *probably meant death in all lands.* But Garth should have died, for desertion, and yet the Empire, Casyn and Dern and ultimately the Emperor, had found another way for him to redeem his failure. *Why not us?*

Time passed. Coarse bread and a cup of water arrived, and with it my pack. I opened it, going through the contents. The books had been returned, and my blood-cloths, but my jar of salve for my scars, my tiny sewing kit, and my flint and tinder had been taken. I slid the history through the bars toward Cillian, telling him which pages to read. He read, squinting in the poor light, then slid the book back to me, shrugging. "So the Emperor has the right to commute a death sentence to exile," he said. "I don't think it matters."

I wanted to scream at him. *Why was he giving up so easily? Because he was right,* I thought. Lorcann would demand death, and regardless of what might be done under the Emperor's prerogative, Callan would stand with Lorcann.

A night and a day and another night passed. My dark thoughts of the first night did not linger; I woke the next morning believing once again that Casyn would find a way to convince the Emperor to pardon us, or at least commute our sentences to exile. I tried to talk to Cillian, but he, sullen and uncommunicative, spent most of his time sitting on his pallet, his knees drawn up, staring at the floor. If I spoke to him, he would answer, but he refused to be drawn into discussion of any possible defense. I gritted my teeth, holding back my frustration: for a man known for his skill in the analysis of strategy, he was not making any effort. As soon as what little light came in through the high, barred, windows faded, he curled himself under the single blanket and slept, or feigned sleep.

My own anger crawled through my gut and my mind, directed now inwardly, at my own choices. I lay awake in the dank cell, in the blackness, asking myself hard, brutal questions. *Why had I gone along with everything asked of me, from the first day Casyn had addressed us in the meeting house at Tirvan? Just who had I been trying to please, or defy?* I tracked my actions, my thoughts, back through the last two years, and beyond, but I found no answers.

A banging on my door awakened me. The cell was dark. I glanced up at the window. The sky was a dark grey, not yet dawn. "What is it?" I asked.

"Get up," the guard said. "You ride today." I heard Cillian mutter something from the opposite cell. I got up, used the bucket, straightened my clothes. I did not look at the door. If the guard watched me, there was nothing I could do about it, except crouch in such a position that only my thigh showed. I picked up my pack—I had used it as a pillow—and waited. My mouth tasted foul, but we had been given no water.

We were escorted out of the prison, one guard for each of us. Outside, two horses stood, tacked and ready: Suran and a dark horse, larger and heavier. "Mount," one of the guards said. I swung up into the saddle. My guard took my bag, pushing it into the saddlebag, before fastening a shackle to one ankle. He passed the attached chain under the belly of my horse, and shackled it to my other leg. I glanced at Cillian; he was chained in the same way. I expected our wrists to be next, but, surprisingly, it was not so. We sat on the horses. Sparrows chirped from under the eaves of the prison. The guards said nothing. I watched the sky pale, the stars growing dimmer, and then I heard the clop of hooves along the cobbled street. Casyn rode up, Siannon's roan coat gleaming in the faint light, Birel beside him.

"Guardswoman," Casyn greeted me. "Cillian na Perras, good morning. We have a long way to ride today; hence, the early start. We are to be at the White Fort the day after tomorrow, by mid-day if we can. We will stop to eat in an hour or so, but let us get underway." The western gates had been opened as he spoke. He rode forward.

"Follow the General," Birel said. "I will bring up the rear." We rode out of the fort. The street became a wider road, swinging south and then east around the wall of the fort. The eastern sky was a pale pink now. I glanced up at the tower at the southern gate, making out the silhouette of a soldier. At this early hour, only the guards on the night watch would see us leave. I wondered if Casyn had planned it that way.

Once past the fort, the road ran parallel to the Wall. The chains jangled quietly as we walked the horses, the weight of the shackles and the chains pulling down on my legs. Shorter stirrups would be more comfortable. I would ask for them to be adjusted, at our first stop.

Casyn slowed Siannon. "Ride beside me, Cillian," he said. "You too, Guardswoman." We did as he asked. "I have questions for you, Cillian na Perras," he said. "Sergeant, fall back, if you please."

"About what, General?" Cillian answered. "I have told you all I know, of the Marai and their ships and their numbers."

"This concerns you, not the Marai," Casyn answered equably. He waited, ensuring, I supposed, that Birel was out of hearing. "Tell me of your mother. Her name, and where she lived."

"Lena has told you her children's tale, then?" he answered. "That I am the Emperor's long-lost son, like a character in one of our *danta*, our story-songs? Based on a fleeting resemblance of dark hair and a grim mouth, or some such?"

"Not only that, although the resemblance is there," Casyn said. "Did you know, Cillian, that the Emperor is my brother? Or that we were in the same regiment for many years, so that he and I were stationed together on the Wall, some thirty-four years past?"

Cillian did not reply for a minute. "No," he said finally, his voice subdued. "I did not know that."

"And so, I am probably the only other man who knows of Callan's love for a young girl called Hafwen, whose family had a small holding perhaps an hour north of the wall, and who brought milk and meat to the fort for trade. That was allowed then, for there was, more or less, peace between Linrathe and the Empire. Callan was on guard duty, the first time Hafwen came with her father. A story that simple, and that old, Cillian. Was Hafwen your mother?"

I looked away from the pain on Cillian's face. "Yes," he said. "That was her name."

"He called her Wenna," Casyn said, his voice soft.

"He deserted her," Cillian said flatly.

"We were ordered south," Casyn said, "unexpectedly, and immediately. There had been a massive storm on the Edanan Sea, with the loss of many ships and extensive damage to both the harbours at Casilla and the Eastern Fort. We rode out with only a few hours notice."

"He could have left word, a letter, something!"

"He did," Casyn said. "He wrote a note, to be left with the quartermaster."

"She never got it," Cillian said flatly. "Why should I believe he ever wrote it?"

"Because I intercepted it," Casyn said. "He was my brother, and he had already risked his life to see Hafwen, and mine, because I covered for him when he left his post. The note was tangible proof. I destroyed it."

"Fuck you," Cillian snarled, clapping his heels into his bay's ribs. The horse sprang forward, running full-out along the road. "Sergeant!" Casyn called. Birel immediately kicked his own horse into a gallop, following him. "Just keep him in sight," Casyn shouted.

"Does the Emperor know?" I asked Casyn after a moment.

He shook his head. "No. I will send him a letter, when we stop, to reach him tomorrow. He needs time to prepare himself."

"He has no other children," I said, half a question.

"No. A few months after we were sent to Casilla, he contracted the swelling complaint. You know it?"

"Of course," I said. "It's a child's illness."

"Yes," he said. "I had it, I remember, before my father came for me. But Callan must not have. He was eighteen, and in grown men there can be swelling here, too," he indicated his groin, "and those that have that sometimes cannot father children, afterwards."

"If he had known of Cillian's birth, what could he have done? You said he risked his life by his liaison with Hafwen, so how could he have acknowledged the child?"

"Ah," he said. "There is a difference between leaving your post to consort with a woman of the north, and at a later time acknowledging a child by the same woman. It was not the liaison itself, but the questions that would have been asked of the how and when, if our commander had discovered the relationship. By our laws, Callan was guilty of desertion, and I of abetting desertion. The penalty for that, as you know, is death."

"Dear gods," I said. "And you have just told Cillian this, knowing how he hates the Empire and the Emperor?"

"A gamble," Casyn said. "Only our reputations can be hurt now, mine and Callan's, and even then, I doubt it would be anything more than a nine-day's whisper."

We rode on. Peewits flew up from the flat land on either side of the road, circling, piping their mournful two notes. As we crested a small rise, I saw ahead of us a watch-tower, a small fort for two or three soldiers, and on the road before it, Cillian and Birel, still mounted. Two soldiers stood with them, one holding Cillian's horse's reins, one standing beside him, sword drawn.

"We'll stop here to eat," Casyn said. He trotted Siannon forward. The soldiers saluted him. "Stand down," I heard him say. "Sergeant, please remove the shackles, so that Guard Lena and Cillian na Perras may dismount."

My legs felt light without the iron shackles. Birel and one soldier led the horses off; the other remained with us, his hand on his sword's grip. Casyn motioned us in through the arched doors of the structure. "The latrine," he said, pointing to a wattled enclosure just inside the gate, "is just there." I glanced at him for permission, and at his nod went to relieve myself.

I emerged to find a soldier waiting for me. "In there," he said, pointing to another wooden hut built against the interior wall of the tiny fort. Inside, once my eyes adjusted to the dim light, I saw Casyn and Cillian seated at a table. Birel was busy at a small stove. I sat. Casyn was writing.

"Do you have anything you wish to say to the Emperor?" he said to Cillian. Cillian shook his head, not looking at Casyn. The general folded the paper. Birel brought over a small brazier. Casyn took his wax from his belt pouch, heated it, and sealed the letter, imprinting the wax with the carved stone in his ring. "This," he said to one of the soldiers, "must reach the Emperor at the White Fort with haste, but daylight riding only. Go now."

"Sir!" A quick salute, and the soldier was gone. Birel brought tea to the table. I heard the clatter of hoofs on the road, already galloping: he would ride at speed for an hour or so, switch horses, and keep going until he was too tired. The note would then be handed over to another rider.

I sipped the tea. From the wooden platter on the table I took a slice of dark bread and a piece of smoked fish, chewy and salt. We ate in silence. The fish made me thirsty. I drank a second mug of tea. Casyn got up and went out. I heard his footsteps on the wooden stairs that led to the watch-tower's platform, and the murmur of voices. I tried to think of what I could say to Cillian. He had eaten almost nothing. In the dark room, his eyes were hollow and black.

Birel finished clearing up. "I'll walk you to the latrine," he said to Cillian. Cillian pushed himself up and went out, followed by the sergeant. I stood too, and went out into the daylight, bending to wipe my greasy hands on a patch of damp grass. Cillian came out of the latrine; Birel went in. I saw Cillian glance at the gate.

"Don't," I said quietly.

He turned his head towards me. "I wasn't going to," he said. "I'm not that stupid."

"Riding off like that wasn't exactly bright," I said. "You're lucky Casyn is a reasonable man."

"You're still defending him," he observed.

"You're a minging idiot," I said. "You went running off as if you were trying to escape. The soldiers here could have killed you, should have, would have, probably, if Birel hadn't been right behind you."

He shook his head. "I wasn't trying to escape. I just needed...some distance. Some space."

"I know," Casyn said from behind us. "That is why I let you go. But not again, Cillian na Perras. Nor do you speak to me again as you did, or you will be riding on a leading rein with your hands bound and your mouth gagged. Do you understand?"

Cillian's mouth twisted. He looked at me, closed his eyes. "Yes, General," he said.

We walked and trotted along the road, not saying much. I watched the rise and fall of the land, and the birds, and the deer that bounded away, letting my mind wander back over the last two years, and beyond. Occasionally Casyn would relate a bit of history to do with the Wall's construction, or the road. At midday, we reached a larger fort, not as big as either the White Fort or Wall's End, but substantially larger than the small watch-towers. Here the horses were unsaddled and fed, and allowed to rest. By now, my legs and back ached, and I too was glad of the break.

Cillian was still quiet, but his face showed less strain. As we walked across to the kitchen, I noticed that the men here were not all Empire's soldiers; a group of Linrathans crossed the open space. One man, with a subtle gesture of hand and chin, pointed us out to his companions.

Birel escorted us to a small room at the back of the fort headquarters. Food and drink were brought. Surprising me, Birel did not stay with us. "The door is guarded," he told us, as he left.

I picked up a piece of bread. There was a small pot of a creamy substance: I prised a little bit out with the wooden knife that had been provided to taste it. Goose fat. The flocks would have been moving north a few weeks earlier, fat from their winter foraging, the hunting parties busy. I spread some on the bread, adding salt. Cillian looked away. "Eat something," I said, beginning to lose patience with his self-pity. "You need the energy."

He made an exasperated sound, but reached forward for the bread. "You saw my countrymen, pointing me out?" he said.

"Pointing us out," I replied, around a mouthful of food. "They could have just been surprised to see a woman at the fort. Most of the other Guards will have gone home to their villages."

He shrugged. "Maybe." He ate a piece of bread. "I thought you said the Emperor was reasonable? If he's anything like his brother, I don't think that's true."

"Why? Because he threatened to gag you, after you swore at him? He's our jailer. What did you think he would do? By the gods, Cillian, he let you ride away. How many men would have done that?"

"You're defending him again," Cillian pointed out.

"I'm not," I protested. "Well, maybe I am, but you're being unfair. I remember Donnalch threatening to send you back to the *Ti'ach* because you couldn't keep a civil tongue towards him, either. Is the problem our leaders, Cillian, or you?"

"And where in this fucking world has your politeness and compliance got you, Lena of the Empire?" Cillian snarled. "You're going to be sentenced to death, just like me. Why do you still believe our leaders are kind and reasonable men?"

Why indeed? "Because they have always treated me that way, I suppose."

"Even when they are trying you for treason? They do not care about us. Get that through your head." He pushed his chair back, standing to pace the tiny room.

"You are wrong, Cillian," I said. "Finn—he was a junior officer—told me they are trained to remember every soldier, and to live their lives to honour those who die, to give those deaths meaning." As I spoke, the reasons I had been trying to find became abruptly clear to me, the pattern obvious, like my sudden understanding of the map on Perras's wall. I already knew why I had given Casyn my trust; I had told my mother, just a couple of days before. Casyn had offered me a wider world, the adventure I sought, but one where I bore little responsibility beyond following orders. *Because the times I had chosen my own path, when I had voted to learn to fight, and again when I had not ridden north when Casyn had first asked, both choices had lost me Maya.*

Hating myself, for what I had not done, and for what I could not be, I had given my allegiance unquestioningly to Casyn and the Emperor, to their strength and knowledge and calm certainties, to their ability to shape the future. *They had seemed*, I realized, *omnipotent.* I went to where I would be welcomed and needed, where most of my choices were made for me, and where I might, just possibly, find a purpose to my life.

But, I thought, with piercing clarity, *neither Casyn, nor even Callan, are the Empire: it is an idea, a political structure, and it does not care about me. Casyn may, does, but the machinations of Empire are not his to command, and they may not even truly be Callan's. The choice that will be made this time isn't about me as a person, but about the value of one Guard in the greater stratagems of war and peace. My purpose is to be something to be bargained, nothing more.*

"They *are* decent men," I said. "You will never make me believe they are not, Cillian. But that does not make the rules of the Empire right, or just, or even some of their decisions the right ones, and," I said, taking a deep breath, "I do not think, any more, that I can trust them, as agents of the Empire, to show mercy to us. And that makes me angry, angry at them, and," I felt tears rising, "angry at myself, for letting myself hope that they would save me, and you."

Cillian sat down at the table. "Forgive yourself," he said, his dark, shuttered eyes holding mine. "Because you are no different than most others: you were told a story and you accepted it. Just like Donnalch let the *torpari* and fisher-folk of Linrathe believe he wanted to invade south to free the oppressed women of the Empire, just like your men believe that the legacy of the Eastern Empire is so sacred that there is no other life for them but the army, we are given reasons, reasons that sound plausible and rational and even unarguable, for why we are to do what our leaders wish. There was a time I tried to believe it all too, but that time is past."

"I think it may be for me, too," I whispered.

"Good," he said. "So what are we going to do?"

"What do you mean?" I asked. "What can we do? You're not suggesting we try to escape?"

He shook his head, impatience visible in every move. "Of course not. How are we going to defend ourselves, at the trial?"

"I tried to ask you that yesterday, and you wouldn't even think about it."

"I was not going to begin planning anything with you while you were still thinking your Emperor would just wave his hand and say, 'forgive them'," he answered. "I have no illusions about Lorcann. He'll have me beheaded as quickly as he can say 'guilty'. I need you to tell me what you know of the Emperor that might help us sway his judgment. How does he want others to see him? That's probably the most important question, but consider not only your own people, but ours. Tell me what you *know*, Lena, not what you feel."

What did I know? "I was told," I began, "that he does not see himself bound by tradition. I would agree with that. At the Midwinter proclamations, before the war with Linrathe began, he announced two changes: one to the military, one to how we—men and women—live our lives."

"Which were?"

"Cadets would have a choice, beyond soldier or medic: they could become builders, without the need to also learn the skills of warfare. And for us, there was to be a new Assembly, a new discussion of our existing Partition agreement, to validate it or to change it."

"Do you know what predicated these changes?" Cillian's voice was calm, his tone one of interest. *He sounded,* I thought, *exactly like his father, asking me questions about my experiences on the road to the Winter Camp.*

"The first one, the choice of becoming a builder, for the cadets, came from his own brother's experiences. Colm, the historian, was Callan's twin, so he knew that whether a man could be a good soldier, or not, had nothing to do with who his father was, or his mother, for that matter." I hesitated. "Do you know what is done to boys who cannot fight, in the Empire?"

"I do," he said. "They are castrated. It is unspeakable."

"Both Casyn and the Emperor agree with you," I said, noting the faint flash of surprise on his face. "That is why they wanted another, honorable path for such boys." I watched as he assimilated this new thought.

"And the Assembly?" he said after a minute.

"The rules of Partition had been broken once we agreed to fight. Callan did not believe we could just go back to those rules, once the need to fight was no longer there. A new Assembly was needed."

"This was his idea?"

"Yes," I said. "And not only his idea, but one I—and I imagine other women like me, on the road after the fighting was done—were charged with spreading, quietly and subtly, to other women, to make it appear that the desire for a new Assembly came from the women's villages."

"Now that is interesting," Cillian said. "Callan understands the importance of stories in shaping choices, it would seem. How can we use that?"

"Cillian," I asked. "What do you see, in your mind, when you are putting all these ideas together?"

"What do I see?" He looked at me, puzzled.

"Yes. All these facts, these ideas, what do they look like, inside your mind?"

He leaned back, his hands behind his head, eyes closed. "Like a map," he said, "with all the ideas connected by lines, or threads. Those that I can't connect are off to the side. If I bring one of those onto the map, it changes the connections and sometimes the positions of the others." He opened his eyes. "Does that make sense to you?"

I nodded. "Listen," I said. "Listen to this: 'He chooses his strategy and deployment based on this picture in his mind, a picture that changes with season and weather, or time of day, and yet he always knows what will happen.'" I quoted. "Someone said that to me about the Emperor once, Cillian. Your father's mind works like yours. Use that."

CHAPTER NINETEEN

CILLIAN HAD OPENED HIS MOUTH TO ANSWER ME when the door swung open to admit Casyn. "Time to ride," he said. "Finish your food."

Five minutes later we were back up on our horses, the shackles reattached, clattering out of the fort. I glanced over at Cillian. His face was shuttered, distant: I guessed he was thinking out possible defenses. The sky had clouded over, and a strong wind gusted from the west, presaging rain. *I had told my mother the weather would hold for her journey to Tirvan,* I thought, but if the winds had been favourable, she could already be home. And this might be only local rain, the coast south of us still sunny and calm. I had seen weather change between one headland and another, when we had explored the coves and inlets for new fishing grounds.

I let my mind drift back to my life in Tirvan, remembering the scent of rain on the dust of the practice field as we learned to use the secca. That thought took me to a conversation with Dern, captain of *Skua*, over wine one night, when I had suggested that I had not followed Maya into exile due to cowardice. *Is that true?* he had asked. I had denied it, telling him that I had chosen to stay because the survival of Tirvan mattered more than one person. *Did I tell him—and myself—the truth,* I wondered? At the time, I thought I had.

But what did it matter now? Whatever my true motives, I was here, facing the consequences of a choice I had made. How that choice followed on from a web of earlier decisions hardly mattered. It could not be changed. All I could do was to tell the Emperor what I believed: I had not considered the possible ramifications of my escape for Donnalch, nor for Darel, nor for the truce. I had been focused on bringing word of the imminent invasion to the Empire. I should have seen the probable consequence, at least for Donnalch. I had known Dagney was afraid for his life, that he was a captive, and that Fritjof had already had Ardan killed. But I had been afraid of the arranged marriage to Leik, and that fear had blinded me to any other consideration.

Anger surged through me again. I *should* have thought about it more, and because I didn't, Donnalch was dead, and Darel. *How would I ever face Turlo? What could I say to him?* My horse tossed his head, uncertain of what my tightened hands and clenched knees asked. I forced myself to relax. "Shh, Suran, it's all right," I murmured to him.

Beside me, Cillian urged his horse up to beside Casyn. They spoke, but the gusty wind made it impossible for me to hear any words. I saw Cillian nod in response to something Casyn said, and then the next gust of wind brought the first drops of rain with it. In less than a minute the rain fell hard and cold, the wind whipping the drops so strongly they stung where they hit bare flesh. I brought Suran to a halt and turned to pull my riding cloak out of the saddlebags. I shrugged it on, pulling the hood over my head; in its deep pockets were leather gloves. Around me, the men did the same.

Suran's chestnut coat turned dark, and water dripped off his mane as we continued eastward. As we approached the next watch-tower, Birel trotted his horse up to beside Casyn. I saw Casyn shake his head. I guessed we would not stop. We had distance to cover, rain or no. Casyn raised our pace to a trot, warming both the horses and ourselves. We passed the watch-tower, situated at the top of a small rise, and continued on, catching up to a small group of carts moving supplies toward the next fort. The men saluted Casyn, staring at us.

The rain came in waves, never really stopping but giving us respite from the drenching every so often. In one of the breaks I turned to look at the sky behind us: it looked lighter toward the horizon. Perhaps the rain would stop soon, I thought. I straightened to see a horseman galloping toward us, a messenger, from the speed he was riding.

Casyn raised a hand for us to stop. The messenger drew his horse up, saluted Casyn, and handed him a sealed note. "From the Emperor, General," he said.

"Thank you," Casyn said. "Are you to take a reply?"

"No, sir."

"Ride with us to the next watch-tower; you can rest yourself and your horse there. We will stop briefly," Casyn ordered. He opened the note, scanning it quickly. He frowned, then refolded the note and slipped it into his saddlebag. "Forward," he said.

I glanced at Cillian, but his face showed me nothing. We rode on. The rain was definitely lighter now, the sky brighter. A curlew called. A stone-bird, flicking its wings, sang its sharp, tapping song from on top of a small bush. Suran snorted and rippled his skin. A pale and watery sun broke through the cloud; I pushed the hood back off my face to let the wind—a breeze now—blow through my hair. My back ached, and I needed a latrine. *I hope the next watch-tower isn't too far,* I thought.

I saw the beacon tower with its iron basket first, rising above a shallow dip in the land and the road. We trotted into the interior yard of the watch-tower; Casyn barely gave us time to relieve ourselves before ordering us into the small guardroom. The messenger had been given responsibility for the horses, instead of Birel.

The door closed firmly behind us, Birel lit a small lamp to give the room some light. "The Emperor tells me," Casyn said without preamble, "that Lorcann was displeased that we rode east without a Linrathan guard, even though he did not send one when he asked us to imprison you, Cillian. He has sent men to meet us. Once they reach us, I doubt any conversation between you will be tolerated. In addition, Lorcann demands, and the Emperor has acceded to this request, that we ride directly to the White Fort, not stopping until we reach it. At which time, your trial, Lena and Cillian, will begin, without time for discussion or counsel."

We were to arrive at the White Fort exhausted, cold and hungry, and go immediately to trial? What chance would we have, to defend ourselves? "That is unfair!" I said. "Why would the Emperor agree to such a request?"

"He will have his reasons," Cillian said.

"Yes," Casyn said sharply, "he will. And one of them may be that your *Teannasach* is now in his debt."

Cillian nodded. "Perhaps," he agreed. "And perhaps another is that tired and hungry, we will not have the energy or spirit to maintain any lies, any collusion."

"Were you planning on such?" Casyn asked.

"We are just going to tell the truth, General," Cillian said. "Calmly, if that concerns you. There is nothing else to do."

Casyn raised an eyebrow. "Does that truth include the subject of my questioning this morning?"

"If needed, yes," Cillian answered. "And it may be. I will not hide behind secrets at the expense of my—or Lena's—life."

"I would not expect you to," Casyn said. "I ask only so I can prepare the Emperor." He turned his head at sounds in the courtyard. "I think your escort has arrived," he said. "I hope for the best, for you both." He offered me his arm, in the soldier's gesture; I gripped it, wishing I could think of something to say. With a brief clasp of his hand on Cillian's shoulder, he opened the door, going out to speak to the men who had arrived.

I turned to Cillian. "I have a plan," he murmured. "I was going to tell you, but now you must trust me." Two men came into the hut, both middle aged, both wearing the tough woven cloth of Linrathe in its muted colours, but over it, leather vests and leggings, and swords on their hips.

"Cillian na Perras," one of them said. "We are sent by the *Teannasach* to guard you on your journey. Please come with us." With one last glance my way, Cillian did as they asked. Outside, we mounted, submitted to the shackles, and began to move away from the watchtower, Cillian and the men of Linrathe riding ahead of Casyn, Birel and me.

The road was wide enough for us to ride three abreast. We trotted, but it was clear to me Suran was tired. "We cannot reach the White Fort tonight on these horses," I said.

"No," Casyn agreed. "At the next fort, we will switch horses, and again once or twice after that. I sent the messenger ahead to ask for replacement mounts to be ready. Be prepared for fast riding, Lena."

"Why did the Emperor agree to this?" I asked again.

Casyn shook his head. "I do not know," he said. "But I know very little of Lorcann, except what I saw of him during the truce negotiations, and even then Donnalch did most of the talking. Callan will have got to know him a bit better over these past weeks. He will have his reasons, but I do not know what they are."

"Cillian says he is hot-headed, quick to anger," I offered.

224

"That fits with what I saw," Casyn agreed. "Things were either right or wrong, and he was impatient, especially with detail. Quite different from the Emperor and Donnalch. I respected Donnalch, for all he was an enemy at the time."

"So did I," I said. "He was considerate, and thoughtful, and curious about different ways of thinking. And he knew how to inspire men to fight, even if it meant not always telling the complete truth, by drawing on what is dear to them to raise their anger. Did you know, General, that the common men of Linrathe thought they were invading us to free the women's villages from our unnatural lives, to let us be free to marry and live with our men and our children?" I did not try to hide the bitterness and anger that insinuated themselves into my voice as I spoke these last sentences. I no longer cared if Casyn knew how I felt.

"I did," he said.

"A common tactic, among military leaders, to tug at our heartstrings so that we will agree to their plans."

"One we use, yes. On occasion."

"As I know," I said, the anger spurting again at this calm admission. We rode a few paces without speaking. "General," I said, when I was sure I had control of my voice. "I find it hard to believe, now, that Donnalch made arrangements with Nevin and Vilnas to breach the Wall as his first course of action. Were there not approaches made for a peaceful alliance?"

"An alliance was not exactly what Donnalch wanted," Casyn replied. "He wanted free movement of people across the border, so that northmen, and women, could come and settle on our lands, but outside of Partition, and have access to the southern trade. In return, men and women of the Empire who wanted a different life would have been free to travel north of the Wall. It was too much, too sudden, even given the Emperor was already considering the need for a review of the Partition agreement, not to mention it was not exactly a fair exchange. Our lands, especially in the fertile south, would have been— are—very attractive to those who battle against long winters and thin and rocky soils in Linrathe."

"So," I said, puzzling it out, "had we had the new Assembly, and the vote had been to change our way of life, then he would have had something different to offer to Donnalch. A compromise, of sorts?"

"Perhaps," Casyn agreed. "That was the plan."

"Then why did Donnalch chose to invade when he did? Surely he could have waited to see the outcome of the new Assembly?"

"For one, he had no idea what Callan was planning. How could he? You know how the threat from Leste played into that idea; once we had asked the women's villages to fight, we had changed the agreement, and had grounds for a new Assembly. Had that not happened, it could have been years before the idea gained support."

"And the Emperor thought Donnalch would wait that long?"

"I think he might have, except—and I am guessing here, Lena, for none of this was ever said to us in any negotiation—that the ill-health and impending death of the Marai king made Donnalch act sooner."

"Yes," I said, "that fits something I heard at the *Ti'ach*." I thought back, remembering candles, and wine, and an evening-dark room. "That if Donnalch could negotiate a treaty of equals with the Emperor, then it would be time to challenge the terms of his treaty with the Marai, especially with a new king."

"Exactly so," Casyn said. "I am glad to have my guess confirmed. And if that treaty of equals with our Empire came after a show of force by Donnalch, all the better to demonstrate to the Marai that they were dealing with a strong opponent."

"Except Donnalch expected Åsmund to be king, not Fritjof, and he and Åsmund were childhood friends."

"Such friendships can mean little, when leaders sit down to negotiate," Callan said. "But Lorcann says they misjudged Fritjof's ambition: even among the Marai, to kill your own brother is nearly unheard of. He rules by threat and blood, and promises of great wealth."

None of this helped me, I thought, but it would give me something to think about, to quell the panic rising in my gut, the closer we got to the White Fort. I had one more question. "Did you really not know about the Marai?" I asked.

"Not really, no," Casyn answered. "We knew there was a king to whom Linrathe paid tribute for their northern borderlands, but beyond that, no. They had never been mentioned as a threat. The peace between them had gone on for so long, you see. Perhaps if Colm had lived, and kept up his correspondence with the scholars of Linrathe, or spent some time north of the Wall, we might have known."

The next fort, lay just ahead of us. We rode through its western gate: horses awaited us. Soldiers helped transfer our saddlebags, and then we were riding again, fast now, galloping along the stones of the road.

It was not yet midnight when we rode through the gates of the White Fort. The sky danced with stars, the clouds and rain of earlier in the day blown further east. The sparks of light blurred as I looked up, exhaustion fogging my vision. I slumped in the saddle, waiting for my shackles to be removed so I could dismount.

I stumbled my way under guard to a latrine. Someone gave me a waterskin; I drank thirstily. We had had neither food nor drink since before the last fort, save for a few bites of dried apple and cheese, eaten as we rode.

I stretched, easing cramped muscles. Torches flickered on the wall outside the great wooden door that led into the antechamber of the hall. Behind those doors waited the Emperor, and the *Teannasach* of Linrathe, our judges. Birel appeared at my side. "Drink this," he said, "just a sip or two, not too much." I took the small flask, tipping a drop of the liquid onto my tongue, tasting smoke and fire. *Fuisce*, Donnalch had called it. I took a larger sip, and handed the flask back to Birel.

"Thank you," I said.

"Now, food," he said. "You're not facing a trial without food inside you, Guardswoman."

I shook my head. "I can't eat."

"You must," he said firmly. He handed me a slice of something. "Just nibble this," he instructed. I did as he asked. *How could I refuse?* The sweetness and spice of a dense, fruit-studded cake filled my mouth, the taste like that of the harvest cakes of Tirvan, baked rich and sweet to fuel the hard work of reaping. It almost made me smile.

"Where did you get this?" I asked.

227

"The Emperor has a liking for sweet things, when he can get them," he said. "I have friends in the kitchens."

"Did you give Cillian a piece, too?"

"His guards would not let me give it to him, nor the *fuisce*," he said, shaking his head. "Just water, they said."

He would be exhausted, I thought. I finished the cake. Birel gave me the flask of *fuisce* again; I swallowed a mouthful, feeling its warmth radiating through me. "Are you ready?" Birel said softly. I shrugged.

"As ever I will be," I answered. "Birel, thank you, for all you have done, now and in the past."

He saluted me; I returned the salute. Behind us, I heard the footsteps of Cillian and his guard. My heart pounded in my throat. I could barely swallow. Birel opened the door. The stone walls of the antechamber seemed to move in the gusting light of the torches. Boots pounded sharp and loud on the stone flags, echoing in the empty space. Birel knocked on the right-hand door of the pair that opened into the great hall; the sound reverberated. A detached, wandering part of my mind wondered what Cillian would make of the floor. My legs trembled.

The doors swung open to light and warmth, the two fireplaces and the wall torches blazing. Birel's hand was on my arm, lightly: I let him propel me forward, towards the long table where the Emperor and the *Teannasach* sat. Callan wore his dark grey robe and the pendant of silver; Lorcann his heather-hued cloak and golden torc. The clothes of power. I heard Cillian and his guard moving behind me. Callan's eyes followed him, watching him steadily as he came to stand beside me, but in the firelight I could read no expression on the Emperor's face, save perhaps a tightening in his jaw.

"Lena, Guardswoman of the Empire," the Emperor said, in his even, quiet voice, switching his gaze to me, "you stand before me tonight charged with treason, namely, the violation of the truce between the Empire and Linrathe, signed in this very hall. Specifically, you are charged with two crimes. One, the murder of a man of Sorham, a land subservient to Linrathe, during the theft of his boat, disregarding these words of the truce: 'no raid nor battle will be undertaken by either side during this time of truce, nor any action that leads to the death by violence of a man or woman of the opposing side'. Second, in escaping your captivity by Fritjof of the Marai, your actions led directly to the execution of Donnalch, *Teannasach* of Linrathe, also held captive by Fritjof, as retaliation for your escape. By the terms of the truce between the Empire and Linrathe, your life is doubly forfeit."

His eyes had been on me steadily as he spoke, only glancing at the paper in front of him once or twice. There seemed to be no opportunity for response. I felt sweat trickling down between my breasts, although I thought I was cold. Lorcann cleared his throat, and began to speak.

"Cillian na Perras," he said, his voice rougher than Donnalch's had been, less musical, "you stand before me tonight charged with two crimes: one being the violation of the truce between Linrathe and the Southern Empire, signed in this very hall. In plotting with the Empire's hostage, the Guard Lena, to steal a boat, you committed a raid that led to the death of a man of Sorham, in direct violation of the words of the truce: 'no raid nor battle will be undertaken'. But that is the lesser of your crimes: the other is not a violation of the truce, but an act that led directly to the death of your *Teannasach*, namely, your flight from the court of King Fritjof of the Marai. For both crimes, the charge is treason, and your life is forfeit."

Beneath my feet, faces grinned and leered in the flickering firelight. I forced my mind to analyze what had just been said, the subtle differences between the Emperor's words and Lorcann's. 'Fritjof of the Marai', Callan had called him; 'King Fritjof' had been Lorcann's words. *Did this matter?*

"Guardswoman." Callan's voice broke into my thoughts. "What have you to say to these charges?"

"Emperor," I tried to say, but the word was a dry croak. Callan nodded to Birel. He walked forward to pour water from a jug, handing me the cup. I drank, a sip or two. Birel took the cup. "Emperor," I said. "The fisherman of Sorham tried to rape me; I killed him in self-defence. I acknowledge that I was trying to steal his boat, but only to bring word of the Marai invasion to you in time. I judged my responsibility to the Empire required that, and that responsibility was what I acted on. I did not think of the words of the truce, but if I had, I would not have considered my actions a raid or a battle."

"And the second charge?"

This was harder. "Again, Emperor," I said. "I knew Fritjof planned an invasion of the Empire; I believed you knew nothing of this threat or of these people. I acted as I did from concern for the Empire, and for our people, and," I added, glancing at Lorcann, "indeed, not only for the Empire, but for Linrathe, too."

"Acknowledged, Guardswoman," the Emperor said. I could smell the tang of my armpits. *Was that all?* I glanced at Cillian. He watched Callan, his face impassive.

"Cillian na Perras," Lorcann said. "What have you to say, to these charges?"

"I admit to the theft of the boat, *Teannasach*," Cillian said clearly, "but the murder of the fisherman was none of my doing. The Guardswoman had convinced me, and she was right, that we could travel faster in a boat than on foot or horseback. While the theft could be construed as a raid, it was in the greater good of Linrathe. And as to the second charge, Donnalch himself knew my plan, and approved it, knowing the risk to his life. Given that, *Teannasach*, there is no charge for me to answer."

Was this true? And if so, why had Cillian not told me? Lorcann leaned back in his chair, his eyes narrowed.

"Can anyone verify this tale," he asked, "other than the Guardswoman, of course?"

"Of course not," Cillian said, almost scornfully. "Donnalch would not have risked anyone else's life by telling them. And whom would he have told? Ardan was dead by then, and that left only the Lady Dagney and the Guardswoman. You know our laws: a *scáeli's* life is not to be risked, nor would the *Teannasach* have confided our plans to a hostage."

"Guardswoman?" Lorcann turned his eyes to me. "Did you know this?"

I shook my head. "No," I said. "I am hearing this for the first time."

"Tell me, then, how you discovered Cillian planned to escape."

I did not trust this man. But all I could do was tell the truth. "He told me," I said.

Lorcann shot his eyes to Cillian. "That is true," Cillian affirmed.

"Why?"

"Had I just disappeared, she—and the Lady Dagney—might have thought me dead, and attempted some rash action. Even though the *Teannasach* knew the truth, they would have little or no opportunity to speak to him privately. I thought it best the women knew."

"Then why did you let the Guardswoman join you? Surely then the Lady Dagney would have thought you both dead. Your logic is at fault, *dalta*," Lorcann said.

"Not at all, *Teannasach*," Cillian said, his voice icy. "Lady Dagney was housed in the women's hall; she would hear the gossip. The Marai women may not have been privy to what happened to me, but they would know that the Guardswoman had escaped. The *scáeli* would have worked out that we had gone together."

Lorcann grunted. "Perhaps," he acceded. "But still I do not understand why you brought her along at all."

"She proposed stealing a boat, saying it would be faster than foot or horseback. I could see she was right. She can sail; I cannot. Speed was of the essence, and so I brought her with me."

"To raid an innocent fisher family of their boat, and thereby their livelihood," Lorcann pointed out. "A crime against the truce, even before the murder."

"Would stealing a horse from a *torp* have been any better?" Cillian countered.

"Yes, man, it would have been," Lorcann said. "Firstly, one horse would not destroy a *torp*. It would be a poor *eirën* who had only one beast. Because you chose to allow the woman to go with you, you left a boy of twelve years an orphan, and with no boat for him to barter or trade for a place in another fishing family, so that he must throw himself on the charity of his *eirën*, or take to the roads in search of work."

"And secondly?" Cillian asked. His insouciance shocked me. *Was he deliberately baiting Lorcann?*

"D'you need to ask?" Lorcann scoffed. "There would have been no murder had you gone alone. Even had you raised the house while stealing the horse, I doubt more than a few blows and bruises would have resulted. The fisherman, himself a widower, found a woman under his hands as he wrestled with the person stealing his boat. What would you expect of him? He had the right to take what he wanted, under the circumstances. The murder is on the southern woman's head, but you are not innocent, man."

"You think that his right?" The words burst out of me. "Do women mean so little to you, *Teannasach*?" I spat the title. "Do you approve of how Fritjof treats the Marai women, then?"

The wall torches seemed to dim, leaving a circle of light around us, and darkness beyond. Lorcann glared at me. "Be silent, and be glad I am not your judge," he said. He turned back to Cillian.

"I believe you not, man," he said. "So, hear your doom. You are a man of Linrathe, and I am your *Teannasach*. I condemn you to death on these charges. At dawn, Cillian na Perras, your head will be on a spear, for the instruction of all."

The words echoed in the silence of the hall. Cillian's guard took him roughly by the upper arm, pulling him away. I looked from Lorcann to Callan, and back again.

"What," Cillian said, his voice almost conversational, "if I am not a man of Linrathe?"

CHAPTER TWENTY

I COULD HEAR MY HEART IN MY EARS. Cillian, head high, stared at the two leaders at the high table. Long moments passed.

"Tell me your mother's name, Cillian na Perras," the Emperor said, his voice pitched low.

"Hafwen," Cillian answered. "Her father was Hael, her mother, Mari. I was born just as winter changed to spring, thirty-three years ago."

"What is this?" Lorcann demanded. "He was a bastard child of a farm girl, it is true, but so are many others. He is still mine to rule and to judge."

"Not if a man of the Empire claims him as his child," Casyn said from beside me. "That agreement was made in Mathon's day, *Teannasach*, if you recall."

"Aye," Lorcann said angrily, "but it was about children, not grown men. Nor has such a claim been made in many years."

"That does not void the agreement," Casyn said.

"So? It is well known that Cillian na Perras's mother never named his father. He has no name to put forward, even if the soldier is still alive and willing to make the claim. You cannot pull yourself out of a well on a thread, man," he said, his eyes on Cillian, "and a thread is all you have. Accept your fate."

"You agree the father was a man of the Empire?" Casyn asked.

"Aye, that was always the story," Lorcann replied, "and I've no reason to believe it a lie. Had the father been a farm lad, there would have been a wedding, with the child born six months later. A nine-days whisper, but no shame to it."

"Then, *Teannasach*, were the father to claim Cillian na Perras, even now, do you agree he has that right? And that Cillian na Perras has the right to accept that claim, and be named a man of the Empire, not of Linrathe, by the agreement made between Mathon, Emperor of the South, and Iaco of Linrathe?" Callan spoke with authority, his voice that of the law-maker, the Emperor. Lorcann glowered.

"Aye, I suppose I do," he muttered.

Callan stood. He looked at his brother, a long gaze, before turning his eyes to Cillian. "Then, in the sight of this court, I, Callan, Emperor of the South, son of Col of the Sixth and Alle of Rigg, acknowledge this man, Cillian, to be my son, borne by Hafwen of Linrathe."

I heard a muffled sound from Cillian's guard, silenced by Lorcann's bark. "What? You claim him?"

"I do," Callan said. "He is my son, although I only learned of his birth yesterday. Do you dispute my right to do so, *Teannasach*?"

Lorcann shot his eyes to the Cillian's guard, and then to the door, and back again. *Like a cornered fox,* I thought. "No," he grunted finally. "If it suits you to be the one who executes him, rather than me, what do I care? It's all the same in the end."

The Emperor turned back to Cillian. "I ask you, Cillian of Linrathe," he said, "if you wish to acknowledge this claim and become Cillian of the Empire, accepting the responsibilities to the Empire that such an acknowledgement would bring."

"I do," Cillian said, his voice steady. "What words must I say?"

"That you acknowledge your mother by name, and me as your father, and that you will serve the Empire."

Cillian nodded. "I, Cillian, son of Hafwen of Linrathe, acknowledge Callan, Emperor of the South, as my father, and I pledge to serve the Empire, and," he added, "to accept the judgement of the Emperor as to my fate."

"I, Casyn, General of the Empire, witness this." Casyn touched my shoulder. I glanced at him. He nodded.

"I, Lena, Guardswoman of the Empire, witness this," I said, my voice barely above a whisper.

All eyes were on Lorcann. Callan gestured politely. "Would you prefer your soldier to witness?" Lorcann's lips clenched. He stood, slowly.

"I, Lorcann, *Teannasach* of Linrathe, witness this," he spat. "Let him go," he said to the guard. He turned to Callan. "He is yours, Emperor. I presume I am welcome to witness the sentencing?"

"You are, of course, *Teannasach*," Callan said. "Shall we sit, and continue the trial?" His eyes held Lorcann's. The northman's jaw twitched. With a bare nod, he sat.

When the scrape of the chairs had subsided, the Emperor spoke again. "Cillian," he said, "tell us what you saw happening between the Guardswoman and the fisherman."

"The Guardswoman fell as she approached the boat," he answered. "The fisherman was in pursuit. That was my fault. I broke a piece of wood underfoot, on the beach, and the sound roused the cot. When he reached her, they struggled, but he was forcing her against him, not pushing her away. That I could see, in the dark, but nothing more. Then he fell into the water. That is all I can say. The night was black."

"Thank you," Callan said. "Guardswoman."

I tried to speak, but my throat was as dry as salt fish. I coughed, and tried again. "Yes, Emperor?" I croaked.

"Cillian na Perras argues that the *Teannasach* of Linrathe approved his plan of escape, knowing it risked his own life. Did the *Teannasach* know of your plan to accompany him?"

"No, sir," I said. "Not that I am aware."

"Did anyone other than Cillian know?"

I shook my head. "No. The Lady Dagney asked, but I did not tell her, thinking it might be dangerous for her."

"Cillian, did you tell the *Teannasach* that the Guardswoman was accompanying you?"

"No, Emperor."

"Guardswoman, you knew your plans were dangerous, as you declined to let the Lady Dagney know them. But you did not think of the danger to the *Teannasach*?"

I hesitated. *How to put this?* "I knew the Lady Dagney thought his life in danger already," I said. "I did not think my escape would add to that danger."

Callan nodded. He looked at Cillian, and then at me, and then at Casyn, a long gaze.

"Guardswoman Lena, of Tirvan," he said. "Cillian of the Empire. I find you both guilty of the second charge, the violation of the truce between the Empire and Linrathe, an action which directly led to the death of the *Teannasach* of Linrathe. The charge is treason. The punishment is death."

I closed my eyes. *Cillian's gamble had been for nothing.* A trembling began deep inside me. I heard a chair scrape as someone stood. I swallowed, and opened my eyes. Callan was on his feet.

"I, Callan, Emperor of the South, sentence the Guardswoman Lena and the man Cillian to death, a sentence I commute to banishment, exile from the bounds of the Empire for all time, as is my right as Emperor. Lena of Tirvan, you are stripped of your rank in the Empire's army. Cillian of the Empire, Lena of Tirvan, you have three days to leave the boundaries of this land."

Banishment. I heard the word. Banishment. *I was not going to die.*

"Nae, Emperor, I cannot support that!" Lorcann cried. The punishment for treason is death, and my brother's fate demands it. You cannot exile them instead!"

"I can," Callan said calmly. "It is within my right as Emperor, and there is precedence, as your brother would have known."

"You tricked me!" Lorcann shouted. "Guard, seize Cillian na Perras!"

Before the man could react, Cillian broke: running, he placed his hands flat on the table, vaulting it to stand beside the Emperor. Casyn pushed me roughly behind him, drawing his sword, shouting. A door flung open. Soldiers rushed into the room, swords drawn. Casyn raised a hand.

"*Teannasach,*" he said, "think again. Think of your own son, and that of your brother. We hold them hostage still, do not forget."

Lorcann looked around him. Outnumbered, Cillian's guard stood with weapons in their hands, but warily. Lorcann gestured to them, and they sheathed their swords. I sagged against Casyn, hearing my heart pounding in my ears. He took my weight with one arm, the other still holding his sword. Lorcann turned to the Emperor.

"Be uncertain of your peace, Callan of the Empire," he snarled. "I must weigh my choices: alliance with the man who killed my brother, or alliance with the man who forgave the instruments of his death. Which is the worse choice, I wonder?"

"I say again, remember your hostages, *Teannasach,*" Callan said softly. "But I too have lost a brother to treachery. I know how you feel."

"Do you?" Lorcann retorted. "And did you not kill both the murderer, and those who made the murder possible? And without trial, I believe?"

"For directly plotting treason, yes," Callan replied. "Not for the unintended consequence of an action to warn of impending invasion."

Lorcann stared at him. "And I say again, be uncertain of your peace. The King of the Marai has made me certain offers. I must consider them, even in light of your threats. Come," he ordered Cillian's guard. He stalked out of the hall, the torches guttering as the massive doors opened and closed.

Callan turned to the soldiers. "Escort them out to their horses," he said. "Be respectful of his position."

When the soldiers had gone, Callan took a deep breath. "Cillian," he said. "Be seated. You too, Lena. Casyn, will you call for food and drink?" I stumbled to a chair. "You must ride in the morning," he said. "There will be an escort, to the Durrains, for that is where you must go, of course."

The Durrains. The wall of mountains on the Empire's eastern edge. *Beyond it, what?* Once, there had been another Empire past those mountains, an Empire of learning and skill and a love of beauty, if the floor of the White Fort told me anything. The east, where no-one in living memory had gone, except Fritjof of the Marai and his men. *Who had not died of disease, and had returned to tell their tales.*

Birel came in with food, more of the rich cake, cheese, wine. I accepted wine, and water. Cillian folded a piece of cake in half and ate it in three bites. I realized how exhausted he must be. Birel poured wine for the Emperor and Casyn, and then withdrew.

Cillian swallowed the last of his cake. He took a cup of wine, sipped, and then put it down. "Did you get what you needed, Emperor?" he asked.

A hint of smile played around Callan's lips. "I did," he said. "Lorcann, as I feared, is untrustworthy. He is still in communication with Fritjof, I would think. It is power he wants, not leadership. I will have to give thought as to what I can offer him, to keep him with me."

"Wait," I said. "This was planned? How?"

"Not planned," Cillian said, with a glance to Callan. "Played, hoping I saw the board rightly. But it was you who told me that the Emperor and I shared a trait, a gift, if you will, for tactics and outcomes. What would I need to know, I wondered, were I the Emperor, in this situation?"

"If Lorcann could be trusted," I said, slowly, working it out. "So," I turned to Callan, "you let him judge Cillian first, and then you overrode him, to discover his reaction."

"Exactly," the Emperor said.

"Once again, Emperor," I said, "we are pieces in your game."

"You could say that," Callan said. "But if so, it was one in which your life was a wager on the outcome, and Cillian was a willing player."

"Not willing, quite," Cillian said. "Compelled, for our lives, I would say."

Callan inclined his head, ceding the point. "Successfully," he noted.

"Yes," I said, all the fear and grief of the last days welling up. "And for that I am grateful. But my life has been a wager in your games for far too long now, Emperor. I thank you for saving it, and Cillian's, and as for mine I take it as fair payment for what you have asked of me, but no more. No more, Emperor. I welcome this banishment, to be beyond your games." White-hot anger flared, goading me into these words. *Did I mean them? Yes,* I realized, *I did. I had had enough.*

"Lena," Casyn began.

"No!" I stopped him. "Casyn, no. I mean what I said. Cillian told me once he had no love for Empires; I understand him now. I am sorry if I disappoint you, but I am not a Guardswoman any more, and can speak my mind to you both. I have had enough of tactics, of intrigues and half-truths. I will be glad to leave."

"We have asked much of you, Lena," Callan said, a note of regret in his voice, "and you have served us well. But do not judge us too harshly. Even my actions, regardless of my reputed gift for strategy, may have unforeseen consequences, no matter how thorough the planning, and half-truths are sometimes all the truths we know." He gave me a smile, his eyes gentle, before turning to his son.

"Cillian," the Emperor said. "Before anything else, I have one thing to ask, and one to tell."

"Ask first," Cillian said.

"Did Donnalch truly approve your escape, knowing the risk to his life?"

A brief smile touched Cillian's lips. "I told him my plan. He said this, and nothing more: 'My brother must know that being *Teannasach* is about serving our people, not having them serve the *Teannasach*.' I took that to mean he knew he would die, and Lorcann would be the *Teannasach*."

"A fair interpretation," Callan said.

"And to tell me, Emperor?"

Callan's eyes were shadowed, the firelight accentuating the planes of his face. "I truly loved her, Cillian. But when I came back to the Wall, Wenna was dead, and no-one told me of a child. Had I known, I would have acknowledged you, Cillian, with pride."

"Had you known," Cillian echoed. "But you did not: I was one of those unforeseen consequences, I suppose. I have lived my life half in exile, so perhaps, like Lena, I am ready to make it full exile, away from those who have judged me on my parentage, or lack of it. I too thank you for my life, twice, I suppose, both in the begetting and the saving." He raised his wine. "To the Emperor, then, for his benevolence."

"To the Emperor," Casyn repeated, standing. I too stood.

"For my life, I thank you, Emperor," I said, as coldly as I could, surprised to feel the prick of tears. We drank the toast.

Callan stood, wearily. "Sleep, now," he said. "Birel will find you beds. Tomorrow you ride east."

"A moment," I said. "I have one more thing to do. Where is Turlo?"

"Not here," Casyn said. "He commands our troops still in Linrathe."

Regret and relief washed through me. "Is there paper?" I said. Casyn found me what I needed. I sat at the great table. 'I will remember Darel. He was brave and stalwart and full of fun,' I wrote. 'I will carry my guilt and sorrow for his death all my life.' Then I signed my name, folded the paper, and handed it to Callan. With a nod, he left the room, Cillian with him.

"Lena," Casyn began, his voice gentle.

"Casyn," I said, forestalling whatever he was about to say. "You told me, once, that you did not want to be a general, when you were my age. Will you tell me why?"

He laughed, a brief, mirthless bark. "Because I too hated the games, the shading of the truth, the stories we told and were told. But Callan was so good at it, at seeing how to make things happen...but he was impulsive, undisciplined: the affair with Wenna, the note he tried to leave, both were proof of that. I had to be by his side, advising him, to keep him safe. He is my brother. So, I did what I had to, although I prefer shoeing horses. I never thought he would rise so high." In the firelight, his face was weary, drawn with fatigue, and, perhaps, regret.

"Thank you," I said. He smiled.

"Sleep now, Lena," he said, "for a few hours. I will not see you again. My duty is to Callan."

I nodded. I felt no surprise, just the bleak realization of the inevitable, like waking on a November morning to see the first snowfall, knowing it presaged the hardship of winter. I had no tears left. My eyes were as dry as autumn leaves, and the taste of ashes was in my mouth.

†††††

The lower slopes of the Durrains were still in shadow, the sun not yet over the peaks. My pack lay on the grass, beside Cillian's, a bird bow and arrows strapped to it. Bedrolls hung below the packs, and two walking staffs leaned against a boulder.

"The track will take you up to some meadows," the soldier holding our horses said. "There's good hunting there, mountain hare and deer and grouse. There are game trails leading out of the meadows, but where they go?" He shrugged. "There are lots of stories. Some of them may be true. I guess you'll find out." He paused. "I envy you that."

I looked up at the path, bending out of sight among the boulders and the scrubby trees. Snow clung to the peaks, even now, halfway to summer. Cillian stood beside me, saying nothing. Part of me wished I was going alone; part of me knew that would be folly. I still did not know if I liked him, or could trust him. I was wary of his cynicism and

240

his cold, tactical, thinking, but I had no choice. He was my companion in exile, at least until we crossed these mountains. *If we crossed these mountains.* He probably felt the same about me.

I turned back to the soldier. "Any advice, Galen?" I asked.

"Stay together. Stay dry. Take it slowly. The higher you go, the harder it is to climb. Let your body get used to it. You're not in any hurry; remember that."

I nodded. "You will send word?" I said.

"I will," he said. "I have your letter. And if the Emperor will allow me to ride as his messenger, I'll go, tell her how proud she should be of you."

Another half-truth. *Better that way,* I thought. *Maybe half-truths were all we ever had, as Callan had suggested.* I picked up the pack, shrugging it onto my shoulders, adjusting the straps. Beside me, Cillian did the same. I reached for my staff, settling my hand around its smooth surface, looping its leather strap around my wrist. I looked up at the path before me. A memory rose, a stone hall, morning light, words spoken: *'What may still lie beyond the mountains and the seas...'*. Deep inside, I felt a frisson of anticipation, almost excitement.

"Lena," my father called. I turned.

"Go with the god," he said. "Both of you."

I nodded. I glanced at Cillian. He gestured me forward. I turned back to the path, away from the Empire, away from Linrathe, and began to climb.

A PREVIEW OF *EMPIRE'S EXILE*
BOOK III OF THE EMPIRE'S LEGACY SERIES

A few hours after sunrise, and already sweat dripped down my back and between my breasts. Overhead, a carrion-bird made slow circles in the sky, gyring higher into the pale, clear blue. No clouds interfered with the sun. Beneath our feet, the soil between the sparse, coarse grasses felt gritty, dry and dusty, chafing when it found its way into our boots.

On a slight rise in the plain, Cillian halted. "Look," he said, pointing. "Is that water?" I shaded my eyes with my hand. Light shimmered and gleamed along the eastern horizon.

"I'm not sure," I answered. "Maybe...but maybe not. It could just be heat haze." I followed the brightness north, then south. The shimmer of haze continued in both directions, but the wavering gleam did not. *A lake?* "I think it's water," I concluded.

"Probably where this game trail goes," he replied. We'd been following the narrow, faint path since dawn, for lack of any other guide. I had checked the sun frequently to ensure it was still heading east. We'd seen nothing of the animals that had made it, although from its width and the occasional mark in the soil, I felt certain they were deer.

Cillian handed me the waterskin. I swallowed a mouthful, took another tiny sip, and gave it back to him. We resumed walking, not speaking: talking increased the need to drink, and we needed to husband our water. Even if that was a lake, it was some miles off, and the sun grew hotter every minute.

The path widened, smaller trails joining it at intervals from both sides. The gleam of light increased, widened, stabilized. *Definitely a lake*, I thought. If we camped on its edge tonight, there would be game to hunt: birds, rabbits—if there were any, here. Better to eat fresh meat when we could, and keep our dried meats for those days when nothing came within bowshot. My eyes went from grass to trail to sky, watching the land, calculating our direction; I did this without thought, long years of training on the sea translating easily to this flat land. Something moved on the path ahead. Cillian strode forward, unconscious of the motion. "Stop!" I shouted.

"What?" he growled, but he stopped walking.

"Snake." A mottled brown viper, as long as my arm, lay in the sun, its tongue flickering. I could see the scales on its flat head, and the sheen of the membrane slipping back and forth across its eyes. "Stand still," I ordered. I thumped my heel into the soil, hard. The viper did not move, although the tongue flickered faster. I searched the ground: no stones.

I had no reason to kill the snake, but I needed to scare it off the path. We could go around it, but were there others in the grass? The shepherd girls, up on the hills above Tirvan, were bitten occasionally; no-one I could remember had died, but the bites were painful and debilitating. We had neither the medicine nor the time to deal with a snake bite—and I wasn't even sure this was the same type of snake.

I unslung my bird bow and pulled an arrow from the quiver. Moving in front of Cillian, I aimed, making the small necessary judgements: no wind, flat land. The arrow flew, burying itself in the earth half a handswidth in front of the snake. Its mouth wide, rearing its upper body at the shaft, the viper struck twice, so quickly I saw only a blur of motion. It stopped, still focused on the arrow, tongue moving in and out—and then it dropped its head, and slid off into the grass.

Cillian let out his held breath. "Well done," he said. I glanced up at him, surprised at his words of praise.

"An easy shot," I countered, stepping forward to retrieve the arrow. I wiped it, point and shaft, on a tuft of grass and tucked it back into the quiver. "Maybe I should go first?" I suggested.

Cillian smiled wryly. "Maybe you should."

Swallows darted over the water, and as we approached a lanky heron launched itself slowly into the air, croaking. Gnats hovered in clouds over the small bushes at the edge. We stopped short of the bank, unsure of its stability, wary of what—or who—else might be here. Slowly we edged forward, keeping behind the bushes, crouching. *Anyone fishing here*, I told myself, *would have seen us coming across the plain long ago. Doesn't mean they're not waiting to ambush us, though.*

From the cover of the bushes, I stood, looking out across the water. I thought I could make out a line of bushes on the far shore. I looked east, then west. Nothing...no people, no animals....and no shoreline. I frowned, watching the water. A mat of grasses floated by, moving south. I kept my eyes on it until I was sure. "Cillian," I said, "this isn't a lake. I think it's a river."

"A river? It's too wide."

"Watch that mat of grasses," I suggested, pointing. He found it, narrowing his eyes. I counted to ten, then twenty. "Well?"

"There's a current, certainly," he said. "But it could just be the outlet for the lake pulling those grasses southward."

"I can't see a shore, south or north," I pointed out, "just the far bank—and if this is a lake it's a remarkably straight one; that bank runs even with this one for as far as I can see." He gazed along the opposite bank, eyes tracing the bushes.

"You may be right," he said eventually. "How are we ever going to cross this?"

"Walk north," I offered, "and hope it narrows? It's flowing south, so it's only going to get wider, in that direction."

"But how far?"

"Until it's narrow enough, or we find a bridge, or a ferryman who doesn't ask questions and accepts a coin he's never seen before to take us across?" I snapped. "How do I know, Cillian? You should know better than I do—don't you remember anything, from the maps you've studied?"

"Let me think," he murmured. His eyes became distant, trying, I realized, to recall the picture the maps made, to overlay it on this land and this water. I waited.

"I think," he said finally, "that you are wrong. We are better to walk south: if this is the river I think it is, it will split into several channels further south, when the land must become rockier, steeper. North of here, I think the land is still flat, and the river will still be wide."

"Does this river have a name?" I asked, but before Cillian could answer, a loud trumpeting split the air. From upriver, several large, greyish-brown birds, long-necked and long-legged, rose from the grasses. "Something disturbed them," I said. "Get down, among the bushes."

We crouched low again, waiting. The birds circled, still calling, going higher, not looking to land. Whatever had flushed them was still out there. Suddenly a pair of ducks launched themselves past us, quacking noisily: the threat grew closer. Cillian crawled forward. I winced at the noise he made, and put a hand out, trying to stop him. He ignored it, crouching at the river's edge, peering out from among the leaves. "Lena," he whispered, "come here. Look!"

I edged forward. Through the twigs and stems I could see the prow of a boat, curved and capped with a carven head, the sweep of oars carrying it forward. Cillian rocked back. "By the gods, Lena," he murmured. "That's a Marai ship."

78347095R00156

Made in the USA
Columbia, SC
15 October 2017